Praise for the David Slaton series

"A stunning thriller . . . The best nail-biting suspense novel I've read in years." —Stephen Coonts, *New York* Times bestselling author, on *Assassin's Game*

"Highly reminiscent of Robert Ludlum's Jason Bourne series." —David Hagberg, *New York Times* bestselling author

"A first-rate thriller with a plot that grabs you hard and won't let go." —Ralph Peters, *New York Times* bestselling author, on *Assassin's Game*

"Sure to entertain fans of Daniel Silva and Robert Ludlum . . . Riveting." —Mark Greaney, *New York Times* bestselling author, on *Assassin's Run*

"The action-filled, high-octane thriller that you have been waiting for. Ward Larsen delivers enough page-turning suspense and globe-spanning action for ten novels." —William Martin, *New York Times* bestselling author, on *Assassin's Silence*

"A superbly written story." —Larry Bond, *New York Times* bestselling author, on *Assassin's Game*

BOOKS BY WARD LARSEN

The Perfect Assassin
Assassin's Game *
Assassin's Silence *
Assassin's Code *
Assassin's Run *
Assassin's Revenge *
Cutting Edge *
Assassin's Strike *
Assassin's Dawn *
Assassin's Edge *
Deep Fake *
Assassin's Mark *

* Published by Forge Books

ASSASSIN'S MARK

WARD LARSEN

TOR PUBLISHING GROUP
NEW YORK

This is a work of fiction. All of the characters, organizations, and events portrayed in this novel are either products of the author's imagination or are used fictitiously.

ASSASSIN'S MARK

Copyright © 2023 by Ward Larsen

All rights reserved.

A Forge Book
Published by Tom Doherty Associates/Tor Publishing Group
120 Broadway
New York, NY 10271

www.torpublishinggroup.com

Forge® is a registered trademark of Macmillan Publishing Group, LLC.

ISBN 978-1-250-79824-4

Our books may be purchased in bulk for promotional, educational, or business use. Please contact your local bookseller or the Macmillan Corporate and Premium Sales Department at 1-800-221-7945, extension 5442, or by email at MacmillanSpecialMarkets@macmillan.com.

First Edition: November 2023
First Mass Market Edition: November 2024

Printed in the United States of America

0 9 8 7 6 5 4 3 2 1

ASSASSIN'S MARK

ONE

The iconic blue-and-white whale that was Air Force One coasted smoothly down the glidepath toward Joint Base Andrews. The skies over Maryland had cleared from an earlier overcast and the sun was poised on the western horizon, a fitting ending to a grueling day that had begun here twelve hours earlier.

President Elayne Cleveland stared vacantly out the oval window beside her. The great chrome-lipped engines reflected the last glimmers of daylight. The terrain below gained definition, small farms giving way to pocket neighborhoods as the city came nearer. In the gathering darkness, traffic on the distant Beltway necklaced the capital in red and white light.

"At some point there has to be a sacrifice, and we all know who's got the target on his back."

Cleveland blinked. Her eyes came back inside. Reluctantly, she tried to process what her Chief of Staff, Ed Markowitz, had just said. He was sitting across from her in a plush aft-facing chair. After the long day he looked no different than he had at the outset, his usual wonkish self: rumpled tweed jacket, bifocals, unkempt hair, and of course the ever-present secure tablet computer. She wondered if Ed, even as a child, had ever gazed out a window and let his thoughts wander.

They'd departed Andrews at daybreak that morning, destined for a long-deferred tour of a new Kansas semiconductor plant. Bringing tech production back to America was one of the few areas on which the parties could agree. After that had been lunch with the governor of Iowa to promote a robotics research initiative. Altogether, it was a pathetic, and all too obvious, attempt at normalcy after weeks of relentless crises. At every stop the reporters had been ruthless, shouting questions that had nothing to do with silicon wafers or AI. Try as she might to lead the country forward, the recent series of attacks against American interests had become a political black hole, an inexorable force that dragged her away from anything productive.

The chain of disasters had begun six weeks ago, and was now referred to by the media as March Madness. First, an Air Force reconnaissance plane had crashed in the Arctic, the wreckage landing on Russian territory. Almost simultaneously, a Navy guided-missile destroyer had sunk in the Black Sea. Both tragedies occurred under suspicious circumstances, and both involved loss of life. Rumors swirled that Russia was responsible. As commander in chief, however, Cleveland could not retaliate based on rumors. She needed hard facts, and while intelligence reports left no doubt that the acts were intentional, attribution for them had proved harder to nail down. Worse yet, making public what they *did* know would be the world's worst poker move. Which meant her only play was to duck the questions and promise "a full and thorough investigation" by the nation's already embarrassed intelligence agencies. More attacks followed, putting America on the precipice of World War Three, yet

Cleveland found herself mired in political quicksand, and with a window for action that was closing fast. She had so far managed to keep America out of a shooting war with Russia, but her poll numbers were dropping like a free-falling anvil.

"Thomas is a good man," she replied, referring to CIA director Thomas Coltrane. "He's done nothing to shake my faith."

"I would never argue otherwise, but we were caught flatfooted. Our intelligence agencies are still drawing blanks. The perception is that they're failing us in our time of need. America was attacked, and we can't even figure out who was behind it."

"It's not for lack of trying. People at the CIA have risked their lives to get to the bottom of this—one man in particular."

"True, but unfortunately that's not something we can share. The operator you're referring to is an off-the-books asset—he's not even a U.S. citizen, for God's sake. And if Congress finds out you authorized the agency to send a gun-for-hire downrange . . ."

The president stared at Markowitz as his words trailed off into the recirculated air. A biting reply began to rise, but then she thought better of it. Ed had been with her for seven years now, first in the Montana governor's mansion, and now in the White House. Was the pressure getting to him? *Or is it getting to me?*

"The midterm elections are closing in," Markowitz pressed, "and the Democrats are baying for a response. Needless to say, national security is not ground we can afford to concede."

"Nobody is conceding anything. Intelligence work takes time." Cleveland spoke from a position of authority—after graduating from college, she had done a stint in the Army Reserve as an intelligence officer. "What's on my calendar tomorrow?" she asked, ready to change the subject.

Markowitz finger-tapped on his tablet. "The standard morning briefings until ten, then you meet with the vice president to discuss border controls."

"I thought he was in Asia."

"He got back this afternoon."

She had put Vice President Lincoln Quarrels in charge of the southern border. It was a thankless job, and a problem that had been festering for decades. In Cleveland's view, it wasn't a uniquely American issue, but rather a regional manifestation of what was happening across the globe. With the world increasingly divided into haves and have-nots, the exodus of the downtrodden had become a torrent. For America, having oceans on either side and a prosperous Canada to the north, the problem was simply hyper-focused.

The president massaged her temples, feeling the onset of a massive headache. Her eyes went back to the window but snagged on her reflection in the inner pane. Her brown hair, styled dutifully this morning, was drooping after the long day. Even in the ghosted image she could see bags under her eyes. Cleveland rarely found time for diversions of vanity, but the thought of a morning makeover crossed her mind.

The ground seemed to rush up suddenly and the great jet settled onto the runway. Its cantilever landing gear, and two of the finest pilots in the Air Force, bonded for a glass-smooth landing. Elayne Cleveland had never come to think of the White House as home, not really, but it was a place where she could rest. The finest bed-and-breakfast in the world.

Runway lights flashed past the window, the time interval between them lengthening as the great plane slowed. She heard the smartphones of staffers chiming notifications in the adjoining cabin. All of it brought her back to reality, and the idea of an early makeover tomorrow vanished.

There's just too damned much to be done.

Five minutes later, Elayne Cleveland was descending red-carpeted stairs to the tarmac. She took care not to stumble—there were only a handful of cameras in the press pen today, but any misstep would go viral within minutes. Such was the aquarium she lived in.

She saluted two airmen at the bottom of the stairs and made a sharp turn toward her connecting flight: the Sikorsky VH-92 known as Marine One. The scrum of reporters was a hundred yards away, and Cleveland pretended not to hear their shouted questions, most of which had to do with the deplorable state of U.S.-Russia relations. Markowitz shadowed a few steps behind her, and nearing the helicopter she paused to let him catch up.

"Are you going to ride back to the White House with me?" she asked.

"Not tonight. I arranged for a car to take me straight home . . . Julie and I have plans to celebrate our anniversary. But if you need me for something—"

"No, no," Cleveland said, cutting him off. "Have a nice time, and give Julie my best. I'll see you in the morning."

She turned away, forced a smile, and waved at the distant press gaggle. Cleveland strode as energetically as she could toward the idling helicopter, and at the steps of Marine One she exchanged another salute, this with a young Marine, before disappearing inside.

TWO

As the four-billion-dollar Boeing 747–800 known as Air Force One crouched on the ramp, its engines ticking away heat from the long flight, and while the most expensive and finely tuned helicopter on earth prepared to deliver the president of the United States the final eleven miles to the White House, a far more ordinary aircraft circled lazily in the humid evening air twelve miles to the east.

The weary Cessna 172 Skyhawk had been purchased thirty days ago for the price of a good used car. It was a cast-off trainer from a North Carolina flight school, and with three inspections pending, antiquated "steam-gauge" instruments, and more than a few dents and dings, the aircraft was fast nearing the end of an exhausting service life. Aside from the fact that it achieved flight, the tiny four-seater was to the aircraft at Andrews what an abacus was to a supercomputer. It had no satellite navigation, no secure communications, no electronic self-defense measures. The only air conditioning involved cracking the side window open, and even that did little to flush out the dank odors inside: forty years of nervous sweat, vomit, and spilled fuel.

The Cessna's two occupants were crammed shoulder to shoulder in the tiny cockpit. They had to nearly shout to be heard over the engine and slipstream noise. Yet if the aircraft itself was a bare-bones platform, its two-person crew leveraged technology that hadn't existed when it was built: one cell phone and an excellent pair of low-light optics.

In the right seat, doing the flying, was a middle-aged Hungarian. His name was Lazlo, and his meaty hands held the yoke with all the deftness of a prisoner gripping the iron bars of a cell door. Hamfisted though he was, Lazlo was a reasonably experienced pilot, with two thousand hours of flight time in various general aviation aircraft. How he had ended up here, floating a quarter mile above the exburbs of Washington, D.C., was nothing less than a testament to his tenacity. He had grown up in a rough quarter of Budapest where he'd learned to fight, first on the streets and later in the bars. A year in a Hungarian prison did nothing to soften his rough edges, yet it also gave Lazlo time to contemplate. All around him he saw men on the same track he was running, many of them years farther along. A scarred and defeated bunch, they sat hunched in their cells, posturing and scheming, and performing prison tattoos on one another with shaking hands. Sensing fate bearing down, Lazlo came to the realization that only drastic measures would alter his own future, and he committed to the most divergent path he could imagine: on the day of his release, he would join the army.

He made good on the promise. To his benefit, public records in Hungary were aspirational at best, and when the recruiters didn't ask about his stint as a guest of the state, Lazlo didn't bring it up. He served in the infantry for three lusterless years, mostly staying out of trouble. Near the end of his service commitment, a short-lived fling with a flight instructor piqued his interest in aviation. Lazlo then made the second good decision of his life: he used his meager savings from the army to take a few flying lessons.

Soon, however, the old ways began to claw back. Lazlo's first flying job, hauling overnight air freight for a fledgling cargo company, was both exhausting and ill-paying. His second, hauling heroin for the Slovakian mafia, was an improvement on both counts. Yet it also, predictably, introduced considerable new risks.

Lazlo's smuggling career ended as most did, badly and on the run from the law. A forced landing near the Moldovan-Romanian border—contaminants in the fuel system, he suspected—had left an undamaged Pilatus PC-12 and nine million dollars of uncut Afghan heroin on a highway median. Fortunately, the forced landing took place in the middle of the night, and Lazlo was able to escape before an epic morning traffic jam ensued. His run of good luck over, the incident put him squarely in a crossfire: on one side was an embarrassed Romanian police force, on the other a furious Slovak *capo*. Lazlo made his way to Ukraine, and it was there that a bolt of providence intervened.

Her name was Magda.

In the course of his brief smuggling career, Lazlo had made a few runs for the SIS, the Slovak Information Service. SIS was Slovakia's one-stop shop for foreign and domestic intelligence. It was also the kind of agency that considered engaging the services of a discreet pilot-for-hire well within bounds. Hiding in Ukraine after his forced landing, Lazlo had called his SIS contact and explained the situation. He'd only met her once before, and on that night, a year earlier in Bratislava, she'd been a vision in black: shapely jeans, leather top, and the barest outline of a holstered

Beretta Nano on her ankle. As it turned out, on his night of desperation, Lazlo's call to bargain for an extraction from Ukraine had found Magda herself at odds with her employer. Money had gone missing from an SIS account she'd overseen, and certain government ministers, for whose benefit the setup had been arranged, were outraged.

One very pretty head was about to roll.

The next morning Magda and Lazlo, both viewed as deserters by their respective employers, rendezvoused in Lviv. By the end of the day a partnership of necessity was born. Magda purchased a small aircraft, using a stack of U.S. dollars taken from a bulging suitcase, and Lazlo assumed the controls to fly them south.

So began their vagabond relationship. The pair crisscrossed the Mediterranean and Africa, seeking out odd jobs that matched their respective skill sets: Lazlo could fly virtually any small aircraft, while Magda had a brimming list of contacts and extensive training in photo-surveillance. It turned out to be a lucrative niche in a conveniently gray world. Cashed-up oligarchs spying on rivals, oil companies looking for illegal taps on pipelines, governments without the means for an air force searching for rebel camps. For three years the pair made a go of it, building a quiet reputation as private aerial contractors.

Slovakian by birth, Magda was two years younger than Lazlo, and as petite as he was burly. She was also the uncontested brains of the outfit. The partnership eventually took a dual track, becoming both intimate and professional. The question of whether they were married remained a point of contention. There had been a ceremony on a Greek island, performed by a drunken priest on the patio of a pub, which might or might not have been legitimate. Neither of them chased any official document to prove the point, but in their hearts, it was enough. Their professional bond, on the other hand, had never been in question.

Today, Lazlo and Magda were both on edge. This was their first job in America, and while they had accepted it without reservation, lured by a stunning payday, the level of risk was beginning to sink in. Tracking warlords across the foot of the Sahara was one thing. Spying on the president of the United States, on the edge of Washington, D.C., was something else entirely.

Magda sat glued to her binoculars. "Hold steady," she ordered in her native Slovakian. "The helicopter's rotors are turning."

Having been raised on the northern border of Hungary, Lazlo was fluent in the language. He squinted, his eyes canvassing the western side of the distant airfield. In the fading light, he could just make out Air Force One, but not the smaller Sikorsky.

Magda called up her phone's encrypted messaging app, and typed: Preparing to depart.

The innocuous message immediately showed DE-LIVERED. Flying a thousand feet in the air, the unobstructed cell signal was stronger here than on the ground. She handed the phone over to Lazlo. The next minutes would be critical and she wanted to stabilize the binoculars with both hands.

"Prepare for the straight-line course," she said.

They had rehearsed the move before—twice in practice, and also on three live missions that had aborted. The failed missions were no fault of their own, and had been anticipated—it was all no more than a matter of odds. On those aborted attempts, Lazlo had simply steered away to the east, blended into the haze, and returned to the tiny airfield in North Carolina that served as their base. As the Americans were fond of saying: no harm, no foul.

"Can't we get closer?" Magda complained.

"I told you, it is out of the question. At this range and altitude we are beneath controlled airspace. That is the only way we can navigate freely, without interference from the air traffic controllers."

Lazlo had plotted the geometry carefully during the planning stage. The Cessna's present orbit put them just high enough to get what they needed—an unobstructed, if distant, view of Joint Base Andrews. Above them was busier airspace, airline traffic and business jets swarming into Reagan National and Dulles airports. Directly below was half a square mile of freshly turned earth, one more farm field being converted into a package fulfillment center.

They had been circling for twenty minutes, having been forewarned that Air Force One was arriving when its pilots checked in with approach control, Potomac TRACON—Lazlo had that frequency tuned in to the Cessna's secondary VHF radio. Their pretense for being where they were depended on who was asking. The flight plan he'd filed implied they were on a cross-country training flight, a round trip out of Plymouth Municipal Airport in North Carolina, with a stop for fuel in southern Maryland. He'd told the mechanic back in North Carolina that he and Magda were headed out for the aviation equivalent of a date, the standard "hundred-dollar hamburger" that included the cost of fuel at some remote airfield.

To the air traffic controllers on VHF-1—they were not under direct control, but had requested traffic advisories—Lazlo explained that they were orbiting in their present position for some photo-surveillance work. Such flights were less common than they had been ten years ago, before the advent of drones, yet there was still some market for it—real estate developers, mostly, yearning for high-resolution overheads of their trophy projects. That this was the fourth time Cessna NUX52 had set up orbit over the same construction site in the past three weeks only backstopped the lie further.

Magda watched as Marine One's rotor blades accelerated to a blur. Soon the aircraft lifted off and banked north, which she relayed to Lazlo.

He released the control column momentarily, and with sausage thumbs pecked out a message: Leaving now.

This was the critical juncture. From Joint Base Andrews to the South Lawn of the White House was a mere eleven miles—roughly a five-minute flight for the big Sikorsky. Magda kept her eyes glued to Marine One, shifting occasionally to search for the others that would join in the next moments. Helicopters, for the most part, flew low and slow, and that made them vulnerable. To enhance security, the VH-92 that carried the president always merged with a group of identical aircraft. Same model, same paint scheme, same squadron. The number ranged from two to four, this variance itself another random element—the Secret Service strove for every variable it could get.

Equally unpredictable was the route the formation would take to reach the South Lawn. Lazlo and Magda had been told there were six tracks in all, and that the pilots had the authority to choose one at will. They had no idea where their employer had gotten this information, or if it was even true, but the tracks on the three aborted missions had correlated with the chart they'd been given. The problem they faced today, as it had been from the outset, was that the attack could only be configured for one particular route. On the previous runs they had struck out.

"How many?" Lazlo asked.

"I still don't see . . . wait . . . they are joining up now."

Like a hawk watching a flock of sparrows, Magda tracked Marine One as it veered north at low altitude. Right on schedule, near the end of Andrews' two big runways, three other VH-92s, perfectly identical, swooped into view.

"Three others . . . four altogether!"

Lazlo sent another message.

The four aircraft began mingling, weaving in a gentle daisy-chain pattern. It was nothing less than an aerial shell game, an effort to conceal which chopper carried the president. The Secret Service used a similar ruse with limousines in motorcades, yet those obfuscations were more easily executed in the concealment of parking garages and tunnels.

Lazlo kept the Cessna flying straight and level, approximating the speed of the distant formation. As the pilot in command, he would normally have occupied the left seat, yet with a northerly course necessary, and the city being on their left side, they'd swapped seats to give Magda an unobstructed view. For Lazlo it made little difference—there wasn't a button or control he couldn't reach with his long arms.

"If we could only fly closer," she fussed as they flew a parallel course twelve miles distant.

"No, we cannot! If we even approach the controlled airspace we will draw attention—especially with the president's bubble being active."

Magda's eyes remained glued to the critical chopper, the others sweeping through the edges of her magnified field of view. For thirty seconds the aerial circus ran, the little band of VH-92s weaving like so many drunks on a sidewalk. Finally, they reached a divergence point and settled on a course.

"They're over the old church!" Having memorized landmarks on all the routes, they knew the path to the White House had narrowed to two possibilities—one of which was the one they were after.

"A coin flip," Lazlo said breathlessly.

There was a final course correction, Marine One tipping slightly to the right at the junction of two minor roads. Today's route was confirmed. Magda felt a flutter in her chest. On any given day it was a one-in-six chance. Today, on their fourth mission, the formation was taking Route Juneau.

"It's Juneau!" she said, trying to keep her voice level.

Lazlo let go of the controls once more, long enough to type out carefully: Juneau! Standby!

Once the message was delivered, he returned a hand to the controls. There were still two messages to be sent, including the most critical. After that, he would shut down the phone, remove the battery, and drop both out the window somewhere over rural Maryland.

"Do you still have the primary in sight?" he asked.

"Yes," Magda replied, her voice barely audible so complete was her concentration. "I am sure of it."

The "bubble" around Marine One was active, air traffic controllers having cleared a corridor to the White House. Two executive helicopters had been vectored away, and the arrival controllers at Reagan National Airport—at its closest point, a mere one mile from the restricted airspace—had built a gap in the flow of oncoming airliners.

It was a routine exercise for everyone.

As the weaving flock of choppers from Marine Helicopter Squadron One neared the confluence of the Potomac and Anacostia Rivers, there was no reason for concern. Their crews were understandably confident. Marine One, as well as its three companion VH-92s, brimmed with self-defense gear. Each had a laser anti-missile system, radar warning receivers, and chaff and flare dispensers to deceive incoming missiles. The pilots, all of whom had seen combat in either Afghanistan or Iraq, were seasoned veterans tested under fire. All those precautions, however, shared one shortcoming—they were geared to defend against, and respond to, known threats.

What lay before them was something else altogether.

THREE

Situated amid a sea of construction equipment, the semi-trailer could not have been more ordinary. Over a half million commuters had crossed the new Frederick Douglass Bridge that week, yet not a single one would have recalled anything special about it. The workers on the job site were equally disinterested; such containers were as common as trees in a forest, and they came and went without notice.

The trailer in question was hidden in plain sight near the edge of a perimeter ditch. All around it was a soil-churning array of dump trucks, payloaders, mobile offices, and no fewer than twenty other box trailers displaying various grimy logos. The construction zone had been active for nearly six years—to the workers, closer to a career than a job site—and while the primary objective of replacing the old South Capitol Street bridge was complete, considerable work remained to revitalize the surrounding Riverwalk and parks.

The trailer sat propped on its rear wheels and forward legs, like a pioneer wagon waiting for a horse. No one could really say when it had arrived or who had left it there. Were anyone to investigate its DOT registration number and license plate—no one ever had—they would learn that it was registered to a company purporting to install sewer lines and stormwater culverts. That vision planted, it was only a small extension to imagine the trailer being filled with pumps, pipes, and trench shoring equipment.

In fact, the generic off-white container held nothing of the sort.

The body of the trailer had undergone subtle modifications. The original access doors in back had been reinforced and strengthened, as had the sidewalls all around. The massive lock on the unit would require nothing short of an acetylene torch to breach. All these fortifications were crude and evident from the outside. This, too, was by design: thievery on construction sites was rampant, and the owner wanted to make clear that there were softer targets elsewhere.

The most significant alteration, however, involved the roof. The forward thirty feet of the trailer's ceiling had been cut into four sections and reinstalled on hinges. The panels folded down and inward, and were actuated by a series of modified garage door openers. These changes could be seen only from above, and even in daylight were barely distinguishable. At night the revisions were all but invisible.

At dusk that Saturday evening, the construction yard was deserted. The trailer near the ditch was as still as the distant monument to Lincoln. There were a handful of pedestrians walking the river's far shore, and the usual weekend traffic buzzed along Capitol Street—altogether, a mere handful of distant passersby.

All of whom were oblivious to what was about to happen.

Inside the trailer a lone figure sat behind a builder's table—eight cinderblocks supporting a section of 5/8-inch plywood. The man was average in height and had a lean build. His features were vaguely Asian, although with something else perhaps mixed in. He sat motionless behind a laptop, staring at his phone. His close-cropped black hair and patchy three-day stubble were floodlit by the computer's screen. The only other illumination in the trailer was a spray of amber cast by a battery-powered work light zip-tied to one wall.

He was getting used to this drill. In truth, more familiar than he wanted to be. For all his attributes—and there were many—patience was not among them. As an experienced operator, he knew that routine was a weakness. He had sat in this same trailer on three previous occasions, waiting and watching, only to see the mission abort. He'd always known it might play out that way, yet each attempt brought an additive measure of risk. Someone might see him a second time, wonder what he was doing inside the trailer.

His index finger tapped the plywood table. Given what was at stake, he was ready to finish this job and get the hell out of town.

He wore construction clothes—frayed jeans, heavy shirt, and steel-toe boots. All of it was worn and dusty, and hung from his wiry frame with the right degree of looseness. Less convincing was the hardhat near the door, a requirement for the job site. He had purchased a used item, only to find that it was far too large—it sat on his head like a football helmet on a deer. Still, the big plastic shell had its uses: it was good for hiding his face from security cameras. He was an expert on surveillance, and had identified three on the work site.

A trickle of sweat rolled down his back, although it wasn't a matter of nerves. A native of Manchuria, he had been born to the cold. The trailer had felt like a sauna when he arrived three hours ago. Leaving the back door open was not an option, so he'd cracked one of the roof panels early. Each week the mission dragged on brought summer that much closer. He would simply have to suffer through it.

While he had never been a religious man—much to his grandmother's disappointment—a few nights ago he'd actually prayed that his time in America would end soon. He was on the cusp of victory, not to mention a once-in-a-lifetime paycheck. He only hoped he would live long enough to see it. If all went as planned, he would be forced to disappear for some time. A year, possibly two. Yet he was not distracted by visions of seaside villas or mountaintop retreats. Not yet. The Manchurian's focus was as singular as ever: an absolute drive to be recognized as the best.

The text he'd been waiting for finally arrived: Juneau! Standby!

The exclamation points were lost on the Manchurian. His body didn't react in the usual way. There was no skipped cardiac beat, no churn in his gut. To the contrary, he felt a palpable sense of liberation. After so much planning, so much risk mitigation, the waiting was over. This was the moment he'd been working toward his entire life, the culmination of years of training and operational expertise. *Execute now, and I will become a legend.*

He entered the preliminary command on the laptop: Power up

For two seconds a clatter of clicking noises filled the stagnant air.

The safety bolts on the roof panels were already loose, and he began the final preparations. The well-practiced sequence took less than thirty seconds: a four panels pivoted inward. The system worked perfectly, leaving the forward half of the trailer open to the soft evening sky. The heat dissipated instantly, fresh evening air taking its place. He looked up into the gray dusk and saw the night's first star, barely visible to the southwest. All his attention returned to the phone, his fingertips poised over the keyboard. The Manchurian's ears reached for any sound, but he heard nothing beyond the din of traffic on the distant bridge.

Soon, very soon, that would be replaced.

They'd run estimates for every conceivable variable, and come up with a window: from the time Route Juneau was confirmed, it would take between two and three and a half minutes for the helicopters to arrive overhead.

His fingertips hovered, ready to input the final commands. To deploy too soon risked discovery and evasion. Launching too late meant missing the chance. Either error would blow the mission entirely. He had one shot to get everything right.

He allowed one glance into the darkened bed of the trailer. One hundred and eighty-six green eyes stared back. Then the Manchurian discerned a vague thumping noise, more by feel than anything audible. For a moment he thought it might be his heartbeat. Then the intensity rose, resolving into the familiar thrum of rotors. He recalled the sound from the previous aborted attempts when, though tantalizingly close, the choppers had passed a mile distant.

His phone vibrated.

Sixty seconds. Route confirmed.

He entered the penultimate command on the laptop: Launch

The great swarm of drones bristled to life, an ocean

of tiny propellers humming in unison. Because the roof opening was not large enough for all of them to launch at once, the aircraft rose in four waves, perfectly spaced and orderly, like a military parade. Twenty seconds later, the entire fleet was airborne, organized in the programmed formation. The swarm hovered above the container, awaiting the final command. The Manchurian was watching the drones, mesmerized, when the final text came.

Target center-west.

He replied to the text: Center-west. Allahu Akbar!

The last two words were something between humor and misdirection. Encryption or not, in a day, possibly two, the NSA would likely uncover the message thread. He quickly typed the targeting command into the laptop, and when he sank the ENTER key, it was fittingly with his trigger finger.

The great flock of weapons responded.

The drones communicated via a discreet network and, using distributed brain technology, arranged themselves not unlike a single organism. The formation climbed in unison, and in the dim light they resembled a flock of birds. From that point, the Manchurian was little more than a spectator. The formation was now autonomous, actively seeking and ready to destroy. He avoided the urge to stand and watch. Whether the mission succeeded or not, it would be recognized within minutes. An hour from now this construction site, this trailer, would become ground zero in a massive manhunt.

He raised the roof panels back up and bolted them in place. Hurrying to the back of the trailer, he unlocked the right-hand door and dropped silently to the ground. He levered the door nearly shut, then attached a pair of uninsulated wires and one of the garage door remote controls to the handle. None of it had any function, but it looked for all the world like a crude booby trap. Enough to give any EOD man pause. It would take time to call in the dogs and the robots. At least an hour, two if he was lucky.

He walked away briskly, scanning the surrounding acres of dirt for signs of life. He saw no one. The thrum of the helicopters was unmistakable now, closing in fast.

Finally, he relented.

The Manchurian paused and looked up into the fast-darkening sky.

FOUR

The drones climbed quickly to their assigned altitude and aligned themselves in perfect formation. They were programmed for optimal spacing: fifteen feet apart both laterally and vertically, arrayed in six rows of thirty-one aircraft. The sum result, within moments, would be an airborne curtain nearly five hundred feet wide and one hundred feet high.

The drones were not off-the-shelf models, but a high-end South Korean-manufactured military variant. This was essential to the mission. Most civilian drones were controlled remotely, receiving commands over a limited frequency range that could be jammed by authorities under times of heightened security—such as presidential movement. Other models could be programmed with preset courses, but that restricted the ability to coordinate. The flock of aircraft rising above the trailer were an entirely different breed.

They were, collectively, a "fire and forget" weapon. Maneuvering was coordinated using artificial intelligence, each aircraft receiving and transmitting information via a sophisticated datalink with frequency-hopping capability. The airframes themselves were a robust quadcopter design, roughly the size of a shoebox. Each aircraft was also a source of intelligence, although not the usual radar or optical data.

Instead, directional acoustic sensors took readings all around. That collective array of data, taken from one hundred eighty-six individual points, was meshed through secondary AI software. Once a target was identified from a library of acoustic signatures, a joint intercept command was formulated. Moving in a wave, the formation would position itself amoeba-like to achieve an intercept.

Presently, the wall of drones was hovering three hundred feet above the ground. There, clear of acoustic ground clutter, and with the formation of helicopters a mere quarter mile distant, four thumping rotors overrode every other sound. The drone's software had been tuned to recognize precisely such signatures, and it quickly resolved the oncoming din into four distinct returns. The third from the left, as instructed, became the focal point. With the end game in sight, the software updated the picture continuously and derived intercept commands. Not unlike a great flock of raptors, the swarm began maneuvering in three-dimensional unison.

Thirty feet higher.

Twenty feet to the west.

Distance three hundred yards, closing fast.

When the range and closure rate reached preset values, the kill mechanisms deployed.

For so much reliance on technology, the lethal blow would be simplicity itself. The drones were effectively modern-day kamikazes, robotic versions of The Divine Wind. They carried no explosives, no projectiles, no offensive electronics of any kind. The devastation promised was far more basic, inspired by a naval armament first utilized five centuries earlier: chain shot, a pair of iron balls connected by a length of chain, was used with devastating effect against the sails and rigging of great navy ships. That principle of destruction remained as valid as ever.

With the lethal curtain established in the flight path of the onrushing helicopters, and twenty seconds remaining to impact, each of the one hundred and eighty-six drones released a two-pound claw connected by a high-strength strap. The strap was fourteen feet in length, a Kevlar composite weave that, while only two inches wide, had demonstrated astonishing tensile strength in testing. Only one limitation had been foreseen by the planners: if the pilots of helicopters were astute, in broad daylight they might see the swarm and have time for an evasive maneuver. Yet in the period from dusk to dawn, they reasoned, or if visibility was restricted, the drones would be virtually impossible to see.

As it turned out, they were proved correct.

The first pilot to see the swarm wasn't flying Marine One, but rather the chopper on its right wing. The lieutenant colonel got off one frantic radio call, but before his warning could register with the pilots of Marine One, they saw it themselves. In the dim light, a confusing image: countless small obstructions directly in their flight path. The natural first thought of both pilots was that they were looking at a flock of birds. Yet the alignment seemed too perfect, too artificial. Within seconds, the flock resolved into something mechanical, and hanging from each tiny aircraft was what appeared to be a rope. From their point of view it was an airborne wall, an onrushing curtain of unknown obstructions.

With the objects a mere hundred feet in front of them, there was no time to process any of that. Marine One was traveling at a hundred and ten knots, giving the aircraft commander less than a second to react. He hauled back instinctively on the controls, but far too late.

The impacts began.

The first two Kevlar straps were shredded by the big Sikorsky's rotor blades, and the lightweight drones connected to them were instantly pulverized. The third impact, however, began a disastrous chain of events. The claw attachment was whipped at lightning speed into the main rotor head, where it lodged firmly. The attached strap spun into the hub and the friction began. Within milliseconds, three other straps became enmeshed in various moving parts.

The hub of a helicopter rotor is an intricate mechanical playground: countless moving parts and carefully dispersed energy. The impact with the drones was the aviation equivalent of throwing a cluster of Mylar balloons into a high-speed ceiling fan. Metal and composites disintegrated in an explosion of opposing forces. Everyone on board, the president included, felt a terrible shudder course through the airframe. Things settled for a moment, like a held breath, until one steel claw ripped out a vital pitch link. Soon shrapnel and debris from the ruined pitch link were chewing through other parts of the rotor assembly. It took only seconds for the out-of-balance forces to induce a crack in a main rotor blade, and a twenty-foot-long section snapped off and went spinning toward the river below.

At that point, the aircraft's fate was sealed. All helicopters are designed with a measure of robustness, having calculated redundancies: they can lose an engine or a gearbox, suffer tail rotor damage. A thrown main rotor blade, however, is nothing short of catastrophic.

The pilot battled the controls, but the aircraft didn't respond. Inside the cabin of Marine One, the two Secret Service officers accompanying the president, who were seated and strapped in nearby, grabbed for handholds against the wild gyrations. For all their training when it came to protecting the president, enduring a helicopter crash had not been in the curriculum. With a selflessness that would earn him a posthumous award for valor, the Marine corporal serving as escort unbuckled his seat belt in the whirling cabin and lunged toward the president. Holding onto the base of her seat as the aircraft plummeted, he wrenched her seatbelt tight and shouted, "Brace yourself, Madame President!" No sooner had he done so than he was thrown across the cabin and knocked unconscious.

From the nearby terminals of Reagan National Airport, the walking paths of East Potomac Park, and the George Washington Parkway, thousands of Americans watched in horror as Marine One plunged toward the Anacostia River like a buckshot quail. It careened sidelong over Buzzard Point and nearly clipped the grand façade of the National War College. Two hundred yards farther south, one of the decoy choppers began spinning to earth on a different angle under a trail of smoke, one of its engines having shredded after sucking in a drone assembly.

The two VH-92s hit the water seconds apart.

Marine One slammed down a hundred yards from the shore of East Potomac Park, a geyser of spray blasting into the evening sky. For a moment there was nothing more, the great helicopter lost in a veil of mist and smoke. When the curtain finally cleared, the chopper was foundering and rolling onto its port side.

And sinking fast.

For all the planning, all the technology and preparation that had gone into the attempted assassination of the president of the United States, there was one variable its architects could never have foreseen.

His name was Humberto Rivas.

Rivas was jogging the curving paths of East Potomac Park, three miles into his five-mile routine, and had just rounded Hains Point when his senses went on alert. He never saw what happened in the sky—Marine One had been behind him, at his five o'clock position—and he never heard anything because AC/DC's "Shot of Love" was cranking in his earbuds. All at once, however, he noticed the people around him—there were scores on the paths at sunset—and it struck him that everyone was looking toward a single point in the sky. A few were actually pointing, hands over mouths, while others seemed transfixed, their faces writ in horror. He turned just in time to see a large helicopter slam into the river a football field away. Seconds later, in the distant periphery, another aircraft did the same, albeit in a more controlled manner. Rivas's first thought, logically, was that there had been a midair collision.

In the next moments, there were a great many reactions among those on the paths. Most stood gawking, while others pulled out their cell phones—some to call for help, others to take video. A few ran for their lives.

Humberto Rivas was of a very different mindset.

Without a thought, he set out on a dead run toward the crash. As a former Navy aircrewman, he was trained in search and rescue. On top of that, in the ten years since leaving the service Rivas had worked as an EMT with the Fairfax County Fire and Rescue Department. The upshot of it all: there wasn't anyone within miles more qualified to respond. Rivas's actions weren't sourced in any sense of patriotism or heroics. He simply went on autopilot, hardwired by twenty-two years of training and operational experience.

He paused for a moment at the water's edge to study the scene. There was still a great deal of smoke around the nearest chopper, and for the first time he realized he was looking at a military bird. This wasn't surprising—a constant stream of helos migrated along the river going to and from the Pentagon. The aircraft was floating on its side, one rotor spiking skyward in a billowing cloud of steam. The tail section was barely visible, the boom having cracked at an odd angle. He glanced back over his shoulder and saw three people talking on their phones—the 911 dispatcher was likely overwhelmed. Help would be on the way. Without further thought, or consideration of risk, Rivas kicked off his running shoes, dumped his phone and earbuds into the grass, and dove headlong into the river.

He covered the gap to the wreckage quickly, and on reaching it he steadied himself by grabbing a wheel that was jutting above the surface. He saw one survivor near the aft rotor, a stunned man in a business suit with an arm hooked over an antenna of some kind. His head was bloody and he appeared to be in shock, and Rivas saw what looked like a wire dangling from one of his ears. The man seemed safe for the moment.

He looked out across the river and saw two boats approaching, one of which had official markings of some kind. Both were still a good distance away, and his training kicked in. The first minutes after a ditching were critical.

The aircraft was floating, but seemed lower than when he'd first seen it. How deep *is* the water here? he wondered. Rivas had no idea, but he assumed it was deep enough to swallow a fast-sinking helo. He side-stroked toward the cockpit, which was almost completely submerged. Through a broken window he saw what he feared: the unmoving shapes of the two pilots. They looked still and lifeless, yet there was no way to be sure. Something about them seemed odd, yet it would be many hours later, as he recounted his actions for investigators, that he realized what it was: the pilots weren't wearing flight suits, but instead Marine Corps dress uniforms. He couldn't reach them from where he was, at least not without an axe to chop through twisted metal and plexiglass. He realized his best chance to save anyone was through the main entry door, which in the aftermath was little more than an opening—the door itself had been either thrown off in the crash or breached during the emergency exit of the survivor near the tail.

He moved aft, walking his hands along the base of the fuselage. Air was venting from every opening, water filling the void—the resulting sound, a churning death rattle, Rivas remembered from his Navy days. The aircraft was going down fast. He was nearly to the entry door when he recognized an emblem painted on the side of the chopper—the seal of the President of the United States.

For the first time, Rivas's autopilot disconnected. He realized what might be at stake.

He hauled himself through the opening, flopping over what had been the top step like a bloated flounder. He gauged the sideways world of the cabin's interior. Thankfully, the emergency lights had kicked on, giving good illumination. The cabin was two-thirds submerged, torrents of water boiling all around. He smelled the unmistakable stench of jet fuel. Rivas saw one body, another Marine in uniform, floating face down, the neck bent at an impossible angle. He looked forward, toward the cockpit, and saw that it was now completely submerged. He then surveyed the back, beyond a floating cushion and a Mae West that had somehow inflated. Against the aft bulkhead, half-hidden by an eddy of swirling foam and flotsam, he saw the top of a head and most of a face.

A face that, when combined with the emblem he'd seen near the door, was instantly recognizable. "Holy shit!" he said to no one.

Rivas looked back once at the entry door. Only seconds remained before it disappeared completely. He fought his way back toward the president, and without even checking for a pulse, he took a deep breath and dove down to search for her lap belt.

Forcing himself to be methodical, Rivas worked by feel, his hands tracking down the president's neck, shoulders, breasts, and finally onto her waist. He felt for the seatbelt latch, found it, and disconnected the belt, then spread the straps as far apart as he could before rising for air. His head struck the angled cabin roof—only a foot-high gap of air remained. Elayne Cleveland had popped up with him, but when he tried to pull her toward the door she stopped as if anchored. Something was hung up, probably her dress or a shoe snagged on twisted metal.

Rivas looked at the door again. The tiny sliver of outside light had nearly disappeared.

He took a massive lungful of air, then dove down one final time.

FIVE

As the disaster on the river unfolded, Vice President Lincoln Quarrels lay sound asleep. He had arrived back in D.C. early that afternoon after a ten-day diplomatic junket to the Far East.

The combination of travel and time zones, not to mention a bout of sushi-induced food poisoning from a state dinner in Tokyo, had left him all but catatonic. After being dropped by his motorcade at the vice president's official residence, Number One Observatory Circle, he'd spent an hour with his wife over a meal—a late lunch according to the official clock at the nearby Naval Observatory—followed by thirty minutes with his chief of staff, Matthew Gross, crafting the best spin for a press release regarding the Far East trip. Neither expected the end product to make waves. Barring any glaring verbal gaffes or tumbles across red carpets, vice presidential trips were largely ignored by the media.

At that point, Quarrels had cleared his calendar until the next morning, professing a need to sleep before his scheduled ten a.m. meeting with Elayne Cleveland. He'd gone upstairs and collapsed into his four-poster bed.

The weeklong Far East junket would have laid any man low, but at seventy-six years old Quarrels was the oldest vice president to ever serve. Even on a good day he looked ten years older. His salt-and-pepper hair, which had begun to turn in his twenties, was now wispy and had gone snow white. The skin on his face and neck was crinkled like old linen, and there was no hiding the stoop in his posture. Still, Quarrels was well-versed in deal making on the Hill, good in a debate, and after four terms in the Senate and a stint as director of national intelligence, he'd been the safe pick to shore up Elayne Cleveland's ticket with foreign policy hawks.

Quarrels had been sleeping for three hours when someone gently shook his shoulder. "Mr. Vice President," said a voice through what seemed like mist.

"Mr. Vice President!"

Quarrels blinked his eyes open and saw a familiar face from his Secret Service detail. "Sir, we have a situation!" the lead agent said. "You need to come immediately!"

Six minutes later, Quarrels was at the front door and being ushered to a car. It turned out not to be his usual ride waiting under the portico, but The Beast— the nine-ton Cadillac behemoth normally reserved for the president. If that wasn't enough of an omen, he noticed an unusually large contingent of Secret Service agents on the perimeter. Virtually all of them were facing outward, scanning and alert.

Quarrels glanced toward a trailing car and saw a familiar military aide, one of the officers who carried the nuclear football, standing outside. He, or someone like him, was tasked to always be near the president. He, too, seemed exceptionally alert.

Quarrels slid into the back seat and found Matt

Gross waiting. "What the hell is going on?" he asked, straightening his miserably knotted tie.

"Marine One has crashed—a terrorist attack of some kind. The president is injured and being taken to Walter Reed."

"Jesus! Is it serious?"

"I just talked to the Treasury Secretary, who's been in direct contact with the Secret Service. Apparently, she's in critical condition."

Quarrels's head snapped back against the headrest as The Beast shot forward. "But she's alive," he said, more to himself than to Gross.

"Yes. As a precaution, we need to get to the White House immediately. I've ordered every member of the cabinet who's in D.C. to convene for an emergency meeting."

The vice president studied his chief of staff guardedly. His bow tie was straight, his shirt crisp. There was no hint of stress whatsoever. Less than half his own age, Gross exuded East Coast money and Ivy League ambition, and although he rankled many of the more experienced staffers, his political instincts were unerringly accurate.

"Emergency meeting," the vice president repeated. "Does that imply what I think it does?"

"It's likely we will have to invoke the Twenty-Fifth Amendment."

It was a contingency Quarrels understood well, the transfer of power during a crisis.

Gross said, "We covered the nuts and bolts of the process in the lead-up to the inauguration and—"

"I know the damned process!" Quarrels snapped. He looked out the window blankly, a hand cupping his chin contemplatively as the Naval Observatory flew past. Like every vice president before him, no doubt, he had gone to bed more than once wondering *what if?*

Now that hypothetical had become reality.

The limo hit Massachusetts Avenue like a tank on nitrous oxide. There were two cars in front, three behind, and a squad of motorcycle police outriggered the formation. As they made their way southeast, Quarrels noticed that the roads had been cleared for the entire three-mile journey to the White House, every side street cordoned off. Major intersections were blocked by military vehicles. His convoy—there was no other word for it—flew effortlessly over District streets that would normally be bogged down with evening traffic. Military helicopters flashed overhead, and he suspected fighters had launched to fly a cap over the city. Quarrels didn't feel like he was in danger, yet the show of force was disquieting—automated protocols taken in response to an attack against the president.

But was it a successful attack?

Gross was on his phone, and as he chattered away Quarrels's gaze settled on a pair of high-end handsets on the console in front of him. The Beast was equipped with a triple-redundant secure communications suite. Shouldn't he call someone? Do *something*? His thoughts drifted, and he wondered how Lyndon Johnson had received word of Kennedy being shot. How had he reacted in those desperate minutes—or was it hours?—when the president's fate hung in the balance as doctors tried to save him?

Quarrels was a lawyer by education, and had once taught constitutional law, so he knew the Twenty-Fifth Amendment chapter-and-verse. He knew it had been sourced from that dark day in Dallas, and tested repeatedly since; the shooting of Ronald Reagan, and when medical procedures were performed on multiple presidents. Never, however, had Section 4, the declaration by others of a president's incapacity, ever been invoked. With Elayne Cleveland's condition unclear, the Constitution was about to be tested again.

The uplit White House abruptly came into view as they approached Lafayette Square. Quarrels sensed a surge of adrenaline unlike anything he'd ever felt. He couldn't say what would happen in the next few hours—much was out of his hands. Yet one thing was clear: tonight, history would be made.

SIX

"I hereby declare, on oath, that I absolutely and entirely renounce and abjure all allegiance and fidelity to any foreign prince, potentate, state, or sovereignty of whom or which I have heretofore been a subject or citizen; that I will support and defend the Constitution and laws of the United States of America against all enemies, foreign and domestic; that I will bear true faith and allegiance to the same; that I will bear arms on behalf of the United States when required by the law; that I will perform noncombatant service in the Armed Forces of the United States when required by the law; that I will perform work of national importance under civilian direction when required by the law; and that I take this obligation freely without any mental reservation or purpose of evasion; so help me God."

Christine gave a polite golf-clap. "Nicely done, not a hitch."

David Slaton set the oath of U.S. citizenship cheat sheet on his bedroom dresser. "You're sure about this." Half question, half statement.

"We've been married long enough, so it's all above board. You qualify for citizenship."

"It says I have to bear arms."

"You've done that already."

"True, but this says 'when required by the law.' The kind of things they ask me to do . . . not so much."

"The kinds of things they ask you to do wouldn't sound very good in an oath of citizenship. Anyway, I thought they'd come up with a workaround, some kind of presidential memorandum to make you legit."

"I don't think anything I've ever done for the CIA was approved by the legal department. That memorandum was about covering asses in Washington in case I screwed up."

"Okay, fair enough. Let's look at it another way. America is a nation of immigrants, and you're a pretty damned good stonemason. We need expertise from all walks of life."

He grinned and laid down on the bed next to her. Christine was comfortably propped back on pillows, her auburn hair showing the first streaks of summer, her long limbs relaxed. He'd begun to notice crinkles at the corners of her eyes, and somehow they made her more beautiful than ever. Five years of marriage or not, she still took his breath away. Slaton was about to say something along those lines when a clatter from the next room interrupted the moment. Their son, Davy, was shoveling through his box of Lego bricks, looking for the perfect piece for his latest project. Romance *did* get harder when you had a kid. And it was about to get harder yet.

Slaton put a hand on his wife's belly, which was starting to show a bump. "Feel anything yet?"

"What, like kicking? Not likely at twelve weeks. But we might see some movement on the ultrasound tomorrow."

"Gender?"

"We should get the results of the genetic testing any day now."

"Is that one hundred percent accurate?"

"One hundred percent? That's asking a lot."

"Maybe we should stay in the dark. You know, come up with both boy and girl names."

She was about to say something when his hand moved on her stomach. "There," he said. "I felt something."

Christine grinned. "Indigestion."

He smiled back at her. "I like having a wife who's a doctor. You can answer all my medical questions."

"Yeah. And also patch you up every time you . . ." she checked what they both knew she was about say, and went with, "when you drop a ten-pound block of stone on your foot."

He looked down at two black-and-blue toes, a minor incident from his latest backyard project, a staircase leading down to the creek behind the house. "Yeah, well, if that's the worst that happens, then—"

His thought was cut off by the sound of the oven timer going off. Christine rolled to one side and got up. "Dinner in ten. But remember, tomorrow night you're the cook."

"Davy and I will come up with something."

She rolled her eyes and disappeared.

Five minutes later Slaton was on the front porch, leaning on a support beam as the sun fell low toward the distant mountain.

As the evening coolness took hold, his eyes swept the open ground in front of their ranch-style house. He'd insisted on a hundred-meter clear area all around, a basic defensive precaution. There were, however, no cameras or motion detectors. Christine had drawn that line. Still, the elbow room was at least a small comfort. The wall of spruce and fir stood still in the evening air, and a patch of aspen on the nearby hill, catching the low western sun, shimmered with new growth. Somewhere in the surrounding forest, out of sight but ever-present, was their agency-issued security detail—a small but highly capable force, and part of the deal he'd made with the devil that was the CIA's clandestine branch.

The job wasn't one Slaton had sought. In truth, it wasn't really a *job* at all. More an accommodation that fit everyone's jagged needs. So far, though, it was working. Christine had recently mentioned that she felt increasingly secure on the ranch, and Slaton sensed it as well. He could never completely discount the possibility of an armed incursion, some settling of an old score from his past, yet the threat seemed increasingly distant. That impression, he knew, sourced from his surroundings. He had a deepening sense of familiarity with this place. The structures, the Northern Rockies, and of course, his family. Eighteen months and counting. It was the longest Slaton had ever lived anywhere. His childhood had been a fractious, vagabond existence. For too many years since, he had simply moved from one mission to another, from safe house to safe house. No chance for a life by any recognizable measure.

Then, in a chance encounter, Christine had saved his life. Perhaps in more ways than one. She was the perfect inverse to the profession that had been consuming him. No secrets, no lies, and from a woman who dedicated her own life to making others well. Now—

"David!" Her voice from inside.

"What's up?" he called back.

"David . . . you need to see this."

Something in her tone. He hurried into the house.

Christine was standing near the dining room table, motionless with a spatula in her hand. Her eyes were locked on something distant, and he followed them to the television on the far side of the room. A newscast was running, and he saw a jerky video playing in a loop. A helicopter crashing into a river. The TV's volume was muted, but a banner scrolled across the bottom to give context.

MARINE ONE CRASHES INTO ANACOSTIA RIVER. PRESIDENT CLEVELAND ON BOARD.

Slaton moved slowly toward his wife, put an arm around her shoulder. They stood that way for a long time, neither saying a word.

It was Christine who finally broke the silence. "David, do you think . . ." Her voice faded to nothing, but the thought transmitted anyway.

"I don't know," he said. "But we'll find out soon enough."

The little Cessna touched down firmly, the tires squeaking to announce its arrival in rural Maryland. There was only one person on the ground to hear it.

The airfield was tiny by any standard. There was no control tower, and the runway had no lights. The lone windsock, knotted by a storm the previous year, had become home to a pair of nesting finches. The narrow runway, twelve hundred feet of ungroomed asphalt, bore a striking resemblance to the cart paths on the nearby golf course. There were two hangars, one of which sheltered not an airplane but the owner's Class A RV. A mere three aircraft resided at the field, and all were tied down sleepily on the parking apron. One had a flat tire, and another was missing its engine. By any measure, it was one of the least busy airstrips in all of Maryland.

Which made it the perfect place for a touch-and-go.

Lazlo never bothered to exit the runway, simply bringing Cessna NUX52 to a stop near the midpoint. He left the engine running. Magda threw open the starboard door, got out, and their passenger appeared out of the nearby treeline. Without a word, the Manchurian clambered in back, shoving a rucksack through to the port-side rear seat.

Magda climbed back inside, and under cover of darkness Lazlo spun a one-eighty and taxied to the spot where they'd touched down. He pirouetted another half turn and, after less than four minutes on the ground, the little airplane lifted off and disappeared into a star-strewn night sky.

SEVEN

Quarrels had expected the meeting to convene in the Situation Room, but he was ushered instead toward the White House State Dining Room. It seemed a strange venue, he thought as he walked down the hall, with décor that was wholly unfitting for what was destined to be a historic meeting. Crystalline chandeliers, fine drapery and valences, gold-trimmed fixtures. A portrait of a thoughtful Lincoln loomed large over the fireplace. When Quarrels finally reached the threshold, however, the logic became clear. The long table at the room's center, normally deployed for champagne-infused state banquets, was surrounded by thirty-odd chairs. The Sit Room would have been far too small for such a meeting.

Only half the seats at the table were presently filled, but then, notice had been short. Dozens of high-ranking officials would be on their way in limousines and private cars, others trotting over from the Capitol and congressional office buildings.

Every seat at the main table had been labeled: cabinet members, mostly, with a smattering of top leadership from the Pentagon and intelligence agencies. The name-tags served, in effect, as an ad hoc roll call. Slightly over half the cabinet was now in place. Gross had advised Quarrels before entering that the Secretaries of Commerce, Agriculture, VA, and Energy were all traveling and unavailable. He explained that they could be linked in electronically, if necessary, but the vice president put that idea on standby.

This was one meeting he was determined to keep behind closed doors.

There were dozens of others around the perimeter. Staffers loitered like hookers against the outer wall, desperate to be seen yet less visible because of it. In a curiously clashing sensation, the aroma of baking bread wafted in from the nearby kitchen. A steward circled with a tray of bottled water with all the propriety of a waiter rounding a cruise ship pool. The Secretary of Education, wearing yoga pants and a ponytail, and with her hair matted in sweat, took two bottles. Overwhelmed Secret Service agents stood at the entrance looking dazed, like nightclub bouncers in a police raid.

As Quarrels took his seat, the Secretary of Transportation and attorney general rushed in breathlessly. Both circled the table in search of their seats, looking for all the world like kids playing musical chairs. Second-tier officials were relegated to the perimeter: House and Senate leaders, National Security Council members, and four military officers of various ranks. The Chairman of the Joint Chiefs had a seat at the table.

Elayne Cleveland's chief of staff, Ed Markowitz, hurried in wearing a well-creased jacket and talking on his phone. Quarrels knew from past meetings that the president's professorial chief of staff didn't always see eye-to-eye with Matt Gross, the young gunner who headed his own team.

Gross leaned in toward the vice president's good ear—he'd lost most of his hearing on the right side a few years earlier—and said in a low voice, "I see about two-thirds of those who were called. Given the importance of what's at stake, I think we should call it a quorum."

Quarrels nodded.

Gross shouted across the room to the Secret Service agents standing by the main entrance, "Shut the doors! No one else enters who isn't a cabinet member!"

That got a few sharp looks from around the table, but no one argued. With the sands of power shifting, the caution in the room was palpable.

The doors sealed with the finality of a tomb, and Quarrels called the meeting to order. "All right, we've all heard bits and pieces of what's happened, but let's start by getting the facts straight. What's the latest on the president's condition?"

A preponderance of gazes fell on the director of the Secret Service, Janet Miller, whose agency was responsible for the president's safety. Having been shunted to the outer ring, she moved toward the table with all the enthusiasm of a woman approaching her firing squad. She paused behind the empty chair labeled COMMERCE.

"At 7:58 p.m. tonight Marine One took off from Andrews. The president had just arrived on Air Force One after a day trip to the Midwest, and she was being shuttled back to the White House. As per standard procedure, Marine One rendezvoused with three identical helicopters. They set out toward the White House on one of the standard routes, and as the formation was nearing the Anacostia River it encountered a large swarm of drone aircraft. An unknown number of these drones impacted Marine One, and also one of the decoy choppers, causing both to crash."

"Drones taking down a helicopter?" the JCS chairman remarked. A burly man, he was sweating visibly after rushing over from the Pentagon. "How the hell does that happen? Were they carrying explosives?"

"We're just beginning to pick up the pieces, but it looks much simpler than that. Each of these drones was carrying a heavy-duty strap connected to an anchor-like device. With so many of them in close proximity, and in the low light of dusk, it effectively created a net that the helicopters flew into. The impacts caused enough damage to bring two of the choppers down. We've collected dozens of these drones so far, and by tomorrow morning we should have a better understanding of the mechanics of the strike."

"Who was controlling them?" asked the secretary of state.

"That's unknown. We have multiple reports, at this point unverified, that they launched from a trailer in a construction site near the Frederick Douglass Bridge. The police are cordoning off the area now. Of the seven people on Marine One, there were two survivors—the president and one member of her Secret Service detail. The Secret Service agent was thrown clear in the crash, while a bystander swam out and was able to pull the president out of the cabin before the aircraft sank. A police boat picked them up minutes later. The second helicopter ditched in the river. Its crew suffered injuries, but none that are life-threatening."

"What's the latest on the president's condition?" Quarrels asked.

"President Cleveland was unconscious after being pulled from the wreckage. She suffered multiple injuries and was taken from the crash site to Walter Reed by ambulance."

The White House physician, who'd discreetly been on his phone in one corner, came front and center, and said, "I've got a stream set up with members of the trauma team at Walter Reed."

The vice president spun a finger in the air to endorse the connection.

Everyone turned to face a monitor that had been set up near the fireplace—incongruously, directly below the portrait of Lincoln. The screen came to life, presenting two men and a woman. They were standing in an office and the look on their faces was collectively grave. All three wore white coats on which their names, followed by M.D., were professionally embroidered. They introduced themselves, but everyone in the room quickly reduced them to their specialties: trauma surgeon, neurosurgeon, and radiologist.

The trauma surgeon started things off by cataloging Elayne Cleveland's injuries: a broken right arm, broken pelvis, two broken ribs, and multiple lacerations. Of greatest concern was that the president had suffered severe head trauma.

The radiologist explained the results of several scans, spending the most time on a CT scan of the brain with ominous shadows indicating a bleed. She then described a procedure the neurosurgeon had performed to relieve the cranial pressure.

The summation was left to the trauma surgeon. "The president has suffered a significant injury to the brain. Her condition is critical but stable. She is presently sedated and intubated, in what's commonly referred to as an induced coma. Driven by concerns about the extent of her brain injury, I reached out to a number of top specialists. All concurred that sedation is the only prudent course for the moment. Hopefully that will give the swelling a chance to subside."

"These specialists you consulted," Gross interjected. "Are they aware of the patient's identity?"

"Absolutely not. The president receives the same confidentiality as anyone."

"Except she doesn't," Gross countered. "News of this crash is breaking all over the world, and when a neurologist from Walter Reed starts asking questions like that—word is bound to get out."

"The colleagues I consulted would never breach—"

"Enough!" the vice president interrupted. "We don't have time for pissing contests. How long do you expect her to remain in this . . . this twilight state?"

"It's impossible to say at this point," the trauma surgeon replied. "The prognosis for brain injuries is vexingly uncertain, particularly so soon after the initial trauma." After a long pause, and perhaps sensing that his answer was deficient, he added, "It is conceivable the president will not survive. If she does pull through, as we all hope, there is some chance she will face impairments."

"What kind of impairments?"

"Movement, balance, speech, mental processing—there's simply no way to tell."

Markowitz said, "Is it possible she could fully recover?"

"Yes, there's a fair chance she'll come through with no adverse long-term effects."

"How long are we talking about in the best case?"

"I really couldn't venture a—"

"Doctor," Gross said, cutting him off, "we are not family members who need to be coddled, nor are we personal injury attorneys. We're trying to run a damned country! We need your best estimate as to when the president *might* be able to resume her duties. Are we talking days? Weeks?"

"I would say a few days is the absolute minimum to be weaned from sedation. In the best case, she might be able to resume her duties in a week or two. But understand, that is highly optimistic. Right now, our goal is to get her through the next seventy-two hours."

In the ensuing silence, Quarrels tried to read the room. He sensed frustration and fear. Sensed powerful men and women weighing dangers. And, as was always the case in Washington, a whiff of opportunity. He instructed the doctors to get in touch if there were any developments, and gave them a stern warning to not divulge information regarding the patient's condition, which was, after all, a matter of national security. Almost as an afterthought, he thanked them for their efforts before having the feed cut.

Again the vice president paused, aware that all eyes in the room were on him. He recalled once being told that the power of the presidency was like gravity. It was an undeniable force which, under normal conditions, kept everything in its place. But the moment that force weakened, chaos took hold.

"Well, you all heard what I did," he finally said. "President Cleveland is not presently capable of fulfilling her duties as commander in chief. Since there is some chance she could return in the near future, the course seems obvious. We are facing, at the very least, a short-term enactment of the Twenty-Fifth Amendment."

He paused briefly, as if waiting for an argument. Ed Markowitz stiffened and his mouth fell open, but then he seemed to pull back. There was no realistic alternative.

Quarrels set his gaze on the heavyset man to his right. "Mr. Attorney General . . . I think it is time for us to review the procedures."

The attorney general cleared his throat. Then, obviously having prepared, he ran through the procedural details. People started taking notes, none more studiously than Ed Markowitz. At the end a vote was taken, and there was no dissent—all eleven attending cabinet members voted in favor of enactment.

Within the hour, as per constitutional requirements, written notice was delivered to the president pro tempore of the Senate and the Speaker of the House of Representatives. After a debate over timing, Quarrels settled on a brief address to the nation later that night. A more scripted and detailed speech would follow the next morning.

None of this altered what was happening outside 1600 Pennsylvania Avenue. As speeches were being written to give the impression of orderliness, and while network air time was coordinated, footage of Marine One slamming into the Anacostia River dominated newscasts. The tragedy had been captured from no fewer than eight angles, a wobbly assemblage of cell phone cameras, CCTV footage, and even one GoPro from the Georgetown University varsity 8 rowing team. The videos went viral on social media, including footage of an unconscious Elayne Cleveland being loaded into an ambulance. Walter Reed National Military Medical Center resembled a fortress, and was surrounded by scrambling reporters.

Against that backdrop, shortly after eleven o'clock, the vice president addressed the nation from the White House briefing room. His two-minute statement covered three essential points.

Someone had attempted to assassinate President Elayne Cleveland.

She had survived, but with critical injuries.

And he, Lincoln Quarrels, longtime Washington

operative and proud American servant, had officially been declared acting president of the United States.

Ten minutes before Quarrels issued the statement, an email was transmitted from central Washington to a little used web-based account.

By an arcane bit of software secretly embedded in the host server, the message was shunted through a series of electronic bypasses and cutouts until it reached its intended recipient eight thousand miles away. He had been waiting patiently in the basement of an opulent residence in the district known as The Peak, on the pinnacle of Hong Kong Island. His ring of black hair was freshly cut, and the chubby fingers addressing the keyboard were well manicured. He wore a business suit, although more out of habit than anything else—it had been more than a year since he'd been in a corporate boardroom.

He read the coded message—coded because, in spite of the circuitous routing, one never knew what new tricks the NSA had up its sleeve—and a smile of relief creased his lips.

Of the four possible outcomes, they had achieved option three.

Not the best result, but a qualified success.

And given what was at stake . . . close enough.

It was time to call a meeting.

EIGHT

Two hundred miles south of the bedlam in Washington, as the vice president was taking control of the nation, Cessna NUX52 skimmed high over the Great Dismal Swamp. An orb of moonlight reflected off the marsh below, tracking steadily across the expansive refuge. After an arduous day, this was the final leg, their destination a tiny grass strip outside Myrtle Beach, South Carolina.

Lazlo was feeling confident. The rain showers alluded to in the weather forecast had never materialized, and the busiest corridors of airspace were behind them. He had turned off the airplane's transponder—air traffic controllers could still see their Cessna, but it would register as little more than an electronic blip.

He glanced at Magda and saw her nodding off, the buzz of the engine having its narcotic effect. His other passenger sat in back, alert and silent as ever. Soon they would part ways, and Lazlo suspected they would never see the man again.

Truth be told, he hoped that was the case.

They had been working with him since early last month. There had been no online feelers, like most of their jobs, no cagy phone calls. The man had simply walked up to their table in a café in Algiers, where they were enjoying a lunch of lamb and couscous, pulled up a third chair, and offered them a job. The man spoke English fluently, with a slightly clipped hue. He could have been from any number of countries, at least a dozen possible ethnicities. Average in height, he had a sinewy build but was otherwise unremarkable. His dark hair was neither short nor long. If there was anything special about him it was a subtle intensity. A sharpness in his gaze and deftly controlled movements.

Despite repeated inquiries that first day, he had deflected all questions about his background. Their prospective employer, on the other hand, knew a great deal about him and Magda. He knew they were vagabond exiles who performed aerial reconnaissance for hire, and that they did so without asking questions or passing judgement. When they expressed cautious interest, and before the specifics of the job were discussed, the man channeled an eyewatering lump of earnest money into their joint account. Right there from the table, with an espresso in his hand. This was enough to convince them that he was serious.

Yet it was also enough to make them wary.

From that point it became an incremental recruitment. They were given money to fly to America. More to purchase the Cessna and cover operational needs. At each juncture, more funds landed in their Bahamian account. Their employer disclosed the mission bit by bit. Where the flights were to take place, how many might be required. Lazlo and Magda went along, providing suggestions for the surveillance of Joint Base Andrews. By the time their employer reached the big reveal—what, or more precisely, *who* they were targeting—they were so deeply enmeshed in the plot that there was no chance of backing out. Or as Magda had put it, "We are waist deep in quicksand, and the only rope is his money."

They had blundered into becoming accessories in a scheme to assassinate the president of the United States. Only the promise of an enormous payday, along with the depth of their involvement, persuaded them to carry through.

"Have we crossed the border?" the man in back asked.

Lazlo turned and saw him looking outside. He had inquired earlier about the North Carolina state line.

"Yes, a few minutes ago."

"And we are on the route I provided?"

"We are." Lazlo didn't know *why* the man had specified a route to their destination, but it was roughly what he would have flown anyway. Monkh clearly had his reasons, and his intel so far had been unfailingly accurate.

That was what they called him—Monkh. It was the name he had provided, and while it likely wasn't legitimate, it fit in an odd sort of way; he seemed socially stunted, prone to meditative stares and arrested conversations. Lazlo guessed him to be Asian, but the region escaped him. Kazakh or Nepalese, possibly Uighur. Perhaps the name was a stab at humor—devotion and piousness were hardly part of his equation.

Lazlo said, "We will land in one hour."

No response from the back, but that was typical. Casual conversation between the three of them was all but nonexistent.

Magda stirred. "Is there any news yet?" she asked, looking expectantly at their passenger.

Monkh was pressing a satellite phone against the window, trying to find a decent signal. Having thrown all their burner phones out the window somewhere over Maryland, the sat-phone was their only remaining connection to the outside world. For the last hour signal reception had been spotty. Monkh had been able to download one video clip of Marine One crashing into the river. It was spectacular, but hardly a revelation since they'd all seen it happen firsthand, albeit from miles away. The accompanying news report had been long on speculation and short on facts. So far, there was no mention of suspects.

"I am getting a weak connection," Monkh said, his eyes glued to the screen.

He said nothing else for a time, and Magda exchanged a cautious glance with Lazlo. Their relationship had reached the point where he knew what she was thinking: *We need to lose this guy soon and get the hell out of the country.*

He gave her a subtle nod.

Their exfil was already arranged. After landing at the tiny airfield, well before dawn, they would take a series of rideshares to the airport in Myrtle Beach. Both of them were booked on the first commercial flight out and, after one connection, by midmorning they would be on their way to Buenos Aires. Yesterday it had seemed a solid plan, quick and direct. Now, with the sobering reality of what they'd done taking hold, paranoia was getting the better of Lazlo. How quickly would the authorities identify the Cessna? Could they track it to South Carolina? He and Magda knew that their images would be captured by cameras when they passed through security in Myrtle Beach. Might the FBI put it all together in the next twenty hours, in time to have them arrested when they landed in Buenos Aires?

Lazlo began to have second thoughts about the plan, and previously discarded options rose back up, like so much operational bile. If they kept going in the

Cessna, he and Magda could make Cuba in time for dinner. Or the Bahamas for lunch. The airplane was sure to be tagged as suspicious, yet he'd filed a flight plan under a fictitious tail number. How long would it take for the FBI to track them down? A revisionist scheme flared into his head. *We could ditch the airplane in the water off some remote island cay, let it sink and swim to shore. Then—*

"The president survived," Monkh said as he scrolled through a news feed.

"What?" Lazlo exclaimed, turning to look at him. "How could that be? We all saw the helicopter crash into the river!"

Magda canted her head, trying to get a look at the screen.

"She was pulled from the wreckage, but is critically injured." Monkh shut down the phone. "The vice president has taken charge of the government."

"So they don't think she will survive," Magda speculated.

"That remains in question."

Lazlo watched their passenger fiddle with his backpack. It was the only luggage he'd brought, and judging by the way he'd hefted it aboard, it was heavy. Hardware of some kind, Lazlo supposed, maybe what he'd used to control the drones.

"None of that matters," Magda said confidently. "Our part is complete. Whether she lives or dies is not our concern. We must make our escape."

She gave Monkh her best SIS stare.

He regarded her curiously, then nodded. "Yes . . . you have done everything asked of you."

"And the rest of our money?" she inquired.

"The transfer has been made. You can check as soon as we land."

NINE

His true name, in fact, was not Monkh. Yet that was all anyone had called him for the best part of twenty years. His birth record had long ago been buried, and the name on his passport changed with striking regularity. The name Monkh had been coined when he was seven years old, and had nothing to do with clandestine work. Since then, only one person on earth had called him by his birth name: the grandmother who had raised him on the steppe of Manchuria.

Monkh continued searching out the window on the left-hand side. The couple in front of him had fallen distracted. They were speaking Slovakian, which he barely knew, but the few words he caught implied a tense discussion about travel arrangements. This made sense, and it was a subject he had no interest in. Monkh was wholly focused on his own exit strategy.

He decided it was time.

He had been mentally rehearsing his next moves for the last half hour. First, he secured the satellite phone in a zippered pocket; right thigh, with the unit upside down and screen inward for easy access. Next his eyes went to the Cessna's instrument panel, which was presently framed by the couple's shoulders. He easily picked out the needed information. Monkh was not a pilot in any sense of the word, yet he'd done his homework. For the last thirty minutes he had been tracking their progress via the instruments, an easy chore once you understood the display.

They were close now. Very close.

He looked outside again, scanning the nighttime horizon, and spotted what he was looking for. Near the eleven o'clock position, a pair of great radio towers spired into the darkness. Each was over fifteen hundred feet high, and they were marked with flashing strobes—a requirement on obstacles to warn away low-flying air traffic. On a clear night the strobes were visible for twenty miles. He estimated that, on their present course, they would pass a few miles west of the towers in the coming minutes.

Monkh checked the altimeter on the instrument panel. 3,500 feet above sea level. From his planning, he knew the ground elevation in this area was only a few hundred feet, putting the Cessna at least three thousand feet above the ground.

Altitude, range, reference. His plan was coming together, although with scant margin for error.

He deftly slid his hand into his backpack.

The swamp remained beneath them, its still waters clear in the muted moonlight. Monkh was thankful the couple had become sidetracked at this critical juncture. He had been prepared to divert their attention if necessary, ask a question about something ahead. As it turned out, that wasn't necessary. Lazlo and Magda were pitching into a minor argument, something about whether Elayne Cleveland's survival bettered their chances of disappearing. She seemed to be winning the contest, as women generally did, by force of superior volume.

Monkh slipped out the Beretta with his dominant right hand, keeping it screened from view behind the right seatback. Magda's head was canted at a nearly perfect 45-degree angle, and he positioned the weapon smoothly using a bent one-arm grip.

With no silencer, the crack of the shot was thunderous in the tiny cockpit. Without bothering to confirm the hit, the assassin expertly shifted his weapon in a smooth flow. Speed was not essential. As expected, the big pilot tensed, his eyes going to the instrument panel. The first instinct in his primitive pilot's brain would be that he was facing an engine problem.

The second shot Monkh executed with the barrel inches from Lazlo's right temple. Just like that, in less than three seconds, it was all over. Monkh checked his victims. Neither showed any signs of life.

He waited.

Monkh had always known the next thirty seconds would require the most nerve. He would not be in control—not really. He sat motionless while things stabilized. The Cessna was not equipped with an autopilot, and with the only pilot on board dead, it reverted to its essence: Monkh was now riding in an unguided airfoil. The little airplane waffled through the sky like a self-propelled leaf. He watched the control yoke nudge vaguely left, then to the right. It looked as if a ghost had taken control.

Satisfied that things were stable, Monkh went to work on the slumped bodies. One at a time, he wrenched them back into their seats and connected the shoulder harnesses to keep them upright. He wiped his fingerprints from the Beretta using the tail of his shirt, then placed the gun firmly in Lazlo's limp right hand, taking care to touch his finger to the trigger.

The airplane rolled slightly left, then seemed to correct itself.

According to his research, airplanes—particularly

light training aircraft—were inherently stable. With no changes to thrust or trim, and barring any shifting of weight, the Cessna would keep flying for a time, meandering through a series of soft climbs and descents. Minor rolls to one side or the other might occur, but with each divergence the airplane would self-correct, seeking equilibrium with no control inputs whatsoever. That free ride, however, would not last forever. As fuel burned off, the airplane would become lighter and the center of gravity would shift. In time, the small oscillations would increase in amplitude, and at some point, long before the airplane ran out of gas, it would either tear itself apart in a dive or stall from low speed and fall from the sky.

Everything was playing out as expected. The Cessna's nose dropped slightly, and the speed increased ten knots. Then the opposite occurred.

Satisfied, Monkh extracted the bulkier item from his backpack: a high-performance ram-air parachute. He shrugged into the harness and made a few last-minute checks. He had packed it with great care the night before. Monkh took one last look outside, searching for his points of reference: the two great radio towers. They were two miles distant now, perhaps a bit more. Half a mile from the base of the southern tower, hidden along a service road, was a motorcycle he had prepositioned—an old but serviceable Kawasaki purchased from a college student using cash.

He again referenced the instrument panel. One of the few modern displays was a GPS readout, which included wind information. The winds were presently eighteen knots from the south-southwest. Slightly in his favor. It was time to make his exit. He pushed forward on the starboard seatback to access the door on the passenger side.

And that was when he encountered the first problem.

With Magda's body strapped in tightly, he couldn't push the seat forward far enough to access the right-hand door. Even without the bulky parachute it would have been tight, but now that he was wearing it Monkh was hopelessly trapped. He processed the problem logically, and came up with a solution. It might detract from the flimsy murder-suicide scenario he was trying to build, but that had never been a priority. It was simply meant to confuse the authorities, perhaps buy a day or two.

He unbuckled Magda, and with considerable effort dragged her bloody body over the seat. He shoved her to the far side of the cabin, and after a pause, decided not to belt her in. He then easily pushed the seatback forward and accessed the side door. As he did so, Monkh noticed that the aircraft's nose had risen slightly. This made sense—weight had shifted aft, so the nose had risen. The same principal as a rowboat.

With a good shove, he pushed the door open into the hundred-knot slipstream. A half-turn put him in the desired position—one foot outside on the wing strut, the other on the seat. He paused one last time to orient himself using the towers. The parachute was steerable, a competition model with a high glide ratio. From this altitude, and with the winds as they were, he could easily travel three miles. That would be more than enough.

Poised to jump, Monkh leaned back inside for his final task: he yanked the little Cessna's throttle to idle. The engine obeyed instantly. The exhaust noise dropped markedly, to the point that he could hear wind washing over the wings and fuselage. The change in flight dynamics was equally notable—the aircraft's nose quickly dropped below the horizon. What had been a mild roller coaster of pilotless flight ended abruptly. Without thrust, the airplane would slow rapidly and enter a series of aerodynamic stalls. There was a fair chance Cessna NUX52 would hit the ground before he did.

Monkh launched himself into space and counted to three, wanting to be clear of the airplane before deploying his chute. He heard a flutter as the canopy deployed, followed by a vicious but comforting tug on his harness. After one half-turn to the right, the chute stabilized nicely.

He scanned the horizon, found the towers, and began steering toward his escape.

TEN

It was not yet dawn the next morning when Slaton's phone chimed a text. The sound cut the silence like a klaxon—nothing to do with the volume, but because his phone was set to allow notifications from only one number on earth at that hour.

He rolled toward the nightstand.

Christine stirred behind him.

The two of them had avoided discussing it, but since seeing last night's news they'd both been on edge. Marine One had crashed, the result of a terror attack, and President Elayne Cleveland was fighting for her life. That tragedy had taken place over a thousand miles from their ranch on the Idaho-Montana border. But it felt much closer.

By no design of his own, Slaton had become Elayne Cleveland's off-the-books operator of choice. It was necessarily a loose arrangement between them, with the CIA acting as intermediary. No written employment contract. No 401K or medical plan. No regular schedule or planned vacations. Two months earlier, Slaton had been dispatched on a mission that took him from the Arctic to the Balkans, and then on to Israel, all in the name of tracking down an obscure organization that was launching strikes against America using high-tech weapons. In the end, Slaton helped to avert a shooting war with Russia by eliminating two commanders at the operational level. Yet the identities of those calling the shots, a group known as The Trident, remained a mystery.

Unavoidably, Slaton had gone to bed the previous night wondering if The Trident was behind this latest attack. According to news reports, verified by amateur video, drones had been used to take down Marine One. This wasn't necessarily damning. Drones were increasingly common on the world's battlefields. Iran had used them to attack Saudi oil fields, and sold them to Russia for use in Ukraine. Turkey had employed them in its Libyan and Syrian campaigns. Yet this attack had a different feel, something deep and menacing. A swarm of drones taking down the most highly protected individual on earth? That implied a very high level of sophistication.

The prospect of a summons from D.C. had been on Slaton's mind since he'd heard the news. He switched on the bedside light and glanced at Christine. Saw the concern on her face. She, too, knew the settings on his phone.

He reached for the handset, but then paused before picking it up. "I could ignore it," he said.

She closed her eyes and heaved out a sigh. "No, David, you can't. Not if you want to be a man of your word . . . support and defend."

Twenty minutes later, Slaton was on the back patio. Christine was inside and he heard the coffee pot gurgling. He had dressed hurriedly, wanting to take the impending call outside. He'd told Christine he preferred the brace of the morning chill. It did nothing to hide the truth. Being outside offered separation between his two lives.

As feared, the text had been from Anna Sorensen, head of the CIA's Directorate of Operations. If Slaton was the president's go-to operator, Sorensen and her Special Activities Center were wedged between them. She was the agency's broker of dirty deeds, tasked to relay orders, assume blame, or do whatever was necessary to keep America safe. Her instructions had been simple enough: call right away using the special phone, a CIA-issued item Slaton kept in a gun safe in the basement.

Now, standing in the cool air of a breaking dawn, with the mountains clinging to moonlight, the phone felt like an anvil in his hand. Slaton had gotten many such call-ups in his years of clandestine work, yet in recent months the crosscurrents had become intolerable. Life as a Mossad assassin seemed simpler in comparison. Not easy, and certainly not safer, but simpler all the same. In those days missions rarely put anyone at risk except himself. Now he had a family, responsibilities, expectations.

Which led to no end of reservations.

Davy and Christine, another child on the way. That was his future. It gave him hope for change, a vision that he could be something other than an assassin. More than once the plan had seemed to be working, only to have some new dirtbag appear who needed eliminating. And Slaton, as the broken record went, was the only operator capable of pulling it off.

Is that where we are this morning? he wondered.

Ever so slowly, he raised the handset and initiated the call.

As the connection ran, he couldn't take his eyes off

the shadowed forest. Somewhere on the perimeter of the ten-acre property was the capable protection detail, supplied by the CIA, that kept constant watch over his family. At that moment, he was very glad to have them.

A series of authentication protocols ensued, and within a minute Sorensen picked up. "Hello, David."

"Anna."

"I need you here ASAP."

And good morning to you too, he thought. Even by her businesslike standards, it was abrupt. Possibly troubling.

"Is this about what happened last night?" he asked.

"I can't talk about it."

"Why not? This is a secure CIA communication device, right?"

No reply.

"Okaaay . . . if it's *that* urgent, should I assume you're sending a plane?" This was their standing arrangement—when time was critical, the head of SAC/SOG had the CIA's tiny air force at her beck and call.

"No, not this time. I'd like you to come commercial. Make your own arrangements, the way you did in Montevideo. But don't bother with the walking. And do it today."

Slaton had begun strolling the terrace, but her words brought him to a stop.

"And when I arrive?" he asked.

"Just make it happen, David . . . please. I'll explain after you arrive at Dulles."

He fully understood the underlying message—and he didn't like it one bit. The CIA had been morphing for years; becoming less an intelligence-gathering agency, more a direct-action military branch. Spec

Ops, drone strikes. War without rules. Of course, it wasn't just America taking such liberties. It seemed like every nation on earth was racing down the same gray road, even if they had no idea where it was taking them.

"Okay," he said. "We'll talk soon."

Slaton ended the call.

There was time for only one cup of coffee, and Slaton downed it as he sat behind the family laptop working his flight reservation.

He was nearly done when he heard a shuffle of cotton behind him. Turning, he saw Davy, dressed in Pooh pajamas, standing behind him. He had come up the hallway silently—not anything he'd been taught, but some natural ability that Slaton feared was inherited.

"Where are you going, Daddy?"

The question took Slaton by surprise, but only for a moment. Davy was deciphering how the world worked at an astonishing rate. The airline's logo was right there on the laptop screen.

"I have to go help someone," David the father said to David the son.

"Who?"

"A friend was in an accident last night. She's in the hospital."

"What will you do for her?"

Slaton reached back and lifted his son into his lap. "I'm not sure exactly, but when a friend needs your help, you go."

"Will you be gone long?"

"I hope not. But I promise to call every chance I get."

"Okay, but . . ." his son's voice trailed off. Then,

suddenly, he slapped his father on the arm and squirmed to the ground. "You're it!" he said, running down the hall.

Slaton smiled and took off in hot pursuit.

Twenty minutes later Slaton approached the front door, his small bag packed and in hand. He'd given Davy one last hug after the game of tag ended. Christine stood awkwardly beside him, as she had so many other times. Would it ever end? he wondered. The collision of his two roles? One part father, one part state-sponsored assassin. Could any two roles be more contradictory?

They passed through the door to the front porch.

"Please be careful," she said once they were alone.

"Aren't I always?"

She glared at him.

"Well, okay . . . point taken." He put a hand on her belly. "Things are different now."

"Are they?"

He looked out toward the horizon. "Maybe not out there. But for us, here . . . yes."

Her expression didn't soften.

He went closer and put a hand to her smooth cheek. "I'll be fine. And you take care as well—I need you more than ever."

"As the mother of our growing brood of children?"

"Yeah, that . . . and you're the only one who knows all our passwords."

It got a half smile.

He leaned in and they touched foreheads, held it for a long moment. Then he was gone.

ELEVEN

By noon that day, the remnants of no fewer than one hundred and sixteen drones had been recovered. The exact number was imprecise since some of the aircraft had been shredded by Marine's One's massive rotors and engines. Fragments were found on the banks of the river and in the nearby park, and hundreds of bits and pieces had been fished out of the murky water by divers. Some of the debris collected was barely identifiable, and investigators separated what was clearly random trash: pens, condoms, hubcaps, and at least two wedding rings.

Fortunately, many of the drones had fallen to earth intact, including the strap-and-claw attachments that had proved so devastating. Those drones that missed their target had simply hovered in place until their batteries discharged, at which point they plummeted to the ground.

The wreckage of Marine One was hauled from the river by a massive barge-mounted crane—a hideously tactless operation given that the shores were lined with news crews—and transported to a shoreside hangar at nearby Joint Base Anacostia-Bolling. For the rest of the day, inglorious images of the bent and battered VH-92 sitting crookedly on a barge, water draining from every orifice, became a ceaseless backdrop on cable newscasts and social media feeds.

The FBI took the lead in the investigation, and within hours they confirmed that the construction trailer had indeed served as the launch point for the drones. After determining that the booby trap on the rear doors was a ruse, an army of evidence technicians combed the interior. They found precious little: a battery charging system for the drones, two flashlights, one work light, a few cable ties, a makeshift table made of bricks and lumber, and three discarded food wrappers. Investigators scoured the interior for fingerprints and DNA, impounded all camera footage from the construction site, and questioned every worker and nearby resident they could track down.

Every shred of new information was immediately sent up the chain of command.

And that was where the dysfunction began.

"Like hell you will!" Ed Markowitz shouted across the table in the White House conference room.

Matt Gross, the acting president's chief of staff, shot back, "You no longer call the shots, Ed. First March Madness, now this. Our intelligence agencies have failed us. And after what happened to Elayne last night, I'd think you of all people would demand some accountability!"

"Enough!" barked the vice president, his hands spreading like a boxing referee trying to separate fighters. "They can hear you two shouting all the way to Capitol Hill."

Both men sank grudgingly back into their chairs.

Markowitz was fuming. He and Gross had gotten

sideways before, but the shift of power had thrown rocket fuel on the fire. Markowitz looked around the room and saw little support—every set of eyes was either fixed on Vice President Quarrels or locked in a thousand-yard stare. At the table were Director of National Intelligence John Nichols, Secretary of State Robert Shawcross, and JCS Chairman General Lou Morris. Quarrels—or more likely Gross—had intentionally kept the morning meeting small, probably thinking it would facilitate a smooth transition of power. With ten minutes gone, it was nothing less than a donnybrook.

The dysfunction was already bleeding into the news. Conflicting press releases had been issued late last night—Markowitz sending one through president Cleveland's usual channels, Quarrels issuing his own. A few minor differences between them were all it took to send the media into a frenzy. In truth, they had a point. America's leadership was shattered, disorganized. Quarrels had been declared "acting president," yet what that meant, what it empowered, had never really been tested. The vagueness regarding Elayne Cleveland's condition only made things worse.

Quarrels, clearly aiming to be the sage voice of reason, hit the reset button. "Gentlemen, now is not the time for division. We have got to look forward. So . . . what's the latest on who's responsible for this attack?"

DNI Nichols took his cue. "We're taking a hard look at the drones. So far, we've recovered over a hundred of them, and we're still pulling more from the river. The kill mechanism was pretty basic—each drone carried a high-strength strap with a claw attachment. Apparently the drones arranged themselves in a vertical wall, creating a virtual net that inflicted critical damage to the two choppers that made contact."

"That doesn't sound very sophisticated," Quarrels commented. He was holding an official White House coffee mug, the presidential seal evident to all.

"On the face of it, no. But our analysts are digging into the circuitry of these devices, and what they've identified so far looks pretty advanced. The drones communicated with one another via some kind of AI software. On top of that, we were jamming the bandwidths used to control most commercially available drones—it's a standard procedure for presidential movement. The fact that it didn't work tells us they were using a different part of the RF spectrum. We also suspect that each unit had an acoustic sensor, and with all of them linked together it effectively formed an array antenna. We've called DARPA in to have a look, but the bottom line—this was *not* something slapped together in Al-Qaeda's basement."

"What about Russia's?" the vice president asked. Quarrels was a lifelong Russia hawk, and the invasion of Ukraine had only hardened his outlook.

"Russia, China, Iran. At this point, we can't say exactly where this technology came from."

Gross said, "I think we've got a bigger problem than figuring out who built these drones. It seems to me someone had foreknowledge of the president's movements. Who could get that kind of intelligence? Does it imply we have a leak?"

"It's a fair question," Quarrels seconded. "The president's schedule is closely held."

"Not as close as you'd think," Nichols replied. "Portions of her schedule are readily available, and yesterday was a good example. There was widespread media coverage of her trip to the Midwest. She also had a public event scheduled the next morning here in Washington, a medal of honor ceremony. Someone could easily have noted Air Force One's departure from Des Moines, which there's no way to hide, and combined that with the event scheduled for the next day . . . her return to Andrews was predictable."

Markowitz took it further. "Figure the average speed of an airliner, and anyone could have estimated her arrival back at Andrews. At least, plus or minus fifteen minutes."

"Another weak point in our security," said Gross.

"Probably," Nichols agreed. "But that doesn't answer the more vexing question: how did they track the president's helicopter? As you all know, Marine One flies varied routes between Andrews and the White House. They're highly randomized with no preplanning, and the pilots are authorized to change routes at will. Then there's the matter of the decoy helicopters—three were used last night. From the video we've seen, this veil of drones wasn't wide enough to take out all of them. The second helicopter that took damage was flying very close to Marine One—so close that it was likely only collateral damage. Somehow, these attackers knew not only which route was being taken, but which aircraft was carrying the president."

"How could that be?" Markowitz asked.

"We can't say for certain, but there are some clues. To begin, there are a limited number of flight paths between Andrews and the White House—six have been charted and vetted thoroughly, designed to minimize just this kind of threat."

"Could the attackers have known this?"

"It seems likely. The routes are closely held, but anyone who watched long enough could figure it out—Marine One makes the trip multiple times each week. Regarding this attack, we've identified a trailer at a construction site where the drones were concealed. It's been there for at least a month, so it's conceivable the attackers have been as well, waiting for the right chance."

"But that doesn't explain how they knew which helicopter to target," Gross said.

"And it doesn't tell us who's behind it," Quarrels added.

General Morris said, "In light of what we've seen in recent months, I think The Trident, whoever they are, has to top our suspect list."

Gross said, "Unfortunately, our intelligence agencies still have no idea who they are. This could be Russia or China playing games through some shadow group. Or a false flag operation from a third party trying to stir up trouble. Whoever's behind it, they're feeling confident enough to go after the president. Since this is clearly an external threat, CIA should be the one getting answers. It's a failure of the first order that they've been shooting blanks for months."

Markowitz sat helplessly, increasingly adrift. He could feel his influence, or more precisely Elayne Cleveland's, fading by the second. The vice president and his COS had been advocating for change at CIA for over a month, but Elayne Cleveland had pushed back.

He said, "Mr. Vice President, it's true that CIA was caught out in March. I won't argue otherwise. But getting accurate, timely answers will require all our agencies working in concert. The last thing we need do is start slashing and burning in the middle of a complex investigation."

"No," Gross said, a terrier not letting go. "Thomas Coltrane at CIA has to go."

"John?" said the vice president, his eyes shifting to DNI Nichols.

Nichols hesitated, then nodded slowly. The vice president visually polled the others. The secretary of state and JCS chairman agreed. Markowitz had already voted.

A tipping point had been reached.

Quarrels cleared his throat once, a prelude to an edict. "Then it's settled. I'm going to replace Thomas Coltrane, effective immediately."

"Who will take his place?" Markowitz asked.

"I have a successor in mind, someone already at the agency. That will minimize any disruption, and hopefully get Senate confirmation fast-tracked."

"Who?"

"Charles Eraclides," Gross replied.

Eyebrows raised all around, but only Markowitz put it to words. *"Eraclides?* He's the agency's inspector general, a lawyer with no operational background. Why not—"

"Ed!" the vice president interrupted forcefully. "I am going to stop you there. We don't have time to spin our wheels. None of us knows if Elayne is going to wake up, or whether she'll be able to resume her duties if she does. It could be weeks or even months. I pray the president will have a full and speedy recovery, but until that time, I am running the show. This attack bears distinct similarities to those we suffered two months ago. It's time for a new course, and Charles Eraclides has been at the agency for over twenty years. I'd argue he is well versed in *all* aspects of the agency's mission."

The vice president's gaze shifted to include the others. "We will find out who's responsible for this attack. When we do, I want options for a response— everything from full scale deployments to SAC/SOG direct action. Questions?"

There were none.

"All right, then. Get to work."

Everyone stood as Quarrels got up to leave.

Minutes later, the vice president entered the Oval Office with only his chief of staff trailing him. When Gross closed the doors behind them, Quarrels said, "I'm concerned about this attack. Clearly whoever is responsible did their homework. Even so, I can't shake the feeling that there's more to it."

"In what way?" asked Gross.

"The attackers knew Marine One's routes. And they knew which one was carrying the president."

Gross seemed to study the royal blue carpet, before saying, "There has to be a leak."

"I can't see it any other way."

The younger man weighed it. "Then we'll find it. But that won't be easy. A lot of agencies have a hand in presidential security. The Secret Service and Capitol Police. The Marine Corps and Air Force."

"I know it's a wide net, but we have to make an effort."

"If there is a leak, it could be at any level. We have to move carefully."

"I disagree. We can't afford to tiptoe around when our nation is under attack. I want you to get with Eraclides, impress on him the importance of finding out who's responsible. If it turns out to be The Trident, we will identify the individuals controlling it and initiate a response."

"What kind of response?"

"The only kind that fits."

TWELVE

Slaton drove to Missoula, and from there he hopped a regional jet to Salt Lake City. His connecting flight touched down at Dulles International Airport at three o'clock that afternoon.

He reached the arrivals curb with Sorensen's words from that morning looping in his head. He'd sensed her tension, her guardedness, and he didn't know what to make of it. *Make your own arrangements, like Montevideo. But don't bother with the walking.*

She was referring to a rendezvous they'd had the previous year in Uruguay. A clandestine meeting far from prying eyes—and a prelude to another risk-laden mission. Slaton had made his own travel arrangements to reach Montevideo, and undertaken an extensive surveillance detection route when he arrived. He didn't think that kind of tradecraft would be necessary today, yet he couldn't shake the caution threaded into Sorensen's words.

He spotted her right away amid heavy airport traffic, sitting calmly behind the wheel of a bland Ford crossover. Just like last time, there was no subtle wave or flash of the headlights. She simply knew he would find her. Slaton opened the passenger door and tossed his carry-on through to the back seat. It held two changes of clothing and a heavy jacket—a lesson learned two months ago, in late winter, when the area of operations for his mission had shifted in a flash from Central Asia to the Arctic.

"Right on time," he said. "I'm guessing you didn't have to bother with the cell lot." As head of SAC/SOG, Sorensen likely knew not only his flight number and arrival time, but also what seat he'd been sitting in. Probably even what Delta had served him for dinner.

She flicked on her blinker and merged into traffic. "Thanks for getting here so quickly."

"Just like a fireman."

"I'm not sure I like that analogy." She shot him a pensive glance, seeming to study his clothing.

"What?"

She shrugged. "I guess I was expecting you might have gone a bit more regional."

He was wearing what he always wore: quality dark pants with plenty of pockets, a loose-fitting shirt, and solid hiking shoes. Clothing that was appropriate for outdoor work, but also tactically sound. "You were expecting jeans and a bolo tie?"

"Never mind. It's nice to see there's at least one constant in the world."

He grinned. "Given what I've seen on the news, I'm guessing the DEFCON at the office is up a few notches?"

"You can't imagine."

"How's Elayne?"

"She's in an induced coma. There's no real timeframe as to when, or even if, she'll recover. The vice president has taken over in the interim."

"Any inside scoop on the attack?"

"There's still a lot we don't know."

Slaton studied her and got that sensation again. Tension. Wariness. Sorensen's features were pure Scandinavian, fair hair and blue eyes. On their last meeting, he'd thought she seemed tense, the stress of the job beginning to take its toll. Now her worry lines were more pronounced than ever, and her posture looked like it was suffering some kind of gravitational overload.

His gaze slewed outside. Slaton was loosely familiar with D.C. geography, enough to recognize that the road Sorensen took exiting the airport—Route 28 South—would not take them toward Langley.

"Can I ask where we're going?"

"I'll explain soon. We need to talk."

Sorensen said nothing else.

Slaton pressed back into his seat and waited.

Slaton expected a CIA safe house in rural Virginia. What he got was a Fairfax County municipal park. The curving access road led to an empty parking area near a trailhead. Sorensen pulled into the lot, gravel popping under the tires like popcorn. She parked and got out, and after Slaton followed suit, she clicked the locks shut.

The only other people in sight were a distant young couple walking a black lab with a wagging tail and a tennis ball in its mouth. Sorensen took a path that led to a clear area, four picnic tables overlooking a burbling creek. She stopped at one of the tables and climbed on, sitting on the tabletop, her feet on the bench.

Slaton saw her arranging her thoughts, figuring out how to say . . . something. Her caution did nothing to lessen his own alertness. His eyes kept moving, checking for people, registering any movement. He noted, with disappointment, that the picnic table was bolted to a concrete slab—tipped on their sides, picnic tables were always the most solid cover in your standard public park.

Since Sorensen's first words that morning, "I need you here ASAP," he'd been trying to guess why he was being summoned. The odds-on favorite was something along the lines of: *Someone has tried to kill the president. We know who it is and want you to fly halfway around the world to put a bullet in his head.* This was Slaton's calling, the dark gift he'd been cursed with—an extravagant aptitude for killing. Now, watching the head of the CIA's clandestine service wrestle her thoughts, he was less sure about his assumptions. She would not have brought him to a public place for that.

"What's going on, Anna?"

"I needed to talk to you privately."

A curious word choice—*privately*. Slaton considered the empty park, the silence in the car. Considered that they were situated in the open and not in a safe house—the CIA kept enough of those in rural Virginia to put an end to homelessness. He also noticed that she'd left her encryption-enabled phone in the car. And the background noise of the brook murmuring behind them? It was a natural acoustic defense.

He said, "Seriously? A deputy director of the CIA, the head of SAC/SOG, has to go for a walk in the woods to get a secure conversation in Virginia?"

"That's . . . part of the problem. I'm not sure how much longer I'll be working for the CIA."

This was a bolt from the blue. Of all the things Slaton had considered, Sorensen getting fired wasn't one of them.

"Thomas Coltrane is getting the axe," she said.

He considered it. "And you think you might be next? Collateral damage?"

"Stands to reason."

He took a seat next to her on the table. "A purge at the agency. I didn't see that coming."

"I did . . . at least as far as Thomas was concerned. Since the attacks in March he's been under tremendous pressure. Congressmen, senators, certain individuals in the administration."

"The vice president?"

"Among others. But yes, Quarrels has been aiming to oust Coltrane, even before yesterday."

"Coltrane wasn't to blame for what happened in March. And probably not for what went down yesterday."

"Doesn't matter. At this point we're talking about politics, appearances. There's been too much bad news on his watch. The CIA can't figure out who's to blame, so it becomes an intelligence failure. The knives are out, and a sacrifice has to be made. Until now, President Cleveland had Coltrane's back. Now she's out of the picture."

"The result of yet another attack."

"Exactly."

"You really think you could go down with him?"

"It's possible."

"That makes absolutely no sense. Nobody was as proactive as you were in countering The Trident two months ago. I know because I was there. Maybe I can talk to someone, explain what we did right."

"Don't worry about me, David. I'll be fine. They won't cut me right away—can't make too many changes with so much going on. Anyway, the truth is . . . I've been thinking about leaving for some time."

"Does Jammer have something to do with that?" For the first time since arriving he caught the trace of a smile. Jammer Davis was her significant other, and Slaton knew him well—they'd been side-by-side on the mission to the Arctic.

"We're engaged."

He leaned forward to catch her gaze. "Congrats, Anna! Really, you guys are great together."

"Yeah, well . . . right now he's up in Canada doing some bush flying in a floatplane. It's possible he doesn't even know what's going on. If it turns out that I *am* out of a job when he gets back, we'll have no excuse for not setting a date." The smile misted away.

"I'm guessing you didn't bring me here to ask me to be best man?"

"I want to give you fair warning, David."

"About what?"

"Coltrane's replacement has been chosen."

"That was quick. Anybody I know?"

"Charles Eraclides has been named acting director."

He shook his head. "Never heard of him."

"With good reason. Until today, he was the agency's inspector general. Career CIA, but no operational experience whatsoever."

Slaton laughed humorlessly. "Seriously? A lawyer?" She nodded.

He was beginning to understand her unease. Slaton had a unique standing at the agency. No employment contract, no personnel file. Correspondingly, and surely by design, he operated outside the usual rules of engagement. He was an unofficial asset, working under the authority of a sealed presidential memorandum—an authorization that might or might not stand up under scrutiny. Any new director, especially a lawyer, would view such a legacy as an unexploded bomb.

"Maybe the new boss will fire me too," he said hopefully. "I could live with that."

"Actually, it's the opposite. I spoke with Eraclides this morning. He wants to make his mark right away by answering this attack."

"*Answering?* What does that mean?"

"He mentioned you by name. Or at least, your code name—Corsair."

Her words hung in the air menacingly, a knife thrown straight up. Slaton stood, moved a few steps away, then turned to face her. "It's one thing to get sent on an op with legitimate objectives, to target somebody who deserves taking out. Everything I'm hearing sounds closer to Beltway politics."

"Could be. But we do have some fresh intel—came in earlier today. We're getting a bead on this Trident organization. We have one name, and a lead on a second. Eraclides doesn't want to wait. He wants to send you after the first target."

"Have you seen this intel? Is it solid?"

"What I saw looked good, but we're still vetting the source, verifying the authenticity of what he gave us. If everything checks out, the op would likely take place in Macau."

"China? That sounds risky. Are we talking about someone official, government or military?"

"Unclear. He used to head up a big defense company, so you could label him as corporate. But nobody runs a big company in China, particularly one that does military business, without the party's seal of approval. It goes without saying, any mission would require the smallest possible footprint."

"One operator? No formal ties to the CIA?"

"That's the general idea."

Slaton realized his first inclination had in fact been dead on. *Halfway around the world* . . . He pulled a step closer and looked her in the eye. "Is it the call you would make, Anna? Send me to Macau?"

"Honestly, given the intel I've seen . . . yeah, probably so. But it's out of my hands. Eraclides has asked for a face-to-face meeting with you."

"When?"

"Now."

"Where?"

"Headquarters."

Slaton tipped his head. "You *are* kidding."

No response.

"He wants me to walk right through the front door at Langley? Should I log in as a visitor too? Maybe sign up for the tour?"

"Look . . . I told him you wouldn't like it."

"You can tell him it's not going to happen. We meet in a secure location or we don't meet."

"I'll forward your well-considered request. Maybe we can switch it to the White House."

Slaton shot her a stony stare. Then her face canted to one side and was illuminated by a streetlight. He saw the trace of a smile.

He eased off and grinned, shook his head. She was winding him up. He heaved a long sigh. "They're idiots if they let you go, Anna."

"Yeah? I was thinking I'm the idiot if I stay."

THIRTEEN

Eleven years earlier

He dropped the first two tangos easily, one running low to his right, the other peeking around the corner of a gray shrapnel-pocked building. A quick dash to the right put him in cover behind a scorched armored personnel carrier. He switched mags expertly, knowing he had but one round remaining in his AN-94 assault rifle. Through all the years, through so many battles, the count in the back of his head had never failed.

He checked the positions of the two remaining members of his team. One man was in solid cover on his right flank. The other, to the left, was running over open ground like a startled deer. "Idiot," he muttered to himself.

Realizing the man on the left was about to die, and not wanting to waste the opportunity, he readied a grenade and scanned ahead. Explosions lit the battlefield, a panorama of the apocalypse. Burning cars and bomb craters, bodies all around. The noise reached a crescendo, blasts overriding the staccato rattle of full automatic fire. He heard indistinct shouting and wails of pain. The most efficient killer on earth tuned it out as he always did.

The chance came precisely as expected, a muzzle flash slightly to the left. His teammate, still in the open, took a hit. Monkh's response was lightning-like. Before his teammate had hit the ground, the grenade was in the air. He scored a direct hit, removing, as it turned out, the last two members of the opposing force.

"Game over, bastards!" said Nikolai, who'd been watching over his shoulder.

And so it was.

Monkh removed his headset and pushed back from the gaming console.

"You are the best ever!" said Nikolai, who at fifteen was two years younger than the friend he idolized. "How many did you kill?"

"One fewer than I will next time."

"What about the prize? How much did you win?"

Shaman44—that was his nom de game—only shrugged. "Not much. Maybe five hundred dollars. This was a small tournament. After I divide it with my worthless teammates, barely enough to buy a keyboard with better backlighting."

"But there are bigger tournaments."

"Yes, far bigger ones. But the problem is always the same. The big-money tournaments draw the best players, and without a strong team it doesn't matter how good I am. And I can never get on a decent team because our internet is throttled down by the government—it's like trying to win an F1 race on two cylinders."

"When you get the money, let's get drunk. The kid who runs my uncle's store at night sells to anybody— you only have to slip him a few yuan."

"I don't like drinking. It dulls my reflexes." Monkh pushed up from his custom three-axis chair and stretched. "You would be a better player if you stayed sober, Nikolai."

"I could never be as good as you. Your speed of play—you have the best kill-death ratio of anyone in the E-Sports rankings."

"It's all about preparation. You have to be a student. Know the scenarios and your opponents." He kicked an empty box across the room, the one that had held his new backup controller. "But rankings mean nothing when you live on a pig farm on the steppe. Without being on a top team there is no way to make a living. And even if I did have a better connection, the best players don't like me. They know I am a threat, so they freeze me out."

A familiar knock on the door behind them. Tentative, but determined.

His grandmother.

Monkh had lived with her since he was four, when his mother had died of cancer. His father had disappeared two years before that, or so he'd been told. By now he had surely drunk himself to death.

Monkh went to the door, expecting the usual admonitions about getting out of the house or tending to the pigs—the farm was down to its last five. He had recently quit school, so at least that battle was behind them.

Monkh opened the door, and what he saw surprised him. It was indeed his grandmother, yet her round, wrinkled face, framed by a colorless scarf, showed none of its usual sternness. His *nai nai* looked . . . befuddled.

"What is it?" he asked.

"Men have come to see you." Her voice was thread-thin.

"*Men?* What men?"

Her face collapsed into a visage that was nothing short of despair. This from a widow to whom life had dealt nothing beyond drought, pestilence, and an abusive husband.

Monkh walked to the front room cautiously—not as Shaman44, gaming wunderkind, but as a gangly, seventeen-year-old son of the Manchurian steppe. There were indeed two men waiting.

The one on the right was easy to assess. His face gave nothing away, but what he wore spoke volumes. Monkh recognized the rank and insignia of a major in the People's Liberation Army.

The second man, wearing an overcoat and fur hat, was something else entirely. Of the two, he was the far more frightening.

Present day

Through the tinted visor of his motorcycle helmet, Monkh watched a blond woman at the adjacent gas pump try to fill her Mercedes convertible. In a tight skirt and ridiculous shoes, she fumbled with the hose, which was twisted near the attach point. An old man, at least seventy, came to her rescue from the opposite side of the pump island. She batted her eyes and smiled as he straightened things out. When he was done, she immediately turned her back on him. The old guy walked away pitifully toward the convenience store, a dog who'd been kicked out of the house.

Monkh had long ago concluded that women were the same everywhere. The schoolgirls in his village outside Hailar had been cliquish and patronizing, uninterested in a boy whose only future involved a failing pig farm. He thought that might change when he left the backwater of Manchuria. For years now, clandestine operations had taken him to cities across the world, expanding the field of play exponentially.

Still, the social awkwardness that had always dogged him, combined with the way he immersed himself in his work, unfailingly got in the way. He found American women particularly vexing. In the month since arriving here, Monkh had regularly tried to strike up conversations with girls in campgrounds, grocery stores, and diners. He'd been rejected every time.

The blond locked the doors on the Mercedes—even though the top was down—and ignored Monkh completely as she walked past him toward the little store, her boobs bouncing and hips swaying.

He didn't like this country. Didn't like Americans for their ignorance and self-absorption. Most people here had no idea how the rest of the world lived. They drank their Starbucks, drove gas-guzzling cars, not knowing or caring where any of it came from. Monkh had been raised differently, imbued in self-reliance. Whether it was keeping a farm running or assassinating government officials, he never counted on outside help.

The pump clicked off, interrupting his musings. He had used a prepaid debit card, of which he kept a pocketful—credit cards required an identity, and paying cash necessitated going inside where there were cameras. He'd acquired the cards from dozens of different sources, and used each of them only once. It was probably overkill, but he wanted no chance of the FBI building a pattern with its digital analytics.

He cradled the pump handle and twisted on the motorcycle's gas cap. The bike was a big Kawasaki touring model, 1200ccs of smooth power. He was presently a few miles outside Boone, North Carolina, having spent the predawn hours working his way toward the Blue Ridge Parkway. It wasn't because he enjoyed scenic vistas, nor was it the shortest route to his destination. It was simply the perfect place to blend in. On a clear Sunday afternoon, he knew the Parkway would be thick with cruising motorcycles. For the last two hours he had fallen in loosely with groups of other bikers and waved cordially to those passing in the opposite lane. Gangs of dentists and accountants, he imagined, all wearing jeans and bandanas, and sporting week-old soul patches.

What could be more American?

His plan was to ditch the bike in a prepaid storage shed in Asheville, and from there make his way to the airport. Assuming he was not the subject of an intense manhunt—and he would have plenty of forewarning if that was the case—he would board a flight to Atlanta, and from there leave the country. Connecting to international flights from regional airports was always his preferred technique, avoiding the more intense security screening at big hubs. If all went well, within twenty-four hours of last night's strike, Monkh would be safely en route to the second, less demanding part of his contract.

Not wanting to enter the store, he decided to stop for a piss somewhere outside town. He remounted the bike, adjusted his helmet, and cranked it to life. Monkh idled toward a nearby curb and then stopped to check his phone. He powered up the satellite device and waited. It was supposedly secure, but Monkh never relied on such promises when it came to electronics.

At last, a notification appeared on the encrypted messaging app: Call immediately.

He wondered what his employer wanted. Monkh had not seen any news since last night, when he'd checked the phone from the back seat of the Cessna. He knew Elayne Cleveland had survived the crash. *But what's happened since then?*

He looked around the busy parking lot, saw cars coming and going. Next to the convenience store groups of people were loitering under shade awnings. Drinking coffee and eating donuts.

Monkh suddenly felt exposed.

"Whatever it is, it can wait," he muttered under his breath.

He turned off the phone and slid it into his riding jacket. With one turn of the throttle, the bike jumped ahead into the cool mountain air.

FOURTEEN

The meeting at the White House had left Ed Markowitz fuming. With his influence there cratering, he retreated to his last base of hope—Walter Reed National Military Medical Center.

Reporters had overrun the main entrance, but Markowitz knew a back door that was reserved for privileged staff—a status he retained, if only just. The place was on virtual lockdown after the attempt on the president's life, and he was forced to clear three rings of security to reach Elayne Cleveland's fourth-floor room. He spotted a familiar face outside her door.

Richard Cleveland, the nation's First Gentleman, was Elayne's husband of thirty-one years. He was a rare sight inside the Beltway, a native Montanan who made no bones about preferring horses to humans. That outlook hadn't helped on the campaign trail, yet since the election, oddly, his disdain for the entire D.C. circus had lifted his approval ratings above any presidential spouse since Jacqueline Kennedy. He spent most of his time on the family ranch outside Bozeman, which was where he had been when Markowitz broke the news to him about the crash of Marine One. Since then, Richard Cleveland's true colors had shone through—he might have been indifferent to his ceremonial station, but his devotion to his wife was unyielding. Eight hours after the accident he had walked into Walter Reed, and he hadn't left the fourth floor since.

The two exchanged greetings and a handshake.

"Any news on her condition?" Markowitz asked.

"No change," Richard said with his Western drawl. He was wearing jeans, a flannel shirt, and scuffed boots. The only thing missing was his signature brown Stetson, and Markowitz figured that was nearby. "The doctor who's runnin' the show is in with her now."

Markowitz nodded. "She's a fighter, but it's going to take time. Have they given you somewhere to stay?"

"Yeah, they set me up a room two floors down."

"Good. Let me know if I can help with anything." He put a supportive hand on Richard's shoulder and then moved toward the room. The door was flanked by two Secret Service agents, both of whom knew Markowitz well. Aside from select hospital staff, he was one of three people allowed access to the room. The lead agent greeted him as he went through.

The air inside was like any hospital room, still and antiseptic. Monitors beeped rhythmically, both proof of life and a reminder of the patient's grim condition. Elayne Cleveland's face was half hidden behind an opaque mask, her breathing being aided by a ventilator. She had a cast on one arm and the left side of her head was bandaged heavily.

Dr. Singh, the critical care pulmonologist whom Markowitz had already met, was standing next to her.

"How is she doing?" Markowitz asked.

The doctor looked up from his tablet. "There is no change, but for now that's a good thing. She remains stable. We're planning to do a scan this afternoon, and hopefully it will verify that the bleeding has stopped."

Dr. Singh catalogued a long list of injuries and tests performed. Markowitz listened attentively, absorbing most of it. At the end he recognized one thing missing.

He said, "Dr. Singh, I know any prognosis is difficult right now. That said, you must understand that I'm not here as a family member. Elayne Cleveland is the leader of this country and serious decisions have to be made. I need some idea of what her prospects are."

A hesitation.

Markowitz added, "You have my word that whatever you say will not go beyond the White House." He knew this was a shaky promise, but he would do his best.

"Elayne is a strong woman," the doctor said, "but she's lucky to be alive. The next forty-eight hours are critical. She has even odds of getting that far. If she does survive, recovery could be a lengthy process."

With sinking spirits, Markowitz asked, "And the best case?"

Singh inhaled deeply. "A full recovery is definitely possible, but right now . . . I think it's better to concentrate on the near term. I know that's not what you want to hear, Mr. Markowitz, but it's the only truthful answer."

Markowitz nodded, and as the doctor turned to leave, he said, "You have my number. Please call if her condition changes—anytime, day or night."

"I will." Singh walked out.

Alone, Markowitz went closer and regarded Elayne Cleveland. He saw bruising on one side of her face, abrasions on her unbandaged shoulder. He recalled the last time he had seen her, on the tarmac at Andrews. She'd invited him to join her on Marine One for the trip to the White House. He recalled telling her that he had an anniversary date with his wife, which was true. He wondered how things might have turned out if he'd gone on that flight. Might he have ended up with her in the wreckage? Might he have helped her in some way?

Or would he himself have died?

How different it all could have turned out.

He looked at the president, battered and broken, her life hanging by a thread, and whispered, "I wish I'd been there for you . . ."

FIFTEEN

The FBI threw everything they had into the investigation. They pored over the spent drones and the trailer they'd launched from. They scoured signal intercepts for traces of attack planning, and analyzed videos of the attack from countless angles. Investigators from Sikorsky, the NTSB, and the Marine Corps went over every bit of wreckage from Marine One.

The drive to collect evidence, however, put the resolution of one great unknown on a back burner: How had the operator of the drones, which were slow-flying and launched from a fixed position, known which helicopter was carrying the president in the final critical moments? As it turned out, the investigators got an answer, and from a completely unexpected source.

An ornithologist named Bernard Smyth.

Smyth had set out early that morning in a canoe, launching from a campground in Dismal Swamp State Park. For hours he paddled the canals, working his way toward the center of the preserve where the previous day he had spotted a pair of mating cerulean warblers. He was thinking about stopping for his brown-bag lunch, and nearing a promising glade, when a distant glint caught his eye.

Smyth extracted his high-power binoculars—the

best of the three optics he carried—and focused on the object. Still not sure what it was, he paddled closer. Vegetation interfered with his view until he was very near, and when he rounded the last stand of tall brush the object lay directly in front of him. There was no question of what he was looking at: the wreckage of a small airplane.

He paddled a few strokes closer and got the shock of his life when he saw two bodies inside. Both were crumpled in a way that ruled out any hope of survival. With shaking hands, Smyth pulled out his cell phone. Not surprisingly, he had no signal. Steeling himself, he took one photo of the wreckage, pocketed his phone, and began paddling frantically toward the campground.

Smyth's 911 call was logged at 12:52 that afternoon.

The first responders arrived by boat ninety minutes later.

The wreckage was right where the ornithologist said it would be. He was also correct that there were two bodies. The complications began when one of the EMTs realized that both victims had suffered gunshot wounds to the head. Neither the man nor the woman carried identity documents of any kind, and there was no luggage in the Cessna's cargo compartment. This seemed suspicious, yet there were no correlating signs of illicit activity: no evidence of drug smuggling or human trafficking.

As was the procedure in any air crash, the FAA was looped in. A safety inspector there, a veteran named Kelleher, was tasked to research the downed aircraft. He began with a search on the aircraft's registration number, and noted a recent change in ownership.

The selling party was a familiar North Carolina flight school, the buyer a murky corporate entity he'd never heard of. He fed the registration number into the FAA's flight management database and discovered that a flight plan had been filed the previous day for a cross-country flight.

Curiosity piqued, Kelleher began the cumbersome process of tracking the aircraft through its previous day's journey. He acquired data from various en route air traffic control centers and approach control facilities. These consisted of both airspace displays and audio files of radio transmissions.

Cobbling everything together, he was able to re-create the path of Cessna NUX52 as it bounced through the mid-Atlantic sky. It was at the midpoint of this sequence, just prior to a landing at a tiny uncontrolled airfield in central Maryland, that Kelleher straightened in his chair. Something about the track stuck him as odd. He backed up the timeline and looped the file a second time.

There could be no doubt.

Near a bend in the Patuxent River, roughly twelve miles east of Joint Base Andrews, Cessna NUX52 had gone into a loose holding pattern. Listening to the audio file, Kelleher noted that the pilot's English, the common language of aviation worldwide, was laced with a hard accent. The pilot explained to the air traffic controller that he was loitering to take pictures of a construction site. This seemed odd given the time of day, which had to be near dusk.

Kelleher found himself wondering how the claim could be proved or disproved. *Was* there a construction site in that spot? If so, had the developers contracted for photos? Had a camera been found in the wreckage? Then all at once it occurred to him *why* those questions were coming to mind: Like everyone in America, the FAA man had watched the news last night, and so he had a good idea of where and when Marine One had crashed.

With his concerns mounting, he called the agency's liaison at the FBI and suggested there might be a connection between the two events. Twenty minutes and three connections later, Kelleher was talking to a very interested deputy director in the J. Edgar Hoover Building.

Sorensen's employment at the CIA might have been in jeopardy, but she still had the keys to the kingdom. She proved the point by procuring a classic safe house in Manassas, Virginia.

The house was ten miles from headquarters, a stately two-story Colonial in a quiet neighborhood with two-acre lots, cinnamon-hued brick, and plenty of elbow room. She told Slaton he could have the place for as long as he needed it, and he laid claim to the upstairs master suite by throwing his bag on the bed.

If it had been an Airbnb, he would have called the host. The bed was unmade, and dirty towels littered the bathroom floor. Next to the nightstand was an empty beer can full of ash and spent cigarettes. Based on the accumulation of dust and a dank odor, he reckoned no one had been here for at least a month. Without complaint, the assassin reverted to housekeeper. He threw the beer can into the outside trash, and found fresh sheets and towels in the linen closet. In truth, Slaton preferred self-help—it was better than introducing a housekeeping crew who had the potential of being compromised. Aside from that, the routine chore of making his own bed was a good mental reset, a few moments of distraction from the trials that loomed.

He went back downstairs and found Sorensen brewing coffee—mercifully, someone had left half a bag of Black Rifle Gunship in the freezer.

"Good news," she said. "I talked to Eraclides and he's agreed to meet us here. He should arrive in about half an hour."

"Was he annoyed?"

"At first. Then I explained that if you went to the headquarters building there would be a video record of it, creating a hard link between you and him."

"And he never considered this?"

"He's not wired to think like you and I, David. Hopefully we can get him up to speed." She handed him a full mug. "There's sugar in the pantry but the cream in the refrigerator is green."

"Black will do."

"Eraclides is going to bring the latest intel on our target."

"Eraclides. Sounds like a Greek philosopher who got sent to the wrong millennium."

"Don't underestimate him. He may not have an operational background, but he's smart and ambitious. We need to be his guides, show him how to put together a solid mission."

"Convince him that my success is his success? I've been trying to make that argument to management my whole clandestine life. Never seems to quite work out."

"Present company excluded, I hope?"

He thought about that, then nodded grudgingly. "Honestly, you're the best boss I've ever had." He held out his mug and they tapped rims. "But don't let that go to your head—it's a *really* low bar."

Charles Eraclides arrived midway through their second cup.

The first thing Slaton noticed was the sound of a big car engine, followed by doors slamming shut. A sharp voice barked instructions. He fingered back a curtain at the kitchen window to see a Mercedes sedan, the biggest and blackest available. Slaton was looking at the side of the car, but he imagined a vanity license plate. Maybe CIA LAW. The suit-clad driver, sporting an obvious shoulder holster and an earbud, stood next to the car, his attention riveted outward.

After a few beats, Eraclides circled into view. His suit belonged on Saville Row, his frown on a winless college football coach. A gold watch glinted in the sun, what people wore not to track the time, but to impress upon others that theirs was valuable. Designer sunglasses sat perched beneath a pair of caterpillar eyebrows. A harried fifty-something woman emerged from the car balancing files and a laptop. They set out toward the house together.

Slaton let the curtain drop.

The doorbell rang. Twice.

Sorensen went to answer it.

Slaton lagged behind, pausing at the kitchen connector. The man who walked in was transformed. The scowl was gone, and Eraclides greeted Sorensen as if they'd connected on an online dating site, an exaggerated smile and an over-held handshake. For two reasons Slaton doubted he was actually hitting on her. First was the obvious wedding band on the director's own hand. Second, and more persuasive, was that he probably had knowledge, on some level, of Sorensen's fiancé, the temperamental and very large Jammer Davis.

The director's gaze drifted to his surroundings. It was likely the first time he had ever set foot in a safe house, and he regarded it with a mix of caution and curiosity, like a priest who'd stumbled into a massage parlor. He was probably wondering where the waterboarding room was when his gaze settled on Slaton. The director's visage turned noticeably wary. He would have had associations with men like Slaton before, but always in the abstract. Legal memoranda and after-action reports. Possibly the occasional interview in a headquarters briefing room. Never would he have encountered such a creature in the wild. Slaton wondered what he'd been expecting. Full beard, tattoos, facial scars? A loose shirt concealing an array of weapons? He was a disappointment on every count.

"Charles Eraclides," the director said, approaching Slaton with a cautiously outstretched hand.

"David," Slaton replied, leaving it at that.

"It wasn't my inclination to meet in a place like this," Eraclides said, gesturing loosely to the room, "but I appreciate your reasoning. Please understand, my time is limited. I'm scheduled to update the Senate leadership in a few hours." He introduced his assistant, a senior analyst from Langley's second floor named Margaret Goode. She was slim and conservatively dressed, her hair tied back sensibly. After a cordial hello, Goode commandeered the dining room table and began setting up her laptop and files.

Eraclides said, "Anna tells me you've been a reliable servant to our country, and on more than one occasion."

"I try to help where I can."

"It seems we may need that help again. Someone has tried to assassinate the president, very likely the same group who's been attacking American interests for months. Fortunately, I think we've finally made some headway on figuring out who it is." He said this as if all the "headway" had been made in the eight hours since he'd assumed control of the agency.

As if he, Charles Eraclides, was the CIA's savior.

"All right," Slaton said. "Show me what you've got."

SIXTEEN

Monkh stopped for the second time ten miles outside Asheville. He still had three hours until his flight departed, and not wanting to spend any more time than necessary at the airport, he turned into a minor scenic overlook.

He stood up the Kawasaki in an empty parking area. An informal trail led up the nearest hill, and he followed it to the crest and then over the top. On the far side he paused, removed his helmet, and rubbed a hand over his mid-length black hair. He'd been wearing the helmet for much of the day, and it felt good to be free of it. After relieving himself on a bush, he sat on a warm rock, cracked open a water bottle, and took a long draw.

The Blue Ridge Mountains spanned out before him, their signature hue evident in the late afternoon sun. He again removed the sat-phone from his jacket, powered it up, and saw a good signal. A second message from his employer bubbled to the screen. He had let the first go unanswered, making no attempt to call back.

This message, however, got his attention.

It wasn't a message in the usual sense; there were no words or emojis. Only a fifteen-digit alphanumeric string, special characters included. It was a code that would mean nothing to anyone else in the world. To Monkh, however, it was a five-alarm fire.

Ignoring an electric jolt in his spine, he quickly switched to his burner phone and called up the app that linked to his crypto wallet. Thirty seconds later, his worst fears were realized.

The account had been zeroed.

He closed his eyes tightly, embracing the darkness for a time. When he opened them, the truth on the screen hadn't changed. Soon, however, the shock waned, and he began to think more clearly. His employer was only making a point, emphasizing who was in charge. Probably piqued that he hadn't responded to the earlier message.

He stood and began pacing back and forth, loose stones crunching under his boots. He wondered how they had done it. He'd employed a secondary authentication app, created a complex private key, and always used clean devices. Still, they had bettered him.

He supposed he shouldn't be surprised. His employer had virtually limitless assets, and would spare nothing to control every aspect of the strike. Monkh had been paid one hundred percent in advance, a highly unusual arrangement, although not out of line given the risks he was taking. He had accepted the most difficult contract on earth: to take out the president of the United States. The success of his strike still hung in the balance, but he'd done precisely what they'd asked him to do, including cleaning up the loose ends last night. There was still a follow-on assignment, but that was child's play compared to eliminating the leader of the free world.

Monkh regarded the encrypted phone, turning it in his hand. He turned off the burner, then initiated a call to the vaulted number on the satellite handset. It was answered after two rings. This was a message in itself—he typically had to wait for a callback.

"Next time don't take so long to reply," said the distant voice. The words were electronically garbled, a method to deny voice identification. Monkh had been hired for this job through the only channel he trusted, a dark web connection with multiple cutouts. As a rule, he didn't need to know the identity of his employers. All they needed to know about him was his reputation for success. Still, there were always clues. The choice of targets generally pointed one in the right direction. As did the prescribed time and manner of elimination. In this case, there was also the garbled voice on the phone. Despite the electronics, there were always tells. American English, no decipherable accent. A decided air of superiority.

"Next time don't steal my money," Monkh replied.

"Yesterday's job is incomplete. She's alive."

If the man had been in front of him, Monkh might have shot him. Almost singlehandedly, he had downed Marine One and then eliminated the only two witnesses who could compromise the operation. The execution of the plan, which was not of his creation, had been flawless. Then, according to the news reports, some do-good idiot at the park had hauled Cleveland out of the sinking wreckage.

"I carried out *your* plan to the letter," he argued. "Any shortcomings were no fault of mine."

"Your protest is noted. In any event, it's still possible you have succeeded. The president may succumb to her injuries."

"Is that what they are saying on the news?"

A humorless snort. "News in America is worthless. It's little more than entertainment, media companies profiting through fearmongering. My information is factual, and sourced from the highest level."

Monkh's phrasing had been deliberate, and he deconstructed the reply. In the end, he decided not to fence. "What do you want?"

"More conclusive results on your next mission. And after that, I may need you to return to Washington."

"*Washington?* For what?"

"A follow-up could be necessary."

"A follow-up? You can't be serious. Her protection would be impossible to breach."

"You overestimate. Difficult, but not impossible. If it comes to that, I'll find a way to get you in."

Monkh hesitated. "And my money?"

"Half will be returned tomorrow, deposited right where you left it. If I were you, I would make arrangements, move it somewhere more secure. You'll get the rest when the job is done."

"I want all of it up front."

"What you want is immaterial."

"And if I decline?"

"Do I really have to say it? You are talented . . . but hardly unique. If I chose to press the matter, you would be hunted to the ends of the earth."

Monkh fell very still. He tried to think of a retort, something clever and defiant. When nothing came to mind, he simply ended the call. His fingers vised around the handset. He briefly wondered if hanging up would be viewed as insolence or defeat. Probably both, he imagined.

He powered down the phone and put it back in his pocket. Monkh wasn't surprised. Not really. Irrespective of who his employer was—and he had narrowed that to a short list—they were both in very deep water. Which meant they were bonded by a necessity of mutual success. Or, barring that, mutually assured destruction.

He started back toward the parking area, no attention whatsoever paid to the stunning vista. It occurred to Monkh that his original contract was morphing, and he wondered if that had been the idea all along. Three possibilities came to mind. First was that his employer had no intention of taking a second shot at the president, and that he considered Monkh a loose end to be eliminated when he returned. The second option was a variation of the first: that his employer would send him into a suicide follow-up, eliminating Elayne Cleveland and at the same time severing the last link to his own complicity. Yet there was a third possibility. Could there truly be a high-level insider? Someone who could pave the way for a second shot at Elayne Cleveland? The drone attack had involved some proprietary intelligence, but at base it was a simple scheme that applied a new weapon against known defenses. The shell game with helicopters, in place for years, hadn't kept up with the times. Yet a second shot at the president would require true insider knowledge. And if Monkh received that kind of intel? Then the list of possibilities as to who he might be working for got very short indeed.

There was, of course, one alternative to all of that. Monkh could simply walk away. He was an expert at disappearing, and he had enough money to lay low for years. But would his ambition, his drive to perfection permit it? His hypercompetitive personality had thrived in the gaming world. Later he had enthralled commanders in the People's Liberation Army and various intelligence agencies, and since going private Monkh could count scores of satisfied clients. After all that, could he sit and do nothing for years?

It seemed tantamount to defeat.

Minutes later Monkh was on the Kawasaki, idling toward the road. He paused at the shoulder to check for traffic. The big bike stood balanced between his legs, the quiet thrum of its engine poised. He was faced with a classically dichotomous question: a digital choice between two outcomes. Cut free and disappear with nothing. Or double down at far greater risk. In a gaming tournament there would have been no question whatsoever. Risk brought reward. Yet in the real world, risk could prove painful. Even terminal.

Monkh looked left, then right. He gave the throttle a turn and the big bike shot into the road.

Goode announced she was ready, and the others semicircled behind her laptop.

She began with a condensed history, everything the CIA had learned about The Trident since March. Slaton himself had acquired some of the information, having tracked down a middleman who confirmed there were three principals in the group. All were wealthy Chinese, and two had once run large corporations—one a supplier of defense electronics, the other a weapons manufacturer—while the third had an academic background with research and development ties to the defense industry. All of them had departed lucrative, high-level positions for a far more shadowed world. Unfortunately, while the middleman Slaton had tracked down knew that much, he claimed to not know their names. He described them only as men who "provide advanced hardware and mission objectives, then pay others to throw the spears." The middleman might have told Slaton more had he not been killed by an assassin. Since then, the trail had gone cold.

Until now.

Goode came to the new intel. "We've finally got a name—it came from a source in Beijing."

"How reliable is this source?" Slaton asked.

Sorensen replied, "We began recruiting him many years ago, while he was working on his doctorate at MIT. There's a popular cliché relating to spying in academia—it basically suggests that Chinese graduate students come to America under the guise of getting an education, then do nothing but steal vital research. That does happen, but it can also work in reverse. These students see the freedoms we enjoy. They make friends, have lovers. The agency approaches some of them, gives them a means of contact. When they go back to China to work on cutting edge projects, a few turn out to be quite useful."

Goode picked up. "As it relates to The Trident, we quietly put out word last month that we were trying to identify former defense industry executives who had overseen development of the weapons used in these recent attacks. We narrowed it down to pulsed lasers and hypersonic missiles, so it was a small net to cast. This source told us the CEO of China Precision Electronics left his post suddenly last year. Once we had the name, dots began connecting."

Goode referenced the laptop, and extensive files appeared on the man in question: his academic and corporate history, personal information, even pattern of life research.

"Looks like you've been busy," Slaton said.

Sorensen replied, "Nothing focuses a search like an assassination attempt on the president."

Goode opened the first file, and said, "His name is Yao Jing . . ."

SEVENTEEN

Yao Jing was a Chinese national who'd risen quickly from relative obscurity—there was nothing in his file more than ten years old—to become the chief executive of China Precision Electronics. In China such rises universally meant one thing: close ties to the party, usually via family. There was nothing in Yao's file to confirm such a connection, but his oversight of CPE was well documented, and the company's products dovetailed perfectly with the advanced technologies seen in the recent attacks. He had left the company suddenly the previous year, and little had been heard from him since. According to the CIA's file, he kept three residences, and was presently in Macau.

"Could Yao and The Trident be working with the Chinese government?" Slaton asked.

"It's a possibility, some kind of new shadow service," Sorensen said. "But so far we've got no evidence of an association."

Eraclides said, "Now that we're getting a bead on who these people are, if there are ties we'll find them."

"I'm not so sure," Slaton argued. "The key to shadow warfare is confusion. You add as many cut-outs as possible. Hiding smoking-gun connections between decision makers and frontline warriors is the whole point. Trust me on that one."

Eraclides shot him a look, but didn't reply.

Goode said, "We managed to correlate some money flows last night. The Trident went to great lengths to conceal its leadership, but we've identified a shell company they set up in Liechtenstein. It's a primary source of their funding, and downstream we found an account in Singapore controlled by Yao. This shell company led to another possible suspect—we're working to confirm the name."

"If it checks out," Eraclides remarked, "that would leave only one to uncover."

"Assuming," Sorensen mused, "that the organization's name, The Trident, isn't itself a bit of misdirection."

Eraclides's face creased in confusion. It wasn't the kind of disruption he typically faced in case law and legal briefs.

"Welcome to the world of smoke and mirrors," Slaton said.

Goode continued for another twenty minutes, at which point Eraclides animatedly checked his watch—a Rolex Submariner, pressure rated to a depth of a thousand feet, that had likely never been deeper than the country club swimming pool.

"Miss Goode and I have to leave," the director said. He fixed his attention on Slaton. "I want you and Anna to come up with a plan for this mission."

"You haven't told me what the mission is. And I haven't told you I'm going to accept it."

Eraclides shot an irritated glance at Sorensen. "The mission is perfectly clear. This Trident group will be stopped, by order of the acting president. Whether they have state support from China, or anyone else for that matter, is immaterial. They have repeatedly attacked America, and now they've tried to kill our president. That demands a response. With your skill-set, you are the least-risk option."

"Least risk for who?"

The director's visage went to stone. It was a look that probably withered lawyers in IG conference rooms. "There is no higher national imperative, and you will have the agency's full support. Travel, gear, funding, insertion, whatever you need. I'll grant you complete freedom to plan the op, but I want every-thing set by tomorrow. Anna will coordinate the lo-gistics and provide intel updates. Sometime in the next forty-eight hours, expect a green light for you to . . ." he hesitated, "eliminate Yao Jing."

Eraclides looked suddenly uncomfortable, which Slaton took as a positive. Condemning a man to death, no matter how deserving, should never be an easy thing. Doubly so when you were doing it for the first time.

"I'm not convinced," Slaton said.

"Of what?"

"First, that Yao is part of The Trident. Second, that The Trident is responsible for the attack on Marine One. Both seem likely, but neither is a slam dunk. I'm also not sure I want to get involved. You're talk-ing about a rushed mission, and in my experience, those are the ones that go sideways. I'm a father now and have a second child on the way. That brings a new constraint for any mission I accept."

"And what's that?"

"Survival."

The director squared his shoulders, a move that fell flat in his tailored Armani jacket. He looked strained and tense.

Slaton's steel-gray eyes never wavered.

None too discreetly, Sorensen edged between them. "David has a point. We can't expect him to—"

Eraclides held up a hand to quiet her, his eyes still locked on Slaton. "Let's be clear, Corsair. You have a delicate relationship with this country. Director Coltrane briefed me at length about your dealings with the agency. He told me you've proven yourself operationally on more than one occasion. He also explained how generous we've been in return. The ranch where you reside was procured at no small expense, and we run round-the-clock protection for your family. This arrangement has worked for both of us, but going forward it could prove . . . problematic if you can't follow orders."

Slaton gave no reply.

"Then there's your application for citizenship to consider."

"His *what*?" Sorensen broke in.

"My staff uncovered a pending application for citizenship . . . it's even in his real name. David is scheduled to take the oath next week."

She shot Slaton a look that asked, *Why did I not know about this?*

He said, "It's something Christine brought up. We've been married over three years, so the requirements have been met. She wants me to become an official American."

"When were you going to inform the agency?" Eraclides asked.

"I don't see that it's any of the agency's business—although I never doubted you'd make the connection."

"It's very much our business. The legal framework you operate under applies only to foreign nationals. If you become a citizen those protections are lost."

"So draw up a new memorandum. The original one was never for *my* protection anyway—it was designed to cover asses inside the Beltway."

"Perhaps. But citizenship is off the table . . . at least, for now."

Slaton's eyes ratcheted between the director and Sorensen. "So that's it? That's your bargain? I fly halfway around the world to kill Yao, maybe one or two other blameworthy individuals, and in exchange my family continues to get protection and I have a *chance* of becoming an American?"

"I'm not here to back you into a corner, David."

"Good choice."

Eraclides motioned to Goode that it was time to go. He then turned back to Slaton. "David, we can't lose sight of the big picture. The Trident has to be stopped. It's a destabilizing force pursuing a reckless agenda. Right now, you're our best chance of putting an end to it."

Not waiting for a reply, he headed toward the front door. Goode left the laptop and files behind. The director paused at a mirror to straighten his tie. On the way out, he actually said, "Good luck. America is counting on you."

And with that, the new director of the CIA disappeared.

EIGHTEEN

Sorensen stood staring at him. If Slaton wasn't mistaken, she was holding her breath.

"I'm glad you're not carrying right now," she ventured.

"You think I'd need a weapon?"

"True, you could have broken his neck. But the vice president might replace him with someone worse."

"*Is* there someone worse?"

She picked up her empty coffee mug. "Refill."

Slaton followed her into the kitchen, trying to throttle down his irritation. After the coffee was poured, he settled in behind the laptop.

She pulled a chair next to his, and said, "Look, I know Eraclides has a lot to learn. But I've had a few dealings with him and he's not an idiot. Give him a chance."

"As if I have a choice?"

He began skimming the files on Yao Jing.

"So . . . are you going to do it?" she asked. "Macau?"

"Head to China, the world's most heavily surveilled nation, and kill three important men?"

"And do it in a way that doesn't drag America into a war."

"Maybe I can find a cure for cancer while I'm at it."

"Right."

"What's your real opinion on this source in Beijing?" he asked.

"Honestly, I don't know much about him. But the name he gave us led to solid supporting data. He put us on the right track. If I was making the call, I'd probably do the same thing. Only I'd be more manipulative than Eraclides."

"How's that?"

"I would have given you the files, knowing you'd come to the same conclusion. That way you'd think it was your decision."

He looked over his shoulder, saw the wry smile.

"I'm a woman," she said, as if that explained something.

"But is putting a target on Yao's back the best solution? Why not go for capture and rendition, sweat him for information?"

"It might surprise you, but Eraclides and I discussed it. It seemed problematic from a number of standpoints. To begin, Yao has decent security at his residence. He lives in Chinese-administered territory, and there's no hint that he'll be traveling soon. At least, not to any place where an abduction might be viable. We also don't have the luxury of time. Our national leadership is lurching through a crisis. We don't even know who our president is going to be next week. The pressure to act is like nothing I've ever seen. Which means, if there's a chance to decapitate The Trident, nobody cares how it gets done. I can also tell you this—if you don't go to Macau, they'll send someone else."

"But a SEAL team or Delta op risks blowback if something goes wrong. On the other hand, if I screw up—no repercussions."

"I'm sure that was part of the director's calculus. As it would have been mine."

He shook his head and smiled. "I wish they'd put you in charge, Anna."

"I'm glad they didn't. SAC/SOG, by definition, stays in the background. I want nothing to do with press conferences and public grillings on Capitol Hill. But Eraclides was right about one thing—we can't lose sight of the bigger picture. If you eliminate Yao, it buys time and sends a concrete message. Whoever he's working with will have serious second thoughts about launching more attacks."

"Yeah . . . second thoughts." He turned away and began typing on the laptop.

While Sorensen excused herself to make a phone call, Slaton launched into his mission prep. He began with overhead reconnaissance of Yao's residence in Macau, and a second building where he kept an office. Both looked like fortresses. To eliminate the man in the timeframe the director wanted, Slaton knew his options would be limited.

As he scrolled through Yao's hastily built dossier, doubts fluttered in the back of his mind. *Am I really going to do this? Rush halfway around the world to protect an ungrateful nation?*

No, he corrected. America wasn't ungrateful. While they would never know his name, know the details of his missions, millions of school teachers and retirees and sales reps counted on the fact that there were men and women like him keeping the world safe. Running toward the gunfire. It was the cast of idiots who ran things that gave Slaton pause. The ones in Washington whose only mission objective was to stay in office or climb to the next level. The corrupt, the power-seekers, the pocket-lining thieves. He'd seen them across the globe, and America was no different.

Yet there *was* something compelling about this mission. The Trident, whoever they were, were intent on blowing the world apart. First a series of terror attacks, and now trying to assassinate the president.

And he, uniquely, was in a position to stop whatever was coming next.

"Well, what do you think?" Sorensen asked when she returned.

Slaton didn't respond right away, risks and rewards battling in his head. He finally shrugged and answered with all the conviction of a teenager being asked to take out the trash. "I guess somebody's got to do it."

Eraclides was on his phone within minutes of leaving the safe house. Margaret Goode had taken a seat in front, next to the driver, and Eraclides raised the privacy screen before placing a secure call.

It was answered immediately.

"Is he on board?" asked Matt Gross, the vice president's chief of staff.

"I think so."

"That's not good enough. The vice president wants a response, and Corsair is our best option."

"You mean he's the option least likely to blow up in our face."

"Whatever."

Eraclides shifted in his seat, supple Bavarian leather crinkling beneath him. "I played the cards we talked about, family security and citizenship. What more is there to persuade him? He didn't strike me as the type who would respond to threats . . . at least, not in the way we want."

"You almost sound as if you're intimidated by him."

"You want to have a word? Be my guest."

Silence from the White House end, then, "Maybe I will. It's vital we press home the importance of what's at stake. I want to ensure his compliance." Gross explained what he had in mind.

Eraclides didn't like the sound of it. "That might work. Or it could backfire completely, create an enemy that neither of us needs."

"It's a simple incentive—an example of what happens if he doesn't come through. Corsair needs to understand who's running things."

Eraclides fell silent, his reluctance clear.

Gross said, "Charles, the vice president put you in charge of CIA for a reason. Don't make him regret it."

Gross went directly to the Oval Office after the call. He found the vice president—no, he corrected, the *acting* president—seated behind the Resolute desk with a pen in hand. It struck him that Quarrels looked suddenly older, as though he'd aged ten years in the last twenty-four hours. His hair was unkempt, and the age spots on his receding hairline seemed more pronounced.

On the blotter before him was one of the ever-present legal pads he relied upon. Half the pages were already filled, outlines of executive orders the two of them had been hatching all afternoon. Trade deals with Central Asian nations, arms support for the Baltic states, redirected funding for three new icebreakers. As a matter of decorum, none of the initiatives would be announced for a few weeks. Still, the foundation was being set.

"Well?" Quarrels asked, looking up from his work as Gross approached.

"Eraclides thinks Corsair is on board."

"Thinks?"

"Lincoln, we're in uncharted waters. Slaton is not officially in our chain of command. But that's what makes him perfect for this operation."

"Is there a chance the Israelis still hold sway over him?"

"I don't think that's an issue—apparently he's applied for U.S. citizenship. Anyway, just to be sure, I'm putting the incentive we discussed into motion."

Quarrels looked questioningly at his chief of staff, as if trying to remember what he was talking about. It wasn't the first time Gross had seen the look—there were definite lapses in his train of thought. Quarrels shook his head and moved on, flipping to a new page on the legal pad.

"So," he said, "about this NATO summit in June."

Gross suppressed a grin. "Yes, I've got some ideas about that . . ."

NINETEEN

Slaton and Sorensen went into planning mode, a deep dive performed in the bastion of the safe house. Two CIA technicians came and went, installing hardware that linked them to Langley's secure network. Their biggest problem soon became parsing through the data—the agency, conspiring with the likes of NSA and NRO, had put so many clandestine magnifying glasses on Yao Jing that Sorensen jested he might die from thermal overload and save Slaton the trouble.

By eight o'clock that evening, their focus had narrowed: their target's most vulnerable moment in the next few days was patently obvious.

"Number five," Slaton said, pushing one high-resolution satellite photo across a kitchen table that was buried in them.

"That's the lucky number?"

"Or unlucky, if you're Yao."

For the last two weeks, as verified by multiple sources—satellite overheads, emails, and multiple intercepted phone calls—Yao had been residing in Macau. A study of his hacked personal calendar showed that his next travel event wasn't for a month, a flight to Beijing for consultations with his banker. That could change, of course, or even be disinformation. Yet a number of crosschecks—the servicing of his personal jet, the schedule of its pilots, hotel reservations, a cancelled dental appointment, and multiple emails—corroborated the timetable.

Also on his schedule was one bright, shiny opportunity: Virtually every week that Yao was in Macau—three months running now, and a habit that had gone on for years—he'd kept a regular golf date with three friends.

Once the opportunity was flagged, the CIA descended on the Macau Golf and Country Club like a multispectral spotlight. Thousands of archived satellite images were retrieved, and the club's computer system was ruthlessly violated. Maps of the course itself, along with the surrounding terrain, were enhanced to extract every topographical detail. Using a look-back of tee times, membership rosters, and financial transactions, the three other members of Yao's regular foursome were quickly identified. It was hoped that at least one them might also be linked to The Trident, giving Slaton the prospect of a sniper's BOGO special—buy-one-get-one-free. Unfortunately, all three men turned out to be friends of Yao's from his university days, and none had ties to the defense industry.

Sorensen studied the photo Slaton had singled out. It was marked in black Sharpie: *5th Hole*.

"What's special about it?" she asked.

"From a golfer's point of view, not much. Long par four, slight dogleg to the left."

"And from a shooter's point of view?"

Slaton leaned over the table and tapped his trigger finger on a thick stand of forest adjacent to the fairway. "There's a lot of dense cover to the north, and it's high ground. Easy access on the backside from a service road. On the way out, you could disappear into the city within minutes. I assume I'll have help on the ground?"

"I'm working on that. We have assets at the consulate, but the Chinese are watching like hawks these days. Hong Kong isn't what it used to be."

"NOCs?"

"That's my inclination, although we don't have any in place at the moment. There are a few holdovers the Brits might share, but we'd have to read them in. I'm not sure that's worth the risk on such a critical op. How many are you thinking?"

"At the very least I need a driver, somebody with local area knowledge. It would be nice to have somebody near the first tee as well—if we can get a positive ID on Yao early, it saves me having to do it. Also, if I know when the group starts, I'll have a good estimate for his arrival at the fifth hole."

"Putting someone at the club in real time might be risky, but I think the consulate can help us there. We could install some cameras ahead of time, use a secure local network so we're not beaming everything around the world. I'll set it up to crosscheck his image with facial recognition software—we've got a solid version for field use now."

"Okay, so that leaves just a driver."

"I'll figure something out." She looked up from the photo. "Complications?"

"The biggest would be weather. If it rains, it's an abort."

"You can't shoot in the rain?"

"*He* can't shoot in the rain."

"Oh, right. Golf was never my thing."

"Mine neither, but let's hope it's not an issue. This group only plays once a week, and right now I'm not seeing a Plan B."

"I'll get a forecast from meteorology."

Slaton tried to absorb that, still not accustomed to the vastness of resources at his command. A CIA meteorologist, or probably a team of them, would soon be tasked to give a two-day forecast for a golf course half a world away. Eraclides might be an ass, but the support of his agency could prove vital.

"We should know what kind of police response to expect afterward," he added.

Sorensen scribbled a note. "What else?"

"A plan for getting me there. And more important, for getting me out."

"Any kind of clandestine insertion is probably out. It would take too long to coordinate, and anyway, we're talking about an urban area. That takes submarines and HALO jumps off the table."

"Agreed," he said. "Which leaves commercial air or a corporate jet."

"Corporate is high profile, hard to pull off without drawing suspicion—especially with the Chinese." After a few beats, Sorensen said, "There might be another option."

"What's that?"

"It's just a loose idea, so let me see what's available. It might require bending some rules."

"You're worried about bending rules? I'm supposed to fly halfway around the world to put a bullet in—"

"Okay," she said, cutting him off. "Point taken."

"If it involves flying, we should use the main Hong Kong airport—it's right across the bay from Macau. If everything goes down like I'm hoping, there won't be any hiding in the aftermath. Exfil will be all about speed. Get in, get out, leave the authorities grasping at straws."

"Got it. Minimum ground time."

Sorensen took it from there, building out the plan. Her confidence was evident, a byproduct of having such extensive assets available: intelligence, logistics, fully backstopped legends. Yet that level of support was a double-edged blade. Headquarters, Hong Kong, the transportation link between them. A lot of people would be involved, and while each only knew his or her small part of the op, word could get out that a swanky country club in Macau was the focal point of . . . something.

It gave Slaton pause.

Assassins, with good reason, were inherently secretive. They preferred shadow to light, silence to noise. Anonymity to recognition. The operation he was committing to would be anything but stealthy. By the time he was crawling through brush to line up Yao Jing in his crosshairs, scores of people would be involved. Aside from Sorensen, Slaton knew none of them. From an operational security standpoint, it was a nightmare. On top of that, Yao was only the first of three targets. Each kill would become progressively more difficult.

To Slaton it all felt rushed and complicated, and the weight of his reservations sank back in. Unfortunately, he saw no way around one hard deadline: the day after tomorrow, at 7:34 a.m., Hong Kong Standard Time, one verified member of The Trident had a tee time.

TWENTY

Davy was an early riser, and just after sunrise Christine's eyes fluttered open as he clambered into bed next to her.

"I'm hungry," he said, squirming his legs under the covers.

"Can you reach the cereal shelf?" she asked.

"Yeah. But I wish Dad was here to make pancakes."

She smiled and mussed his hair. "Yeah, me too, buckaroo. But maybe you and I can figure it out."

Thirty minutes later they were dropping sticky plates and forks into the dishwasher, and ten after that they were on a bench on the back porch. Davy was burrowed deep in the crook of her arm, listening raptly to her rendition of *The Cat in the Hat,* when the sound of an arriving vehicle broke the still morning air.

Christine quickly checked her phone but saw no messages. Anytime someone approached the house, she was supposed to get a notification from the protection detail.

"Is somebody coming, Mom?" Davy asked.

"Sounds like it."

"Maybe it's Dad!"

"Let's go see."

She took Davy by the hand and together they walked to the side of the house. She saw one of the familiar SUVs used by her security team pulling into the gray-gravel parking apron. Mike, a shift lead, got out and stood by the driver's-side door.

"Hey, Mike."

"Morning, Dr. Palmer." His usual easy demeanor seemed absent.

"Is something wrong?" she asked.

Mike frowned openly. "Well, not wrong exactly, but we've gotten some new orders. Looks like there are going be some changes around here . . ."

Slaton arrived at Joint Base Andrews at ten that morning. The base was on a hard security lockdown, the events of two days earlier having had their effect. Their agency car had to pass through three checkpoints to reach the flight line.

Sorensen was by his side in the back seat, the two of them having spent the night at the safe house shaping details of the mission. After a few hours' sleep and a rushed breakfast, a driver had shown up in an SUV to deliver them here. Even with departure imminent, Sorensen hadn't yet explained the details of his flight. In fact, based on her most recent phone call, the plan was still being ironed out during the drive to the airport.

Through the tinted windows Slaton saw a neat row of executive transports on the far side of the airfield. All were painted in the white-and-blue livery of the 89th Airlift Wing, and their spit and polish was clear from a mile away: shiny chrome-lipped engines, gleaming fuselages, prominent American flags. The

89th was Air Force's elite transport unit, flying not only Air Force One, but a comprehensive squadron of business jets that shuttled government officials across the world.

That ramp, however, was not their destination.

Ahead lay the corner pocket of the airfield. Not red carpets and honor guards, but anonymous hangars and generic air freight containers. Arrayed on the ramp were a motley collection of freight dogs—everything from battered turboprops to a whitewashed Boeing 747.

"I take it you've finalized my ride?" he asked, his eyes sweeping the tarmac.

"I have," Sorensen replied, putting down her phone. She looked exhausted, having been up most of the night managing logistics. "It wasn't easy. Our mission requirement was to get you halfway around the world in minimum time, then extract you again within a couple of hours. One cover struck me as a natural fit—you're going to pose as a cargo pilot."

Slaton considered it. "Not bad. Legend?"

She handed over a wallet and Slaton looked inside.

"All the usual docs," she said. "Plus a pilot's license, FAA medical certificate, and a radiotelephone operator's permit."

Next came a dark blue United States passport. Slaton flicked it open and saw what looked like a mug shot. "I don't recall sitting for this picture."

"You didn't—it's all CGI, based on a couple of others we had."

"A deep fake passport? So much for Kodak moments. Nobody's going to expect me to fly, are they?"

"Don't worry. The airplane we're using requires a good bit of training."

As if on cue, the driver pulled to a stop in front of

the most conspicuous airplane on the ramp: the massive B-747.

"Seriously?"

"It's perfect. Boeing 747 freighters are a dime a dozen in Hong Kong. The company that operates this one is an occasional business partner of ours."

"The new Air America?" he suggested, referring to the shady air cargo outfit run by the CIA during the Vietnam War.

"This one's a legitimate business, and we occasionally contract with them for heavy lift. This particular airplane has a nice advantage. It's certified for two pilots, but longer flights require an augmented crew—a third pilot who rotates in so the others can rest."

"And let me guess—the two on board aren't going to get a lunch break?"

"Don't worry, both are volunteers—they know what they're getting into."

Slaton liked the concept. Entering Hong Kong on a leviathan like this would be so overt, so over the top, it would generate little suspicion. Like pulling into Monaco's harbor on a superyacht. Slaton and Sorensen stepped outside.

The airplane loomed like a mountain. The engines on the port wing were the size of railroad cars, and the tires belonged on a farm combine.

Two pilots loped down the boarding stairs, looking every bit the part in dark polyester trousers and epauleted white shirts. The four-striper was a woman, the copilot a man, both mid-forties with a professional bearing. Slaton guessed they were former military, probably retired lieutenant colonels who wanted to keep flying, but something more challenging than the Washington–Newark shuttle.

After introductions and handshakes, the captain,

whose name was Melanie Lyle, gave Slaton a basic rundown of the plan. "The first leg will take us to Anchorage, roughly nine hours. We'll do a quick gas-and-go there, then eleven hours to Hong Kong."

"That's a long day for you guys," Slaton said.

"True, but we've got you as a relief pilot."

Slaton shot Sorensen a hard look.

"Don't worry," the skipper said with a grin, "no stick time involved. Just keep telling jokes so the guy on duty stays awake."

Slaton smiled.

"Pilots like nothing better than getting paid to sleep," added Dan Raymond, the copilot. "We call it dozing for dollars."

Lyle said, "We've been briefed to expect a short stay in Hong Kong, so we may be your outbound crew as well. But that would be a shorter flight."

"Where to?" Slaton asked.

"I'm still working that out," said Sorensen. "Probably the Philippines, but it could change."

Slaton caught a slight nod from Sorensen, and immediately he understood. The Philippines would serve as his staging point for phase two. The CIA had a lead on a second member of The Trident, and the third could be uncovered soon. The hope was to take out all three. Slaton knew, however, that the level of difficulty would be progressive: each successive hit would become harder, the targets being forewarned.

Lyle and Raymond, of course, knew nothing about that. Their mission was as simple as it was narrow: deliver Slaton halfway around the world on a strict schedule. The pilots returned to the flight deck to finish their preflight checks. Sorensen took a new call on her phone.

Slaton drew in a deep breath. The acrid scent of

spent jet fuel laced the air, which only accentuated how far he was from the evergreen mountains of home.

Things were happening fast now, the mission about to launch.

It was all becoming real.

TWENTY-ONE

Sorensen climbed up to the flight deck, professing a need to finalize communications protocols with the pilots. No sooner had she disappeared than a limo arrived at the distant main gate.

Slaton watched closely as the big car was admitted and made a beeline in their direction. He was an expert on cars—all snipers were—and this one got his attention. He noticed a heaviness in the way it cornered, a thickness in the tires. The windows belonged on a deep-sea submersible. Altogether, closer to a tank than a luxury sedan. The antennas on the roof blended seamlessly, and every inch of chrome was shined to perfection. The most telling giveaway of all: on the two front fenders were twin empty sleeves waiting for flags.

If this wasn't a presidential ride, it was borrowed from the same motor pool. Based on what he knew, Slaton presumed that one of two people would climb out. He was proved right moments later.

The car coasted to a stop in the shade of jet's port wingtip. What emerged looked like it had teleported from Yale. Like Eraclides yesterday, there was an expensive suit, stiff and sharply creased. But this one was worn by a pale and thinly built man. The tie hanging from his starched collar could only be an Italian item. He walked toward Slaton with strained casualness, his shoes gleaming in the midday sun. It was not the vice president. But Slaton guessed it was his right-hand man.

He stopped two steps away, removed a pair of Cartier sunglasses, and said, "I'm Matt Gross, the acting president's—"

"I know who you are," Slaton said. "What do you want?"

A pause for recalibration. "Cooperation."

Slaton looked around obviously. At the airplane. At the suitcase next to his right leg. "It appears you have it."

"To this point. But the acting president wants to be sure we have a clear understanding."

"Then the acting president should tell me that himself."

Gross ignored the comment. "Miss Sorensen has confirmed that we have a lead on one member of The Trident. She also tells us that the others could be identified soon. I'd like your personal assurance that you'll see this mission through."

Something about Gross rankled Slaton. Which was probably why he'd come. "See it through to what?"

"Whatever it takes to ensure your country's security."

"*My* country?"

A furrowed brow between the Cartier logos.

"I'm not an American," Slaton said. "Not officially."

"In due course," Gross said, adding a cavalier wave. "In the meantime, certain changes are being made."

"Changes?"

"I realize that your family is foremost in your mind,

so I've ordered a few adjustments on that front. A new protection detail is going to take over, an upgrade over what was in place."

Slaton felt a clench in his gut—a sensation he usually associated with incoming fire. "First of all," he said in a level voice, "I was happy with the existing team. Second, I don't see how *you* have the authority to order any kind of changes. You serve the vice president in an advisory capacity."

"David . . ." Gross said, his voice dripping with patience, "I realize you've spent most of your life in the field, so I'll excuse you for not understanding how things work in the upper echelon. As chief of staff, I issue instructions as an extension of the acting president's authority."

Slaton was about to reply when Sorensen appeared at the top of the airstairs. She took one look at the two of them and clearly sensed a crisis. She hurried down and exchanged a measured handshake with Gross—more than Slaton had been offered—and began briefing him on the operation. It was little more than an executive overview, most key details left unmentioned. Slaton appreciated that—the fewer people read in on the op, the better.

He was also glad for the distraction, since he suddenly had more important matters to attend to. Slaton climbed the stairs, turned into the mostly empty cargo bay, and pulled out his phone.

Christine answered on the very first ring.

TWENTY-TWO

"Did you know this was coming?" Slaton asked Sorensen ten minutes later.

They were standing side by side on the warming tarmac, each holding a dormant phone. The big limo carrying Gross was lumbering through the exit gate. Slaton was glad for that—his citizenship application might hit a hitch if he choked out the vice president's chief of staff.

He'd just gotten off the phone with Christine, and she confirmed what was happening—a new protection detail had arrived at the ranch that morning. She'd met the new team leader, who assured her that staffing and procedures would remain unchanged. This was little solace for Slaton. Without being there in person, he had no way to vet the new crew. He wanted to know their backgrounds, gauge their competency. And most critical of all, he wanted to know who they took their orders from.

"I knew nothing about it," Sorensen replied, having put in a call to her new boss to find out more. "Eraclides confirmed the change, but he says it wasn't his idea."

"I know whose idea it was," Slaton said, watching the armored limo disappear behind a hangar. "What I don't understand is *why*."

She tracked his gaze. "You have to choose your battles, David."

"That's exactly what I'm doing."

"Please don't—"

"The team we had was solid, Anna! I won't entrust my family to people I don't know!"

"I told Eraclides you would see it that way. He promised to work something out when you get back from the op."

"There's not going to be any op—not the way it stands."

Sorensen looked skyward, as if pleading for divine intervention. "If Eraclides was the one pushing it," she said, "I might have leverage. But I can't fight the White House."

"Does that not strike you as odd, Anna? I mean, this new administration has taken charge virtually overnight. One minute the vice president is giving speeches at plumber's union conventions, going to state funerals in Ecuador, then suddenly he's running the country. You'd think his chief of staff would have bigger worries than who's running security on a ranch in Idaho."

Sorensen pocketed her phone, then hooked her right thumb on an unused belt loop. It was something near a gunslinger's stance. "Maybe I can work around it," she offered. "I could divert a few SAC/SOG assets to supplement the force until you get back."

"No. If Gross found out, and I'm betting he would, he'd only shut it down and lash out at Eraclides, who would then lash out at you." He looked up at the big jet and shook his head. "I'm sorry, Anna, but this doesn't work. It's not the op that worries me, it's the thought of traveling halfway around the world and leaving my family vulnerable. I won't go downrange with that hanging over my head."

"Have you really thought this through? If you bail on the op, you're going to piss off the new regime. Chances are, by the time you get back to Idaho there won't be *anyone* watching your place. They'll cut you loose in a heartbeat."

Slaton knew she was right. If he backed out, he would be forced to conjure up an entirely new life plan. It would mean taking his family back off-grid, nationless and wandering. All at a time when Davy needed stability—a home, a school, friends, the same bed every night. And when Christine and their unborn child needed an obstetrician and prenatal care. It was a lot to give up.

Sorensen said, "I get where you're coming from, David, and if you bail I'd understand. On the other hand, if you go ahead with the mission, make it a success, you'd have something to bargain with."

"I can't bargain with people I don't trust."

"What about Elayne Cleveland? You trust her, right?"

His silence conceded the point, but also underscored the uncertainty of the situation. Would she ever be in the picture again?

The word "trust" caught in Slaton's mind. In his line of work it was an absolute, and the corrosive situation in the White House spoke for itself. He needed someone he could rely on, someone to look out for his family until things settled. One name naturally came to mind. He looked at Sorensen for a long moment.

"What?" she asked cautiously.

Slaton explained his idea, not even knowing if it was possible.

An agonized look spread across her face, and for reasons Slaton understood all too well.

"That's asking a lot," she said.

"I know. And I wouldn't ask if there was a better way."

"I'm not even sure he could do it."

"Would you at least run it by him?"

She heaved a sigh.

Captain Lyle appeared at the upper entry door. "All systems are go up here!" she called down. "We need to leave soon if we're going to keep the schedule."

"One more minute," Slaton shouted up. He and Sorensen exchanged a long look, one that had nothing to do with their roles of special operator and commander. More like a prizefighter and manager facing a bout five weight classes too high.

Sorensen nodded. "I'll make the call, hopefully have an answer for you by the time you land in Alaska."

"Thank you." He made a move toward the boarding stairs.

"Be careful, David."

"Funny . . . Christine said the same thing."

"I can't imagine why."

Ed Markowitz was completely out of breath when he reached the fourth-floor corridor at Walter Reed. He found Dr. Singh outside Elayne Cleveland's room, dictating into a handheld recorder.

Markowitz glanced through the window into the room, saw an empty bed, and his thoughts ran away. "I got here as quickly as I could!" he said breathlessly.

The doctor looked up and ended his recording, but his face gave away nothing. He surveyed the hall and tipped his head toward a door on the opposite side. It turned out to be an office of sorts, a scatter-shot place with a single desk buried under files and a white board overrun by so much scrawl it looked like subway station graffiti.

Singh eased the door closed. "There's been a set-back," he said. "The president has developed a second-ary brain hemorrhage."

"How bad is it?" Markowitz asked, measuring every word.

"She is being prepped for surgery. It's a risky pro-cedure, and there is no guarantee of a positive out-come. Her chances are probably less than even. If we do nothing, however . . . her condition will almost surely degrade. The surgeon and I have discussed the options at length with her husband. He gave the au-thorization to go ahead."

"Has the vice president been advised?" Markowitz asked reflexively.

"It was my understanding that you were the point of contact for the White House. That's why I called."

"Yes . . . of course. I'll get word to the acting presi-dent right away."

TWENTY-THREE

Eight years earlier
Yunnan Province, China

"At least it wasn't a complete waste of time," Colonel Huang remarked acidly.

"I am still not convinced," said the man next to him. Deng Yoo headed Bureau 19 of the Ministry of State Security, an emphatically veiled directorate whose mission was little known outside the inner sanctums of Beijing.

They were standing on an observation platform, watching a recruit work his way through the tactical shooting range. Tall and athletically built, the young man moved quickly, if not smoothly, through a gauntlet of obstacles. His exchange of fire with the instructors, via a laser scoring system, was haphazard, but according to the display he was getting a few hits. Candidate 21, as he was known, came within thirty meters of his objective before the red light illuminated and a horn sounded. Everyone stood down, the instructors repositioning and Candidate 21 returning to the base of the platform.

"Not bad," Deng said. "I might make use of him. Language skills?"

"Fair English, a bit of French."

Without further comment, Deng turned his attention to Candidate 13, who was preparing for his final run. This one was built differently, having the lean frame of a distance runner. Deng watched the young man adjust the vest he was wearing, which carried the scoring sensors, tightening here and loosening there. He next practiced handling his weapon—left hand to right, then back again—and touching his extra magazines. Curiously, he did it all with his eyes closed, everything done by feel.

"What is he doing?" Deng asked.

Huang, who had been both a PLA weapons instructor and commander of the Sea Dragon Assault Team, said, "The training facsimiles are polymer and steel. They resemble standard service weapons, but do not have the precise weight and balance of the real thing."

The trainee's movements became smoother with each cycle.

Deng shrugged, still unconvinced. He himself had never been operational. He'd entered the ministry based on family connections, risen by the usual institutional politics. Successes were to be crowed about, failures swept aside. This project, in his view, had always seemed a dim prospect. "For all the time and effort, two seems a small return."

"When the program was forced on us, I also had doubts. But after three years, I have to tell you . . . Candidate 13, he is special."

The initiative, codenamed Zhong, or Loyal, had been hatched following a series of operational debacles across the globe. Congo, Syria, Thailand—the direct-action killers of Bureau 19, a tiny but vital force, had suffered a string of embarrassing failures. The bureau's leaders had gotten lazy, hiring local amateurs to do wet work, not keeping its own stable of assassins sharp. Too many missions had failed, resulting in operatives being captured and held for show trials. A complete reset was ordered by the president himself: the bureau was to be rebuilt from the ground up, its old leadership swept aside. Deng took control of the Bureau, and Huang was reassigned from the PLA to manage training. They were given complete authority to remake the unit.

And that, all too typically, was where the meddling began.

Spurred on by an obscure research paper, a member of the Standing Committee—the seven most powerful men in China outside the president—proposed that elite teenage gamers, in particular those who specialized in first-person shooter games, had all the requisite skills to become assassins. Quick reflexes, experts in multitasking, familiarity with the latest weapons.

Deng and Huang both thought the idea absurd, yet neither were going to sacrifice their careers over the point. Deng authorized a trial. Two officers— one from Bureau 19, and a second from the Sea Dragons—researched nearly a thousand of the top gamers in China. In the end, thirty-two candidates were recruited. The prospects were told they would be part of a research program designed to better train PLA soldiers. They would get a chance to leverage their unique abilities in real-world scenarios, as well as help the country better its defenses, all while earning a decent paycheck. None, at least at the outset, were told the true goal of the program: to identify and train a handful of elite assassins.

The recruits were sent to a secret base in western

Yunnan Province. Unfortunately, no sooner had the training commenced than the hopelessness of the effort became apparent. Of the thirty-two original candidates, twenty were gone in the first week. Most were physically unfit, the result of childhoods spent on couches in front of computer monitors. Others were wholly ill-suited to military discipline: waking before dawn, running in the middle of winter, suffering crewcut sergeants shouting in their faces. The academic fantasy of cyber-honed military warriors smacked headlong into reality. After one month, a mere six candidates remained, and most of those demonstrated only average abilities.

There were, however, two exceptions. Huang had not been completely surprised. Take enough young men, whatever their backgrounds, abuse them properly, and a few would rise to the top. He had long studied BUD/S, the American Navy's SEAL training program, and took pride that his culling was even more ruthless.

"Even if these two can run your course," Deng said speculatively, "I wonder how useful they can be to the ministry. Your Sea Dragons are effective for a military assault, but they lack tradecraft. Give them a knife and they can flay open a Uighur in seconds. But to do it in a crowd, without anyone noticing—that is a very different kind of skill."

The second man began the course. Both sets of eyes on the platform tracked him. Deng had not seen Thirteen since last winter, and the progress was stunning. He moved through the obstacles like water, yet did so unpredictably. His marksmanship was unerring, his timing that of a Swiss watch.

The two men exchanged an uneasy glance.

Huang said, "His English is faultless."

Deng pursed his grouper-like lips. "He is Manchurian as I recall?"

"Yes, a farm boy from a tiny village outside Hailar."

"That's something. If he is from a farm he is used to privation and hard work. He knows how to solve problems."

Two instructors took hits as the student advanced.

"He also grew up as a hunter," Huang added.

"He told you this?"

"He didn't have to. Hunters are always the best shooters. Note how he moves. He is not simply trying to stay alive . . . every switchback seizes an advantage. He is not hiding from his adversaries. He is stalking them."

A tentative nod from the bureau man. "For all the failures . . . perhaps we have stumbled on something."

The student darted low across a gap, rolled across the ground, and from a solid prone position tagged the final instructor.

"Has he been told yet?" Deng asked. "What he's being groomed for?"

"By now he must have some idea."

Deng was silent for a time, digesting what he'd seen. "Congratulations, then. Perhaps we've found the asset we've been looking for."

TWENTY-FOUR

"Her prognosis is good," Markowitz lied.

He was standing in the Oval Office, facing the vice president and his chief of staff.

"Good?" Gross remarked. "Brain surgery?"

"We all know how strong she is," Markowitz said, hoping there was confidence in his voice.

"Are the physicians planning a press conference?" Quarrels asked.

"Yes, they're going to hold one after the procedure is complete. In the meantime, we have to put out something regarding the surgery. I suggest we word it positively."

"I'm not sure that's the right tack," the vice president said. "We don't want to give the country false hope. Matt, why don't you get with Susan, draw something up." Susan Reyes was Quarrels's chief speechwriter.

"I'm on it," Gross said.

"Even in the best case," Quarrels thought aloud, "her recovery is going to take longer."

"I'm confident she'll bounce back," said Markowitz. He felt an urge to shift gears. "Is there anything new on the investigation?"

"The FBI sent an update an hour ago," Gross said. "Apparently you're not part of that loop any more. They identified the bodies from the Cessna that crashed in the swamp. The woman is a Slovakian national named Magda Bartos. Former Slovakian intelligence."

"SIS?" Markowitz asked.

"That's right. It seems she left the service under suspicious circumstances a few years back, and didn't leave a forwarding address. The pilot's name was Lazlo Kovac. His background is equally shady. We know he spent a year in a Budapest jail, then three in the Hungarian army. After that he apparently learned how to fly, and at some point, he hooked up with Magda. For the last couple of years they've been running a sketchy fly-for-hire operation, mostly in Africa and the Middle East. They spent a week last February tracking a rival for a Russian oligarch. In December they were helping a Nigerian crime syndicate steal oil from pipelines. Before that, the Syrian minister of agriculture had them doing god-knows-what in Darfur."

"The FBI thinks they were involved in this attack?"

"Almost certainly. The details are still being hashed out, but the premise is that these two served as spotters for whoever was in the trailer. It's been confirmed that this aircraft was circling nearby when Marine One took off, close enough to have eyes on Joint Base Andrews. With a decent pair of binoculars, they could have seen Air Force One land, watched the president transfer to Marine One, and then tracked her to the point where the drones launched."

Markowitz nodded. It made sense. "So the man at the construction site had help."

"Apparently. But there was something else notable about the two victims in the Cessna—they didn't die from the crash."

Markowitz took on a befuddled look. "What do you mean?"

"Our suspects, Magda and Lazlo, each died of a single gunshot wound to the head. The investigators have pretty much ruled out a murder-suicide scenario."

"Which means—"

"Which means someone else was on that plane."

"I saw the pictures of the crash," Markowitz said. "There's no way anyone could have survived."

"True. The operating theory is that a third individual, in all likelihood the man who launched the drones, was picked up from a small airfield in Maryland—the FAA has raw radar data showing the Cessna landing there. Then they took off again, headed toward North Carolina, and at some point our drone operator shot the others and parachuted to safety."

"*Parachuted?* Is that possible?"

"No less possible than a bunch of drones taking down Marine One. The FBI couldn't figure any other way to make it all fit together. They also found evidence to back the theory up—after scouring the area around the crash site, they found a discarded parachute along the access road to a nearby radio tower."

Quarrels interjected, "Which means we still have one person to track down. And whoever he is, he's a highly proficient killer."

"Are there any leads?"

"A few," Gross said. "A tiny amount of DNA from the trailer where the drones launched, a bit of grainy video from a camera near the river. The FBI is working to enhance the video. One way or another, we'll find him."

Gross addressed his phone momentarily, then said,

"A message from Charles Eraclides. He says the transport heading to Hong Kong is running on schedule."

"And we're sure Corsair is on board?" Quarrels asked, the double meaning obvious.

"David Slaton?" Markowitz wondered aloud before Gross could respond. He noted a subtle visual exchange between the vice president and his COS.

"That's right," Gross said.

For two days now, Markowitz had been adrift, outside the Oval Office and looking in. Yet he knew perfectly well who David Slaton was. And what he did. Markowitz was also still copied in on the president's daily briefing: one member of The Trident had been identified and traced to Hong Kong. The nexus between the two was simplicity itself, and it brought conflicting reactions. He knew a retaliatory strike against The Trident was necessary, and perfectly justifiable in terms of national defense. He also understood that Slaton was the perfect weapon.

On the other hand, he wished Elayne Cleveland could have given the order.

"What's the timeframe of this mission?" Markowitz asked.

After another swapped glance, the vice president simply said, "Soon. Very soon."

The hastily drafted press release was set to be issued later that evening. President Elayne Cleveland would undergo emergency surgery for a brain hemorrhage. Her condition was grave, and her doctors would provide an update after the procedure was complete. The wording of the statement was bland, succinct, and infused with all the cheer of an obituary.

Thirty minutes before it was released, at precisely 9:30 p.m. Eastern time, a text message streamed from the West Wing of the White House to a very secure phone in Hong Kong: No changes. Proceed as planned.

TWENTY-FIVE

"Be careful," Christine said. "Knives are sharp."

"Triangles or rectangles?" Davy asked, the butter knife poised.

"You're the cook."

Her son cut the PB&J, corner to corner, with surgical precision. His father's genes dominating again. He'd built the sandwich himself, an essential life skill in her motherly view, and a bit of relief from cooking on a night when she didn't feel up to it.

After finishing, he looked up for her approval.

"Nice job."

"What now?"

The mother smiled.

All meticulousness disappeared as he crammed the first gooey corner into his mouth.

Christine put a hand to her belly. As she found herself doing often.

She still hadn't felt any kicks, but those would start soon. Nausea, on the other hand, was her constant companion, and she decided a cup of tea would suffice for her own dinner. She took the butter knife to the sink, and as she washed it her eyes drifted to the window overlooking the backyard. The usual scene stared back: a happy patch of green grass littered with colorful toys, the stoic mountains in the distance.

More disconcerting was what lay between the two. Somewhere, lost in the treeline, a group of armed men stood waiting. For whom, or what, Christine never cared to contemplate.

She had met some of the new crew earlier, and to her untrained eye they seemed competent. Yet where the old guard had given a sense of security, this one imbued something else. Not protectors as much as jailors. Christine couldn't pinpoint the reason for the shift in her impression, but she guessed it had to do with David's tone when they'd talked. He had sounded cautious and doubtful. Christine never liked any of it, and more than once she'd told him she didn't want their home encircled by armed guards. She craved a normal life, one free from the specter of his past.

It had come up only last week, and David's response was typical: *If we stay in one place, we're predictable. I need help protecting you.* His usual logic was followed by his usual lame attempt at humor. *At we least won't get Jehovah's Witnesses coming to the door.*

She turned away from the window, set the knife in the drying rack. She was reaching for the kettle when her phone trilled. She picked it up and saw a text from David: FaceTime. Tomorrow morning. Back patio.

The phone began to tremble, nothing to do with its internal vibrator.

Christine tried to steady her hands, and deliberately typed out the prescribed reply: We'll be waiting.

She set down the phone.

Christine was not prone to extremes. She lived life in the calm and careful middle. Reason over emotion. Even so, with that one simple text exchange, the world as she knew it capsized. It was a prearranged signal, their private version of an air raid siren. Emergency orders sent and received.

The concerns she'd been brushing away all day, the nagging signals, hardened in an instant to stone cold fear. Unavoidably, her eyes returned to the kitchen window and back patio. The surrounding woods, moments ago peaceful, acquired a new menace. She had no idea what was behind David's message. Did it relate to the change in their protection detail? To the mission he'd been called on to perform? Or was it somehow tied to an attempted assassination of the president of the United States?

Whatever the source, the upshot was clear. Tectonic change for her and Davy. Possibly for the nation.

In the end, Christine knew there was no choice. She would do what she always did.

She would trust her husband.

Tomorrow morning, on the back patio, she and Davy would be ready. Ready for whatever came.

In the meantime, there was a great deal to be done.

Slaton stood on the tarmac at Anchorage International Airport, the distant panorama of Denali ominous beneath brooding clouds. He had moved under the wing of the B-747 as protection from the light rain, the world's biggest awning, while he texted Christine. After receiving an immediate reply, he powered down the phone.

Nearby the fueler was unhooking hoses from the underside of the airplane's wing, two trucks having transferred fifty thousand gallons of jet fuel. It was a big carbon footprint for the elimination of one man, and yet another reminder that no expense was being spared.

So far, every facet of the mission was running on schedule. Slaton had never bothered to count how many covert ops he'd been involved in, but between Mossad and the CIA, it had to be in the hundreds. In all that time, he'd never performed an ingress as rushed as this one. Still, the flight to Anchorage had gone off without a hitch. His documents and legend appeared faultless.

The timetable had them on the ground in Anchorage for an hour, and he'd been assured there would be no inspections of either the crew or the load. There were a few pallets tied down in the cargo bay—if the manifest could be believed, auto parts and precision tooling. He guessed it was all legitimate, because there *would* be inspections on the Hong Kong end. The aircraft's owners might make a few extra dollars on the shipment, or perhaps the CIA's expenses would be offset. Accounting aside, Sorensen appeared to have everything in hand.

Slaton began pacing beneath the wing, wanting to move before the next long flight. Somewhere over Canada he had tried to sleep in one of the crew bunks, yet couldn't quite drift off. An Ambien had done the trick, but also induced dreams that strayed into the surreal. Images of Davy on horseback, a lone man on a Chinese golf course. His wife battling the helm of a sailboat in a storm while he fumbled over an endless nautical chart. Slaton had never experienced such vivid dreams before, and he didn't know what they meant. His world had long been one of precision, a place where mission objectives overrode all else. Now, new priorities had taken hold.

He looked out at Denali, just visible beneath broken clouds on the horizon, only to have his thoughts stray again. Details of the topo chart for tomorrow's op flickered into in his head, a schizophrenic series of snapshots: contour lines, high points, a creek bed that seemed perfect for egress. He visualized the sight picture from the expected range: one man in gaudy clothes and spiked shoes, lined up squarely in the crosshairs.

All of that was imminent. Briefed and predictable.

So why, then, did everything feel wrong?

"Ready in ten."

Slaton turned to see Captain Lyle walking across the tarmac and waving a stack of papers. "The weather looks good," she said. "Food's been provisioned, and no issues with the airplane."

"I wish all airlines ran like this one."

"I wish I had your clout every time I flew."

Slaton saw her wrestling a question, probably something along the lines of, *So what are you going to do in Hong Kong that's so important?* The captain never put it to words.

The great jet lifted off twenty minutes later, Denali disappearing in a gathering mist. Slaton chatted with the crew for a time, and they answered all of his questions. When would they arrive? How long it would take to get airborne when they departed Hong Kong? Lyle pulled up an airfield diagram on an iPad and showed him where they would park. She also highlighted the nearby customs and immigration building.

Slaton eventually excused himself to the rest berths in back. There, for better or worse, he lay alone with his thoughts. The mélange of scenes that had filled his head earlier didn't interrupt. Instead, he ran through the mission, as far as he knew it, from beginning to end, making a laundry list of items to be accomplished when they arrived. Intel updates, communications, a thorough inspection of the weapon that was to be provided.

He went over the entire sequence once. Then he did it again. His third attempt fell short.

Somewhere over the Bering Sea, a deep sleep prevailed.

The surgery on Elayne Cleveland, a six-hour marathon, went flawlessly. But then, one would expect no less from the head of neurosurgery at Johns Hopkins, who had been flown in to perform the procedure.

As promised, the surgeon and Dr. Singh, both visibly weary, delivered tandem statements afterward. From a lectern at the head of the packed hospital conference room, they assured Americans the president was resting comfortably, and that the surgery had stabilized her condition. Both men expressed cautious optimism, as doctors were hardwired to do, and no questions were taken.

Their update spread across the nation at light speed, and the vigil on Room 407 at Walter Reed resumed unabated. Because news abhors a vacuum, reporters at the hospital's entrance descended on anyone wearing a white coat. Little else came and, in living rooms and break rooms across the country, Americans held their collective breath.

Nowhere was the wait more interminable than at 1600 Pennsylvania Avenue.

TWENTY-SIX

On final approach to Hong Kong's Chek Lap Kok Airport, Slaton was invited to ride the flight deck jump seat behind Captain Lyle. It was the third best seat in the house, giving a panoramic view of the city during the approach to landing. It was a clear and cloudless night, the sun having set hours ago, and the darkness accentuated the city's vibrant neon glow. The twin strips of landing lights bordering the runway seemed inconsequential as the big jet lined up for touchdown.

To support his legend, Slaton had been given a uniform to wear: polyester pants and a pilot's shirt with epaulets, four stripes on each shoulder. All of it fit as if tailored, and was by now badly wrinkled—he'd put it on hours ago, determined to look like a pilot who'd just flown an eleven-hour trans-Pacific leg. He was posing as a "cruise captain," a relief pilot who would normally rotate with the others on a long flight. In reality, Lyle and Raymond had taken short breaks during cruise, leaving one pilot up front. This wasn't to regulation, but over the vast North Pacific the workload was minimal. He himself had managed five hours' sleep, which would hopefully counter the circadian disruption of eleven time zones.

The runway rushed up to meet them, and the massive

widebody touched down with surprising smoothness. Slaton checked his watch and saw that they were three minutes early—this based on a schedule set thirty hours ago halfway around the world. The timetable had seemed impossibly compressed, but so far was dead on. Yao Jing's tee time was in slightly over nine hours.

As they taxied to the air cargo ramp, riding high in the cockpit, Slaton felt as though he was on the third floor of a moving building. The anonymous off-white jet turned into a vacant parking spot, slotting between like-sized aircraft with more recognizable logos: FedEx and Cathay Pacific Cargo.

As a ground crewman was wheeling airstairs to the entry door, a message chimed to the airplane's datalink. Lyle gave Slaton the highlights. "There's a crew van on the way. It'll take you to immigration, and on the other side a driver will make contact." She told him where to find the crew transportation queue, and read out the license plate number of his ride. "According to the message, the driver will have comm set up and all the equipment you asked for." She paused there, giving Slaton a chance to explain what that equipment might be. When he didn't, she condensed the rest. "Looks like we're going to be your ride out, but that could change depending on the timing."

"Okay, all good. If I don't see you again, thanks for the help."

Both pilots smiled, and Raymond said, "Buh-bye. And thanks for flying the new Air America."

Christine and Davy were on the patio early, ostensibly for an improvised breakfast on the stone bench David had built. What sat beside them was more telling: two backpacks full of clothes, a blanket, documents supporting false identities, one blue burner phone, and a thick wad of cash.

This wouldn't be the first time Christine had taken her son into hiding, which was a sad commentary on the wobbly pattern of their lives. On the most recent occasion, a few years earlier, she and Davy had been forced to go on the run, abandoning their sailboat at a marina in Gibraltar. That escape had ended disastrously, and only a last-ditch effort by David had saved their lives. She hoped today's getaway, however it played out, was only a matter of her husband being proactive.

She had tried to distract Davy with a donut—a rare weak moment for Christine, both as a mother and a physician—but it wasn't really working. He was becoming more curious, more worldly. He was also starting to read her moods, and probably her evasions. When he had asked about the backpacks, she told him they were going on an adventure. That got a smile, and she'd done her best to return it. Even so, she could sense his wheels turning.

She'd been freighted all night by an inner heaviness, apprehension taking hold. The change of the security team, David's coded message. Whatever was happening, she guessed it was some downstream consequence of the assassination attempt on the president. And that was about as serious as things got.

They had been on the patio for nearly an hour, waiting and watching. Time and again, Christine scanned the treeline as if expecting David to appear, beckoning them to come running. It was pure fantasy, of course, but it helped pass the time—she really had no idea what to expect. All she could do was carry through on David's instructions. Sit outside, bags packed, and wait for . . . *what?*

Christine shot a glance at the utility shed in the distance. Inside was another part of their contingency plan, fueled and ready to go. The specific wording of David's message, one of three prearranged "bailout" codes, had been the variant that included the ATV. She knew other married couples had code words, but those usually involved escaping parties or picking up the tab in a restaurant. *At least things are never boring around here.*

Christine checked her phone as it clicked past eight o'clock. She watched and listened.

8:02. Still nothing.

And then . . . something.

It began as a barely audible buzz, like a great insect in the distance. Soon the sound morphed into something recognizable: an aircraft. Christine canted her gaze up into the robin's-egg-blue sky but saw nothing. Whatever it was, it had to be small.

After a brief decision tree, she discounted the idea that it might be coming to her and Davy's rescue. The nearest airport, a tiny dirt strip she'd once seen from a rural road, was fifteen miles away. A flash of motion caught her eye above the trees to the north, and sure enough, an airplane materialized.

It wasn't what she expected. She saw a small single-engine plane, which was in line with the engine noise. Yet in place of wheels the aircraft had floats. She was looking at a small seaplane, white fuselage with a blue stripe.

"Look, Mom," Davy said, standing and pointing into the sky. "An airplane."

She put an arm around him. "Yes, I see."

The aircraft turned toward the house and began to descend. It wasn't quite skimming the trees, but seemed unusually low, perhaps five hundred feet up.

The seaplane kept a steady course toward the house, and then, just before it was overhead, Christine saw something fall from the side window. She and Davy watched a small object, trailing a bright yellow streamer, drop like a stone. It landed dead center in the backyard, between the swing set and the fire pit. A tiny puff of dust bloomed on impact. The airplane disappeared behind the trees to the south, and its engine noise faded.

She and Davy didn't move for a time. They simply looked at the lump in the middle of the yard, stunned and curious. The cloud of white around the object dissipated. The yellow streamer fluttered in the soft breeze.

"What is it?" he asked.

"I don't know. Let's go see."

She held her son's hand and they approached the object carefully. It turned out to be a small canvas bag, the size of a one-gallon Ziploc. Attached was a yard-long ribbon that resembled the tail of a kite. The bag had burst open on impact and white powder of some kind had burst out. Had Christine been of a more conspiratorial mindset she might have imagined the powder to be something harmful. She instead bent down, touched it, and was convinced it was baking flour.

"I see a letter," Davy said.

She looked where he was pointing and saw it for the first time—attached to the end of the streamer, a thin manila envelope. She pulled it free of a spring clip, opened it, and inside found a handwritten message scrawled on hotel stationery.

Christine read it once quickly, then again more carefully. All at once, everything made sense.

"Is it time for the adventure now, Mom?"

"Yeah, baby . . . and you're going to like this one."

TWENTY-SEVEN

Sorensen was at headquarters when she got a message from Eraclides to meet immediately in his seventh-floor office. When she arrived he wasn't there, but she was sent into his suite by the receptionist, who explained that the director would be along shortly.

While she waited, Sorensen surveyed the office Thomas Coltrane had vacated only days earlier. She might have expected empty walls with a few exposed nails, faded rectangles of paint to denote where wall hangings had been. What she saw was a statement: Eraclides's own framed pictures and mementos were already in place, and, based on both appearance and scent, the walls had been freshly painted, a tasteful gray hue.

"Looks like he's got his priorities straight," she muttered.

"What?" Eraclides said, entering in a rush from the anteroom.

"Oh . . . I was just saying, I hope I'm not late."

The director veered behind his desk, distracted by a stack of file folders. He opened one as Margaret Goode trailed inside, carrying the laptop that seemed surgically attached to her hand. She set it up on a writing table that buttressed the far wall.

"We've gotten fresh intel on the second member of The Trident," Eraclides said.

"Same source?" Sorensen wondered. "The repatriated academic?"

"Same source," the director said distractedly, flicking through the file. He then looked up suddenly. "Why do you ask? Has anything about the first target not held up?"

"No, so far everything is running straight and true. Yao is still set for his tee time tomorrow morning, and Slaton just arrived. Even the weather report is good."

He seemed to be trying to read her. "Any doubts at all?"

"Doubts are my job. But no, everything seems solid. That said, I'll be happier after the mission goes off without a hitch."

"Agreed. And if it does, we can't waste any time—we go straight after the second target." He looked at Goode, nodded once, and she launched into a briefing on another member of The Trident.

From the middle of her backyard, Christine scanned the surrounding forest. There was no one in sight, but the new protection detail was out there somewhere. Their job was to keep strangers out, not hold the protectees in. At least, that was how it was supposed to work. If she kept to the plan, executed it quickly enough, she decided the security team wouldn't enter the equation either way.

She hurried back to the bench and grabbed their backpacks, slinging one over each shoulder, and then led Davy toward the shed. Christine heaved the big door open, and seconds later Davy and the backpacks were loaded onto the ATV. They donned helmets and she fired up the engine, the bike seeming louder than ever before. There was no way to hide their departure, but she was reasonably sure that the western trail, which spurred from the backyard into the woods, would not be closely watched. It was the least approachable side of the property, with steep terrain and no paved roads for miles.

She gave the throttle a twist and the bike jumped ahead. She easily found the trail, and took the first turn without slowing. Davy's hands gripped her belt loops and he giggled with every bump.

She turned right onto the old logging road, an abandoned path that terminated near Moose Lake. The lake was remote, with no public access, but it was one of the largest in the county. It probably had an official name, but there wasn't any listed on the topo map they used for hiking, so they had anointed it themselves after seeing a big bull moose along the shoreline while camping there last year. The lake was six miles from the house, but the logging road was in decent shape after the winter thaw, allowing Christine to keep her speed up.

Twenty minutes later, columns of deep blue began flickering through the stands of aspen, and soon the lake spread out before them. Christine didn't see the seaplane at first, and her spirits sank. Had she gotten something wrong? Had there been a specific time in the message? Was she at the wrong end of the lake? Then she spotted it, nestled tight to the eastern shore. She motored closer, not taking her eyes off the aircraft for a second. As she pulled the ATV to a stop, a mountain of a man emerged from the cockpit, squeezing out like an oversized mollusk from a shell.

It could only be Jammer Davis. Christine had never met the man, but she knew him by reputation: he was

Anna Sorensen's significant other, and had accompanied David on his previous mission. He moved forward on the port pontoon, one hand walking along a tree limb that reached out across the water.

Christine killed the engine and the mountain's silence took hold.

She dismounted, removed their helmets, and hauled Davy down. Grabbing their backpacks, they shuffled downhill toward the plane.

"I heard you need a ride," Davis called across the divide.

"Apparently. Although I'm not sure why." Christine drew to a stop at the shoreline, a few feet of water separating them.

"I don't know what's behind it either," he said. "But I got a call from Anna late yesterday, so here I am."

"Well, it's good to finally meet you. David has spoken highly of you."

"I could say the same about you two."

Christine felt her son hugging one leg. "This is Mr. Davis, honey."

The pilot kneeled down to Davy's level. "You can call me Jammer, buddy. Everybody else does."

"Okay, Yammer."

Christine smiled. "We're working on our J's—they digress a bit when he's excited."

"Hey, I'm excited too! Ever been on a seaplane?"

Davy shook his head.

"Well, today's your lucky day. This is a de Havilland Beaver, an oldie but a goodie. Two floats, one engine, and a whole lot of noise." Davis looked at the two backpacks. "Is that all you're bringing?"

"It is. If this goes on for any length of time, we might need a trip to the mall."

"Well . . . that's the thing. Where we're going, the

nearest mall is a ninety-mile walk, and there aren't any sidewalks. Did you at least bring jackets?"

"We did."

"You'll get by then." Davis stood to full height and studied the forest behind them. "I was told you might have company?"

"Possible . . . but I think we got a good head start."

"In that case, how about we load up and get out of here?"

"Sounds like a plan."

Jammer snapped to attention and gave his best version of a bosun's whistle. "All aboard that's coming aboard!"

Davy jumped across the divide like a rabbit shot from a cannon. Jammer kept him from falling into the lake, then guided him along the float toward the door. Christine handed the backpacks across and pocketed the key to the ATV. She stepped across cautiously, Davis holding her hand like he was helping a countess over a puddle.

Ten minutes later they were skimming over the mirror-flat lake, the roar of the engine drowning out every other sound. Christine was in back of the four-seater, Davy up front in the copilot's seat. The look on his face was one of unreserved wonderment as the little plane broke its bond with the water and lifted gently into the sky.

Six miles away, the new security team was frantically searching the house. They'd been alerted by the sound of an engine, undoubtedly the ATV they'd been briefed on, which was now missing from the shed. Minutes before that, they had seen a suspicious airplane fly directly over the house.

The man who'd been tasked to search the basement appeared from the stairwell. He looked at his commander and shook his head. "They're definitely not here, boss."

The team of contractors were all ex-military. The man in charge, a retired Army major, cursed a blue streak.

"Maybe they just went for a ride."

Another man joined from the back door. He was carrying what looked like a torn sack of flour with a long ribbon. Though they had no way of knowing it, the message that had been attached was gone. "I found this in the yard," he said.

The major studied it, then looked at his men.

"Maybe they'll come back tomorrow," one of them said hopefully.

"Yeah. And the chances of that are about the same as us having a job tomorrow."

"This isn't our fault," another complained. "We were tasked with keeping people out, not keeping them in."

The major didn't respond. The full orders he'd received, which he hadn't shared with the rest of the team, had made clear that they were responsible on both counts. And now? A mere twelve hours after taking over, they'd lost their protectees.

He pulled out his phone for what was going to be a very unpleasant call.

Margaret Goode's briefing ran the best part of an hour. They had made good headway on identifying a second member of the Trident, and Eraclides promised the agency would spare no resources in validating the information.

Sorensen and Goode left the director's office together, and soon they were back on the first floor. There was no one within earshot as they traversed the checkerboard-tiled atrium, but Sorensen found herself edging closer all the same.

"Maggie, there are a lot of moving parts to this mission, which means there are a lot of ways it could derail. I want to move someone forward, in theater, but that presents some problems. To begin, I want to keep this at the highest level, which means bringing in a SOG operator isn't an option. I need someone who's already briefed in, and preferably someone David knows. Most important of all, I need somebody I trust. I can only think of one person who fills all those squares."

Goode looked at her questioningly, not yet understanding.

When Sorensen explained what she wanted, Goode's librarian-like demeanor collapsed.

"But . . . I have no operational training."

"All the better." The spymaster smiled.

The analyst didn't smile back.

Then a tentative nod. "How will I get there?"

"Just let me handle that."

TWENTY-EIGHT

The crew van was waiting as Slaton and Captain Lyle came down the boarding stairs. Slaton was hauling a big roller bag that contained all of his clothes, as well as a few of First Officer Raymond's. It had been Lyle's idea. She'd explained that the bag Slaton was carrying was far smaller than what any pilot would travel with internationally. It was a fair point, and Raymond had offered to switch with Slaton, leaving a few of his things inside to make it appear full should any immigration officer actually perform an inspection. It made Slaton think the pilots had done this kind of thing before, and again he was silently thankful for Sorensen's networks.

"We're going to split with you here," Lyle said. "We've got a few postflight duties, and our instructions were to cut you loose."

"Okay, thanks for the help. Maybe I'll see you on the way out."

"Always here to help," she said.

He walked to the van and took a seat in back with two other crews. Slaton glanced at their ID lanyards and saw that one worked for Asiana, the other KLM. South Koreans and Dutch. He nodded to everyone cordially, but had no interest in striking up a conversation. Anything beyond the basics, and he could quickly be caught out as not being a legitimate crew-member. As it turned out, it wasn't a problem. Every-one looked spent, dead tired from what were probably very long flights.

As the van pulled away, the massive jet that had brought him here faded into the darkness.

Slaton followed the other crews into the immigra-tion building, a charmless warren of concrete walls and linoleum flooring. There were a dozen uniformed agents inside, all of whom looked as weary as the crewmembers they were scrutinizing. Air freight was a round-the-clock operation, and he guessed this group of inspectors was nearing the end of its shift. Had Slaton been planning the op, he would have cho-sen precisely this hour to arrive.

He kept to the back of the line and watched the routine closely as the other crews queued up to the passport desk. The art of forged identities had been transitioning in recent years. In an era of facial recog-nition and digital accuracy, disguises were a quaint memory, carbon-dated relics of another era. The goal today was not to defeat a sharp-eyed inspector trying to match a face to a passport photo, but to control the primary database and implant a perfectly convincing image.

When it was his turn, Slaton handed over his pass-port and a declaration form Raymond had helped him complete. He took a few questions, in broken English, that he'd been told to expect. The agent scanned his passport, saw the image the CIA had generated, and no red flags appeared.

It all took no more than a minute.

Formalities complete, Slaton stepped outside into a

deepening night. The access road outside the cargo terminal was quiet; there was only one other aircrew waiting along the curb. In the distance, a disinterested policeman chatted with a female parking attendant.

Slaton quickly spotted the license plate he'd memorized: a hundred feet away, an idling minivan. In the window of the van he noticed a sign that said, *Lucky Transportation, Aircrew Shuttle.* The rear hatch popped open as he approached, which he took as a cue to meet the driver at the rear bumper. It turned out to be an Asian man, early thirties, wearing a standard chauffeur's livery: black coat and cap, slightly scuffed oxfords. His hair was neatly trimmed and he wore a pair of glasses with clear round lenses.

The driver took his bag without greeting and loaded it into the cargo well next to another suitcase, slightly larger, that had a luggage tag with his fictitious name already filled in.

They really do think of everything, Slaton thought.

Without comment, the driver closed the tailgate, ushered Slaton toward the sliding side door, and said in a hushed voice, "It will look better if you ride in back." His English came with a mild British lilt, as was typical in the territories formerly administered by The Crown. Slaton decided he could only be a NOC—not a registered consulate employee, but a deep cover asset. One more by-product of Sorensen's labyrinthine connections.

Slaton took a seat in the middle of three rows.

"Welcome to Hong Kong," said the driver after sliding behind the wheel.

"Glad to be here . . . I think."

"My name is Thomas," the man said, no indication as to whether this was his first or last name. Slaton decided it didn't matter because neither would be true. "Miss Sorensen sends her regards."

"She always does," he replied, meeting Thomas's eyes in the rearview mirror.

"I've booked a room for you at the Altira in Macau. It's the usual crew hotel for the airline you flew in on. The drive should take roughly thirty minutes."

Slaton had discussed with Sorensen the option of using a safe house instead of a hotel. Each carried risks and rewards, but in the end, because his stay would be brief, and hoping to keep his cover intact as a cargo pilot on a short layover, they had settled on a hotel.

"You should check in as soon as we arrive," Thomas continued. "While we're driving please transfer anything you need out of your luggage to the roller bag in back—a pilot wouldn't carry two bags, and everything you requested is in the one I've provided. If there is anything missing, you must tell me soon—time is running short."

Slaton set to work. He maneuvered into the back-row seat, half of which had been folded forward, to access the new bag. He unzipped the cover, took a careful inventory, and saw everything from the list he'd given Sorensen. He added his own clothing and shaving gear, then zipped both bags closed.

"It looks like everything is here."

"I will be your only local contact. Miss Sorensen insisted we keep your mission as tightly held as possible."

"What's the transportation plan in the morning?"

"I'll pick you up at the hotel, outside the main entrance. Be in uniform and have your bag packed. The plan is to head straight to the airport once your mission is complete."

"Did you get the tactical map I drew up?"

"Yes. I checked the insertion point, and it looks ideal. The access road you selected will also work. But I would recommend a different egress route—construction south of the bridge has been backing up traffic near the university. There's a map in the bag on which I've highlighted an alternate route."

Slaton appreciated Thomas's acumen. All the same, he would verify the route later. "I'll look it over. What about the timing?"

"The driving time from the lobby to your drop-off point is fourteen minutes—I've run the route four times. Traffic won't be an issue at that time of day. The exact schedule, of course, is up to you."

Slaton had been building his timetable all the way across the Pacific. "Be on the curb at 6:15."

"6:15 it is."

Thomas covered a few more points, then went silent—perhaps because he was done, or more likely to give Slaton time to process it all.

Slaton's attention went outside as they began traversing the Hong Kong–Zhuhai–Macau connector, thirty miles of bridges and tunnels that both soared above and sank beneath the Pearl River estuary. The first bridge graded down toward a man-made island, and then the road dropped into a long tunnel. When they again emerged into the night, minutes later, Macau lay before them.

The city glowed against the darkness, brassy and bold, its reflection shimmering off the calm water. A twelve-square-mile postage stamp of urban verticality, Macau was the most densely populated place on earth. Like Hong Kong, the city was designated by China as a "special administrative region." Also like Hong Kong, it was inexorably being consumed by its giant neighbor. Freedom and rule of law, hallmarks established under Portuguese rule, were systematically being eroded, capitalist breakwaters failing against the unyielding tide of authoritarianism.

Slaton had been here once before, years ago to help Mossad track down a terrorist financier. That mission, like so many others, had turned into a tail-chase, two weeks lost pursuing ghosts across the city. From a distance he saw the familiar skyline, vibrant and alive with light. Up close, however, the changes wrought by China were metastasizing. He saw countless billboards with nationalist slogans, and patriotic murals impressing the glorious history of the revolution. The president's image was everywhere, on shop windows, bus benches, and municipal buildings. Every delivery truck seemed to display his image in the windshield, like a de facto registration certificate.

The real changes, of course, were far more insidious. Going to bed wondering whether your neighbor would report you for having dinner with foreigners. Knowing that your phone was being monitored. Watching newscasts that gave only the Party line. Such was life under autocracy, blind trust and fear replacing liberty and enterprise.

"You will need this," Thomas said, handing over the ersatz iPhone Sorensen had promised. Trying to bring it through customs, they'd agreed, could have caused complications. The handset looked like a billion others, but most certainly was different. Langley had issued Slaton a similar model on his previous mission, although he was sure this one had the latest upgrades, courtesy of the agency's Directorate of Science and Technology.

"You'll find it preloaded with contact information," Thomas added. "Most of the numbers are from the

U.S. and verifiable, but there are only two you will need. You can reach me at Lucky Transportation, and Miss Sorensen is listed under A-1 Cleaners."

Slaton smiled and pocketed the phone.

Soon the Altira came into view, forty-odd stories of glass and blinking neon. Like every other hotel in Macau, the world's highest-grossing gambling mecca, it included a casino. *Good thing I took Lucky Transportation,* he mused.

Thomas wheeled the van through a grand portico and came to a stop along a vacant segment of curb. Slaton noticed that he ended the maneuver by canting the wheels toward the open road. He also left the engine running, and checked both sideview mirrors before getting out. Every bit of it was instinctive, baked in by some distant training program. Slaton decided not to dwell on where that might have been, simply taking the win that he had competent support.

Moments later, Thomas was setting the new and heavier roller bag on the sidewalk. Slaton tipped him twenty bucks.

"Very kind of you, sir," Thomas said with a grateful smile and a tip of his chauffeur's cap. "Enjoy your stay. I will see you in the morning."

"See you then."

TWENTY-NINE

When Sorensen was summoned to the director's office a second time it came out of the blue. She'd barely passed through the door when Eraclides launched on her.

"Do you know what I just heard from our protection team in Idaho? Slaton's wife and son have given them the slip."

"The slip?" she repeated, a commendable look of surprise on her face.

"The two of them climbed onto an ATV, and without telling anyone they rode to a nearby lake and disappeared. A seaplane was seen in the area, so it stands to reason they were flown out. Does this not sound like something Corsair would put together?"

"I can't imagine anyone else."

"You know him better than anyone. Where the hell would they go?"

"I have no idea," Sorensen said, which was technically true.

Eraclides sat fuming.

"Why does it matter where they went?" she asked.

"For Christ's sake, he set up an escape for them!"

"So what? If it gives him peace of mind on this mission, I don't see any problem with it."

"The problem is that if we're not watching them,

we can't guarantee their safety. It means we lose control of . . ."

And there his words cut off, snagged on the truth. *We lose control . . .*

Sorensen waited.

"We need to find them," Eraclides said.

"How?"

While the director considered it, Sorensen weighed how to proceed. Tracking down missing persons, particularly on U.S. soil, was completely outside SAC/SOG's purview—it was like asking a tank commander to drive an ocean liner. But the alternative was to get the FBI involved. Sorensen threw caution to the wind.

"Let me work on it," she suggested.

The director's eyes narrowed. "SAC/SOG?"

"Well . . . it's not my department's usual mission, but in this situation, it provides some advantages."

"Such as?"

"If you use any other agency, questions are going to get asked. Who is Slaton? Why is the CIA providing protection for his family? For everyone's sake, including David's, I think it's best to keep this in-house."

Eraclides eyed her. Interagency politics, standard on the operational side of the CIA, wasn't something he was used to navigating.

He nodded slowly.

Sorensen glossed over a few ideas on how to proceed, and when she left his office ten minutes later she chalked the meeting up as a victory. Thankfully, it was one crisis she had seen coming.

By the time she reached the elevator, however, doubts began creeping in. It struck her that Eraclides had given in quite easily.

Did he have that much confidence in her?

Was he distracted by recent events?

Or am I missing something?

By the time a car arrived, she was sure of only one thing. The dysfunction around her, and the suspicion it bred, was only going to get worse.

Slaton was in his room soon after arriving at the hotel. Following a check of the room, he laid the suitcase on a couch, removed the rifle, and gave it a thorough inspection.

Sorensen had provided a shortlist of weapons to choose from—local availability was extremely limited, and bringing a rifle in through customs was a nonstarter. He'd been happy to find a Desert Tech SRS-A2 on the list. It was a compact bullpup design, and came with a Vortex Razor scope and bipod. The SRS was smaller than most sniper rifles, a bonus when it came to concealment and maneuverability, and it easily had enough range to execute the shot he was contemplating. There were also two five-round box magazines and enough .338 Lapua Magnum rounds to fill them. Slaton made a few adjustments until he was satisfied with the rifle's feel and balance. He would normally have wanted to zero the weapon on a range, but the rushed nature of the mission precluded it. If everything went to script, it wouldn't matter—he would be a mere two hundred yards from his target. A simple shot.

And if I had a dollar for every time I'd thought that, he mused.

After spending twenty minutes going over the weapon, Slaton went through the rest of what Thomas had provided: a Leupold spotting scope, Merrell trail shoes, and a GPS navigation device. He repacked it all carefully. The short barrel fit perfectly inside the suitcase, and he wedged the rest in the gaps, then used one set of tactical clothing to keep everything in place. He took off his pilot uniform, hung it neatly in the closet, and then ironed a fresh uniform shirt for the morning. He would wear the uniform to the lobby, and then switch out to tactical clothing once he was in the van.

It was nearly midnight when he finished.

With everything in place, the surreal nature of the mission dominated his thoughts. The timetable had seemed impossibly tight, yet here he was, a few miles removed from his objective with everything in place. In spite of having caught some sleep on the plane, he decided the best use of the next few hours would be rest.

He grabbed a bottle of hotel water from the dresser, broke the cap, and strolled to the eighth-floor window. Slaton pulled open the curtains and was awed. The Macau skyline was frenetic, bright electric against a dark sky. Tourists circled the casino across the street like Muslims orbiting the Kaaba in Mecca. This city, he thought, seemed the opposite of timeless, a place built for the moment. There was a harshness to it, a visual staccato where nothing blended. The din below was surely cacophonous, yet it was cut to nothing by double-pane windows built for a hurricane.

He felt a twinge of unease. A stunning view from a superior room in a high-end resort—it was hardly what he was accustomed to. Mossad took pride in being a bare-bones operation. Even his previous work with the CIA had involved basic accommodations. This setting felt discordant, less a clandestine operation than a James Bond trailer.

And Slaton didn't like it one damned bit.

Of course, it wasn't merely the pretentiousness.

Looking down to the street Slaton saw a sheer drop of a hundred feet. No way out there. There were stairwells outside his room, at either end of the hall; to most guests they were fire escapes, but to Slaton they were funnels. His routes for egress were severely limited. Easily covered. He'd spotted a plethora of cameras on the way up, the usual casino watchfulness, but he'd had no time to truly research the hotel's security. Across the street was another hotel, a hundred windows staring back, any of which could be used to watch his room. On the busy streets outside, surveillance was everywhere. Half the cameras on earth were in China, most keeping an eye on its own citizens. Transportation hubs, grocery stores, gathering halls. Software that identified faces, voices, and irises. One could try to minimize exposure, but there was no true escape.

Because this mission was rushed, basic precautions were lacking. He and Sorensen had spent the bulk of their time plotting tomorrow's strike. It wasn't an unprecedented situation; operations often came with time constraints, a need to act on perishable intelligence. All the same, Slaton felt unusually vulnerable. He was playing all offense, ignoring caution in the name of speed.

He drew the curtains shut, cutting the vivid scene. It seemed a hopeless and flimsy gesture. The good news was that by this time tomorrow, if all went as planned, Yao Jing would be dead and Slaton would be out of the country. *If all went as planned.*

He went to the nightstand next to the bed and unplugged the house phone, wondering why hotels even bothered with them anymore. He laid down and tied to get comfortable. The clock in his head was uncannily reliable, and would probably wake him in time.

Probably, however, didn't cut it tonight. Not wanting to be mugged by the fog of ten time zones, he set the alarm on his phone as a backup.

He stared at the phone for a time, weighing the prospect of two calls: one he didn't want to make, and another he very much did. Slaton deferred both for the time being. He closed his eyes and tried for sleep.

THIRTY

Slaton didn't need the alarm after all.

His eyes cracked open and were immediately drawn to the red LEDs of the bedside clock: 5:25. The first thing he did was check his phone. He saw one message from Sorensen, received thirty minutes earlier: No changes. Expect updates for follow-on assignment after completion.

On the former he was encouraged; no changes meant fewer complications. The "follow-on assignment" he would worry about later.

He showered and dressed in the pilot's uniform, adding a base layer beneath that would work with his tactical clothing. He reached the lobby twenty minutes early, purchased a bagel and a cup of coffee at the hotel coffee shop.

Thomas was ten seconds early—the kind of precision Slaton appreciated. Same van, same chauffeur's uniform, same loading drill at the tailgate. They were soon running smoothly through early morning traffic.

"No changes," Slaton said.

"I was told the same. The road we are going to access is rarely used. It's a gravel path that was built during construction. There are no gates or barriers, and the groundkeepers still use it occasionally for course maintenance. For that reason, I plan to circle the area after dropping you off. I designed a route that will never put me more than five minutes from the pickup point."

"Perfect," Slaton said. "I should be back at the rendezvous point between 8:30 and 8:50. That assumes they start on schedule, and the exact timing will depend on how fast they're playing."

"If you give me ten minutes notice it will simplify things."

"All right. I'll send a text ten minutes prior to pickup. As a backup, if you don't hear anything by 8:40, plan to be at the exfil point at 8:50."

Thomas said that he would. Slaton sent him an innocuous text to verify comm integrity, and Thomas did the same in reverse.

"Okay," Slaton said, "time to gear up." He shrugged off his pilot's coat and began loosening his tie.

"They flew away in a seaplane," Sorensen said.

"A seaplane," Matt Gross repeated.

Sorensen held steady, her hands clasped coolly on the conference table. They were sitting in a minor White House briefing room she had never seen before. Gross had been waiting for her, expecting an update on the situation. The vice president was not in attendance, but Sorensen knew he would be filled in.

She had spent the first few minutes going over Slaton's progress in Macau. Satisfied everything was going to plan, Gross diverted to the subject of how Slaton's family had gone missing. CIA director Eraclides, apparently, had forwarded that gem.

"To begin with," Gross said skeptically, "what's a seaplane doing in Idaho?"

"There are a lot of lakes in those parts. Including one near Slaton's home."

Gross looked unconvinced.

Sorensen realized a few more facts would be required. "I spoke at length with the leader of the protection team. He said they heard an ATV crank up, so they went to investigate and found the house empty. They'd seen a seaplane fly past minutes earlier, so they put two and two together. Your team eventually found the ATV abandoned near a lake." The word *your* was perfectly deliberate, and nothing short of an accusation. She didn't know precisely how the changing of the guard had come to pass, but she knew Gross and Eraclides had conspired to make it happen. She hoped to imply that it was *their* move that had precipitated Christine and Davy's disappearance. Conveniently omitted was the fact that Sorensen's own fiancé was the getaway driver.

"Will we be able to track down this airplane?" Gross asked.

"I'm working on that, but it won't be easy. No one saw the aircraft registration number, and since it was flying through mountainous terrain at low altitude, there won't be any consistent radar return."

"Consistent?"

"I'm told there were a few hits on a slow-moving target east of Coeur d'Alene—that's north of the lake—but we're not even sure it was the aircraft in question."

"Could they have gone into Canada?" Gross wondered aloud.

"No telling."

"Is it possible they've been abducted?"

"I doubt that. They obviously drove to the lake of their own volition. I suppose it bears mentioning that

Corsair wasn't happy with the new security situation."

Gross nodded in agreement. "That's it then," he said harshly. "This is all Slaton's doing."

"Most likely. But if it was, it's nothing sinister. He's only looking out for his family."

"The man is a loose cannon," Gross fumed.

"I would agree. But right now he's a cannon we're very much counting on. Slaton has pulled America's ass out of the fire more than once." She glanced obviously at a clock on the wall. "And in less than an hour, he's going to do it again."

The access road was in good shape, a raised gravel roadbed that the van had no trouble negotiating. Slaton and Thomas had already agreed that if they encountered anyone on the property, they would claim Slaton was an environmental consultant performing a survey for Beijing. As covers went, it was soft, but the very mention of the Chinese capital was sure to buy time.

The drop-off point was half a mile from the main road. As the path curved through trees and high brush, the surrounding city disappeared. Slaton concentrated on the terrain. He'd seen countless overheads of the area, but there were always nuances from ground level. They had arrived early enough that he could modify the plan if necessary—possibly alter his ingress route, and take his time scoping out a shooting position.

The road degraded near the end, the van's chassis groaning over ruts, stones skittering in the wheel wells. Thomas pulled to a stop on a broad parking apron where heavy equipment had probably been staged during the golf course's construction. On the edges were old railroad ties and unused sections of concrete pipe, grass growing high between them.

Slaton took a final look around, saw no people or vehicles. He gathered his weapon and equipment, and said, "Okay, as briefed."

"Happy hunting," Thomas said.

Slaton momentarily locked eyes with his driver. Then he slid outside and disappeared.

THIRTY-ONE

If any sport had been invented by a sniper, surely it was golf.

Like no other pastime, it was a shooter's dream. Your target was guaranteed to appear in the center of a large, elevated open space, no obstructions whatsoever save for a few gauchely dressed playing partners. The target's approach to the kill zone was also over open ground, offering a predictable arrival as he strove to get as close as possible to a central point. Then, after loitering for a few minutes at one or two spots, he would eventually bend down to pluck his ball from a cup. Conveniently, that focal point was marked by a flagstick—in today's case, a triangular pennant emblazoned with the logo of the Macau Golf and Country Club. Even the flag had utility. Presently hanging limp on its pole, it showed the wind to be dead calm.

For a professional like Slaton, golf was tailor made for success.

As he sought out a shooting position, the bizarre ease of the mission persisted. He found a perfect hide in the forest, a slight rise that gave concealment from virtually every angle, and with a commanding view of the entire fifth-hole green. He settled onto the damp forest floor and grounded his rifle on a downed tree trunk—solid hardwood, not yet rotted, embedded firmly in the soil. With a clean line of sight to the target area, through thirty yards of vegetation, Slaton was as happy with the setup as he could be.

Which meant he was only moderately worried.

A great deal, he knew, could still go wrong.

One major variable remained: the speed at which play was progressing on the club's front nine. Yao's group had a tee time of 7:34, and Slaton had already received two messages from Sorensen, who was getting updates via a pair of surreptitiously placed cameras. Yao had been identified, and his group had started on time.

It was now 8:28.

Slaton stepped his weapon's optic over a group of four Asian men who were chipping onto the green—poorly in two cases. This was not Yao's foursome, but they were perfect stand-ins for practice. Slaton settled his crosshairs on an unsuspecting man in a wide straw hat who was lining up a putt. This would be the ideal moment, he decided. His target would stand perfectly still for roughly ten seconds. A few practice swings over the ball, hit the putt, then wait to see if the ball fell in the cup.

It truly was a shooter's fantasy.

As he watched the straw-hatted man, a second golfer began strolling the green. He came to a stop leaning on his putter, and ended up blocking Slaton's line of sight perfectly.

Good to know.

At 8:33 the group departed in their carts and the next group came into view. Slaton shifted to the Leupold spotting scope and focused on the new pair of carts, each of which carried two men. All were dressed in long pants and color-splashed shirts, with a variety of hats and sunglasses mixed in.

190 | WARD LARSEN

Slaton had seen numerous pictures of Yao Jing, and also one video—as the former CEO of China Precision Electronics, there were plenty of images online. The man Slaton had been tasked to kill was slightly on the tall side and carried thirty extra pounds. His most distinctive features, derived from the video, were a long-boned frame and a noticeably stiff, almost limping gait.

The carts came to a stop a hundred yards from the green, and of the four men who emerged, two fit the general profile. Under the highly magnified optic, Slaton concentrated on the pair to the right, and within ten seconds he was convinced. Face, movement, stance. There was no doubt: the man on the far right, in a sunflower-yellow shirt, was Yao Jing.

The first player hit his approach shot, his ball plunking straight into a sand trap. Yao went next, coming up a bit short of the green. Slaton was suddenly thankful he hadn't set up closer—a wildly overhit approach shot could have sent the group into the woods in search of a stray ball. After all four men had played their shots, the group zoomed closer in the carts.

Slaton settled comfortably behind his weapon. The scent of the forest was heavy in the morning air. The canopy above remained calm and silent, no wind whatsoever.

He tracked Yao Jing, one of the three members of The Trident, as he strolled along the inclined shoulder of the green toward his dimpled ball. This was a man who had, only months earlier, orchestrated the mass murder of dozens of American sailors and airmen. A man whose organization had more recently tried to assassinate President Elayne Cleveland.

Important as all of that was, none of it weighed on Slaton's mind as he lay prone in the shadowed stillness. The time for evidence and reason, the establishment of crimes and punishments, was long past. He was, perhaps, mildly disappointed that Yao's playing partners were not also part of The Trident. With little extra effort, he could take out the entire organization with three tightly spaced shots. Tactically, it would be simplicity itself. No security, high startle factor. Five-round magazine. All at a range, by his estimate, of a mere one hundred and ninety meters. How easy it would have been.

Slaton pushed the idea away. His objective was clear. It was simple.

His body relaxed.

All four white balls were quickly on the green, the players converging with putters in hand. The first man, wearing a red visor, missed his putt. Slaton could hear a bit of distant banter—the Chinese words escaped him, but the heckling tone was universal. It told him the men were relaxed. Completely unaware.

Yao's turn to putt arrived, and he positioned himself over his ball in a slightly crooked stance; his back was facing Slaton squarely, shoulders canted forward twenty degrees. He stood motionless with his eyes directly over the ball. Through the optic, at less than two hundred meters, the yellow shirt looked like a billboard.

Slaton began his pressure, and the trigger broke quickly. The bullet arrived in the moment Yao released his own shot.

His last putt was a good one.

Unfortunately, Yao never saw his ball disappear into the hole.

THIRTY-TWO

Slaton quickly recovered from the recoil and worked the bolt to charge a second round. He took in the scene using his scope. Yao was down, splayed motionless on the ground, a splotch of red centered on the back of his crisp yellow shirt. He'd fallen forward onto his putter, which had somehow impaled into the turf. It stood beside him like a country club headstone.

The reactions of his playing partners were mixed. One of them rushed to Yao's side and kneeled, trying to help a man who was beyond help. Another pulled out his phone, presumably to call for emergency services. The third was running for cover, his head on a swivel. He knew instinctively what had just happened, which Slaton took as evidence of either military service or a life in crime.

He'd seen enough.

He quickly sent a text to Thomas to initiate the extraction plan. Next, he retrieved the lone casing from the leaf-covered forest bed and placed it in his pocket. After gathering his gear, he took one last look around. The police would find this spot, sooner or later, and he intended to leave behind as little as possible. Seeing nothing else, he set out toward the exfil point.

He moved as quickly as the terrain allowed, trotting

along a creek bed before veering toward the saddle of a minor hill. He emerged from the woods to find Thomas waiting.

Slaton slid into the back, and without a word the van shot off. Thomas drove quickly but with control, and there was little traffic on the route he'd suggested. Slaton heard the first sirens in the distance.

Minutes later they were crossing the Pearl River. Slaton fired off a quick message to Sorensen. She responded by confirming the details of his outbound flight. He then turned to the luggage area and put everything back as it had been the previous day. The weapon went into the bag Thomas had provided, along with his tactical clothing and gear. He put on his pilot uniform as they were transiting the long tunnel, and repacked his personal clothing in First Officer Raymond's bag.

No sooner had he finished when they reached the airport.

As they neared the drop-off point, Thomas said, "I take it all went well?"

The two hadn't exchanged a word since the pickup. Once again, Slaton met his eyes in the rearview mirror, saw them full of interest.

"Well enough," he said.

Slaton sensed another question brewing, but it never came. "Thanks for the help," he added.

The van came to a stop at the curb, and soon they were going through the drill at the rear bumper.

As Slaton entered the cargo terminal, he tried to put on the fresh face of a well-rested flight crew member. The security checkpoint was quicker than any passenger terminal, and after a short ride on the aircrew shuttle, he reached the same B-747 that had brought him here. Slaton went straight up the airstairs to the cabin, as any pilot would, and was slightly out of breath when he reached the flight deck.

Two familiar faces were waiting.

"We good?" Lyle asked, her hands flying over switches.

"All good. Let's get out of here."

Slaton buckled into the flight deck jump seat, and within minutes the airplane began its push back. Raymond started the first of the big jet's four engines.

Slaton referenced his watch.

Fifty-two minutes after Yao Jing had dropped on a tightly manicured green, and as the first detectives were likely arriving at the Macau Golf and Country Club, the airplane carrying his assassin was pushing back on the cargo ramp at Chek Lap Kok Airport.

Twelve minutes later, Logic Air Flight 410 was airborne, en route to Manila.

The big jet's departure track arced southeast from the airport, and through the right-side cockpit window Slaton looked down over Macau. Working from big to small, he easily picked out the country club, and from there the fifth hole—an aerial view he had committed to memory. It was presently surrounded by flashing lights and uniformed police.

Well, he thought to himself, his breathing returning to something near normal, *that was easy.*

Word of Yao Jing's demise spread quickly through the corridors of Washington, where it was late evening.

Anna Sorensen, waiting and watching at the CIA's operations center, was among the first to hear the news. Minutes after receiving Slaton's message about the successful op, confirmation began arriving from other sources: an agency asset in Hong Kong, one special-request electro-optic satellite feed, and NSA intercepts of police communications.

The distribution list for the relay of this information was acutely short. It first went to CIA director Eraclides, who in turn forwarded the good news to the White House. Matt Gross, working late in his West Wing office, was the first in line to see it. He read the message twice, smiled once, and sent it up the final rung of the ladder.

Vice president Quarrels received the news as he was retiring in the Lincoln Bedroom. He had taken up temporary residence there, not wanting to leave the White House for Number One Observatory Circle every night, but also knowing that, at least for the time being, optics prevented any notion of taking over Elayne Cleveland's quarters. Quarrels read the message carefully, then set the secure handset on the nightstand.

One down, two to go, he said to no one.

THIRTY-THREE

Compared to his previous flights, the two-hour crossing of the South China Sea to Manila felt like jumping a puddle. This time, after landing, Slaton stayed with the crew for the immigration gauntlet. They all arrived together at a resort hotel on the south shore of Manila Bay.

Having woken up seven hours ago in a garish casino, Slaton now found himself enmeshed in an overmanaged tropical theme, all palm trees and tiki bars and sunburned tourists. Captain Lyle signed everyone in, and when she was done the desk clerk began handing out keys. When she reached Slaton, the clerk said, "We received your message about your wife joining you—she has already checked in."

Slaton stared at the woman, trying not to look dumbfounded. "My wife."

"Yes, sir."

Recovering, he said, "Great, thanks very much."

Setting off toward the elevators, Lyle said, "Wife?"

"I have one, but I wasn't expecting her here."

They split up in the third-floor hallway, and Slaton approached his room ruminating on who would be inside. He saw two possibilities. The less likely of the two was that Christine had indeed come, perhaps owing to some failure in the extraction plan he'd concocted with Sorensen. Yet the woman at the desk hadn't mentioned a son, and Christine would never have traveled without Davy. Which meant the odds-on favorite was that Sorensen herself had come. The deputy director in charge of SAC/SOG had proved herself a hands-on leader—one of the reasons he liked her.

Then a third possibility came to mind.

Not carrying a weapon, Slaton approached the door cautiously. With his body bladed against the wall, he swiped his key card and pushed the door open with an extended arm.

He peered into the room, and saw that he was wrong on all counts.

A wide-eyed Margaret Goode stood staring at the open door, a look of sheer terror on her face. Her fear softened when she recognized Slaton.

"Thank God, it's you!" she said breathlessly.

Slaton stepped inside and eased the door shut. Behind Goode he saw her ever-present laptop on the small hotel desk. The computer's mouse was in her hand, and she was gripping it in a way that suggested she might fling it across the room.

"The clothes iron is a better weapon," he said. "Especially if you have time to heat it up."

She set down the mouse awkwardly.

"Whose idea was this?" Slaton asked.

"Deputy Director Sorensen."

It was the answer Slaton wanted to hear, as opposed to Director Eraclides. And he didn't think lying was in Goode's skill set.

"She chose me because I'm briefed in on the mission and she wants to keep everything as closely held as possible."

Slaton heaved his bag—he was back to his original

one—onto the nearest of two double beds. "Closely held is good, although that's a bit less of an issue now that the job is done."

"Actually, it's not . . . which is why she sent me."

He considered it. "You've nailed down another member of The Trident?"

"Yes."

"I don't suppose he's a golfer."

This seemed to throw Goode, but she recovered quickly. "If he is, I doubt he'll be playing anytime soon."

Slaton grinned. "True. So have you gotten any feedback from this morning's op?"

"We've been tracking the situation in Macau closely. So far, we've seen nothing unexpected."

"And what generally *is* expected when the former CEO of one of China's biggest defense companies is gunned down in broad daylight?"

"The police response was nothing out of the ordinary. And so far, there's been no diplomatic finger-pointing. One of the big questions we've been pondering is whether this Trident organization is linked to the Chinese government."

"And since there's no unusual thrashing, that suggests no ties?"

"Exactly. Even communist paradises have mob hits and jilted lovers."

Slaton agreed with the logic, in a general way, although he weighed arguing that jilted lovers were more inclined to employ kitchen knives than sniper rifles. He moved on. "So who is this second member of The Trident?"

Goode took a seat behind her laptop.

Slaton pulled a chair toward the desk and settled in beside her.

THIRTY-FOUR

Ed Markowitz arrived at Walter Reed at eight that morning. He had gone home ten hours earlier in the hope of getting a decent night's sleep. He'd failed miserably.

The fourth-floor corridor looked little changed since he'd left, save for a new Secret Service shift posted outside the Elayne Cleveland's room. They cleared him through, and Markowitz was reaching for the door handle when he registered the scene inside through the inset glass pane. Richard Cleveland, standing next to his wife and clasping her hand, was engaged in an intense conversation with Dr. Singh. The doctor, who was situated on the opposite side of the bed, looked highly displeased.

Markowitz took his hand off the handle and backed away to watch. The hospital-grade door prevented any words from escaping, but tension radiated from the room with the all heat of a summer sun. He saw Singh give what looked like a reluctant nod. The doctor then circled around the bed and made his way toward the door.

Markowitz backed away, and as soon as Singh emerged, he said, "Is everything all right?"

The doctor paused. Markowitz could see him shifting mental gears, gnashing through a decision.

"Has there been a change?" Markowitz implored, this time more insistently.

"Ask her husband." Singh spun away and whirled down the hall, a vision of white-coated irritation.

Markowitz edged inside, cautious but determined.

Richard Cleveland looked up at him, his anger also clear.

"What happened?" Markowitz asked.

"Nuthin'," said the Montanan, who remained by his wife's side.

"Richard, I—"

Cleveland held up an open palm in a *stop right there* gesture.

Markowitz did. He regarded the president, and thought she appeared much as she had on his last visit. Same bandages, same bruises, same ventilator. The monitors arrayed behind the bed looked equally unchanged. No flashing red lights, everything holding a steady rhythm.

It stayed that way for a few minutes. Cleveland holding his wife's hand, Markowitz keeping a respectful distance. Finally, Richard said, "Ed, could you give us a minute . . . please."

There could be only one response.

Markowitz stepped out of the room, but kept a line of sight through the window. Still holding his wife's hand, Richard bent down over her. At first Markowitz thought he was going to kiss her, but then he saw something else—he whispered into her ear. Markowitz tried to imagine the words.

Goodbye, I love you?

Don't worry, I'm still with you?

Richard finally backed away and headed for the door. Stepping out into the hall, he locked eyes with Markowitz, and said, "Wanna buy me a coffee?"

"Yes . . . I could use one myself."

There was no line at the hospital café, and after ordering two coffees—sugar and cream for Markowitz, black for Cleveland—they took up a window-side table in the expansive sitting area. Hospital staff were sprinkled around the nearby tables, weary mid-shift nurses and lab techs, none of whom seemed to recognize the First Spouse. Markowitz himself was virtually anonymous outside the West Wing, a status he worked to maintain by ducking the press at every opportunity. This was a departure from how many of his predecessors had handled the job, but that was how he wanted it, and his unremarkable features and accountant's demeanor cemented his obscurity.

They sat in silence for a time. Markowitz, determined to let Richard lead, simply stared into the blonde swirl of his cup, a fortune teller who was off his game.

"Elayne knew this attack was coming," Richard finally said.

Markowitz looked up at him dumbly. "What? How?"

"I don't mean the specifics, with Marine One and all. But she knew something was brewing. She first mentioned it to me a couple of months ago."

Markowitz thought back. "I don't remember hearing about any potential threats to the president in our intelligence briefings."

"Wasn't in any briefing."

"Then how could—"

"I'm not gonna get into that. There was a lot of fuss about this Trident organization, and she reckoned they might try something."

"Apparently that's what happened. According to the CIA, they're almost certainly responsible for the attack."

"Yeah, maybe . . . but there's more to it. Elayne told me there might be someone on our end involved."

"*Our end?* As in—"

Richard's voice went to a harsh whisper. "As in someone in the damned White House!" His even-tempered cowboy visage turned to stone.

"A *mole?*"

"Call it what you want."

"Who?"

Richard paused long enough to look around the room, then answered in a barely audible voice. "She never figured that out. Or if she did, she never told me."

Markowitz sat staring, slack-jawed. "I need to—"

"No!" the Montanan said. "You don't need to do a *damn* thing! Not yet. And I'm not gonna say any more. The reason I'm telling you this much is because I need your help."

"In what way?"

"Somebody has got to figure this out, and there's only one person Elayne would trust with something like this. I want to talk to Anna Sorensen."

"Sorensen?"

A slow cowboy nod.

"Well, all right. I could get you in to see her at Langley as soon as—"

"No, I ain't leavin' Elayne! You tell her to come here."

Before Markowitz could respond, Richard tipped

back the dregs of his coffee, got up, and ambled away with an old cowhand's gait. He dropped his crushed cup into a recycle bin before disappearing down the hallway.

Markowitz sat thunderstruck, weighing the ramifications of what Richard had said. Looking both backward and forward, it introduced a dizzying array of complications. He was a methodical man, steeped in the machinations of government. The minutiae of emails and meetings, the fine art of Capitol Hill arm-twisting. What Richard Cleveland was suggesting pushed him onto entirely foreign ground. The steady, comfortable world in which Markowitz existed, wobbly in recent days, had now flipped completely on its head.

If what Richard had said was true, the country was indeed in peril. Dire peril.

And it was up to Markowitz to save it.

THIRTY-FIVE

Davy's smile was a mile wide as the little seaplane tracked a river canyon through virgin wilderness. They were flying at treetop level, mountains soaring majestically on either side. From the back seat, Christine gazed down to the river's twin banks, endless lines of gray rock interrupted by the occasional fallen tree.

"Faster, Yammer, faster!"

Jammer stole a glance back at her.

Christine could only smile. She had promised her son adventures before, but this one was off the scale.

"I wanna fly again!" Davy said.

Christine rolled her eyes, but nodded.

Jammer guided the plane higher, and then said to Davy, "You have the airplane, copilot."

Christine watched her son put his hands on the right-side control column. The aircraft banked gently left and right, Jammer's distant hand discreetly guiding things from the left.

"When will we get there?" Christine asked, sounding like the four-year-old of the group.

"Another hour."

She could not say with any precision where they were. Somewhere west of Calgary, on the upside of the Canadian Rockies. Deep British Columbia, but below the Yukon.

They'd crossed into Canada late the previous afternoon, and Jammer had set the little seaplane down on a bucolic lake. He'd pulled up to an untouched shoreline, extracted a tent and camping gear from the cargo bay, and an hour later they were all circled around a campfire and sitting on logs, bellies full and jackets donned. It was the kind of night city dwellers would pay thousands of dollars to experience; and one Christine would have appreciated far more had they not been on the run.

This morning, an hour before sunrise, they'd loaded back up, and by daybreak Jammer was landing for a pit stop. They put down on another glass-smooth lake and coasted up to an outfitters' shack that belonged on the set of a Hollywood western. After topping off the tanks and buying a bag of elk jerky, they were back in the air. That had been two hours ago, and Christine hadn't seen a man-made object since. No roads, no power lines, not even a contrail from a passing airliner. It was as if civilization no longer existed.

Which, of course, was the point.

"Okay," Jammer said, "time for me to take her back."

"Your airplane, Captain," said Davy, moving his hands away from the controls.

Jammer guided them down low again, the river rushing past just beneath the twin floats. After Davy had fallen asleep last night, he'd explained to Christine that the low altitude flying wasn't merely a scenic excursion. By keeping low, masking behind mountains, there was little chance they could be picked up by ground-based radar.

"Will we be camping again tonight?" she asked.

"Nope, we'll have proper accommodations." Jammer

then amended his answer with, "Well, I mean . . . it's not exactly the Ritz."

"I thought Ritz was a cracker," Davy chimed in.

Jammer broke out laughing.

Christine couldn't resist a chuckle. "I'm sure it will be fine."

Slaton and Goode spent the entire day working, a freeform pool and luxuriant tropical gardens going to waste outside their window. They ordered room service twice—the hairy crab special proved far better than the sandwiches—and by ten o'clock that evening both were exhausted.

The good news, if it could be characterized as such, was that they'd acquired excellent intelligence on not one, but both remaining members of The Trident.

The CIA's Chinese source, after fingering Yao Jing, had come through with a second name. Li Qiang was the former chief executive of China Eastern Industries Corporation, one of the country's largest defense contractors. Eighteen months ago he had abruptly resigned. In China such departures usually indicated a falling-out with the Party. In Li's case there were hints of scandal and disgrace, but nothing specific. In all likelihood, he'd been ensnared in one of the Party's periodic corruption sweeps. Whatever the reason, in a matter of days Li went from holding one of the most lucrative jobs in the People's Republic to completely falling off radar.

The CIA launched a deep dive, focusing on Li from every conceivable angle; the results came in an avalanche. They discovered where he lived, where he had recently traveled, and most surprisingly, where his money was hidden. The agency charted every person

Li had recently associated with, and crosshatched a similar list they'd made for Yao Jing; this unearthed a trove of commonalities, yet one particular name flashed in red neon: a man with a comparable *curriculum vitae* whose travels had intersected with both Yao and Li no fewer than ten times in the previous year.

Zhao Hu held a doctorate in physics, specializing in signals analysis, and until recently he had managed one of China's most secretive research institutes. All this meshed with the intel Slaton had acquired months earlier, further sealing the connection between the three men. A similar investigative sledgehammer came down on Zhao, and the hits were equally convincing.

By agency standards, it was a slam dunk. In less than half a day, the CIA had built a rock-solid case that Li and Zhao were the last two tips of The Trident. The string of luck continued when the NSA, who had been called in to assist, cracked the encryption on both men's personal phones. According to intercepted calls and messaging, Li and Zhao were planning an urgent meeting. In less than twenty-four hours, they would be not only in the same city, but bunkered up at the same address: Li's hillside mansion on Hong Kong Island.

Slaton had long harbored a healthy dislike of coincidences, and at first glance this one seemed all but providential. Yet the more he considered it, the more it made sense. The two surviving members of The Trident had seen their compatriot gunned down this morning in what was clearly a well-planned hit—not the kind of thing retired corporate chieftains typically faced. They would be nervous, running scared. The secrecy of The Trident had been pierced, and they would wonder how deep the damage went. More importantly, they would wonder who they were up against. It seemed only natural that Li and Zhao would want to discuss the situation. From a security standpoint, it was a reckless move.

But precisely the kind of move that panicked men made.

Slaton pushed away a file folder, rubbed his eyes, and rose from his chair at the tiny hotel-room desk. On whole, he was convinced the intel was solid. But that was all it was—good analytics. *He* would be the one tasked with translating that research into his own, more tangible domain: the ballistic end game.

"All right," he said, stretching his arms over his head as he paced the floor behind Goode. "Let's go over it one last time."

She remained at the small desk, hunched over her laptop. Goode called up the pertinent files, and Slaton tapped on an overhead photo of the mansion in question.

She opened it and adjusted the orientation.

"What's the date on that image?" he asked. He had been burned before by dated intel.

"Today—nine hours ago."

"Okay, that'll do. Can we get updates going forward?"

"Probably."

He gave her a hard look.

"Definitely," she corrected.

Slaton studied the photo for a full two minutes, then switched to topography, nautical charts of the bay, and street maps of nearby neighborhoods.

"Okay, here's a list of what I need . . ."

She retrieved a notepad and a pen.

"Plans for all utilities within a mile of the property—gas, electric, water, sewer, garbage, internet. Find out if Li has dogs."

"Dogs? Like guard dogs?"

"That would be particularly good to know, but even chihuahuas can yap up a storm."

Goode scribbled feverishly.

"Parse out everything you can about who's on security for both of these guys. You might get names through banking or payroll records, and also search for job postings and résumés. I want backgrounds for whoever's protecting him. Are they military, police, rent-a-cop, organized crime? For Li I want to know how big his usual contingent is. For Zhao go back over travel records and figure out the size of his travel team." Slaton paused there.

"Is that all?" she asked.

"No, but it's a start. In the meantime, I need to talk to Anna."

THIRTY-SIX

As busy as Slaton was, he guessed Sorensen was busier. For that reason, he asked Goode to send her a message requesting a call. Even assassins had to tolerate some degree of corporate etiquette.

Slaton viewed every minute of preparation as insurance, so while he waited for Sorensen's call, he went back to the photo surveillance. He began with the God's-eye view of Li Qiang's residence, a high-res image acquired only hours earlier. What he saw was mostly predictable, an executive mansion that was part fortress, part playground. The house was set on the side of a mountain on Hong Kong Island, overlooking the high-rises and tenements of the greater city across Kowloon Bay.

The main house was large, as were a handful of surrounding residences in what had to be an exclusive enclave. Wealth disparities were extreme in the communist "People's Republic," and for the fortunate few discretion was mandatory. The lone access road that snaked up from the city was protected by a gate at the bottom—nothing particularly secure, but more a message to the commoners. The road climbed steeply, offering sweeping views all the way to Victoria Peak. The peak itself was home to a cluster of radio and telecommunications antennae.

As he studied it all, Slaton ran headlong into a shooter's most common problem—geometry. The gradient of the hillside was steep all around. The undisputed high ground was the nest of towers on Victoria Peak, but setting up there was problematic for two reasons. The first involved the tower array itself. He saw strong security around the base of the complex; dual fences, gated access, and while there was no sign of guards, he was sure the place would be riddled with surveillance cameras. The second drawback was even more damning—the towers looked down over the front of the residence. From that vantage point, Slaton's only opportunity to target both men would be to catch them arriving or departing. Not only did this give a narrow window of opportunity, but an expansive portico above the front entrance restricted the line of sight. He also saw few windows in front offering a "look" inside the mansion, and the angles would be acute.

He moved on.

As expected, the backside of the house was a virtual theater of glass, the usual architectural cliché for drinking in urban vistas. It was a weakness Slaton had often exploited: designers and builders, by nature, emphasized aesthetics and grandeur over security. And when they installed glass on half a mansion's rear-facing wall, it was rarely the expensive, bullet-resistant variety. Even so, he made a mental note to have Goode try to chase down the construction records. Outside all those back windows, a broad balcony ran the width of the main floor.

From there Slaton scanned down the hill and tried to read the terrain, looking for possible avenues of approach. Everywhere he saw challenges.

His phone rang.

He looked down and saw a padlock symbol, which supposedly guaranteed the call was secure. *If only it were so easy,* he thought as he picked up the call.

"Hello, David."

"Anna."

"It looks like things went smoothly this morning. Well done."

"No blowback?"

"Not yet. We're seeing the usual police involvement, and there's been nothing ominous on the diplomatic front."

"You made it easy—I was in and out in record time."

"Did the local help work out?"

"Thomas? Very competent. Where did you find him?"

"He was recommended by the British. They still have the best networks in China's administrative areas."

"Well, they did have ninety-nine years to work on it."

"True. So, tell me how you want to approach the next one."

It struck Slaton that she hadn't asked *if* he wanted to approach the second mission. He let it go, knowing he would have done the same if he was in her place.

"The biggest variable is timing," he said. "What's the latest on this supposed meeting?"

"We've been monitoring their phones closely. There was a flurry of calls between the two this morning, roughly thirty minutes after your op. Zhao is in Indonesia—no idea why, but he seems to go there frequently, stays at a condo he owns. Soon after these calls, Zhao got in touch with the crew of his jet, told them to plan on a flight to Hong Kong tomorrow morning. He'll definitely be staying with Li—we intercepted messages between their security teams making arrangements—but we don't know for how long."

"I'd guess no more than one night. They'll strategize, try to figure out if The Trident is still viable. Or maybe come up with a plan to wind it down. They could amend or cancel any attacks that are still on the books. None of that would take long. I'd be shocked if Zhao didn't leave the next morning."

"I agree. Hopefully we'll get some intel to back it up soon."

"How much security?"

"According to the message traffic, between six and eight combined. Not bad."

"Easy for you to say. I'm flying solo over here."

"Point taken."

"What about Zhao's jet?"

"We're watching it like a hawk. When the crew shows up, or if a flight plan is filed on that tail number, we'll know immediately. So far, nothing firm."

"That gives us a little time. If Zhao and Li really are going to have a sleepover tomorrow, it gives me a window of twelve, maybe eighteen hours, starting around midday."

"That's how I see it. And we might not get an opportunity like this again—to take them both out at once."

Silence took hold, until Slaton said, "Are you thinking what I'm thinking?"

"That it seems too good to be true?"

"Something along those lines. About the only thing missing is intel on when they'll be standing next to each another. I could do it with one bullet and save the taxpayers a few bucks."

He sensed Sorensen about to reply, but nothing came. Perhaps she was recalling a rumor, one Slaton had never confirmed or denied, that he'd once done precisely that.

"So the way things stand," he said, "we're looking at tomorrow night."

"Unless Zhao's travel plans change. Have you looked at Li's residence? Is it doable?"

"Working on that now. Getting in is going to be tough, getting out even worse. There's only one road that goes anywhere near the place, and given the income bracket of that neighborhood, I'm guessing it's thick with cameras."

"Actually, I've got some bad news on that front. Apparently, a couple of government ministers live on the same hill. There's private security at the gate, and the police make regular passes."

"So the road is out."

"There must be another way in," Sorensen said.

"I could rough it, climb up from the edge of the city. It's a steep grade, but the area is heavily wooded. That works in my favor to a point, but it also makes for tough reconnaissance—there's no telling what else is under that canopy."

"The best satellite imagery for penetrating vegetation is synthetic aperture radar. Unfortunately, those birds belong to NASA and NOAA. I might be able to get some coverage, but it would take time."

"That's the one thing we don't have. If I'm going in hot tomorrow, the plan has to be set in the next few hours. What about weapons? Can you get me something with more range than the gun I used yesterday? Some stand-off would give me more options."

"Doubtful—the time issue again. We don't exactly have an armory at our disposal."

Slaton didn't complain; it was a big ask, and he knew she was only being level with him. "Okay, I'll plan on the SRS."

"Hang on," she said. "I'm getting a new message."

Silence ensued for a time.

In the gap Slaton found his thoughts drifting to his family. He wondered where they were right now, whether they were safe. He trusted Jammer Davis without reservation. Problem was, he mistrusted the Washington hierarchy more. At the risk of distracting Sorensen, he said, "Did everything go okay with that pickup we arranged yesterday?"

He sensed her shifting mental gears, before saying, "No news is good news."

Slaton understood, and appreciated her brevity. Even if their CIA line was as secure as the lock symbol implied, the mission he was alluding to was known to no one else, Margaret Goode included. Sorensen would have heard from Jammer by now if something had gone wrong. No news *was* the best he could hope for.

"I just got an update from meteorology," she said. "For what it's worth, starting tomorrow afternoon the weather's turning much worse. Heavy rain and wind, a tropical system."

This should have gotten Slaton's full attention, a raft of new variables to be considered. Instead, he filed it away for later. His thoughts, as much as he wished otherwise, were somewhere in the sky eight thousand miles away.

THIRTY-SEVEN

Jammer skimmed in low over a thick stand of forest, aiming for a smooth spot on the upwind side of the lake. "You can use the water to see the direction of the wind," he said, his flight instruction to Davy ongoing as he pointed out patterns of ripples on the surface.

The touchdown was silky, and the Beaver decelerated quickly as it settled. Jammer steered left and Christine spotted their destination: a hundred yards ahead, a log cabin with a few outbuildings and a tiny floating dock. The place looked unoccupied, no smoke rising from the chimney despite the morning chill, no light in the lone window to counter the early gloom.

Jammer coaxed the airplane gently, aiming for a point along the shore next to the dock. He killed the engine when they were thirty feet away, then opened the door and stepped out onto a float. Momentum carried them the rest of the way, a light breeze pushing them nearer the dock.

Christine looked down into water so clear it felt like they were floating on a sheet of glass.

Jammer tied the airplane to the dock before announcing, "All ashore that's going ashore."

Davy scrambled down, leapt onto the dock, and bolted for the cabin.

Christine squirmed out of the backseat to reach the float. She sized up the cabin. "Looks pretty rustic."

"Yeah, well . . . it's not exactly a cookie-cutter home."

"Are we alone?"

"We are. A friend of mine owns the place, fellow seaplane enthusiast. That's the only way you can get here. He doesn't use it until summer, so I usually come up for a few weeks this time of year. I was actually here when I got the call from Anna."

"Call? I can't imagine there's cell service."

Jammer laughed. "Not a chance. At this latitude, even sat-phone service is iffy."

Christine thought about the blue burner phone in her travel bag as she looked out across the lake. "And I thought our ranch was remote."

"The nearest road is thirty miles west, and that's a dirt and gravel path put in by a mining company. To reach asphalt you're talking another twenty miles. The closest town, if you can call it that, is a thirty-minute flight."

"Does David know where we are?"

"Nope. Even Anna didn't want to know. We've got provisions for twenty days, thirty if you don't mind losing a few pounds. Of course, I can always make a milk run if necessary."

Davy was running circles around the cabin. Jammer gave her a circumspect look before saying, "By the way . . . it's not a major issue, but I wouldn't let him stray too far. It's spring, and there are a lot of mama bears around. I also saw a pack of wolves a few days ago."

"Those are the kind of predators I can deal with."

Jammer laughed, a growl that heaved up from deep

in his chest. "Any idea how long you'll be wanting to stay off-grid?"

"Not really."

"Well, as long as it doesn't go into winter we should be fine. I'll bet we can even make it fun for Davy. I've got fishing gear, lots of hand tools. I even saw an old bow and some arrows in the shed."

"You make it sound like summer camp."

"Not a bad way to think of it."

But Christine couldn't think of it that way. In the course of two days her family, her life, had been uprooted. She and Davy had been exiled to the back of beyond, and David was somewhere in the world solving America's latest problem. If felt as if everything had spun apart by centrifugal force, all thanks to a terrorist attack that had occurred thousands of miles away.

Christine's next question surprised even her. "Are there any weapons?"

Jammer's eyes narrowed. "Aside from the bow, a couple of hunting rifles, a Glock for the varmints. Plenty of ammo."

She felt a shiver.

"But we're not gonna need any of that," he said a little too easily. "Why don't you guys help me unload, then we'll get started on dinner."

"Sounds like a plan."

For Slaton, the weather introduced multiple complications.

If Sorensen's forecast held—rain and wind all night—he wasn't going to find his targets swilling a digestif on the midlevel balcony. Then again, if they were truly security-conscious, they wouldn't show their faces at all—they would bunker up in the most thick-walled interior room. If that was how it played out, Slaton would simply have to adapt, search for a glimpse of his targets or maneuver in close.

More confounding than the weather was the geometry. Slaton needed to acquire a line of sight to both targets, and while the most obvious opportunity involved the windows in back, the terrain fell away sharply in that direction. There was no chance of a shot from ground level, and setting up on either side introduced secondary problems: the neighboring residences, both east and west, had highly restrictive look angles. Worse yet, both appeared to be occupied.

Slaton scoured the photos for any kind of elevation on the favored north side, but found nothing. No towers, no rooftops, no convenient terrain outcroppings. The trees weren't high enough to compensate for the incline angle, and at any rate, climbing one to establish a platform stable enough for a multiple-shot sequence wasn't realistic.

He pored over images on the tablet, searching for anything within three hundred meters of the residence—his self-imposed limit given the weapon he would be using, the expected conditions, and a two-target engagement.

His eyes shifted east and settled on a trussed concrete slab surrounded by freshly turned earth. Based the surrounding piles of material and debris, it could only be a residence under construction. The property was two lots away from Li's residence, at the edge of his maximum range.

Goode's overheads of the neighborhood went back eighteen months, and after stepping through a few Slaton decided the place had been under construction for roughly a year. The photos provided a visual sequence of the builder's work. The first four months were foundation work, moving dirt and installing retaining walls. Then concrete footers outlined the lower floor. At that point it had been little more than a graceless slab protruding toward the city like a giant tongue. In the most recent photos, however, the structure was taking shape. The walls were mostly in place, although there was still no roof. The shell of the house was presently surrounded by scaffolding.

Slaton measured the most critical detail, and got three hundred and ten meters to the center of Li's residence. It was the absolute maximum. He gave it ten more minutes of thought, most of which was spent striving for alternatives.

There were none.

Working against the clock, this was the best possible solution. Not ideal under any circumstances, but it *could* work.

Or . . . it could fail spectacularly.

THIRTY-EIGHT

Matt Gross entered the Oval Office to find Quarrels alone, looking out contemplatively across the tree-studded South Lawn.

"I've got some news," Gross said to announce himself.

Quarrels turned, and he blinked a few times as if recalibrating his thoughts. "Good news, I hope?"

"Yes. I just took a call from Anna Sorensen. She says the intelligence on the last two members of The Trident looks solid. Better yet, an opportunity has come up to eliminate them both. Sometime in the next thirty-six hours, we expect them to meet in a house outside Hong Kong."

Quarrels looked mildly surprised. "That all happened quickly."

"I agree. Seems like poor security on their part, given what happened to Yao Jing. Sorensen thinks they're running scared, making bad choices. Whatever the reason, it's not a chance we should miss."

"Slaton again?"

"He's already in the area. Sorensen's got him in planning mode."

"Let's hope it goes as well as the first strike."

"If it does, The Trident will soon be history."

A look of concern dawned over Quarrels's face. "We

never really discovered their motive, did we? Why all these attacks?"

"We might figure it out someday. Or maybe not. As long as Slaton puts an end to it, I'd say mission accomplished."

"I guess so," Quarrels agreed. "And then we can move on to more important business, like a new package of sanctions on Russia."

"What about Slaton?" Gross asked.

"Slaton?"

"I was wondering . . . how do we handle him when it's done?"

"We treat him like any of our warriors. We bring him home and let him get on with his life."

Sorensen was in the CIA operations center, refocusing after a long and guarded conversation with Matt Gross, when a call came in from her own office.

"What's up, Travis?" she asked, picking up the local line. Travis McCall was her assistant.

"You've got a visitor up here, ma'am."

Sorensen referenced the wall clock. "I don't have any appointments this morning."

"No, ma'am, this wasn't on your calendar. When I came in this morning, Ed Markowitz was waiting outside your office. He's President Cleveland's—"

"I know who he is," Sorensen cut in. "Tell him we'll have to meet later. I've got a high priority mission about to go critical."

A pause, followed by muffled voices. Travis said, "Apparently he's been trying to track you down since yesterday. He says it's imperative that he sees you right away."

Sorensen heaved out a long sigh. Corsair wasn't

set to arrive in Hong Kong for another hour, and Markowitz *was* the president's chief of staff. A dark thought struck: Had Elayne Cleveland taken a turn for the worse?

"Okay," she said. "I'll be right up."

As she navigated to her office, Sorensen wondered why Markowitz would want to corner her in her own office. If it wasn't bad news about the president's condition, she guessed it probably involved a power struggle. She was already sensing White House efforts to sideline him, so it was possible Markowitz was making an end run for some privileged intelligence. Whatever his intentions, she could think of no scenario where meeting him was going to make her day easier.

Markowitz was waiting in her office. He looked more disheveled than usual. His suit was rumpled, his hair mussed. Yet it was the look on his face that put her on edge—a stare that looked sourced from a stun grenade.

"Good morning, Ed," she said tentatively. "What can I do for you?"

"Actually," Markowitz replied, "I'm not the one who needs your help."

Sorensen tried not to look irritated. "Okay. Then who does?"

"You need to go to Walter Reed and see Richard Cleveland."

"Is it about the president? Has her condition worsened?"

"No, it's not that. But trust me . . . you need to hear what he has to say."

THIRTY-NINE

The flight back to Hong Kong continued Slaton's streak of successes. His private Boeing 747, flown by his dedicated crew, set up on final approach to Chek Lap Kok Airport right on time. Even Captain Lyle remarked on their run of good fortune. "It's a good thing this approaching weather front didn't get here any sooner. In a few hours, there are going to be some wicked air traffic delays."

The jet touched down at the onset of dusk, a time-table set by necessity; Slaton had utilized most of the day for planning and rest, but the operational window when his targets would be vulnerable had already begun—he'd gotten confirmation that Zhao had indeed arrived at Li's residence roughly an hour earlier. This information came from the Bumblehive—the NSA's Utah Data Center—which was vacuuming every possible SIGINT channel to track the two men.

NSA also confirmed that Zhao was planning to fly out the next morning. It gave Slaton one night in which to work, and even that was frontloaded; the construction site where he planned to set up had a good look angle into the main living area and dining room, but no line of sight whatsoever to the four bedrooms, including the top-floor master suite. Chances were, once the men went to bed, he would have no shot at either until morning.

It was raining lightly as Captain Lyle set the big jet's parking brake. Before leaving the flight deck, Slaton asked her for the latest aviation weather report; it showed winds out of the northwest at eighteen miles an hour, gusting to twenty-five. The forecast was for conditions to deteriorate over the next twelve hours. Hardly ideal for precision marksmanship.

Strike one, Slaton thought.

The familiar drill ran its course. Immigration was uneventful, and Thomas was as punctual as ever; Slaton found the van waiting at the same curb. Thomas began driving, and Slaton moved to the back; the SRS was in the luggage well, this time concealed in a nylon sports bag. Slaton went to work as they blended into traffic, transforming from aviator to operator in the back seat of the van. There was still mud on his trail shoes from the previous op.

It all felt like déjà vu until Thomas took a different road departing the airport, the Lantau Highway. Instead of crossing the sprawling bridge to Macau, they headed east. The lights of Hong Kong filled the windshield like an apparition out of the mist.

They drove in near silence, Thomas making no attempt to discuss anything that wasn't related to the mission. In any social situation it would have been awkward, but here it fit perfectly. NOCs operated at great risk, and polite conversation was generally counterproductive. They didn't want to know you. And they didn't want you to know them.

Slaton understood.

As he began checking his weapon, the first flash of lightning flickered in the distance.

———

Five miles away, sheltered in a derelict pump shed at the base of Victoria Peak, eight men were going through similar motions. All were Filipino, all were mercenaries. Beneath a leaky corrugated roof they checked their comm nets, gear, and weapons one last time. That done, the group gathered around a make-shift table, and by the illumination of a shielded light they made one last study of a map of their target area: a hillside mansion surrounded by acres of forest.

"Both men are in the house," said the leader of the team. A former master sergeant in the Philippine Army, and a veteran of minor campaigns throughout Southeast Asia, he spoke in their native Filipino.

"Do we know what they did to deserve this?" some-one asked.

The sergeant shrugged. "They pissed off the wrong people. Not our concern. We do what we've been paid to do."

There were discussions about tactics and ap-proaches, which could only be expected for such an unusual mission. Silence then fell. It was the standard pre-mission hush; the time when soldiers harbored a few private thoughts before the shit hit the fan.

At that point there was nothing to do but wait for the "Go" command. All eyes went to the comm unit on the table. It was big and heavy, the size of a paver brick, and had been provided by the man who'd hired them. While none of them had ever seen a tactical ra-dio like it, it worked well enough, and was suppos-edly secure.

The man they knew as Monkh had promised that much.

FORTY

Sorensen found Richard Cleveland outside his wife's room at Walter Reed. She had never met the First Spouse before, but he was instantly recognizable in his cowboy regalia, complete with scarred boots and a silver belt buckle. When the two locked eyes, he seemed to recognize her as well—not necessarily a good thing for the head of CIA clandestine operations.

After a quick handshake and greeting, Sorensen asked, "How is Elayne?"

"She's hangin' in," he muttered. He seemed unsettled.

Sorensen waited, but nothing more came. She glanced at a hospital clock on the far wall; there had never been any question of whether to come, but with Slaton's mission looming, she needed to get back to the ops center. "I don't mean to push," she prompted, "but Ed Markowitz said you wanted to see me about something. I'm afraid I don't have much time."

Richard nodded, then jerked his head down the hall. He led her to the patient room adjacent to his wife's, which turned out to be empty. Sorensen suspected it had less to do with a lack of patients than a need for a security buffer. Richard closed the door behind them.

"Thanks for comin'," he said.

"Ed said it was important."

"Yeah, it is. A couple of months ago, Elayne told

me a few things about this Trident bunch. I know you think they're responsible for shooting down Marine One, and you're probably right. But they might have had some help."

Sorensen nodded guardedly, realizing how awkward the conversation had turned already. Richard Cleveland had no official standing, no security clearance. Yet he also might have uniquely intimate knowledge of Elayne Cleveland's thinking. She said, "We always suspected The Trident was getting support. China or maybe Russia."

"That was her inclination too. But then some new information came to light. Something that made her think it wasn't any country."

"What information?"

Cleveland checked the steel toes of his boots before saying, "About six weeks ago I was with Elayne—she'd come back to Montana for the weekend. We saddled up a couple of horses and went for a ride. It usually lightens her mood, but I could see something was weighin' heavy on her. She eventually told me what it was. Seems the head of Homeland Security came to see her, a one-on-one meeting at the White House."

"Vince Seward?"

"That's him. Apparently, as part of its usual security routine, the Secret Service monitors phone calls going in and out of the White House. In past years, that was pretty much what went through the switchboard. But the Secret Service has been trying to catch up with the times. They brought in NSA and asked them to build a system that could track all electronic communications."

"As in cell calls."

"Actually, more than that. According to Elayne,

this gadget they put together sweeps up pretty much everything—you know, all the bandwidths and such."

"I've never heard of anything like that," said Sorensen, who knew a great deal about signals intelligence.

"Neither had Elayne. It started out as just sort of an experiment, people wanting to see if it could be done. As it turned out, this system worked. Seward said they captured a lot of calls that surprised them. Now there were privacy issues, and all that, and most of what they found was harmless. But one batch of calls got Seward worried."

"And this is why he called a meeting with the president?"

"Yep. Seems they intercepted a number of calls from some sort of satellite device. It was supposed to be encrypted, but I guess that doesn't mean much to NSA when they set their mind to it. Bottom line, these calls were made shortly before and after the attacks in March, and what was in them built a pretty good case that somebody was talking to The Trident."

Sorensen's thoughts began to slow. The urgency she felt to get back to the operations center evaporated. "You're saying someone in the White House is communicating with The Trident?"

"Not me sayin' it. That's what Seward told Elayne."

"Who was it?" Sorensen asked breathlessly.

"That's the catch. The system wasn't good enough to pinpoint exactly who was making the calls or from where. At least not yet. So Elayne gave Seward his marching orders, told him to figure it out. She also warned him to not share the news with anyone but her until they got to the bottom of it. And she meant *anyone*. That's where things sat a few days ago when Marine One went down."

Sorensen stood speechless, her thoughts pinging in countless directions. She eventually asked, "I appreciate your sharing this, Richard, but I have to ask . . . why me?"

"It's a fair question. You and I aren't really acquainted, but Elayne told me she trusts you more than anyone in this damned city. I had to tell someone, so stands to reason I picked you."

"Okay." Hoping to organize her thoughts, Sorensen built a mental timeline for the events. "And she confided all this to you in Montana last month?"

Richard actually cocked a slight smile. "Well, that brings us to the other thing you oughta' know . . ."

FORTY-ONE

The van's tires hissed over wet asphalt; the rain was steady, its scent heavy on the air. Slaton looked back through the rear window and studied the cars behind them. In the deepening night he could only distinguish headlights, but that was enough; he classified each pair by size, shape, and brightness, as well as the configuration of parking and fog lights. None of the cars appeared to be following them, but he watched all the same. Slaton had no specific reason to expect a threat, but running his second mission in two days, in the same general area, made countersurveillance mandatory.

The highway was new and smooth, the traffic moving fast. An exit sign for Hong Kong Disneyland mocked Slaton's intentions. Soon a mile-long bridge deposited them on the city's waterfront. Thomas held to the shoreline road, keeping pace with the traffic. The bay's briny scent took hold, and furious waves smacked into the rip rap seawall, spray clawing out toward the boulevard. He saw only two boats braving the churning sound, a passenger ferry and a heavyset tug, both plowing ahead stoically as they went about their business.

Again, Slaton felt a twinge of unease. The fact that he couldn't nail down the source only heightened his concern. It probably had to do with the bizarre execution of this mission. He had flown halfway around the world on a private widebody jet, and now, for the second time in two days, he was being chauffeured to a kill. It was beginning to feel almost theatrical. An op that belonged in a screenplay, everything orderly and without risk, the details arranged by the most capable intelligence service on earth. Aside from the vagaries of the weather, everything tonight was going to plan, exactly as it had two days ago when he'd executed a flawless shot. There had so far been no repercussions whatsoever regarding the death of Yao Jing.

And now, here he was, engaged in another silk-smooth mission.

So why does it all feel so wrong?

This was the cautionary background voice all good operators had. One that Slaton had heard before, and that he invariably listened to. Still, he couldn't see the problem.

His thoughts looped back to tonight's targets, the remaining two-thirds of The Trident. Li Qiang and Zhao Hu. Who were they really?

Cash-hungry oligarchs angling for a payday?

Chinese government minions trying to deflect accountability for the attacks?

Could they represent some new variant of organized crime?

Answer that question, determine who he was up against, and he might feel more comfortable. Try as he might, Slaton couldn't.

The skies cleared briefly, and across the bay he picked out the district of Sheung Wan. Above that was Victoria Peak, a great blotter of black dotted by the lights of large homes. From across the bay each residence looked distinctive, unique silhouettes shaped by high-end LED interiors and uplit landscaping. At the summit of the peak Slaton could just make out the tower farm, antennae reaching up like steel fingers into the gloom, red lights flashing a warning.

He tried to pick out Li's residence, but in the marginal visibility it was hopeless. As the final bridge dumped them onto Hong Kong Island, the view of Victoria Peak was blotted out by buildings. Thomas wheeled the van left and right, battling heavy traffic through Sheung Wan. Slaton saw shops and restaurants on street level, apartments above. Most of it was lower-end, a blue-collar variation of the greater city. The farther they got from the waterfront, the more things degraded. The buildings looked older, the streets less clean.

The faces he saw on the sidewalks were a mix. Many were Asian, but there were a considerable number of Occidentals as well. This was one of the few places in Asia where Slaton, with his fair hair and Nordic features, wouldn't stand out. The foul weather also worked to his advantage—as requested, Thomas had provided a light jacket with a hood to help muddy his appearance.

"Two minutes," Thomas called over his shoulder. The warning made Slaton think of an airborne jump-master.

Tonight's ingress would be different from the previous mission. Slaton would be dropped near the city's edge, and from there he would make his way to a landmark that would guide him toward his objective.

Thomas pulled the van to a stop beside a rain-sotted gutter.

"Fifteen minutes," Slaton said.

"Fifteen minutes," Thomas repeated.

This was their "on call" agreement. Thomas would

keep the van on the island, moving as necessary to avoid suspicion, until they rendezvoused again here; unlike the op at the country club, there could be no set window. The precise timing of tonight's operation was dependent on factors out of Slaton's control, so he'd simply told Thomas to expect a fifteen-minute heads-up.

The SRS was concealed in a sports equipment bag, and Slaton slung it over his non-dominant left shoulder. Wearing loose clothing, a rain jacket, and hauling the bag, he might have been an expat Brit or Aussie returning home after a rained-out cricket match.

With one last check of the street, Slaton got out and made for the first intersection. By the time he reached it, Thomas and the van had blended away. Slaton double-checked the street name—the sign was conveniently scribed in both English and Chinese, something the communist party hadn't gotten around to correcting—and he turned right at the corner.

He continued up a dead-end road with a steep grade, three-and four-story apartment blocks stair-stepping upward. Thanks to the rain, he saw virtually no one. At the end of the street Slaton found what he expected: a red-and-white traffic barricade, signifying the end of the street, and beyond that a prodigious slab of concrete.

It marked the place where the city ended. And where the risks began.

Sorensen followed Richard Cleveland to his wife's room. He paused at the door to have a word with the Secret Service detail, and the team leader cleared them both inside.

Sorensen went through tentatively. She wasn't completely prepared for what she saw: the president, a woman she called a friend, laid out motionless on a gurney, leads and tubes snaking around her body. Her face was barely visible, half hidden by a breathing mask. There was a cast on her right arm and multiple bandages.

Together they stood by her side for a full minute, neither speaking. Sorensen sensed it was Richard's way of letting her acclimatize to the reality of Elayne's condition. It was one thing to hear about the president's injuries, quite another to see them firsthand. When the shock subsided, Sorensen looked expectantly at Richard, wondering why he'd brought her here.

Without comment, he returned to the door and pulled a privacy shade across the room's only window. "I asked them to install that," he explained. "Told them I didn't want anyone taking pictures."

He came back bedside and took his wife's hand. Richard then bent down and whispered something in her ear.

To Sorensen's astonishment, Elayne Cleveland's eyes cracked open.

"My god! She's conscious again!"

Richard looked at Sorensen knowingly.

Finally, she understood. "When did this happen?"

"She began squeezing my hand two nights ago. Late yesterday she opened her eyes."

"What are the doctors saying?" Sorensen asked.

"That's something we need to discuss. The only other person who knows about this is the team leader, Dr. Singh. We want to keep it that way."

"*What?* But how will the staff—"

Richard cut her off by holding up a finger. He beckoned Sorensen closer. She complied, and he took her hand and placed it in the president's. Her skin was warm and soft.

Richard said, "One squeeze means yes, two for no. That's how we've been communicating. She can get out a word now and again, but talking seems to tire her. She's starting to breathe on her own, which the doctor says is a really good sign." He turned toward Elayne. "Darlin', you need to convince Miss Sorensen of a few things. First, is it true that you want your recovery kept completely private for now?"

With Elayne Cleveland looking squarely at her, Sorensen felt one soft but distinct squeeze.

Richard went on. "And is it true that you believe there is a traitor in the White House?"

One squeeze.

"And that they are controlling The Trident?"

One squeeze.

He looked at Sorensen, and said, "Are you on board here, Anna?"

"Yes," Sorensen said. Instinctively, she found herself squeezing the president's hand once.

Richard said, "Dr. Singh says this is excellent progress, but I . . . or actually, Elayne . . . convinced him that her recovery has to be kept secret, at least for a few days. As it stands, someone tried to kill her, and we're convinced the plot involved someone in the White House. I'm not gonna get into legalities, but Elayne believes strongly, and I back her up, that the safest place for her at the moment is right where she is. What she needs is for one person, someone she trusts completely, to get to the bottom of what's going on. That would be you, Miss Sorensen." He shifted his eyes to his wife. "Is all that right, Darlin'?"

Richard pulled away the breathing mask, and Elayne Cleveland spoke, one raspy word escaping her dry, cracked lips. "Yes."

Sorensen could think of only one reply, "If that's what you want, Madame President, then that's what I'll do."

The lips twisted into a weak smile.

"But if that's how we're playing it," Sorensen added, "I do have a few questions. Are you up for it?"

One squeeze.

And so began the most astonishing interrogation Anna Sorensen had ever performed.

Twenty minutes later Sorensen was outside, walking quickly to her car. Elayne Cleveland's recovery was spectacularly good news. Yet it introduced a host of complications, one of which overrode all others. Slaton was about to engage in a strike halfway around the world. If there truly was a leak, might his mission be compromised? Sorensen considered that the previous mission had gone off without a hitch.

There was simply no good answer.

She reached her car, climbed in, and sat still for a moment. Sorensen gnawed her lower lip, realizing how limited her options were.

Should she contact Slaton immediately, tell him to abort?

Or was it already too late?

FORTY-TWO

The massive edifice was impossible to miss, a ten-meters-wide strait of ungroomed concrete. Had it been situated on mainland China, or somewhere in Russia, Slaton might have taken the great slab for some manner of Brutalist architecture. In the reconnaissance photos he had studied, cold snapshots taken from hundreds of miles above, the channel stood out like a river on a parched desert.

In the greater scheme of things, it was little more than a foundational patch, a repair to rectify decades of careless top-down municipal planning. Twenty years ago, Hong Kong Island had begun to suffer routine seasonal flooding, a consequence of shifting weather patterns and unchecked development. The Hong Kong North Tunnel was the four-billion-dollar answer, a massive man-made network designed to divert and capture stormwater.

Tonight the tunnel was Slaton's guide.

He followed the big sluice as it rose gently uphill. With the rain increasing in intensity, the system was doing its job, filling quickly to divert the deluge into voluminous underground storage tanks, with the overflow spilling harmlessly into the bay. Slaton tracked the system for a hundred yards, at which point the giant gutter dropped into the earth. From that point, the main pipe ran underground, although a cleared easement above highlighted its buried course.

It made for a simple hike.

Slaton pulled out the GPS navigation device Thomas had provided and crosschecked his orientation. By following the easement another four hundred yards, bypassing six tributary collection points, he would reach the closest point to his objective. From there he would turn uphill and follow a creek bed through the forest for the final mile.

He reached the junction quickly, and from there he slogged across a secondary channel that was capturing water from an uphill creek. The water was ankle-deep, burbling down in a steady churn. When he reached the creek itself, the gradient increased significantly. Within minutes, Slaton was breathing hard, his thighs burning as he ascended the steep hillside. Thankfully, enough light spilled in from the city to make the dense foliage visible.

Ten minutes later, after checking his position again, Slaton veered away from the creek, heading eastward. He was getting close. His footfalls were silent on the loamy earth, and the sound of rain on the forest canopy drowned out the din of the city. He paused near a natural clearing, and saw what he expected on the hillside above—the house under construction.

Slaton held there, at the edge of the forest, for a full five minutes. Waiting and listening, searching for any trace of light, motion, or sound that didn't belong. He presumed there would be no workers at this time of night, especially given the conditions, yet a few minutes spent confirming it seemed like a good investment. The storm was becoming a dominant factor; wind shook the trees, putting leaves in a constant swirl and downing old branches. The lights of the city reflected off scudding clouds overhead. He heard sheets of plastic, presumably protecting equipment or piles of construction material, snapping against tie-downs. At one point, Slaton thought he heard an asynchronous rustle in the nearby forest. He wrote it off to the wind and rain.

Satisfied, he ascended the last fifty meters. The skeletal home gained definition as he closed in. Its concrete foundation was finished, but the cinderblock walls above were a work in progress. On the highest floor the wood frame stood restlessly in the wind, topped by a partially trussed roof. Slaton veered toward a network of scaffolding on the home's east side. A ladder leaned against the frame, giving a path upward toward the midlevel balcony. With a last look around, he shrugged his gear higher on his shoulder and began climbing.

The ladder reached a landing, but he was still ten feet below his objective—the outer deck ringing three sides of the main floor. Seeing no simple way to reach it, Slaton began climbing the scaffolding's metal frame. He made it to the balcony, stood, and got his first direct look at Li's home.

The lights were on.

But is anybody home?

Sorensen hurried into the Langley operations center, and moved toward the comm workstations on a near-run. The question that had been rumbling in her head all the way from Walter Reed still had no answer. On one hand, Slaton was in position, his assault on Li and Zhao imminent. On the other, if there really was a high-level leak, the mission could be jeopardized, putting him in danger.

Abort or let it run? Sorensen skidded to a stop behind a desk labeled Mission Comm.

"Ask Corsair for a status update," she ordered.

The young man at the desk began typing. They both watched the monitor, waiting for a reply. A minute passed. Then two. One side of the split main screen began filling with technical jargon that meant nothing to Sorensen. She shifted her attention from the screen to the young man behind it.

He began typing again—far more keystrokes this time.

"What's wrong?" she asked, sensing his urgency.

"I'm not sure, ma'am . . . but it appears we've lost his signal. Corsair's comm has gone down."

FORTY-THREE

Every mission has its critical juncture, the moment when research smacks headlong into reality. No matter how many photos you studied or how well you measured your angles, the actual picture on the ground always brought surprises. Sometimes the differences were minor, a simple matter of skewed geometry. Sometimes man-made changes intervened. Had someone planted a new tree since the reconnaissance photos had been taken? Put up curtains in a window? Turned on a bright exterior light that shined directly in your eyes? Slaton was, after all, standing in the middle of a construction zone, where change was the objective.

He eased behind a pile of cinderblocks, set down his bag, and removed the weapon. After giving the gun a brief check, he settled in behind the waist-high stack of blocks. He pulled out the spotting scope and trained it on Li's residence.

Slaton began on the far left where a modest balcony, the wood a reddish hue in the flood of light from the house, extended out over the precipice. There, the first thing that got his attention were two security men. They were standing against the house, in the shelter of a narrow eave. They looked wet and miserable. Their hands were in their pockets, their heads bent low. Watching but bored. Thinking about the next break and a hot cup of coffee. Slaton guessed that another man, or possibly two, would be stationed out front. Which, if his research was correct, left a minimum of three inside.

All as expected.

He shifted the optic and noted an outdoor table and chairs. A furled umbrella flapped in the wind, and two cushioned chaise lounges lay sodden in the thickening rain. Slaton walked the optic from left to right, pausing on each of the home's windows. Altogether, nine were visible from his perch. Most, unfortunately, were on the north-facing back side, abutting the back terrace, leaving an impossibly narrow look-angle into the house. Better were the three eastern windows, which were situated almost perpendicular to Slaton's position. The rightmost of these, he knew, was the least promising—an architect's diagram Goode had unearthed pegged this window as little more than an architectural accent, mounted high on the wall of the laundry room. That window remained dark. Also of limited use was a high transom window on the left.

He shifted to his gun-mounted sight and settled it on the best option—front-and-center, a broad ten-by six-foot panoramic window overlooking the main living area. Slaton could see half of the dining room table, and at that moment a laptop computer sat glowing at the end seat. Deeper in the room were two plush chairs and an armoire filled with porcelain figurines and framed photos. The floor plan Slaton had memorized told him the main living area was behind the wall to the window's left. Altogether, he was mildly disappointed—he'd expected to have a clear view of the entire dining room where, with any luck, Li and Zhao might join for what he hoped would be their last supper.

Slaton lowered the gun and moved to his right along the brick stack, all the way to the point where the balcony ended. It altered the geometry, but not enough—he still could see only three dining room chairs. He was scoping out the half-built home around him, contemplating an alternate perch, when a flash of motion at the house caught his eye. He quickly slewed the sight to the left side of the big window and saw a burly man wearing a cook's apron. Slaton tracked him, noting that he was carrying a tray loaded with what looked like appetizers, until he disappeared to the right—the kitchen connector.

It was encouraging. His targets were very possibly behind the leftmost wall at that moment, out of sight by no more than ten or fifteen feet. Slaton was close, very close, but saw no way to get a better angle.

A strong gust of wind swept in, and the distant window grew dimmer as rain began hammering down. Slaton backed away from his scope and wiped water from his face using the barely dry collar of his shirt. He'd had to pull back the hood on his jacket in the swirling wind.

He decided that the big window was his best option. If his targets were indeed just out of sight behind the wall to the left, at some point they would move. To reach any other point in the house—a bathroom, the kitchen, or a bedroom—they would have to cross behind the big window.

This, however, underscored his second problem. He needed to eliminate both men. What were the chances of them appearing simultaneously? It was possible, he thought, but any opportunity would be fleeting. He'd already decided to not engage a single target if only one man appeared. At least, not yet. Tomorrow, with Zhao's departure pending, and with work crews likely returning here, his calculations might change. For now, he simply had to be patient.

Slaton stacked two cinder blocks into a makeshift seat. The rain was sheeting down, and he looked for protection. His gaze snagged on a canvas tarpaulin big enough to cover a small car; it was draped over a nearby pile of lumber, snapping in the wind but anchored securely by ropes on four corners. Slaton detached the ropes and rearranged the tarp over his shooting position. It was hardly perfect, but kept most of the rain at bay, and also gave some concealment.

He settled in to wait and watch. If a chance came, it might be fleeting, so he built a simple decision matrix. A quick positive ID was essential for anyone who came into view. If both targets showed themselves, he would immediately take out the man farthest from the center of the window, then quickly shift to the second. Given the atrocious conditions, he knew a follow-up shot might be necessary. Fortunately, the window was tall, and unless his target fell very close to the knee-high base, he would still retain line-of-sight.

Slaton used the GPS receiver to verify his exact position, then input the stored coordinates of the distant window. Three hundred and six meters. A straight-forward shot under ideal conditions—but that wasn't what he had. The effect of the rain, ballistically speaking, would be minimal, yet it did introduce a degree of unpredictability. More problematic was the gusting wind. Confirming hits would be vitally important.

With everything in place, he pulled out his CIA-issued sat-phone. He had been expecting a final intel update, yet the handset showed no signal. This seemed odd—satellite signals were largely impervious to weather. He pocketed the phone and settled back behind his sight.

The brightly lit window less than a quarter of a mile away became the center of his universe. Rain pelted the outer panes and beaded along the edges. The interior lights were dazzling in contrast to the storm-driven night. The weather continued to deteriorate. Strong gusts came with sheeting rain, and then for a time conditions would ease. Slaton sensed a pattern developing, a signature tropical flow—rain and wind organizing in intense bands, periods of calm between. He wagged estimates for the wind, the greater and lesser extremes of what he was seeing, then banded his sight picture for a range of options. In all likelihood, if an opportunity appeared, there would be no time for math.

He was concentrating intently on the reticle, applying his notional corrections on a lampshade slightly over three hundred meters away, when a branch snapped somewhere in the forest below.

Slaton froze.

FORTY-FOUR

Slaton pulled away from the tarp, wanting no buffers to the world around him. He fell still, watching and listening. Rain peppered his face. The wind seemed to swirl in from every direction, whipping the forest into a frenzy and splattering rain all around.

But he *had* heard something.

The snap of a branch? It could have been the storm, a rotted limb falling, but his gut told him otherwise. He recalled hearing something earlier, moments before climbing the scaffolding. Now the inoperative sat-phone began to weigh.

Too many warnings.

Too many coincidences.

His eyes swept the darkness, every tree, boulder, and hill. He looked toward the narrow road fronting the house, and that was when he saw them; two figures ghosting through the foliage just beyond the road. Then a third.

Slaton turned very slowly and checked in the other direction, down the hill to his left. He spotted two more there, moving left to right, lacing up the incline. The thought came to mind that they might be here for the same reason he was—to kill Li and Zhao. Yet that didn't compute—the two groups were moving in the wrong direction. Could it be Li and Zhao's security making some kind of regular sweep? According to the intel, each had a few guards. That didn't feel right either. There were too many, and the geometry of their approach was all wrong. In the end, Slaton came to two conclusions.

He was looking at a team of unknowns.

And they were coming for him.

Was he completely surrounded? How many was he up against?

Before answers could filter in, his eye was caught by a burst of motion at the distant window. In the rain-driven gloom the scene resembled a TV screen in a dark room. Two men had appeared.

He quickly lifted the SRS, settled the scope, and had no trouble identifying two faces he had memorized. Li and Zhao were there, standing, inexplicably, dead center in the wide window. The sticklike figure of Zhao was talking on his phone. Li stood next to him, rounder and doughy, a mushroom of black hair topping his head. Both were referencing the laptop at the end of the big table, and seemed completely engrossed in whatever was being discussed.

The rain came harder, as if to conceal what was about to happen.

With both men in view, Slaton amended his targeting plan for the most ruthless of reasons. Because Li was a bigger target, and might react more slowly, he settled his sight on Zhao, center of mass.

Every sound seemed magnified. The wind in the trees. The rustling of footsteps left and right.

Everything felt wrong.

Slaton was engaging a target while he himself was being hunted. It was a game with three teams, and while he was playing offense, a vise was closing around him.

His targets stood dumbly, motionless, just off-center in the great window. They seemed as still as paper targets on a range. Slaton's finger touched the trigger, doubts coursing through his head.

This entire mission suddenly felt upside down. The flights, the logistics, the intel. All so seamless, so faultlessly on schedule. An operational juggernaut catered to his whims, delivered by the Gatsby of the world's intelligence agencies.

How easy it had all been until now.

And how wrong it had turned in a matter of seconds.

Enlightenment came in a rush, a cascade of interrelated decisions. Life and death choices, both for Slaton and others.

Time seemed to compress.

Tune out what you can. Focus on the task at hand.

His finger began the pressure. Zhao's chest filled the scope in its tapered view. Slaton instinctively applied the wind correction. The rifle was motionless, rock-steady on the makeshift stand. By the smallest of mercies, the rain seemed to lessen.

The trigger broke. Slaton absorbed the recoil and instantly shifted to Li, centering his adjusted sight picture on a second chest. Through the glass, in the periphery, Slaton saw Zhao shudder, his phone flying away. Li seemed to freeze, his brain processing what had just happened.

That hesitation gave Slaton the moment he needed. He was on the trigger again, smooth and sure . . .

And then . . . *No. Too much is wrong.*

Slaton adjusted his sight picture one last time and fired.

———

"Still nothing," said the comm tech.

Sorensen shifted to the supervisor's desk and addressed a bespectacled Black man. "Could the signal be getting jammed?" she asked.

"We've tested these handsets against all known Chinese jamming systems, but that's no guarantee. Electronic warfare is a constantly moving target."

Sorensen sank into a vacant chair and stared at banks of useless monitors. The bombshell dropped on her at Walter Reed loomed larger than ever. Her command and control of a critical mission had been interrupted. That wasn't proof positive, but it came close.

There *was* a leak, and at a very high level.

Her thoughts dove deeper into the abyss when she realized that if Slaton's comm had been compromised, there was a good chance the entire mission would be sabotaged.

And she had no way to warn him.

FORTY-FIVE

Recovering from the recoil, Slaton pulled away from the scope and checked his three o'clock position.

He saw them clearly now, three . . . no, four figures in the treeline beyond the road. They moved in a way that suggested training, one man on point, the others staggered behind. All were crouched low, weapons in hand, and wearing night optical devices.

He shifted back to the window just in time to catch a glimpse of Li running deep into the house. He'd clearly not been hit. An instant later, he was gone— and with him, any chance of a second clean kill.

Slaton looked left, down the sloping hillside, and spotted the second group. Four figures were converging on the half-built house Slaton had commandeered. Altogether that made eight, but there could easily be more. Their movement and tactics convinced him that this was no security team. He was looking at an assault force.

He was trapped, encircled on the high ground. No way out, every angle cut off. Any attempt at engagement, given the odds and the weapon in his hands, would border on suicidal. That thought ended presciently when the first shot rang in, chips of concrete stinging his wrist. The shots hadn't been preceded by any command to surrender, which meant this wasn't any kind of police force. A hail of gunfire erupted from his right, splintering a nearby stack of lumber. He kept low and listened closely to the incoming fire, trying to get a bead on how many weapons he was facing, where they were grouped.

Slaton swung his rifle toward the road, sighted on the nearest attacker. In a tight two-shot sequence, he dropped him, then sent a second man pitchpoling down an embankment. The incoming fire only doubled, now coming from the left as well. He threw himself against the nearest wall. The position was more concealment than cover, enough to buy a few seconds. In that amount of time, he had to find a way out.

His eyes scoured the balcony, desperate for inspiration. The options for escape ranged from poor to irrational. Going out the way he'd arrived was a nonstarter—the shooters on the low side had a clear view of the scaffolding. The road was completely covered.

Every avenue of egress seemed a tactical disaster.

He kept looking, searching.

What came to mind was more a nightmare than a memory. A moment of madness in Malta so many years ago. He sized up the canvas tarp he'd been using to keep the rain at bay. It might be wide enough, strong enough for what he had in mind—or it might not be. The ropes attached to grommets on each corner were the key. He set down his weapon, lunged out, and yanked the tarp toward him; the bricks anchoring the ropes avalanched down. Slaton gathered the canvas close to his chest. If he'd had more time he would have thought things through, folded the tarp in some practical way. As it was, he fumbled only long enough to gather the four ropes attached to the corners. As rounds smacked in all around, he looked at the SRS. He didn't like leaving his only weapon behind, but his hand was forced.

A more devout man would have uttered a prayer before his next move. In two giant strides, Slaton launched himself headlong off the balcony. He flew through space, holding the ropes in a death grip, and snapped the tarp upward like a maid sheeting a bed.

Slaton had parachuted many times in his life, so he was familiar with the painful, yet always comforting, shock of getting a full canopy—energy absorbed and translated into a well-fitted harness. What he felt now was infinitely less reassuring. Not swinging securely beneath a full chute; more like clinging by his fingertips to an overburdened kite.

He saw muzzle flashes in the periphery, heard a staccato chorus of semi-automatic fire as he plunged toward the hillside. For a few seconds he would be completely vulnerable, little more than a giant clay pigeon hurtling through the night sky; surprised shooters all around would be trying to track him in the dim light. The tarp seemed to barely arrest his rate of descent. He guessed the vertical drop was at least eighty feet, but with luck he might land in thick vegetation on the downslope. Rocks would be the worst-case scenario, trees somewhere in the middle.

It all came as no more than a jumble of fleeting thoughts. Slaton's grip on the ropes was wobbly, and in a burst of inspiration he twisted both hands to loop the lines around his wrists.

It was a desperate gamble—completely exposed, he was relying on a combination of surprise and his enemy's poor marksmanship. Never a good bet, but it was all Slaton had. He focused on the only thing he could control: a landing that was going to bring immediate hurt.

In training, airborne instructors always said, "Don't look down. Keep your eyes on the horizon."

Slaton looked down anyway.

In the barest of light, he saw the forest rushing at him like a train. At the last instant he discerned trees, and the same ancient voice reminded him to tuck his chin to protect vital arteries. It seemed like a great idea.

He smacked squarely into a big trunk, his right hip taking the brunt of the impact. He flailed through branches for a time, and then his arms were nearly pulled from their sockets when the tarp caught like an anchor on something. The ropes around his wrists jerked taut, twin nooses breaking his momentum.

Stunned, Slaton hung there for a moment, pain the only thing telling him he was still alive. He tried to acquire his bearings in the ebony darkness. He tasted blood in his mouth, and something had impaled his abdomen. He looked down, trying to gauge how far above the ground he was. He couldn't tell.

There was good news: the gunfire had stopped, at least for the moment, and he'd survived the fall. The less happy reality: the gunfire would start again very soon, and he hadn't yet reached the ground.

The ropes around his left wrist were slack, so he disengaged and reached down toward his abdomen. He felt a broken branch stabbing him. Taking hold of its base, he grimaced and pushed away using his knees. Slaton nearly passed out from the pain, but managed to hold on and got clear.

His right arm was bearing most of his weight, and he explored blindly with his boots, searching for a foothold. On the left side he found a branch, and he tested it with some weight. This gave him another point of contact with the tree. He heard shouting from uphill in an unfamiliar language. Slaton didn't need a translation to know what was being said. *Find him!*

Unwrapping his right wrist, he began to move, and for the best part of a minute he laddered downward. He felt blindly for hand and foot holds, hoping with each move that the next step would reach the forest floor. A gap in the vegetation finally gave him a look down, and Slaton discerned a vague outline beneath him: a great wet boulder glistening in the dim light. Then he saw more problems. He was still twenty feet up, and the old limbs at the bottom of the tree were mostly gone, rotted and broken away—a point proven when the one that was taking most of his weight snapped and sent him into a free-fall.

FORTY-SIX

Sorensen kept trying. She stood behind the duty chief, who presided over an elaborate workstation. Every regional agency asset was lasered in on Hong Kong Island. Unfortunately, it wasn't a particular hotspot in terms of global security, meaning their options were limited.

"Do we not have any overheads at all?" she asked.

"If NRO had repositioned something, it would be different, but that takes days to arrange. As it stands, the only satellite in place at the moment is an electro-optic bird—and that's useless in this storm."

"So we're blind."

"Pretty much."

Sorensen saw a flicker of messages light to the monitor. "What's that?"

The duty chief opened a series of updates, and explained them to Sorensen. "We've tapped into the emergency services switchboard. About three minutes ago, a call of interest was flagged. It looks like gunfire is being reported in the neighborhood where Slaton is working. The police are responding."

Another message arrived.

"Hang on," he said. "There's more."

He opened the new message, but it was so full of

jargon and raw data, Sorensen couldn't make sense of it. It took every bit of restraint she possessed to wait for the translation.

The chief finally said, "We have some new software that automatically analyzes the background noise of selected intercepts. The switchboard call about the gunfire was run immediately, and according to the analysis, at least six weapons could be distinguished in the background. Sounds like quite a firefight." He looked up at Sorensen uneasily. "Any way you look at it, Corsair is in trouble."

Slaton lay in a heap, dazed—his head had hit something hard. He blinked and tried to collect his misfiring thoughts. There was still no gunfire but he distinctly heard voices; that brought an adrenaline surge to get him to his feet. He nearly fell right back over, his hip stinging in pain. He began staggering downhill, moving as fast as the darkness allowed, more feeling than seeing his way through the underbrush. Each step was a battle, and he knew he was making too much noise—a mistake that was proved when a bullet snapped past his head and shredded bark from a nearby tree.

He pushed himself faster, half running, half falling down the steep grade. He tumbled to the ground, but tuned out the agony and got back up. Frantic shouting from behind as more shots cascaded in. He veered right, searching for the creek bed that would guide him to his starting point. If he could reach that, at the edge of the city, his heavily armed pursuers might not follow. At the very least, the gunfire would bring a police response.

Unless it's the police behind me now, he thought, reconsidering his earlier assumption.

He recalled telling Thomas that he would give fifteen minutes notice, and without stopping he reached into his thigh pocket for his phone. As soon as he touched it his spirits sank. He pulled it free, and in the dim light his fears were realized. The screen was shattered beyond repair, the plastic case destroyed. *So much for the hardened model,* he thought. Had it happened when he'd hit the tree? Or when he'd fallen out of it? It hardly mattered—last he'd checked, he had no signal anyway. Slaton threw the phone aside and kept moving.

The time spent studying Goode's maps proved invaluable. He found the creek and tracked it downhill, sloshing through shin-deep water in the center. He made better time, and the gunfire paused again. He could just make out lights through the foliage ahead, a rain-swept blur of yellow in the distance.

The creek began to deepen, swollen by the deluge. Then it became a torrent. He had to move to the edge to keep his balance. Finally Slaton reached the bottom, where the creek spilled into the drainage channel. The scene had changed massively since he'd first gone by. Water cascaded down a series of baffles, and the churning concrete staircase ended in what looked like a river. To his right the channel plunged into the underground portion of the network, a waterfall tumbling into a great pipe that looked big enough to drive a bus through. The main sluice, a mere trickle an hour ago, had gone to whitewater, runoff from the entire mountainside funneling into the system.

He looked back and saw his pursuers fifty yards distant, dark shapes slashing through the trees. His only chance was to cross the channel, yet even if he hadn't been injured Slaton doubted he could reach the far side without being swept away. In the condition he was in, damaged and beaten, it seemed suicidal.

He was weighing a short list of very bad options when movement on the opposite side of the rapids caught his eye. By the spray of a distant streetlight, Thomas's familiar silhouette appeared. He drew to a stop fifty feet to Slaton's left, standing on the far edge casually in his chauffeur's get-up. A handgun was hanging loosely at his side.

Slaton took one step into the torrent, and was about to shout for cover fire when something made him hesitate. The stillness in Thomas's stance, the steadiness of his gaze, flicked a switch in Slaton's head.

The weapon rose quickly, smoothly, aimed not at his pursuers, but squarely at Slaton.

Slaton lunged toward the stair-steps as gunfire erupted from two directions, twisting as he did so. He took a grazing hit across the beltline that sent him sprawling into a concrete pillar. He caromed off, and fell down the last two steps like a salmon tumbling down a ladder. Bullets raked in, their strikes lost in the torrent of whitewater. Slaton hit the main spillway and was immediately swept toward the immense pipe.

Bullets kept coming, their aqueous explosions lost in the maelstrom. Slaton disappeared briefly, bobbed once to the surface, then was pulled under as the deluge swept him away.

The last thing any of the shooters saw was a rag-dolling body disappearing into the great underground spillway.

———

Within a minute the team of mercs were assembled at the shoulder of the spillway. Only six remained, and the commander, a sergeant-major, called across the divide to their employer.

"We lost two men at the top."

"Wounded or killed?" Monkh replied, shouting to be heard over the roiling whitewater.

The sergeant shook his head as a reply.

Monkh, who for some reason was wearing a chauffeur's uniform, nodded. He then removed a handset and motioned for the commander to initiate a call—the roar of the whitewater was deafening.

The sergeant turned, held out his hand, and one of his men produced the big radio from his backpack. The connection went through, and the sergeant said, "We don't have much time. The police will be slow, but they are not completely incompetent."

"You and your men did well. I want to tell them about the bonus each of you can expect."

The sergeant motioned to his men, and they edged closer to hear, everyone's attention piqued. They were in a tight arc around him, their weapons at their sides and their thoughts halfway home, when Monkh tapped up a keypad on his phone and input a three-digit sequence.

The explosion was muted from across the raging divide, but the shaped Semtex charge inside the comm brick, surrounded by five hundred flechettes, was devastating. All six men were cut down by the razor-sharp projectiles. For a moment Monkh stood still, waiting for the smoke to be swept clear by the pulsing wind. Once it was, he noted that only one man was still moving. The bloodiest of the bunch, his hands clutched his shredded throat.

Monkh had to work quickly now. Even against the storm, the sound of the explosion would have carried.

Speed. Speed has always been my advantage.

He pocketed his phone and pulled out his Glock a second time. In an act he rationalized as mercy, he settled the red dot on the man who was moving. Two shots later, he stepped through the others, each of the team taking two rounds to the head. The count in Monkh's head, reliable as ever, told him he had one round remaining. He instinctively switched to a fresh magazine, then secured the weapon in a concealed holster.

Monkh reflected on the outcome. Things had gone largely as planned. There had been, from the outset, only one real question. Would his hirelings kill the assassin at the top of the hill, or would they drive him into Monkh's own sight like so many hunting dogs?

Now he had his answer.

He picked up a small backpack near his feet and removed a full kilo of heroin. Taking a knife sheathed beneath his uniform vest, he slashed the plastic packaging twice, took careful aim, and launched the brick of brown powder across the torrent. It landed squarely amid the corpses, some of the heroin spilling out onto the ground. He kicked the empty backpack into the raging current and watched it tumble downstream.

Monkh turned and walked back toward the city.

On the way to the van he sent two text messages using different phones. The first was received in the basement engine room of the United Kingdom's Hong Kong consulate, and would soon be relayed to the CIA operations center in Langley, Virginia. The most pertinent words came at the end: Mission aborted. Asset lost.

The second message was routed directly, and received on a secure handset seven miles southeast of CIA headquarters. The lone recipient read it in a quiet corner of the White House: Mission complete. Corsair eliminated.

FORTY-SEVEN

Slaton gasped for breath, his body giving out. He was tumbling through darkness, the only illumination coming from overhead floodlights that swept past at regular intervals. He submerged again and again, the water surging relentlessly. His lungs were filling fast with muddy mountain runoff.

His hands thrashed wildly, grasping for any purchase. They found only smooth concrete walls all around. He surfaced briefly, and coughed out water before sucking in another desperate breath. Debris swirled around him, plastic water bottles, tree branches, and discarded surgical masks. He bounded from one wall to the other, a hellish water park ride without end.

Yet there *would* be an end. His strength was ebbing fast, his injuries compounding. The equation was simple—get out soon or die.

Slaton concentrated, trying to recall the diagram he had seen of the drainage system. He'd viewed the network as little more than a reference, a guide for infil and exfil. It was so massive, so complex, he never could have memorized it all. But there had to be a way out. As far as he could remember, one of two destinations awaited: he was either headed for a storage reservoir deep underground, or he would be swept

into the sea. One carried the promise of never seeing daylight again, while the other guaranteed miles of
battering ahead. Either would be fatal.

It was all Slaton could to keep his head above
water, steal the occasional lungful of air. Another
light swept past above, and as it did one of his hands
smacked something metallic. The pain barely registered. He twisted his hips, trying to rise higher in the
water, and in the dim light he caught a glimpse of sal-
vation: disappearing behind him, a metal ladder rising out of the torrent.

Through the haze of pain, logic took hold. Municipal tunnels had to be serviced, and that required
access. Ladders and lighting. He spun again, using
his last reserve of strength to stabilize in the deluge.
The tunnel seemed to be curving, and for a time he
saw nothing. Then a jaundiced yellow orb appeared
ahead. The ladder he'd seen was on the right. Were all
of them on that side? Did every light correlate to a
ladder? The tunnel was twenty feet wide, and at the
speed he was traveling Slaton was forced to choose.

He paddled awkwardly toward the right wall, and
thirty feet away he spotted it—tight to the vertical
wall, the skeletal frame of a metal ladder. Near the
edge he spun into an eddy and momentarily lost sight
of it. He twisted back forward with his hands outstretched, only to be struck squarely in the face by the
metal siderail.

Slaton saw stars, but clutched with both hands,
searching blindly for a handhold. He caught the rail
with his right hand, yet the force of the current nearly
tore it free. With three clawing fingertips, he twisted
closer, his body rippling like a flag in a gale. His left
arm wasn't fully functional, but he managed to get a
hand on a step. Pulling in tight, he barnacled against

the wall. Then he got a knee to the bottom rung. With a final surge, Slaton hauled himself upward.

Each step was like a mountain, every movement mired in quicksand, but at last he was free of the torrent. He kept climbing, and six rungs later the ladder topped out on a long metal catwalk. Slaton had no idea where it led, and didn't care. He only knew he was out of the water.

He struggled onto a knee, but wobbled when he tried to stand. He felt a warm wetness on his beltline that had nothing to do with stormwater. The world seemed to waver, and he clutched a handrail near the wall. Slaton touched it briefly, but his fingers slipped away. He hovered for a moment, poised like a breaking wave. Then he face-planted on the metal-mesh walkway and passed out cold.

It was a fail on so many levels.

Sorensen sank into a chair behind a vacant ops center workstation as the battery of reports arrived. Gunfire on Victoria Peak. A possible explosion. The Hong Kong police were responding, but so far there were no intercepts to suggest what they'd found. Slaton's phone remained off line.

Just when she thought her day couldn't get worse, word came that the White House wanted an update on the mission.

Of course they do, she thought cynically.

The request was for a videoconference, as soon as possible, yet there was nothing to suggest who might be on the other end. The vice president seemed likely, but assuredly there would be others. And somewhere among them, very possibly, a traitor.

It occurred to Sorensen that she needed time to

prepare. There were things that needed to be said. Others that didn't. As far as she knew, no one other than herself, Richard Cleveland, and one doctor knew that Elayne Cleveland had regained consciousness. And by order of the president—the real president— she had to keep it that way. Never in her life had Sorensen gone into a meeting with so much baggage. She was in a vise, trapped between the two most powerful politicians in the country, both of whom considered themselves to be in charge. And with the wild card of a high-level traitor floating in their midst.

She replied to the White House request with the first of what would be many lies. She said the mission was still ongoing, and that she would call with a briefing as soon as events permitted. The equivalent of putting the acting president on hold.

The fabrication didn't bother Sorensen one bit. Her first loyalty, in that moment, was to neither king nor country. She had always considered herself a thoughtful leader, one who backed those under her command. In this case, she couldn't deny a special bond with Slaton. She trusted him unfailingly, and knew that he, in turn, trusted her. With his mission going horribly wrong, Sorensen would do everything in her power to make it right.

I don't know what I've gotten you into, David. But I will do my damnedest get you out.

FORTY-EIGHT

Chen Jing stopped at the curb before chasing his ball into the street. Six years old, his mother had taught him to be careful.

"Go on!" said his friend Yulong, who'd kicked the ball over the fence.

Jing wasn't bothered by his friend's impatience. The rain had finally let up, and they'd been itching to get outside and play under the streetlights before being sent to bed. He looked both ways, not that it was really necessary. They lived in the last building on a dead-end street, and few cars ever made it this far.

Jing crossed uneventfully and pulled his bright blue kickball out of a muddy gutter. He kicked it back over the courtyard fence where Yulong was waiting. He had just started back across the street when something moved in the middle of the road.

Jing stopped a few steps away, his eyes fixed on the square metal plate built into the street. He was certain it had moved, and one edge now rested crookedly on the rim. He had seen the big plate a thousand times, yet wasn't quite sure what it was. His father had told him it covered some kind of drain, and also that in most countries they were round. His big brother had warned him it sealed a hole where monsters lived.

Jing didn't believe in monsters.

The heavy plate moved a second time, and then began sliding to one side with a heavy scraping sound.

Transfixed, and perhaps a little frightened, Jing looked up and down the street, hoping for a familiar face. He saw no one. His eyes went wide when a hand emerged from the opening, clawing as if from out of a grave. Without thinking, he took a step back, and to his amazement a man crawled out.

At least, he thought it was a man.

His hair was wet and matted, and his tattered clothing sodden with mud. He moved like a crab at first, sidling clear of the hole. Then, with what looked like considerable effort, he stood crookedly in the spill of a streetlight. Jing saw what looked like a bloodstain on the man's trousers. His features were Western, his hair light in color, although it was hard to be sure given how muddy he was.

The man, if that's what it was, settled his eyes momentarily on Jing. The boy stood paralyzed, even after the creature smiled at him.

Then, without a word, the figure went limping up the street.

Chen Jing shivered once, took a deep breath, and ran toward home.

Slaton heard sirens wailing on nearby streets, no doubt responding to the chaos on the hillside. He was moving through an alley, and just ahead a bustling street loomed. Pausing in an alcove with a decent spray of light, he gingerly pulled the waistband of his pants lower to get a look at his abdomen. A wave of pain sent him reeling into the nearby wall. He took a deep breath and kept going. The wound was six inches long, just below the beltline. There was no entry or exit, just a deep, continuous graze. It was presently oozing blood, but he saw no pulsing flow. Slaton recalled twisting in the instant before the last volley of shots came. That dumb-luck move had saved him from a gunshot that would have been fatal.

He had no idea how long he'd lain unconscious on the subterranean catwalk, but the stiffness of his limbs and the deepness of the night suggested it had been at least an hour. He continued his self-triage. He could barely put weight on his right hip, but the damage seemed internal. The most critical injury, he suspected, was the puncture wound he'd suffered colliding with the tree. Just beneath his lowest right rib, it was deep, bleeding badly, and hurt like hell. There were any number of vital organs in the area that might be damaged. More ominously for the mid-term, Slaton had been tumbling like a shoe in a washing machine through filthy stormwater—he reckoned his chances of getting an infection were exceedingly high. He chided himself for not carrying a field first aid kit. A packet of clotting agent and some antibiotics would have been a godsend. He noted a half dozen other cuts and bruises, but none seemed serious.

Slaton started moving again, his shoes squishing like wet sponges with every step. At least they had stayed attached through the rapids, he thought—plus one point for wearing good tactical clothing. He stole a clean shirt from the clothesline of an apartment porch, and two corners later he stopped to put it on. Removing his old shirt was an exercise in pain. Once it was off, he gripped a torn edge and began tearing off strips of fabric. He used the cleanest strips as makeshift bandages for his two worst wounds, wrapping as tightly as he could. The rest he used to wipe away mud and bloodstains before tossing them in a nearby garbage bin. He donned the new shirt—it was still damp from being laundered, but that could be written off to the rain. After finger combing his hair into place, and wiping the last of the blood from his hands, he decided his appearance was something near normal.

With two minor victories behind him—escaping from the deluge and cleaning up his appearance— Slaton began to think more positively. He was alive. He was functioning.

More sirens in the distance. On the matter of police, Slaton was thankful to be in Hong Kong, and now of all times. The once-efficient British colony was being subsumed by communist China, and even decades after the transition, according to a CIA report he'd seen, its police and security services were shambolic. Senior administrators had been replaced by party sycophants, while drowsy middle managers coasted toward retirement. It was a recipe for infighting, for operational disarray. The storm would only hamper the response further.

Still, relying on incompetence was hardly a strategy. Slaton had significant near-term needs to address. Sutures, antibiotics, food, a place to rest. He needed all of that. And he needed it soon.

The plan that had brought him here, so well-executed in the beginning, had gone completely off the rails. The question of who or what was responsible had to be left for later. Tonight was about survival.

Slaton limped off toward the lights of the boulevard ahead.

FORTY-NINE

Desperate for information, Sorensen tried to approach her problem logically. All at once, it occurred to her that another source had gone silent.

"What about our NOC?" she asked the comm officer. "Is his handset still offline?"

It took the young man thirty seconds to confirm it. "He's still dark as well."

Of course he is, she thought.

Sorensen hadn't liked the idea of using outside help to begin with, but given the time constraints there had been little choice. And in Hong Kong, there was only one ally available for assistance.

Cultivated over a century of administration, the British had long run the best networks in Hong Kong. That being the case, Sorensen had reached out to Louis Rudbart, chief of MI-6's Hong Kong station. She had worked with Rudbart years ago in Europe, and knew him to be a steady hand. In recent days she had spoken with him twice to coordinate backing for Slaton's mission. Sorensen had shared little about the greater objective, but that was hardly uncommon. Rudbart had put her in contact with a local, non-official-cover asset who the Brits had used previously and deemed reliable. For two days it had worked brilliantly. According to Slaton, the NOC, who went by the name

Thomas, had been integral to the successful mission that eliminated Yao.

Tonight's mission, however, had gone very differently. She'd been told an hour ago that the comm unit carried by the NOC was also offline. Sorensen saw two possibilities. He was either running scared and had shut his phone down, or it had been compromised in the same manner as Slaton's.

With no direct link to anyone involved in the op, Sorensen decided to go back to square one. She put through a call to the British consulate in Hong Kong. The line was secure, and after one shunt from an operator, Rudbart picked up immediately. It wasn't lost on Sorensen that it was after ten o'clock in Hong Kong.

"Hello, Anna. I was about to call you," Rudbart said. His accent reflected Eton and Oxford.

She said, "We've lost touch with both our asset and the NOC you recommended, Louis. On top of that, we're getting intel that suggests our mission may have gone south. What can you tell me?"

"I'll assume we're talking about the ruckus over on Hong Kong Island?"

"We are," she replied.

"The chatter we're hearing isn't good, but I can tell you we just received a message from the NOC—that's why I was about to call you."

"Why would he reach out to you? This was our op." Sorensen immediately regretted the comment. It was pushy, bordering on mistrustful. "I'm sorry, Louis. My frustration level is high."

"Not to worry. I know how stressful it can be when things don't go to script. The message from the NOC arrived via a comm channel we'd previously set up with him."

"Like I said, we lost our own link. Maybe that was he only way he felt safe reaching out."

"Possibly. I'll read you the entire message." After . pause and a few keystrokes in the background, he aid, "'Pickup and infil successful. While waiting for gress, heard gunfire on hill, multiple weapons. At ally point saw asset taken down. Mission aborted. As-et lost. Going dark.'"

Sorensen felt the world fall away under her. She •layed the words back in her mind, searching for some race of hope. There was none. *Asset lost.*

A prolonged silence ensued before Rudbart said, I'm sorry, Anna. I wish I had more positive news. If ve hear anything more from him, I'll pass it along nmediately. As soon as I read this, I reached out to ny best police source for details. He told me there was major dustup on Hong Kong Island. The police re-ponded to multiple reports of gunfire at the base of /ictoria Peak. The first units to arrive heard a firefight 1 the distance, but by the time they reached the scene he worst had played out. Six bodies were discovered t the head of the island's spillway network."

Sorensen braced herself. "Any descriptions of the ictims?"

"Curiously, all appear to be Filipino."

"Filipino?"

"That's right. Even more curious, they appear to ave been killed by some kind of explosive device."

"Explosive device?" She felt the situation bounding ito the surreal. "My asset would never have used any-hing like that."

"I thought it seemed a bit over the top. For what 's worth, whoever was responsible added an assas-in's coup de grace—two rounds to the head for each ictim, almost assuredly after the explosion. There was also a significant amount of heroin scattered around the scene."

"Heroin," Sorensen repeated. "Anything else?"

"Is that not enough?"

She took a moment to process everything, and it occurred to her that no mention was made of gunfire at the top of the hill. Had Slaton ever reached it? Were Li and Zhao unharmed, or had the police simply not discovered that crime scene yet? She recalled Thomas's report: Slaton had gone down at the "rally point." Having been briefed on the plan, she knew this to be the spillway.

She said, "If these Filipinos were executed, as you say, then they were collateral damage. I don't see any connection to what my asset was undertaking."

"Perhaps not directly. But if you're suggesting that your man stumbled into a drug transfer—"

"No, of course not. Someone brought this team in, but it wasn't our doing. I'd guess that whoever hired these men killed them as an operational security measure, then added the drugs in the aftermath to muddy the waters, make it look like organized crime."

"Not the rules you or I would play by, but it makes a certain sense. And I suspect it will be effective. Since coming under Chinese administration, the police here always lean toward the easy answer."

"But you're sure *none* of the victims were Western in appearance?"

"That's what I was told."

"So it's possible—"

"There *is* one other thing, Anna. I'm told a significant bloodstain was found not far away, on a column by the spillway. The police are operating on the assumption that one body might have been swept away in what was a very strong current. A search of the tunnel network is taking place as we speak. Combine this with the NOC's account of your asset's fate . . ."

"I understand," Sorensen said. Except she didn't.

Filipinos, explosions, heroin, six bodies. And no word whatsoever regarding the fate of the true targets of the mission. She tried to put it all together, a hopelessly incoherent array of facts. In the end, she said, "Do you expect any further updates?"

Rudbart hesitated. "Anna, please understand . . . my source at the police department is very high level. And, given the difficult situation here, one that we can't afford to compromise. Every communication increases the level of risk."

Sorensen let it go—she knew how protective station chiefs could be of hard-won local sources. "I understand, Louis."

"He did promise to notify me if another body was recovered. Unfortunately, the rain last night was torrential, and under conditions like that the spillway goes to whitewater. When the reservoirs fill, the overflow goes out to sea. If remains are ever recovered, it will likely take days."

Sorensen could think of no reply.

"If it should come to that," he ventured, "would you like us to claim the body?"

"Just keep me posted," she managed. After a thoughtful pause, she added, "Tell me, Louis . . . do you trust this NOC?"

"As much as I trust any foreign national in this business."

It was a problematic answer. And an honest one. "All right. If you hear from him, tell him it's imperative that he contact us."

"I will. But based on our previous dealings with him . . . I wouldn't count on it. He's proven himself useful in the field, but when operations end he has a distinct tendency to go off-grid. Given the chaos level last night . . . I don't expect to hear from him anytime soon."

Sorensen retreated to her office after the call ended. She sat behind a desk stacked with ignored file folders, and never considered waking the nearby computer. The clutter in her head took a far higher priority.

Zhao and Li might be alive. A team of armed Filipinos were dead and covered in heroin. Slaton, by all accounts, was also a casualty. And an asset on loan from the Brits might never be heard from again. Her head spun with possibilities, yet the one thing that kept recurring was what she'd heard at Walter Reed: Elayne Cleveland suspected a mole high in the U.S. government.

This was central to everything. And, she was quite sure, what had doomed Slaton's mission.

Regardless of who had hired these Filipino paramilitaries, the fact that they'd appeared at such a critical juncture was unconditionally damning. Operational security had been breached. Someone had learned that Slaton was coming for Zhao and Li. They knew when and where the op was going down. Could that same person have fingered Zhao and Li to begin with? Perhaps manipulated the CIA's source in Beijing? It seemed likely.

Sorensen needed to identify the traitor, and she knew precisely where to begin: the Director of Homeland Security. Vince Seward had been ordered by the president to get to the bottom of the leak. He was to identify who had been making calls from the White House to members of The Trident, and to do it with the utmost of secrecy. Might Seward have already succeeded? It was possible, she decided. But according to Richard Cleveland, he was to report his findings to no one but the president herself.

One more complication.

Sorensen's thoughts snapped back to her most pressing problem.

Where was David?

She had lost operators before, and it always hit hard. Yet this mission, and Slaton's involvement in it, was wholly on her shoulders. She had talked him into it, hammered through the logistics. Even spirited his family to a safe place. Never before had an op felt so . . . personal.

Might Slaton have at last crossed the fine line? Put himself in a position where he could no longer beat the odds? *Or did I push him over that line?* Not for the first time, Sorensen wondered whether she'd condemned an asset to becoming a star on the agency's Memorial Wall.

If only for the sake of her own sanity, she had to verify what had happened. But how?

She recalled Rudbart mentioning blood evidence on a concrete pillar. If no body was found, might the authorities in Hong Kong test the sample for DNA? China was gathering DNA profiles on all its citizens, so it seemed a natural step. If that happened, could Rudbart access the results? Possibly. Yet when Sorensen extended the idea, she ended up in as depressing a cul de sac as she'd ever faced. The CIA had no sample of David Slaton's DNA on file to compare. Even more disconcertingly, she realized where she would have to go to obtain the nearest genetic match.

To a four-year-old boy now lost in the wilds of Canada.

FIFTY

Slaton had one immediate objective: avoid drawing attention while he came up with a plan.

He had left his wallet, containing his ID and money, in Thomas's van. What seemed a sound precaution at the time had proved an egregious error. The voice of an old Mossad instructor pinballed in the back of his mind: *Always, always carry cash.*

What else had he screwed up?

Only hours ago everything had been going to script. Now he was badly injured, and his only in-country help, Thomas, had tried to kill him. That, above all else, turned the op on its head. He thought back to his first meeting with Thomas, the van ride to Macau. Slaton had sensed the man had training, yet he'd taken it as a positive. Trusted that others had vetted him. *One more mistake.*

If that wasn't enough, the backing he'd enjoyed from the world's most capable intelligence agency was now off the table. He recalled his sat-phone losing its signal in the final critical moments. At the time he'd written it off to a technical glitch, never considering that the connection was being jammed or intentionally disabled. Now that seemed a near certainly, and the phone was destroyed anyway.

Slaton thought back to the two shots he'd taken

from the balcony. He'd put Zhao down with the first, and then had Li in his sight. Then, for reasons he couldn't quantify, he'd hesitated. Even more inexplicably, he'd deliberately pushed the second shot wide at the last instant. Why?

No immediate answer came, and he forced it away. Now wasn't the time for mission eulogies or analysis.

Tonight was all about survival.

There had been no time to procure a safe house—a standard contingency on most missions—so finding a place to hole up became the highest priority. He kept moving, keeping to alleys wherever possible, and tried to imitate a normal stride when forced to walk in the open. Slaton was sweating despite the cool rain, his heart racing from the combination of shock and exertion. He stopped once to lean on a bus stop bench, but started moving again when a police car appeared up the street. He was nearing the center of Sheung Wan, which took him away from known threats, and hopefully closer to opportunities for recovery.

The rain was abating, but thanks to the storm the streets were uncrowded and the traffic was light. The sounds of the city were lost to the rush of rain through gutters. Slaton crossed a quiet street, tucking his chin low as people did in inclement weather. He ducked into an alley on the far side, little more than a walking path between two buildings. On both sides he saw service doors for various small businesses; the floors above appeared to be apartments. He studied the doors, a few of which were labeled in both English and Cantonese. A hair salon, a coffee shop, a convenience store. All were presumably closed this time of night. Slaton tried the doors but found them locked tight. None would have been an ideal refuge, but he had to find something. A wave of nausea struck, and he paused to let it pass, holding onto a doorknob for support.

He moved toward the next street and paused at the top of the alley. This block looked different than the one behind him. Instead of grocery stores and electronics shops, he saw massage parlors and cheap hotels. Neon signs, in every imaginable hue, blinked and beckoned, as if sin was a holiday to be celebrated. Lone men stopped to chat with girls in alcoves. A woman in a tight black dress and spiked heels talked animatedly to what looked like a hotel proprietor, and on the wall behind them prices were listed like a coffee shop menu. Slaton had stumbled into Sheung Wan's dark heart, and he felt its arrhythmia.

He knew little about prostitution in Hong Kong, aside from the fact that it was legal. The CCP would never promote red light districts, but it was an institution that had been here far longer than communism, and would, invariably, outlast the glorious leader of the moment. Like most places these days, he supposed assignations were arranged online, consummated in cheap hourly rooms. Slaton studied the sidewalks carefully. Like the rest of the city, he saw a smattering of Western faces. Everyone seemed to move cautiously, slouching and wary. All of which was good. He would not stand out.

A pair of jagged voices suddenly seized his attention. One was male, loud and accusative. The other female, low and pleading. Slaton tracked the sounds to an opposing alley, across the street and to the right. A woman had her back to a mildewed wall. Three men faced her in a crescent formation. The man in the middle, the tallest of the three, was wearing a long black jacket. From across the street Slaton saw a gold chain around his neck that would have anchored a boat. The other two men were a few steps back. Both stood still and rigid, twin bastions at the entrance of a fort.

The girl's shoulders were pressed against the wall as chain man put a bony finger to her chest, just above her bosom. She was wearing a short skirt and tight low-cut blouse. Her features were Asian, although perhaps not Chinese. Her black hair was tinged with streaks of magenta, and even from across the street her red lips glinted in the light.

Slaton shifted to his right, deeper into the shadows. The twisting motion brought an electric jolt down his right leg. He steadied himself against a brick wall, and the pain ebbed. He looked at his shirt and saw blood—the puncture wound bleeding again. His right leg was trembling.

As much as he didn't want to admit it, his situation was increasingly dire. His condition was worsening, and after the stormwater bath, infection of his wounds seemed a virtual lock. Slaton didn't just need a first aid kit—he was going to need a doctor, meds, a place to rest. A place where no one would alert the authorities.

Bottom line—he had to get someone on his side.

With his options narrowing, and time critical, he looked across the street and strategized a way to get it all.

FIFTY-ONE

There is only one city in the world. It is home to count-less people, each with public dreams and private wor-ries. Their essential needs are stacked in the usual pyramid. Food and clothing, shelter and security, sex and spirituality. The interplay between them all—contests of haves and have-nots, the hard-working and the lazy, the devout and the bohemian—is the fire of daily life. No matter the continent or country, the architecture or language, sweeping similarities are hardwired. There is only one city in the world because there is only one kind of human.

The pimp kept shouting.

The girl had gone quiet.

Slaton checked up and down the street from the re-cesses of the alley, saw perhaps ten people in either direction. Inside a nearby doorway a group of young girls were sitting on stools, all of them smoking and chatting. No one seemed interested in the altercation in the alley.

Slaton heard a few of the man's words. He was speaking English, which was notable in itself.

. . . back to Thailand.

. . . you are lying!

He raised his hand to her face.

The girl shrank back. She was thin, bordering on

emaciated. A good gust of wind might sweep her away.

Slaton tensed. Fifty feet away, and well concealed, he was facing no risk. Yet he knew where his thoughts were headed. It wasn't an ideal scenario. He was looking at three men, all of whom would be comfortable with violence. He himself was severely injured. Slaton tried to not view the situation from a moral standpoint—not as a matter of right and wrong, but rather as a tactical opportunity. He saw a strong chance of procuring money, and he could gain an ally. An ally who, through some combination of bribery, coercion, or trust, might conceivably help him out of his bind.

Slaton was contemplating the situation, weighing whether he might find a better one, when things went downhill. The pimp reared back and punched the girl in the face. She fell to her knees, one hand going to her cheek.

Operational needs went out the window.

Slaton didn't move. At least, not yet. Something didn't make sense. The blow had been full force, delivered directly to her face. A pimp might slap a girl, but damaging the merchandise seemed self-defeating. Had she stolen money? Said too much to a cop? Whatever the transgression, it had to be serious. Possibly career-ending.

The pimp lifted the girl forcibly to her feet and shoved her back against the wall. When his hand threatened a second strike, Slaton's decision was made.

Since leaving the storm drain, he had struggled to maintain a normal appearance. Walking in a straight line was a challenge, some muscles working, others misfiring. Before committing to something that might be beyond his abilities, Slaton tested the waters. He rotated his arms, one at a time, mimicking a truncated striking motion. Both seemed more or less operable. He next checked the legs, planting and shifting weight. He could set his right leg in a solid stance, but twisting from that hip was agony.

So adapt.

He saw a fist-size lump of cement on the ground nearby. He picked it up, palmed it in his right hand, and set out across the street.

Slaton made no attempt to mask his limp, which could easily pass for inebriation. He stooped a bit to lessen his height, and locked his eyes on the woman. Twenty feet away, he tried for what he thought was a leer. A lonely male tourist looking for a good time. A man with a predilection for hard drink and soft women.

It seemed to work. The two heavies noticed his approach, but were clearly switched off. Both looked bored. The nearest of the two was beefy and muscled up, with bowl-cut black hair that fit his head like a helmet. He was wearing tight clothes—good for projecting bulk, but lousy for hiding weapons, which Slaton saw no sign of. In the local league of thugs, he would be a serious player. Possibly a regional champ. The other man, smaller and hatched-faced, worried Slaton more. Scrawny guys invariably carried weapons, and the fact that his shirttail was hanging loosely over his pants almost guaranteed it. Slaton figured him for a knife, but a small-caliber handgun wasn't out of the question.

He was five steps away when the pimp noticed him. Slaton discreetly checked up and down the street. There were still a few people in sight, a mix of shady characters, but no one that concerned him.

"Hello there," Slaton began, going for a slurred British accent.

The pimp turned and looked him over with a king-of-the-jungle stare. He was round and fair-skinned, with a receding hairline and reptilian eyes. Up close he bore a vague resemblance to Mao.

"How much?" Slaton asked, addressing the pimp as if the woman was a piece of chattel.

The pimp scratched his tattooed neck, contemplating. "I get you another girl."

"No, I want this one," Slaton argued. He almost added something about liking a girl who could take a punch, but didn't want to overplay his hand. Instead, he suggested he would pay a good price. As he talked, Slaton edged slightly toward the bigger guard, ending up an arm's length away. Close enough to smell his sour breath.

Both guards seemed bemused by the drunk Brit. The pugilist's meaty arms were crossed indifferently. The hatchet-faced man began texting on his phone. Slaton doubted he was calling for backup.

"Come back tomorrow," said the pimp.

"I can't, my business is done and I'm leaving early."

The pimp looked Slaton up and down, suddenly skeptical. "What kind of business is that?"

Slaton planted his feet precisely, measured the distance to the big man on his right. He took a firmer grip on the lump of cement in his right hand. Behind a drunken smile, he looked conspiratorially left and right along the street, and then said, "I'm a CIA assassin."

The two guards looked up abruptly. Apparently, they spoke English after all. All three men regarded Slaton, his crooked posture and grubby countenance.

The beefy man chuckled first, and soon all three were laughing unreservedly.

Slaton smiled like a man who'd delivered the perfect punch line. With lightning speed, he swung the cement chunk in a roundhouse blow that landed squarely on the big man's temple. It was a vicious strike, delivered with all the force he could muster. On contact, Slaton lost his grip on the concrete.

As the man began to collapse, Slaton spun toward the hatchet-faced man. He was already reacting, core aggression circuitry in his brain going on autopilot. His hand was behind his back, reaching along the belt-line. Slaton seized his right arm as the blade of a knife appeared. But knives were only good if you could control them, and the moment it cleared the man's hip Slaton took over.

He leveraged his superior size and ignored the pain in his hip. Knowing the man would naturally draw the blade up and forward, he used all his strength to redirect motion: farther up and toward the man's throat. He twisted the cutting edge toward his neck, just below the jawline, the vital juncture where nerves and arteries bundled toward the brain.

The man realized too late what was happening, and the blade sliced deep into the soft flesh of his neck. With firm control of the blade, Slaton shoved it deeper and the man sank to the asphalt clutching his bloody throat.

He whirled toward the pimp.

The man looked more livid than scared, a thunderhead in black leather. The wild look in his eyes made Slaton think he was amped up on something. He pulled his right arm back and stepped in with a punch. Slaton surged toward him, giving the swing no chance to develop. He met the pimp chest to chest, reached down, and got both hands on his heavy gold chain. Slaton tried to spin right, but his hip gave out and pain shot through his ribcage. He collapsed to the ground, but his hands never lost their grip. Slaton ended up on his back, with the pimp on top of him and facing away. The massive chain was still around his neck.

Slaton twisted the chain tighter. The pimp gagged and flailed, but his hands were useless with Slaton behind him. A wrestler might have gotten out of it, managed a reversal against an injured opponent. But this man was no trained fighter. The pimp's struggles only used more oxygen, and thirty seconds later he stopped moving. Slaton's hands were nearly numb from torquing the chain, but he didn't let go. Not until he was absolutely sure.

He pushed the body away and tried to stand. Pain flared in his abdomen and he dropped back to one knee. He managed to stand on the second try.

For the first time since the melee began, Slaton looked at the girl. She hadn't moved, but was frozen against the grimy wall. He was thankful she hadn't bolted, which he knew was a possibility. He was in no condition to chase her.

"Why you do that?" she asked in pidgin English.

"You're welcome."

"You kill them."

He looked down at the three men. The skinny guard was bleeding out, while the pimp lay on the sidewalk flat on his back, his legs together and arms wide in a Jesus pose. Slaton pointed to the unconscious third man. "That one will come around."

Her expression went from astonishment to angst. "What will I do now?"

"Maybe something different," he suggested.

She pointed to the dead pimp, and said in a wobbly voice, "His brother will come. He will kill me."

"Not if he can't find you. Is there somewhere—" Slaton suddenly felt lightheaded. He leaned into the wall to stay upright.

The girl looked up and down the street. The bodies were deep enough in the alley that none were readily visible. Slaton saw no sign of an alarm being raised . . . not yet.

"We need to leave," he said, floating the plural pronoun.

She looked at him, then cautiously came closer. She was staring at his shirt. Slaton looked down and saw blood on his abdomen. A *lot* of blood.

"You are hurt," she said.

"Yes."

"The knife?"

"No, something else, before this."

He saw thoughts spinning in her head, decisions being made. Perhaps he should have lied, told her it *was* from the knife, implying he'd been hurt coming to her rescue. Slaton was fading fast, with no Plan B.

She finally said, "You come with me."

He felt a wash of relief.

She put an arm around his back and together they limped away.

The police didn't arrive at the alley for nearly half an hour. They might have been quicker if they hadn't been preoccupied with a massacre at the base of Victoria Peak. On top of that, the local precinct was long anesthetized to violence in the red light district.

They found only one man alive in the alley. He was dazed and seeing double, with a welt on his head the size of a golf ball; he probably would have run away if he could have figured out which of the two sidewalks in front of him was real. All three victims were familiar, minor local ruffians who worked for the neighborhood boss. When ambulances came to remove them, there was plenty of gawking from the gathered crowd but not a single shed tear.

The junior investigator assigned to the case arrived soon after. He was already piqued to have not drawn the more spectacular crime two miles away. On appearances, the scenes could not have appeared more different, one a military-grade spectacle, the other senseless gang warfare. For that reason, no link was drawn between them that night.

Nor would it ever be.

FIFTY-TWO

With each step Slaton felt weaker. He could no longer walk without help—her arm around his waist was the only thing keeping him going. How long had they been walking? Twenty minutes? Thirty?

He had no idea where they were going. His senses of time and direction, typically unerring, were falling offline fast. The rain had stopped, but the temperature was dropping and Slaton was shivering uncontrollably. Hypothermia, augmented by loss of blood and shock. He had never felt so vulnerable. He needed first aid, security, and rest, in that order.

For all of it he was dependent on a stranger.

"We are close now," she said reassuringly. The unsteadiness he'd heard in her voice earlier was gone. She looked over her shoulder occasionally, searching for recurring silhouettes or familiar cars. In terms of surveillance detection, it was nothing polished. Closer to simple street smarts. The difference between the two was often subtle, little more than style points. Yet for Slaton it was convincing—it told him she was on his side.

He coughed up more stormwater, and asked raggedly, "Where are we going?"

"Safe place. I take care of you."

"We can't go to your place," he said, some part of

his tactical brain still functioning. "Not after what happened."

"No, much better."

Slaton turned and studied her. What he saw raised no alarms. No calculation or deceit; something closer to humanitarianism. A woman helping a dog that had been struck by a car. Beyond motive, he sensed something else . . . she was confident. They stumbled along in unison, a hooker and a drunk. Not invisible, but unremarkable.

At last, they arrived.

The entrance to the building was charmless, thirty feet of scuffed linoleum and stained plasterboard. They encountered no one on the way to the stairwell—it was, after all, close to midnight. She helped him up the stairs, and after five flights he could barely stand.

They turned into a hall, and she drew to a stop at the second door on the right. She produced a key, and held him upright with one hand while she battled a corroded lock with the other. He instinctively checked the door frame for wires or sensors, only to realize there would be no alarm—it wasn't that kind of place. Slaton was losing focus, his mind swirling toward incoherence. He concentrated on the hallway, and it reinforced what he'd seen outside. Small building, dated and worn; six floors, maybe ten units per floor. The air was tinged with mildew and burned cooking oil. He heard a TV down the hall.

His dizziness returned, worse than ever. Shock was winning.

He felt the need so say something, if for no other reason than to hear his own voice. "I don't know your name."

"Suzy," she said automatically.

"No . . . your real name."

She stopped fumbling and regarded him. "My name is Mali."

Slaton heard the clank of the deadbolt. "It's good to meet you, Mali. My name is . . . is . . ."

Before Slaton could finish, the world began spinning. And then it was gone.

"What the hell happened?" bristled the acting president of the United States.

"We're trying to work it out," Sorensen replied, surprised by Quarrels's venom.

Thankfully, he wasn't in the same room. Sorensen was at Langley, beaming a secure videoconference to the White House Situation Room. Also on the other end were Matt Gross, CIA director Eraclides, DNI John Nichols, and Secretary of State Robert Shawcross. Sorensen suspected there might be others present, aides and NSC staff, but they weren't in view. It hardly mattered. She could only assume that somewhere in the room lay a traitor.

And her briefing would reflect it.

"We've been leveraging every available asset—local sources, our own SIGINT, and the British have been very helpful. We're also closely monitoring communications between the authorities in Hong Kong and mainland China." Sorensen launched into a five-minute overview of how the mission had been drawn up. "By all accounts, the insertion went well. Our first hint of trouble came when Corsair's communications went down. It appears he was able to get into position, but after that things get hazy. We intercepted a burst of phone traffic among Li's security detail, right about the time Corsair would have been on the hill. It takes some reading between the lines, but it appears that he took one shot that removed Zhao. A second shot, presumably aimed at Li, missed."

"Your gunslinger missed?" Gross said. "I thought he was your best!"

Checking an impulse to knock Gross down a notch, Sorensen ignored the comment. "We've also obtained acoustic evidence from Zhao's phone—he was on a call when all this went down. At almost the precise moment Corsair took his second shot, we believe that he himself came under heavy fire."

"Heavy fire from who?" Quarrels asked.

"Some kind of assault team."

"Were they police?" asked Eraclides

Sorensen forwarded what she'd been told by Louis Rudbart, ending with the *asset lost* message regarding Corsair. She hoped this might give pause for reflection.

Instead, Matt Gross immediately countered with, "So the way it stands, Slaton is dead, Li survived, and eight Filipino mercenaries were killed by a bomb? Do you *realize* what a debacle this is?"

Sorensen lost it and shot back, "I realize that a man I sent on a dangerous mission, one who has a wife and a child, has apparently paid the ultimate price for *your* freedom!"

Gross stared seethingly at the camera, but was silenced for the moment.

"We will make sure he gets his star," the vice president said.

Sorensen found herself shaking her head. "No. Until I have firm proof, I am not giving up on Slaton."

"We need to focus on the mission," Eraclides said. "As I understand it, the only clear survivors of this disaster are Li and the NOC who was recommended by the British?"

"To the best of our knowledge, yes."

"Then it seems simple enough," Quarrels surmised. "We finish the job. Li is still out there, and it has to be addressed."

"That might not be easy," Eraclides warned. "His two cohorts are dead, and Li himself was targeted. If he has any sense at all, he's going to bunker up big time."

"I don't care if he's in Fort damned Knox—I want options! And what about this other loose end, the NOC you relied on?"

After a prolonged silence, Sorensen filled the void with, "We're trying to track him down."

Quarrels said, "All right. The priority is to deal with Li. If anything changes, I want to hear about it right away." He picked up a remote control and cut the connection.

The screen in front of Sorensen went blank. Even so, she couldn't stop staring at it. Questions continued to mount. Was one of the men she'd just spoken with a traitor? Or was it someone else, someone not on her radar? And what of the NOC the British had recommended? He'd disappeared at the worst possible moment. Could he be involved as well?

The most troubling question, however, seemed unanswerable: Could Slaton have survived?

Sorensen realized she would soon have to give the same briefing to Elayne Cleveland. Hopefully, by then, she would have a few answers.

FIFTY-THREE

Li Qiang sat unmoving in the basement of his residence, rooted in a soft recliner in the darkest corner. He was frozen with fear. A loaded shotgun was within reach, leaning against the nearby wall. Li was barely proficient with guns, but one of his men had handed it to him, probably hoping it would give him a sense of security. After witnessing the fatal shooting of his business partner hours earlier, it would take more than that.

Morning had dawned, although there were no windows in the basement to prove the point. Some hours ago there had been a heated debate about running, making a dash to the airport for a flight out of the country. Li kept a residence in Singapore. Traveling, however, seemed the highest risk option. And would that home be any safer? In the end, Li had decided they would stay here, yet he couldn't stop thinking about Singapore. The distant sea. The soft blue swimming pool. Palm trees swaying in the trade winds. It seemed a world away.

He was brought back to reality by a pair of boots stomping down the stairs. He saw his security chief, Junfeng, who had been with him five years now, since retiring from the local PLA garrison.

"We have finished another sweep," Junfeng reported.

"There is nothing to report, and the police have still not come."

This was the other great variable. Would the authorities realize that the gunfire had started at the top of the hill? "Good," Li replied, "at least that is in our favor." They had expected the police to come knocking immediately after the shooting. Yet moments after Zhao was killed, the entire battle had cascaded downhill. The sounds of gunfire faded into the storm. Since then, there had been nothing. No one had come to the door all night.

"I spoke to my friend at police headquarters," Junfeng said. "He is a senior investigator, and I explained that I had concerns about the gunfire last night. He told me not to worry. He said there was an altercation at the edge of the city, but that the police have the situation well under control. They are treating the matter as a war between rival drug merchants."

"Drug merchants?" Li said disbelievingly. With Zhao dead and a near miss for him, it was obvious they'd been targeted. Still, he wasn't sure what to make of it all.

"It confirms that we have taken the right approach," Junfeng said.

The "right approach" had been in the works for two hours now. Dumbfounded by the violent events, and lacking sufficient mental bandwidth to come up with a plan, Li had asked Junfeng for advice. The ex-policeman's plan had been simple: Dispose of Zhao's body, take care of a window with two bullet holes, and hope the police never came. The window had been easy—one of the men had shattered it completely, then dragged a broken tree branch to the ground beneath. The opening was covered with two pieces of plywood. Bullet holes gone, storm damage implied.

"There is one additional complication," Junfeng said. "One of my men was performing a search of the nearby area, and he discovered two additional bodies near the house under construction." Li barely reacted as his security man explained that all three bodies were now in the trunk of Zhao's limo, wrapped ingloriously in a half dozen garbage bags. They would soon be at the bottom of the bay.

His report complete, Junfeng went back upstairs.

Li sat immobile, reflecting on how far his life had sunk. Three years earlier he had been the chief executive of China Eastern Industries Corporation, the third largest defense manufacturer in the country. Yet what The Party gave, The Party could take away. Li had been kicked to the curb in a routine corruption sweep, along with Zhao Hu and Yao Jing. All three of them, of course, had taken bribes and kickbacks, but no more than a hundred other executives. They had merely been targeted as scapegoats, cannon fodder to distract from the Party's rotten core.

With the system turned against them, the three men had combined for the most purely entrepreneurial move any of them had ever made: They quietly moved money out of the country, stole some cast-off hardware from their companies, and set up shop in the black world. And just like that, The Trident, an arms supplier like no other on earth, was born. The Chinese government turned a blind eye to the scheme. The corruption purge had run its course, and as long as the weapons were not sold to China's enemies, the powermongers of Beijing had more important fish to fry.

For a year, The Trident discreetly shopped its high-end hardware. The list of potential customers was small, yet all three men had connections. When they acquired their first, and as it turned out only, customer it came from a place they could never have imagined. Instead of selling high-tech arms, they found themselves shaping the world.

Three months ago the strikes had begun and money was pouring in. Now Li's partners were dead, and he was a hunted man.

His eyes swept the room.

Two guards were with him, while the other six— three of whom had hours ago worked for Zhao Hu—were upstairs maintaining watch. Li began to think more positively. If he could bunker up for a time, survive the coming weeks, he might be able to hire a bigger security team. Money, of course, was not a problem. The key to his future was in Washington.

Had their distant employer put a target on their backs? Almost certainly. But what would happen if he himself was uncovered? This, Li recognized, was his best leverage. Any way he viewed it, The Trident had reached its end, a black hole collapsing on itself. What had happened last night was always going to be the endgame. He and the others knew too much. Yet Li had survived, and his suspicions about his employer's identity might be exchanged for survival.

But how to make such a bargain?

He regarded the shotgun, and then the special phone on the nearby table. The handset, always their lone link to their employer, had been ominously silent for weeks. It would now remain so forever—Li had turned it off and removed the battery. He would never again speak to the overseer who'd hired them, the man who had selected the weapons and chosen the targets. For a time it had gone flawlessly. Money paid and spectacular strikes delivered. Yet with each attack the pressure had intensified. Two months ago their conduits, an Israeli and an Albanian, had been uncovered and eliminated. Then a major strike had failed.

And now?

As the sole survivor, Li could do nothing but sit in a hole in the ground. There would be no more strikes. No more calls from Washington. Yet he also knew that the traitor would be desperate—because he had more to lose than any of them.

FIFTY-FOUR

"You failed," said the voice from Washington on the encrypted line. "Zhao is dead, but Li is alive."

Monkh took a moment to process this. He was seated at a table in his safe house, a decrepit flat in a lost tenement on the outskirts of Tai Po. On the table before him was a disassembled Glock 19, along with rags and a tube of gun oil. He set down the gun's slide gently.

"If Li is alive, it was not my failing. You can thank your so-called legendary assassin."

"Corsair clearly wasn't as good a marksman as we were led to believe. Are you sure you eliminated him?"

"My shot didn't miss."

"Let's hope. You seem to have acquired a habit of not completing your assignments."

Monkh held back on the first response that came to mind. "I will take care of Li. Send me a fresh intel package."

"I can't. With Corsair eliminated, we no longer have a dog in the fight. The agency will go after Li again, but not anytime soon. Things are too hot at the moment, and if I ask for intelligence it will draw attention. You'll have to handle this on your own."

Monkh considered it. "It's possible . . . but I will

have to be cautious. Li will be wary, and if he leaves the country I'll have to track him down."

"I don't care how you do it . . . just do it."

The line went dead.

Monkh turned off the phone and pushed it across the table.

"Incompetent," he said to no one, not sure if it was directed at his employer or the dead assassin. An image came to mind of Corsair being swept away in the raging deluge, the only remnant a streak of his blood on a pillar. Only Li remained now, but that would require caution.

He began reassembling the gun, barely looking as his hands went through the familiar motions. Things had nearly fallen perfectly. The CIA had sent their assassin to remove the last two members of The Trident. Monkh, in turn, had planned to kill the killer. Then the idiot had gone and missed. Had his Filipino mercs gone in too soon? He'd given them precise instructions not to engage Corsair until after his second shot. What had gone wrong?

Monkh chided himself for constructing a plan that was too elaborate. The mercs had offered degrees of separation, both in eliminating Corsair and, after being eliminated themselves, adding confusion to the resulting investigation. Now the job was only two-thirds done, and it was his mess to clean up.

Monkh jacked a fresh magazine into the Glock, racked the slide to chamber a round. He trained the sight on a wall-mounted picture across the room, the ever-present smiling visage of China's Dear Leader.

Sometimes you simply have to do things yourself.

———

The gunshot woke Christine out of a sound sleep.

She rolled instinctively toward Davy. He was sleeping with a toddler's somnolence. She looked around the cabin and didn't see Jammer, but she did notice that the gun rack on the wall was unlocked and a rifle was missing. She got up, edged toward the window, and peered into the gloom. She saw him near the dock, the Remington in his hand. He didn't look particularly troubled.

She shrugged on her jacket and went outside. "Everything okay?" she asked tentatively as he strolled back toward the cabin.

"All good," Jammer said. "Just fired a round into the water. I was working on this gun earlier. The action was a little gummy and the ammo looked old, so I figured a live fire was in order. Better now than when you need it." He went inside, secured the rifle, then came back out and dropped into one of the rockers on the porch.

Christine took a seat in the other. Even in late spring, there was bite to the morning air, frost tinging the windows. She pulled a blanket off the chair's back and covered herself. Christine dug the blue phone out of her jacket and checked the battery—she'd charged it last night off the generator.

"I should try for a signal soon," she said.

"That requires flying, but we won't have to go far. There's a little town about thirty miles west of here. We don't even have to land—cell signals are strong when you fly as low as I do." He gestured to the phone. "Did David give you any instructions to go with that, like a particular time of day to reach out?"

"No. This is our last-ditch lifeline. He said if it comes down to the blue phone, things have gotten dire. I'd like to check it once a day, maybe twice."

"Doesn't look very fancy."

"It's not. Just a standard burner. What about you? Does Anna have to way to reach you?"

"Satellite phone. According to Anna, the security is top-notch. I wouldn't mention that to your husband. He was pretty adamant about me not bringing any comm."

"Yeah, he's a pain that way. But in his line of work, it goes with the territory. Have you heard from her?"

"Not yet."

Christine turned the burner in her hand. "How about we make a run this afternoon."

"I'll have the airplane ready."

"I'm guessing it might take a few days. Won't the airplane need fuel if we start making daily flights?"

"We won't be going far, and the tanks are three-quarters full. Like I said earlier, between that and the supplies we've got on hand, we could stay off-grid for weeks."

"Let's hope it doesn't take that long," she said.

"Don't worry. If I know David, he'll be in touch soon."

FIFTY-FIVE

For three days, from high ground over half a mile away, Monkh observed the compound on Victoria Peak. He kept a log of how many guards were present and where they were positioned. He saw no sign of his target, but the fact that security remained tight was proof enough that Li was inside. This was further reinforced, on day two, when he saw one of the men deliver a consignment of groceries.

Monkh was encouraged. They were settling in for a lengthy stay, at least another week based on the volume of provisions. It alleviated the pressure of time. The longer Li waited, the more time he would have to prepare.

And the more complacent the security team would become.

For three days, Li Qiang waited in his home, paranoia his constant companion. He had taken to sleeping in the office, which had no exterior walls and a reasonably comfortable couch. His housekeeper took to doubling as a cook, feeding both him and his security men with surprisingly hearty fare.

The police never did come to his door, and at this point it appeared certain they would not. According to Junfeng's friend on the police force, the investigation into the killings at the bottom of the hill was fading quickly. The reasons were threefold. First was a glaring lack of suspects. Second was a distinct lack of empathy for the victims, who were likely themselves criminals. Most damning of all was a police commissioner who knew a losing cause when he saw one. All but one detective had been reassigned to other cases, and the one who remained was scheduled to retire in three weeks.

On only one occasion since the attack, in a moment of self-inflicted panic the previous night, had Li loaded the battery into his special phone. He turned it on, saw a solid signal, and waited with shaking hands to learn if any new messages had been sent from Washington. There was nothing. He had quickly disassembled the phone again.

Li couldn't say what was happening across the Pacific, but so far things seemed calm. He was increasingly convinced that bunkering in place had been the right choice.

For three successive mornings, Mali woke to find her patient unmoved. This was how she thought of him now—her patient.

His near-catatonic state was, according to the doctor, to be expected—the combined effect of drugs and a serious infection. When the patient rescued her that night, Mali had viewed his intervention with mixed feelings. Sami, her pimp, had been getting increasingly violent. It was a relief to know he could no longer hurt her. That said, Mali had been trying to escape for months, and was close to a path home. Now she'd been forced into hiding, and the bloody altercation would only deepen her bad situation. And then there was the matter of her rescuer—his injuries proved he was a man with his own problems.

The bedroom was eerily silent. There were no beeping monitors or alarms, as there would be in a hospital, no chatter from doctors or nurses. The only medical equipment in sight was a standard IV pole, at the top of which was a bag containing antibiotics and a sedative.

Mali heard soft footsteps from the apartment above. She had no idea who lived there, but the footfalls seemed light and unhurried. This flat was not her own, but that of a friend who'd escaped to Thailand the previous month after stealing her passport back from her pimp. Mali had often imagined such a getaway, yet her situation was more complex. And now even more so.

The place was a wreck, her friend having left in a rush. There were books and papers on the floor, dirty dishes in the sink. The dresser drawers were ajar, still half full of clothing. The refrigerator was thick with leftover takeout containers. Her friend had texted Mali on her way to the airport, told her about the hiding spot for the key. The rent was paid through the end of this month. At the time, Mali wasn't sure what use the place would be. Then, three nights ago, the key had proved a godsend.

It gave her refuge.

Gave her two weeks to find a way out of her predicament.

After what happened on the street, she had to get out of the country. One of her friends confirmed the obvious, that two of the three men had died that night, including Sami. None of it was her fault—the man on the bed had initiated the fight—but she was certain Sami's brother would be looking for her.

When her wounded white knight had collapsed on the doorstep on arriving, she'd been forced to drag him inside. After getting him into the bed, she'd considered simply leaving and running away. Then she'd watched him in the dim light, injured and fading in and out of consciousness. She simply couldn't screw up the courage to leave.

Mali went to the sparsely furnished kitchen and made a cup of green tea.

Ten minutes later she went back to check the IV. She was studying the drip when she heard a soft groan. His eyes fluttered open, then closed again.

Mali took a step back, then remembered what she'd been told to do.

She quickly slipped on her shoes and went to fetch the doctor.

FIFTY-SIX

Charles Eraclides sat patiently outside the Oval Office, waiting to be admitted. He considered the agency's previous directors and imagined that all had, at some point, been in this exact position: sitting in a chair picked out by Eleanor Roosevelt while waiting to relay the nation's greatest secrets to the most powerful man on earth. He couldn't deny that it was intoxicating.

After one week at the top of the agency, he was still getting used the job, both the burden of its demands and the intrinsic benefits. There was a time when he would never have imagined rising so far. After graduating from college—bachelors from Brown and a law degree from Yale—he had meandered around Washington for a rudderless five years. One federal court clerkship, staff attorney at the Justice Department, and a brief stint at DOD. When the job posting had opened up at the CIA's Office of Inspector General, it seemed little more than another stepping stone, although to where he couldn't say.

That had been twenty years ago.

In retrospect, Eraclides had arrived at the agency at a critical juncture, as its legal arm was transforming in the face of groundbreaking issues. The integration of direct-action agencies with the laws that governed them had always been a messy business, but the post-9/11 wars in Iraq and Afghanistan had taken things to a new level. Torture, rendition, targeted assassinations, drone strikes. For an up-and-coming young lawyer, it was heady stuff, and a place where careers were made. Eraclides had shone, and the promotions cascaded. Still, he never imagined that journey would take him to the White House.

The door beside him opened, and a steward appeared. "The acting president will see you now."

Acting president. The title still sounded odd, Eraclides thought, but he supposed the steward was using it on his own initiative. Americans everywhere were confused and anxious, adjusting to a transfer of power that might or might not be permanent, all while America was under attack.

He went through and found Quarrels huddled over the Resolute desk. Matt Gross was at his side, as he invariably seemed to be. Gross was explaining something in an open file folder. Even from across the room, Eraclides recognized the hatched border on the folder—Special Access, President's Eyes Only.

Quarrels appeared mildly befuddled.

"Good afternoon," Eraclides said, announcing himself.

Gross and Quarrels both looked up.

"Well?" Gross said speculatively. "Have you made any progress in Hong Kong?"

"No . . . at least, nothing new since yesterday. We think Li is still in his residence. We're putting together options for another strike, but we have to wait until things cool down."

"And Corsair?"

"His body hasn't turned up yet, if that's what you're asking. Police interest in the whole affair seems to be fading." Neither man commented, and Eraclides moved on. "There has been one development relating to the takedown of Marine One."

"We already know who's responsible," Gross said. "It was The Trident."

"True, they were involved. But it's also increasingly clear that this attack, as well as those of last March, didn't occur in a vacuum. This wasn't chaos for the sake of chaos. There has to be some greater purpose, someone steering the agenda. This new evidence points to a suspect."

"A suspect?" Quarrels repeated. "What do you mean?"

"I received a report from our technology division a few hours ago. Working alongside DARPA, they've made excellent headway in sourcing this swarm of drones. The actual drones are high-end off-the-shelf models, made in South Korea. Anyone could have purchased them. But from there it gets more interesting. The first clue involves the AI software that controlled them. About two years ago the NSA cracked into a research lab run by one of our adversaries. They were able to download a number of this lab's latest coding algorithms before the breach was detected and shut down. It appears that the code is a near-perfect match for the swarm that almost killed the president. The acoustic sensors added to each drone have also been identified. It's actually a system designed by a Canadian company, but we have good intel that it was stolen about a year ago by a hostile intelligence service."

"You're telling me this attack came from another country?"

"Well, The Trident were directly responsible, along with others they hired as intermediaries. But if you look at this new evidence, together with what we confirmed regarding the weapons used in March . . . everything is sourced from China."

A silence fell. Eraclides and Gross both looked at Quarrels, realizing it was his moment to lead.

After a full minute of thought, the vice president shook his head. "No. This was the Russians. If you look at the attacks in March, their fingerprints were on every one."

When neither subordinate responded, Quarrels continued, "The Chinese clone all their equipment from Russian designs. Virtually every Chinese jet and tank and warship are copies of Russian equivalents, are they not?"

Eraclides said, "That might have been true twenty years ago. But since then China has come up with more and more indigenous hardware. And when it comes to software and AI, they're far ahead of Russia."

Slowly, the vice president's expression went to muted fury. He looked at Eraclides, then shifted to Gross. "Russia is responsible for all of this, I feel it in my marrow. First the Ukraine war, then March Madness. It's not a nation state, it's an organized crime syndicate with nuclear weapons. And this time, gentlemen . . . this time they have gone too far!"

Across town, Sorensen left her office and headed to the parking garage. It had been a long day at work, and a frustrating one at that.

She had long viewed it as her duty to insulate her operators from high-level politics. For no one had she gone farther out on that limb than David Slaton. Yet acting as a buffer was a double-edged sword. It meant isolating the operative, which left few backup channels. Now, with Slaton reported to be a casualty, and all lines of communication severed, Sorensen was nearing desperation. She could think of one only life-line that might remain.

Unfortunately, it was one she didn't control.

She got in her car, closed the door, and sat deep in thought. The silence cleared her head.

It was time, she decided, to do what she should have done days ago.

Thirty minutes later, Sorensen pulled her Honda sedan onto a remote gravel road in rural Loudoun County. She drew to a stop, removed a satellite phone that was protected by top-tier encryption, and sent a brief mes-sage: Need to meet. Your place.

Within ninety seconds a reply chimed to the handset.

133.51321

59.71316

2100.0514

Sorensen heaved a sigh of relief.

Latitude. Longitude. Time and date.

She would be there.

FIFTY-SEVEN

His first sensation was touch. A deft softness beneath his arms, fabric behind his neck. He was in a bed, his breathing slow and rhythmic. Sound arrived next, although there seemed to be little—either that, or his hearing was impaired. A clock ticking faintly, distant traffic noise.

Ever so slowly, Slaton opened his eyes. He struggled against the brightness, but gradually things came into focus. He tried to make sense of his surroundings, ignoring the invisible vise that seemed clamped on his head.

The first thing he noticed was an IV pole hovering over him, a tube snaking down to a needle in his left arm. He wasn't in any kind of hospital, but a small bedroom, and through the open door he saw a compact living area. Beyond that was a tiny kitchen, a shipwreck of dirty dishes on the counter. A Mickey Mouse clock on the nearby dresser suggested it was seven thirty, and the window on his right, covered with butcher block paper and tape, allowed enough light to suggest that it was morning.

He studied the room beyond and saw a threadbare couch, two mismatched chairs, a rickety dinette. Yet something about the place seemed off, and he realized what it was. There was nothing here of a personal nature. No family photos or travel souvenirs. No coat hanging on the hook by the door. The only thing that came close was an empty picture frame on one wall.

Empty?

Slaton blinked a few times and his gaze sharpened. He tried to recall how he'd gotten here, and bits and pieces flooded back. The gunfight on Victoria Peak, his near-death encounter with Thomas. Almost drowning, then picking a fight with three men in an alley. And of course, the girl.

Was this her place?

He vaguely recalled her saying her name. *Mali.* He remembered her helping him walk across town. They arrived at a building, and then . . . nothing. Hearing no sounds whatsoever from the main room, Slaton guessed he was alone.

His first instinct was to run. Get up, rip out the IV, and leave. Experimentally, he tried to push himself onto his elbows. The strain on his abdomen brought immediate pain, and he laid back down. He worked his right hand down and raised the blanket covering his chest. He was naked beneath, and he saw the two wounds on his abdomen—one made by a tree branch, the other by a bullet. With great care, he reached down and, one at a time, pulled up the edges of bandages. Both wounds looked red and ragged, but had been stitched closed.

"Okay," he said to himself. "Maybe I'll just stay here a bit."

The gravity of his predicament, and the futility of his instinct to flee, sank in next. He was trapped inside China, the most intrusive surveillance state on earth. No ID, no weapon, no transportation. And with serious injuries.

Slaton was ruminating on it all when the distinct sound of a key turning a deadbolt interrupted. A door somewhere in the main room opened on squeaking hinges. He instinctively looked for weapons within reach. A metal IV pole. The needle in his arm. An empty picture frame. Which was to say, not much at all.

He distinguished two voices, both female, both whispering. One was vaguely familiar. They were speaking an Asian language he couldn't place. Mali appeared, framed by the open doorway. She looked different than when he'd last seen her. No makeup, casual clothes, black hair tied back in a neat ponytail. After a few moments, another woman appeared. Similar features, more mature.

"Hello," Mali said with a tentative smile.

"Hello again," he replied.

"I bring you doctor."

Slaton regarded the second woman. Her features were Southeast Asian, and she was built more solidly than Mali. She had a streak of blue dyed into her black hair, and a small stud decorated one side of her nose.

"I am Doctor Niran. You can call me Chinda." She came closer and inspected the IV. The doctor was wearing civilian clothes: a conservative blouse, pants, and sensible flats. "How are you feeling?"

"Not bad, all considered."

"You have two serious wounds. I cleaned and closed both. The IV contains antibiotics. You had an infection, but it seems to be lessening." Her English was excellent, almost without accent.

"An infection? Is that based on bloodwork? A CBC?"

The doctor's eyes narrowed. "It is based on your appearance and temperature. Also my experience. Ordering such tests is not an easy thing here. At least, not for a noncitizen who carries no identity documents."

"What about my hip? That was really bothering me."

"I see significant bruising, but I doubt you've done any lasting damage. Without an X-ray, it's hard to be sure." She looked around the room obviously. "We are not a hospital. But then, based on the nature of your injuries, I think you might prefer a more private setting."

He nodded, allowing the point. "How long have I been here?"

"Three days. But you won't be able to stay much longer."

Slaton sensed a new crosscurrent. Wanting to explore it, he shifted gears. "I can pay you for your work."

"Can you?"

For the first time he smiled. The girls had gone through his things. Checked for an ID, wallet, anything to explain who he was and how he had ended up in a Sheung Wan alley coming to Mali's rescue. And with preexisting injuries that included a gunshot wound.

"I will make good on it," he insisted.

Slaton attempted to sit up, but she immediately pushed him back down and tick-tocked her finger in his face. "Not yet."

She retrieved gauze, a roll of tape, and a tube of ointment from a nearby shelf. Chinda pulled back the sheet and began gently removing the bandage from his gunshot wound. Slaton saw an eight-inch gash just below the beltline. Had the bullet struck at a deeper angle it surely would have been fatal. Any practiced assassin—which Thomas indisputably was—would use hollow points, and a more direct hit would have expanded on contact to rip apart blood vessels and tissue. As to the puncture wound on his abdomen, Slaton had feared some vital organ might have been perforated. That, apparently, wasn't the case—once again, dumb luck.

"Are you really a doctor?" he asked as she worked.

She paused and looked at him directly. "I'm an oral surgeon."

"A dentist?"

"Some oral surgeons are MDs, but I attended a dental school in Canada."

"Attended? Does that imply you didn't graduate?"

Her gaze went to stone. "My doctorate was nearly complete. Unfortunately, sometimes life intervenes. I took a leave of absence because my sister was victimized by a human trafficking network. I came to Hong Kong to find her and get her out."

Slaton was beginning to understand. He addressed Mali. "You're Thai?"

The younger woman looked at him guardedly.

"The man who hit you . . . I heard him say something about going back to Thailand."

Mali nodded. "Yes. I was brought here against my will, forced into . . . working."

"Forced how?"

Mali's eyes flicked once toward the open doorway, and she nearly said something before the doctor interrupted. "That is not important. I left school to come here and take my sister home. The man who brought

Mali to Hong Kong—the one you killed—said that if I could raise enough money, he would return her passport. I have been in Sheung Wan, working, for five months."

"Doing what?"

"Essentially what I have done for you."

It made sense, Slaton thought. There was always a market, in dark urban corners, for off-the-books medical help. A cottage industry of STDs, minor fractures, knife wounds, and infected body art; patients who didn't want any record of their treatments. Much of that care could be performed by anyone with basic medical training and access to black market medications.

Chinda said, "Twenty thousand British pounds, that's what they were asking. I nearly had enough until you came along and ruined everything."

"You want me to apologize for stopping a man from beating your sister?"

"Stopping?" Chinda said curtly. "Is that what you call it?" Her expression softened. "I will never condone killing . . . but I will also shed no tears for any of those men. I only want to get Mali home, and that was nearly within our grasp."

"In my experience, bargains with men like that have a way of not being honored."

"I am not naïve, but there was a chance."

"Will there be repercussions?" he asked.

"Sami was a well-known pimp, so the police won't do much. But others in his organization, especially his brother, will come looking for Mali. If they find her, they might let her live. Or they might make an example of her. Either way, any chance of freedom is gone."

"I'm sorry to have ruined your plans," he said.

"Your motives were noble . . . at least, in part. But the truth now is that Mali has no path to getting her passport back. We will be safe here for another week, but after that I'm not sure where we'll go. I could say the same for you."

"Were there witnesses to what happened?"

"Probably," Mali said. "And it is difficult to escape the cameras. I don't know whether it will be the police or the Triad . . . but sooner or later, someone will find us."

Slaton didn't know which was more of a threat, the police or the local organized crime syndicate. He preferred to stay clear of both. As to his motives that night, he wasn't going to defend them. There had, in the moment, been a trace of chivalry. Yet there had also been self-interest. In the end, he had protected Mali from a brutal thug, and also fulfilled his own needs. Rest, sanctuary, medical care. His instincts had proved right.

He said, "What if I told you I could get you both out of the country."

The sisters exchanged a look.

"How?" Chinda asked.

"I'm not exactly sure, but I know important people."

"Important people where?"

Slaton didn't answer right away.

The doctor's eyes narrowed. "You are American," she said.

"What makes you say that?"

"The crown on your back molar. It's a new type of porcelain, presently used only in North America."

"I was born in Israel. After that . . . it gets complicated. But yes, I have connections to the U.S. government. If I ask them to get the two of you out, they'll find a way."

"Actually," Mali said, "it is not only the two of us. There is another."

Slaton looked at her blankly, waiting to be told their mother was also involved. Mali left the room, then reappeared moments later carrying a small girl. She was not quite Davy's age, probably three years old. Poised on her mother's hip, she rubbed sleepy eyes with her fists. This was why they'd been whispering when they first arrived. Nap time.

The girl had likely been used as leverage by the Triad.

Slaton heaved a long sigh. As so often happened, his mission going forward was getting more and more complex. He nodded, and said, "Three of you . . . right. But if I'm going to do that, I need to get out of this bed."

The doctor crossed her arms defiantly. "We'll see about that tomorrow."

The second time Sorensen entered Elayne Cleveland's room, she was alone. She looked back through the inset glass and saw Richard Cleveland in the hall. He looked around, and then gave her a slight nod. Sorensen pulled the makeshift privacy curtain shut.

She walked slowly to the president's bedside, thinking the scene looked much as it had on her first visit. Elayne resting peacefully, surrounded by the same equipment, wrapped in bandages. Yet there was one encouraging change: the ventilator was gone and she was breathing on her own.

Sorensen stopped at the bedside and regarded the president's hand, wondering if the same drill would be necessary. Squeezes for every yes and no. As she reached out to try, the patient's eyes opened and focused immediately. "What took you so damned long!" the president said.

Sorensen startled, but couldn't contain a smile. "Looks like someone is feeling better."

Elayne coughed weakly. "I feel like shit," she said, her voice dry and brittle.

"Understandable, given what you've been through."

"I tire easily. You have five minutes to tell me everything new."

Sorensen paused only long enough to gather her thoughts, then launched into a briefing like none she'd ever given. "I met with Vince Seward an hour ago. I confided in him, explained your condition."

The president's gaze turned severe.

"Elayne, I know you wanted to keep it close, but I didn't see any other way. If there's a traitor in the White House, we can't move until we know who it is. I came up with two parallel ways to approach it. The first is to bring Seward on board by telling him what's at stake. I did, and he's on our side. As far as unraveling those comm intercepts from the White House, his techs don't have an answer yet. He seems confident they can source the calls, but it's going to take time."

The president nodded. "And the second track?" she rasped.

"That's a little more speculative. It involves Corsair."

"Slaton?"

Sorensen gave a condensed version of what had happened in both Macau and Hong Kong. "So we have two problems," she said at the end. "Li is still alive and Slaton might not be. But I'm not giving up on him."

"You . . ." the president's voice faltered and her eyes flickered shut for a moment. When they opened again, she said, "You need to find Corsair."

"I'm working on it," Sorensen promised. "Wherever he is, I'll find him."

FIFTY-EIGHT

Slaton's acting physician was good to her word. She arrived early the next morning and began with a cursory examination. Slaton winced as she probed the area around his beltline. His entire body was scraped and bruised. He never bothered to explain how it had all happened. *First, I fell eighty feet and landed in a tree. Then I tumbled down rapids for half a mile.*

He wouldn't have believed it either.

To her credit, Chinda never asked. He did notice her eyes pause, however, on some of his old scars. They were anything but typical, an intimate map of operational mistakes and bad luck. Or maybe good luck, since he was still wearing them. Chinda didn't comment on these either.

"All right," she said. "Let's get you out of bed."

She disconnected the IV, leaving the needle in place, and pulled him into a sitting position. She helped him dress in his stolen clothes—someone had laundered them during his catatonic state.

"You said I was unconscious for three days?" he asked.

"Propofol fentanyl. Works very well."

She took his vitals with the usual instruments. Combined with the IV equipment, it proved she had access to basic medical supplies. Slaton didn't care where it had come from, although he hoped the fentanyl derivative dripping into his arm wasn't some kind of street-purchased concoction.

"I'll help you stand," she said.

He rose to his feet unsteadily. His hip was sore, but he could bear full weight. For the first few steps, it felt like his joints had rusted in place. The more he moved, however, the better things got.

"What other meds have you been giving me?" he asked.

"Aside from the sedative, a wide-spectrum antibiotic. After we stop the IV, I can offer you a milder opioid for the pain."

Slaton recognized a distinct fogginess in his thoughts. "No, I'm good."

"You're going to need to sleep in order to heal."

"I should tell you right off the bat, I'm not an easy patient. My wife is a doctor and she tells me that all the time."

"Lucky girl."

Slaton saw the trace of a smile. It was a positive sign in an awkward relationship. He went into the main room and saw the little girl playing on the floor with her mother. She looked tiny and delicate, her glossy black hair tucked behind twin seashell ears. She regarded Slaton warily and he gave her his best Dad smile.

"What's her name?" he asked.

"Aranya," Chinda said.

"She's Mali's daughter?"

"Yes. It's complicated, but she's been staying with me. Are you hungry?" she asked.

"Yeah, actually, I am."

"That's a good sign."

Chinda went to the kitchen, and Slaton retreated to the bedroom, finger-waving to the little girl as he did. The apartment was small space, but it seemed safe, which was all that mattered at the moment. He approached the window, instinctively shouldering to the wall beside it. He fingered back one edge of the paper curtain and saw a rusty fire escape six floors above a grimy alley. The side of the neighboring apartment building filled the view otherwise. All good to know.

Three days, he thought. That was how long it had been since the disaster on the hill. It was a long time, and the clock was running. The apartment seemed secure, and for the moment there was no alternative. It was only a matter of time, however, before someone—the local Triad or China's Ministry of State Security—battered down the door in the middle of the night.

Questions began flooding his mind. What had happened in the interim on Victoria Peak? Was Li Qiang still alive? How would the powers in D.C. react to his mission gone bad? Where was Thomas, the assassin who'd nearly gotten the better of him?

And lastly, how much did Sorensen know about the outcome?

The answer to this final question seemed apparent. The mission had ended in disaster, and Slaton hadn't sent a sitrep in three days. The obvious implication: the CIA's most secret operative, codename Corsair, had not survived.

In all likelihood, he had been written off as KIA. Yet that wasn't all bad. It was a card Slaton had held before, and one that he knew how to play. He had time to recover, and a relatively safe space. If the sisters Niran were correct, and assuming they kept a low profile, they could all remain here anonymously for another week. In that time, he needed to unravel what had gone wrong.

But how to go about it? Could he trust anyone in Washington right now?

With the possible exception of Sorensen, absolutely not.

Was his family safe?

Probably.

And with that, his next step became clear.

Every decision going forward was contingent on his family's safety, so he would to reach out to them using the last comm link available. Only then could he move to the next step—figuring out who had betrayed him.

On that count, Slaton knew precisely where to start. Indeed, it was a deduction he had made three days earlier as he lay motionless behind a gun sight on a balcony.

Li Qiang.

He'd had the man in his crosshairs, dead to rights. Then in the last instant Slaton had intentionally pulled his shot wide. It had been a strange and obscure impulse, a kind of sixth sense. This mission had been too easy, too perfect, and not until that critical moment had Slaton recognized it for what it was: the setup of all setups.

Now he was immensely thankful he'd altered that shot. Li Qiang was his best, and perhaps only remaining, source of information regarding The Trident. The organization had been attacking America for months, yet on that rainswept balcony, with tactical teams closing in all around, the truth had finally dawned on Slaton. He had been sent to eliminate the last vestiges of The Trident. At the same time, someone had been sent to eliminate him. Which meant he was getting close, one answer removed from blowing up the entire scheme.

Slaton committed then and there to finding out who the ultimate controller was.

And when he did?

He was going to return the favor.

FIFTY-NINE

The Beaver skimmed to a smooth landing on the light chop of Atlin Lake. The little airplane settled, and soon the propeller was kicking up a storm of spray as Jammer steered toward the dock at the water aerodrome.

"Right on time," he announced.

Christine looked tentatively shoreward. "Do you really think Anna will come?"

In answer, Jammer smiled and pointed toward the top of the distant pier. Even from a distance, Christine recognized Sorensen's trim figure. She was waiting at the midpoint of the dock, a hand shielding her eyes from the late afternoon sun.

Jammer eased the Beaver to the dock, then got out to secure lines.

"You got here quick," he called out as Sorensen walked up the weathered wood-plank pier.

"My jet is over at the real airport, the one with a runway—you know, asphalt and big numbers."

"Highly overrated. Which jet did you choose?"

"Gulfstream G650."

"Nice. Big range."

She paused within reach of the starboard float. "I have unlimited CIA assets at my disposal. You should never forget that."

"I'm sure you'll never let me."

They leaned across the narrow gap of water and exchanged an extended kiss.

Christine bundled out of the airplane, then helped Davy get down. Soon they were all on the dock exchanging greetings, but the intimacy Sorensen had displayed with Jammer was lost on Christine.

She was increasingly racked by anxiety and doubt. The very fact that Sorensen had requested this meeting had been weighing for half a day. If David had perished, or if he was severely injured, wasn't this how it would play out? A one-on-one notification by his commander? Extending her torment further, Sorensen bent down and engaged Davy, who was soon regaling the head of the CIA's clandestine service with tales of his flying adventures.

The situation turned awkward until Jammer took charge. He diverted Davy's attention to the far end of the dock where a big tugboat was moored. Christine nodded, and the two of them launched off on a trot.

"What do you hear from David?" Christine asked as soon as they were out of earshot, days of tension flooding out.

"He hasn't checked in lately," Sorensen said, keeping to the truth. "I was actually hoping you might have heard something. He hinted that the two of you have some way of communicating."

Christine hesitated, then pulled out her blue handset. "I've checked each of the last three days. So far, nothing."

"It's one way?"

She nodded. "He can call or message this number, but there's no line in the other direction."

Sorensen appeared to steel herself. "We have heard some troubling secondhand accounts. David was in Hong Kong and something went wrong with his mission. There was a firefight, and it's possible he was injured."

Christine felt her legs go weak. She reached out to a dock piling for support. It seemed to help. "It's going to be all right," she said. "He's out there, I know it."

"I like your attitude."

"I've been married to David a long time, and that's the only way it works. I keep faith in him, no matter what."

"I do as well. That said, Christine, I want to be honest. We've been pressing every possible source for information, but we haven't heard from him in four days. That might be good . . . or it might not be. I just can't get a bead on exactly what happened."

"I appreciate your being straight with me." In the distance, Davy was spinning circles around Jammer, pointing up at the tugboat.

"How is Davy holding up?"

"He's good. Jammer has been outstanding."

Sorensen hesitated, then said, "There is something else you should know. It's the reason I came here in person. There are some worrisome things going on in Washington, and while I can't get into specifics . . . I think David's mission may have been sabotaged. It's possible there's a traitor very high in our government."

Christine tried to compute this. "Sabotage? You mean . . . someone tried to kill David?"

"I don't think that was the objective, but they compromised his mission."

"Do you know who it is?"

"Not yet. But the point I want to make is this— security is more vital than ever. Trust Jammer, and if you do hear from David, get in touch with me immediately. No one else."

Christine tried to read Sorensen. "This leak came from someone high up?"

"Yes."

"Can you find out who it is?"

"I'm working on that."

Christine nodded. "All right. But when I do hear from David, I'm going to tell him. If there is a traitor, he needs to know."

"Yes, he does."

SIXTY

Slaton woke the next morning and, notwithstanding two partial sponge baths, showered for the first time in nearly a week. It felt good to wash away the grime, sweat, and blood of his mission-gone-bad. A sense of betrayal, however, was not so easily rinsed away. He didn't allow a descent into bleakness. He had learned early on in his career that self-pity was the most destructive of emotions. It sowed distraction, poor decision-making.

Anger, on the other hand, had its uses.

He examined himself in the mirror as he toweled off. The scattering of bruises across his body were in peak color, but the pain was lessening. His two most serious wounds were healing, no redness or discharge to imply infection. After putting on fresh bandages, he got dressed, moving freely but not without pain.

When he was done, he went to the main room, clicked on the TV, and stepped through channels to find a morning newscast. The tiny television had been left behind by the apartment's owner and wasn't connected to a cable or satellite box, but a simple aerial antenna captured a few local channels. Slaton actually preferred it that way—it meant there was no two-way connection to be exploited.

He could find only one newscast in English. He

watched a segment on the launch of a glorious new navy ship, a Party leader breaking a bottle of champagne across its bow. That image alone—a Chinese politician christening the nation's newest warship with a bottle of French sparkling wine—was ruefully symbolic of the disconnects in the ruling CCP.

A flash of motion near the bedroom doorway caught Slaton's eye. By the time he turned to get a better look it was gone. He smiled. Not so many years ago, he wouldn't have known how this game was played. The tiny face appeared again, just above the floorboard. Slaton quickly pointed a finger, and Aranya ducked out of sight. He heard her giggle. Even if the tone was different, it was identical in spirit to another laugh he knew all too well.

Slaton desperately missed his son. Right now, part of him wanted to do nothing more than go home. Find a way across the Pacific and walk into his house. Take hold of his family and never let go. But another part of him clung to reality—if he gave up and went home, the threat might follow him there. Closure was needed. And no one was in a better position to bring it than he was.

"Is there news?" Mali asked as she arrived from the kitchen with a hot breakfast and a smile. Toast, a boiled egg, and tea. Her Thai accent remained heavy, but Slaton was growing attuned to it.

"Nothing that changes our situation. Last night there was mention of an altercation between drug gangs on Hong Kong Island. Nothing about Sami and his boys."

"That is good."

"Thanks, this looks great." Slaton sat behind the tray at the tiny dining table. Next to the food was a big white pill—his daily antibiotic.

She smiled cautiously, which he found encouraging. Mali wasn't afraid of him—given how the world had treated her, he wouldn't have blamed her for being guarded. He hoped he could work out a deal with Sorensen, find some way to spirit all three of them to the States. If not, Slaton would make it happen some other way. They had housed him, fed him, nursed him back to health. He owed these two women his life, and little Aranya was part of the bargain. But before any of that could happen, there were more pressing matters.

Aranya scurried past the bedroom door, begging to be chased.

"She likes you," Mali said.

Slaton grinned. "I like her back."

Mali diverted to the bedroom and came out with Aranya on her hip. She set her daughter down at the kitchen counter where her own breakfast was waiting.

"I have high hopes for her," Mali said.

"And you should. I feel the same about my son. You wonder what life will bring them. Will they play soccer? Are they a math whiz or will they turn into a bookworm?"

"Worm?"

"Figure of speech. It's someone who likes to read."

Mali nodded, then said flatly, "I only hope she does not become like me."

Slaton regarded her, saw her trepidation. Then he silently admitted feeling a trace of it himself. Wasn't it true that children often aspired to follow in their parents' footsteps? If so, he would move heaven and earth to steer his children into taking their mother's path. Or was that wrong? What would his own father, who had died defending Israel, think of what his son had become? Were Slaton's missions, eliminating individuals who threatened others, more noble than they seemed on face value?

A metered triple knock on the front door vaporized the thought. Slaton pushed away the tray, got up, and went to the door. He was moving more freely, his hip less of a hindrance. From beside the door he waved his dinner napkin once in front of the peephole.

"It's me." Chinda's voice from the other side. Had she said, "It's Chinda," Slaton would have assumed duress. The dentist took directions well. He peered through, saw nothing amiss, and opened the door.

She came in looking slightly winded—the building had no elevator and they were on the sixth floor.

"Did you find everything?" he asked.

She dug into a shopping bag and pulled out her purchases. One hard-shell plastic package containing a prepaid mobile phone. One set of quality binoculars. One baseball cap and a pair of trail shoes. Two pairs of men's pants and two shirts. All of the clothing was used and bland and styleless.

"Just what I would have bought," he said.

"I believe you."

"I hope you're keeping track of my expenses."

"I am," she promised.

"All right," he said, trying one shoe on for size. "The sooner I get to work, the sooner we can get out of here."

SIXTY-ONE

Death, for Slaton, was peculiarly liberating. There were no superiors to answer to, no sitreps to file. It gave absolute freedom to set mission objectives and parameters. It also, unfortunately, introduced serious complications. Chief among them: getting around in the surveillance state that was modern China. Most forms of transportation—taxis, airplanes, trains, and rideshares—required a smart phone app, ostensibly as a method of payment, but more surreptitiously as a form of government tracking.

Yet there was one exception.

The walk to the bus stop was Slaton's first test. Four days after the disaster on Victoria Peak, he was moving well, although not without hitches. He could walk without limping, bend over with only a slight wince. On the downside, he didn't see himself sprinting away to separate from a threat. He carried no weapon, and close-quarters combat was a last resort. Altogether, it meant that avoiding trouble was paramount.

Chinda had sized the clothing perfectly. The pants and shirt fit loosely, and the shoes were comfortable. He would have no trouble blending in as a Western expat.

Slaton decided an afternoon of reconnaissance was

the next step, even if it went against his dentist's medical advice—Chinda didn't think he was ready. In the end she had relented and done her best to facilitate things. Her first suggestion was that he should move about the district using the Green minibus network. He told her where he wanted to go, and she recommended a route.

The bus arrived right on schedule.

Slaton climbed on and paid the fare using coins raided from Aranya's piggy bank—not the most desperate move in his long operational history, but unquestionably the most humiliating. It also raised his running tab to the family a few dollars more.

Wearing the baseball cap, pulled low, and a cheap pair of borrowed sunglasses, no one gave him a second look as made his way to the back of the bus. There were only three other people on board—Chinda had recommended a slack time of day—and Slaton ended up with a two-row buffer from his nearest seatmate. He'd run a solid surveillance detection route after leaving the flat and seen nothing worrisome.

Now, safely on the bus for a twenty-minute ride, he gave countersurveillance a break to concentrate on the big picture. His entire operating theory on the mission had shifted seismically in one moment on the balcony. With Li squarely in his sight, and threats closing in all around, the reservations that had been gnawing at him resolved into something firmer. The Trident, he and Sorensen had sensed all along, was a shadowed organization built to mask the identity of its true controllers. China and Russia topped that list, with an outside chance that it was a private group leveraging advanced weaponry for some unseen profit motive. What had never occurred to Slaton, until that instant, was that the actual control might be closer to home.

Once the idea of a traitor surfaced, it easily gained traction. Had Sorensen been aware of a conspiracy when they'd diverted to the remote park in Virginia? At the very least, she had sensed it. Now a massive power shift had taken place in Washington, the direct result of another attack by The Trident. Once Slaton made that connection, the existence of a traitor seemed all but certain. And with his trigger finger poised to eliminate the last surviving member of the organization, Slaton realized that six pounds of pull would terminate his best chance of uncovering the truth.

He'd taken the shot, but intentionally pulled it wide, hoping that would provide options going forward. Slaton was sure his bullet had missed Li, yet he had no idea what happened at the residence afterward. Had another element of the team that attacked Slaton gone in to eliminate Li? Or had someone else, perhaps Thomas, gone after him later?

It all distilled to two questions, both of which Slaton hoped to answer today. Was Li Qiang still alive? And if so, was he still in his home on the hill?

The minibus groaned across uneven pavement. It was nearing the stop where he would pull the string above his seat to ring the bell for the driver—China hoped to one day lead the world in technology, but it still had a long way to go.

Before setting out on the streets for answers, Slaton had one more task to perform. It was, in his mind, the most critical of all, and it had taken every bit of self-control he possessed to wait until now. His tactical reasoning was sound: he was now ten blocks removed from the apartment that had become his refuge, and also a moving target as the minibus weaved through traffic.

Slaton pulled out the burner phone Chinda had purchased and powered it up. He entered the only contact the phone would ever have, and sent a single two-word message.

I'm safe.

Christine and Davy arrived at the pier loaded down with grocery bags. They had gone on an outing for provisions—food mostly, and a few layers of clothing. Jammer had broken away to get the Beaver refueled and, probably more critically, to have a quiet cup of coffee with Sorensen. Christine knew they needed time alone, and the shopping excursion was a necessary distraction; something to keep her from overthinking what Sorensen had told her about David.

"What's wrong, Mommy?"

Her son's voice interrupted her spiraling mood. "What makes you think something's wrong, honey?"

"You look worried." Davy shifted the bag he was carrying to the opposite hand.

He really was getting more attuned to the world around him. More attuned to her. "I just miss your Dad."

"Me too. When can we see him again?"

"I don't know. But I'm hoping very soon."

They turned a corner and saw Jammer at the end of the pier with Anna. By their closeness and body language, it was clearly more personal than business. Christine took that as a good sign.

"Can I give Jammer the elk jerky we bought for him?" Davy asked. It had been his idea.

"Absolutely. Why don't you—" Her thought was interrupted when the phone in her pocket vibrated. *The blue phone.*

She nearly dropped the bag containing the eggs as she snatched it out. Christine read the two-word message, and then drew in a great lungful of fresh mountain air.

It felt like she hadn't breathed in a week.

SIXTY-TWO

When Sorensen saw the message she relaxed. But only a little.

"You just got this?" she asked.

"Two minutes ago," Christine replied.

"It's from Dad!" Davy piped in. "Is he going to come flying with us?"

"Not right now," Christine said distractedly.

Sorensen held out her hand, and Christine gave her the handset. Sorensen studied the screen, but saw little of use. She noted the time the text had been sent, and saw decent signal strength. The nature of the message implied that there would be no immediate follow-on. Which, in turn, implied something else.

"What now?" Christine asked.

Sorensen took a moment to think it through. She gave Jammer a subtle tilt of her head, and he understood immediately.

He bent down to meet Davy eye-to-eye. "Ready for our preflight inspection?"

Davy nodded vigorously and off they went.

"Shouldn't I stay here?" Christine asked when they were gone. "If we go back to the lake we won't have a signal if David messages again."

Sorensen turned the blue phone in her hand. "If he was going to say something else, he would have. This text was for your peace of mind. And . . . maybe also a message for me."

Christine looked at her thoughtfully. "There's no way he could know you're here with me."

"True. But he knows you can reach me."

"So what's the message?"

"The usual."

Christine looked perplexed.

Sorensen said, "Those with Y chromosomes have trouble asking for help."

It got a half smile.

Sorensen studied the phone and weighed her options. If she gave the handset to the CIA's techs, there was a chance they could tear it apart digitally, trace where the call had come from. There was also a chance that news of David's survival could leak out and create more problems than it solved. She handed the phone back to Christine. "You should go back to the cabin. I think that's what David would want. But check the phone every day; at least once, twice if you can. Have Jammer get in touch with me if you hear anything else."

Christine promised that she would.

Twenty minutes later, Sorensen watched the float-plane skim across the glass-smooth lake and rise into the sky. Thirty after that her own jet was lifting off from the municipal airport.

She had the cabin to herself, no distractions other than the well-insulated drone of the engines and slip-stream. She fell deep into thought.

Slaton was alive. Yet beyond one short message, he'd given her little to work with.

Or had he?

He'd said he was safe, but in his line of work that was a maddeningly relative term. The more Sorensen thought about it, the fact that he'd gone silent, not reported in for five days, was acutely telling. *He knows there's been a breach. He doesn't know who to trust.*

She had come to Canada to pursue the thinnest of threads—to find a way to reconnect with Corsair. The fact that she had done so obviated the need for her fallback mission—to obtain a sample of his son's DNA for matching purposes. Sorensen heaved out a long sigh of relief. An hour ago, that was what she'd been contemplating. What had passed for hope.

Where to go from here? she wondered.

Her pilots had filed a flight plan back to Joint Base Andrews. Was that her best move, or simply a reflex motion? How could she immerse herself at headquarters, with all its institutional complexity, now that an unidentified traitor was lurking?

The thought of going back to Washington felt like a mission behind enemy lines. *And how crazy is that?*

Sorensen realized there was only one alternative. She reached for the intercom handset and buzzed the pilots.

She was finished with armchair quarterbacking.

It was time to get in the game.

Slaton rang the bell, and at the next intersection the brakes of the minibus hissed. He got off, turned right, and immediately began another surveillance detection routine. That took nearly an hour.

The streets of Sheung Wan were vibrant on a Monday morning, the sidewalks bustling, cars and scooters flying past. The weather was glorious, far different from the recent night when an assassin had chauffeured him to the base of Victoria Peak.

He ended up three blocks away from where the bus

had dropped him; he saw no sign of anyone trailing him. The building that stood before him was one of two he'd identified early in the planning stages. It was a ten-story hotel, rated at three stars in most travel guides, that sat perched on a small plateau at the edge of town. Slaton hoped it would provide at least a partial view of Li's residence, albeit from half a mile away.

The hotel proved easy to breach. It wasn't the kind of place where Party members would stay, and probably not even local city councilmen. There was one sleepy guard in a surveillance closet near the front desk, easily visible through an open door, and a few cameras dotted the main lobby. The emergency stairwell, Slaton quickly determined, had no surveillance whatsoever.

He began climbing.

His hip was sore at the outset, but by the time he reached the tenth floor things had smoothed out. He was more winded at the top than he should have been, a reminder that he'd been bedridden for days. At the top Slaton got his first good break of the day—the roof access door was conveniently blocked open with a scrap of wood.

He pushed the fire door open cautiously and looked around. There was no one else on the flat, tar-encrusted rooftop, but he saw signs that it did get traffic. A sodden blanket in one corner, a few discarded food wrappers and beer cans. He guessed that hotel employees came here on their breaks, or perhaps to loiter after the end of a long shift to enjoy the nighttime view.

Slaton walked the length of the roof to get his bearings, and easily picked out Li's residence in the distance. After a quick scan of the rooftop, he decided to conceal himself amid a forest of air handlers. From there he had a good line of sight to the home half a mile away. He could see both upper floors, although the front driveway and back balcony were partially obscured by trees. Slaton settled in and pulled out the binoculars Chinda had purchased.

For the next two hours he kept a constant watch on the house. What he saw was encouraging. The most obvious difference from his previous surveillance of the home was that the window through which he'd fired two bullets was now boarded up. There were five guards in view, three of whom Slaton recognized. He didn't doubt there were more inside, some sleeping, others staying close to the boss.

And the boss, Li Qiang, *was* definitely inside.

Slaton never actually spotted Li, but there was no other explanation for such watchfulness. If Li had bolted immediately after Slaton's raid, he would have taken every available man with him. Slaton recalled from the floorplan Goode had dredged up that there was a basement of sorts on the bottom level. That's where Li most likely was at that moment.

At various times, Slaton noted lights inside the home switching on and off, notwithstanding the bright midday sun. At the two-hour mark he saw the most damning proof of all: a delivery driver pulled up to the front entrance and handed over a stack of takeout food, including what looked like four pizza boxes. Slaton guessed it was enough to feed between eight and twelve people, which backstopped the profile building in his head. The attack had occurred five days ago, yet since that time things had settled. Li and his crew were probably tired of cooking, and with the situation stabilized, the security men would feel confident, emboldened enough to order out. A little morale boost after so many days under siege.

Slaton planned while he observed, looking for weak points, for opportunity.

He paid special attention to the exterior of the house. He located the garbage cans and mailbox, saw a stack of firewood beneath the balcony. A pair of faux boulders, the kind used to hide outdoor speakers or equipment boxes, lay overturned near the wood pile. He identified the main electrical feed where power routed into the house, and also a big generator that would carry the load in an emergency. Two air conditioners were mounted near the foundation, as was a water pipe with a shutoff valve, surely the main connection. Old outdoor furniture sat stacked against the wall near an exterior storage closet, along with a rusty bicycle. It was the usual detritus that gathered around homes across the world.

Slaton shifted outward and studied the road in front for a full two minutes, his plan slowly building momentum. Li was home now, yet there was no telling for how long. Slaton decided to act tonight, in the early morning hours. Ultimately, he had one but goal: to get Li alone and extract one much-needed answer. More than anyone on earth, he would have insight into who really controlled The Trident.

Slaton checked his watch. He had been on the hotel roof for four hours. In that time, he'd seen no employees come through the blocked-open door behind him. Guessing that might change with the approach of nightfall, he decided there was no sense in tempting fate. Anyway, he had what he needed. Slaton packed up his optic, descended the stairs, and lowered the brim of his baseball cap before traversing the lobby.

The evening air was soft, the heavy rains having given way to a cooler dryness. He headed back into the honeycomb of streets, wanting to walk some distance before picking up a different bus to return to his makeshift safe house. The sidewalks remained busy.

Two blocks down the hill his route paralleled a dated cemetery. Every society had their gardens for the dead, and, perhaps fittingly, the conditions for the dearly departed in Hong Kong reflected those of the living—too many bodies, not enough space. In recent years, most Chinese had begun opting for cremation and group memorials, but that hadn't always been the case. Slaton looked out over a seemingly endless sea of stone markers wedged into concrete terraces. A young couple stood reverently near one marker, their hushed words to the occupant inaudible.

The more Slaton thought about his plan, the less certain he was it would work. He saw too many variables, too few assets at his disposal. Instead of worrying about it, he considered the cemetery. Everyone ended up here, or someplace like it. The challenge was to make a difference before that day came.

Success or failure tonight would not be a matter of planning. Nor would it involve teamwork or troves of intelligence. He was a coalition of one, dependent on experience and real-time decision-making. For the sake of America and his family, not to mention his own well-being, he simply had to make it work.

Though Slaton couldn't know it, at that moment a man with very similar ambitions was gliding up a parallel street on the opposing side of the graveyard. He had been watching Li's residence from a different building, the headquarters of a second-tier maritime insurance company—indeed, a building Slaton himself had identified as a backup to the hotel.

Monkh had used his most powerful optic today—it was his fourth visit to the insurance company's rooftop—and nailed down the last details of his plan to eliminate Li. Like Slaton, he had left just before sunset, with many of the same conclusions reached, and for mostly the same reasons. Monkh had what he needed, and he too realized that the window for action was narrowing.

Neither man was ever aware of the other's presence, and at one point the two assassins were less than two hundred yards apart. Unlike his counterpart, Monkh's eyes and thoughts never held on the cemetery, other than a few necessary glances in the name of countersurveillance. Monkh retained a young man's bulletproof surety, and so he saw little need for an afterlife, or for that matter, "making arrangements."

For Monkh, the concept of mortality was analogous to failure. He had always known the risks would be extreme on this mission, yet that, admittedly, was part of the appeal. To achieve the impossible. To pull off the toughest hit ever attempted.

The protections he once relied upon had gone razor-thin. Monkh had begun his lethal career as a state-sponsored actor. Recruited as a teen, he'd advanced through four years of training, and survived five years in the field. By then he was growing wary of his Chinese controllers, whose criteria for assigning missions seemed increasingly tied to their personal agendas as opposed to any kind of national interest. Monkh cared about neither. When a government minister simply ordered him to eliminate a rival, Monkh realized he was playing a fool's game.

So he walked away and went private.

He erased his previous existence, at least, as well as one could in the digital age, and began acquiring business via the dark web. For three years he succeeded spectacularly, gunning down titans of business, heads of state, and heavily guarded crime bosses. In doing so, he acquired wealth far beyond what any spy service could offer. His reputation escalated, bordering on legend. And then the holy grail of assassinations had landed in his shadowed inbox.

Now he wondered where it would all lead. Had he taken a job that exceeded his abilities?

In the beginning he hadn't been sure who he was working for, which was intrinsic to the dark web bargain. Yet as time passed, as the details of the strike became clear, the number of possible suspects narrowed. Thanks to his years working in the Chinese intelligence services, Monkh knew the question to ask.

Who benefits?

Given the power shift in Washington, it was a lengthy list. With enough time, Monkh was sure he could figure it out. But perhaps it was better not to know. If he could finish the job, eliminate Li, he could put all of it in the rearview mirror.

At the bottom of the hill, where the cemetery ended, he turned right and headed toward the room he had rented. It was a pitiful hovel, but he would be leaving soon, and the place had one redeeming quality: it was a mere hundred meters from the gated access road that led to the residences of Victoria Peak.

SIXTY-THREE

The second night Slaton climbed toward Li's home was different from the first. The storm had passed, leaving less visual and audible cover, and the lights of the city were clearer, illuminating open areas. The forest, thankfully, remained shot with shadow.

The other distinction, of course, had nothing to do with his surroundings.

Tonight Slaton carried no sniper rifle, no spare magazines. He wasn't working off reams of fresh intel provided by the CIA. Nor was there a traitorous chauffeur waiting at the base of the hill. Tonight's mission was personal. He was here to find out who had betrayed him.

Like the first night, on reaching the clear area below Li's residence, Slaton stopped to look and listen. His primary focus was on the guards around the house. He saw three at that moment: two on the mid-level balcony, one at the front portico. In all the time he had observed the place, he'd seen no one sweep the perimeter at ground level.

He checked his watch: 10:45 local.

There were lights on throughout the home, but some would soon extinguish. Li, and most likely the commanders of his security team, would turn in for the night. Slaton waited another thirty minutes. When a light flicked off in the main living area, he began moving cautiously toward the house. He took angles that would keep him out of sight from the balcony.

His preparations took twenty-nine minutes, at which point he returned to the edge of the forest. Slaton pulled out his phone and waited. Watched.

The action would begin soon, and when it did he would lose a degree of control. While his objective was clear—getting access to Li—his path to attaining it would be complete improvisation.

Recognizing weak points. Seizing opportunities.

All he needed was for the show to begin.

It was time for a Chinese fire drill.

It all began perfectly. The delay was provided by a switch, a simple mechanical timer. The power source was a stolen motorcycle battery. The makeshift initiator had been purchased by a suspicious Chinda at a fireworks store.

The first flames flickered.

Dryer lint, along with some fuel from a cheap butane lighter, was all the accelerant needed at the outset. Next in line were a pile of greasy rags taken from the ground-floor closet, and old cushions from the discarded patio furniture. Strategically placed fireplace logs raised the temperature, and the bicycle tires and two plastic garbage cans added convincing waves of coal-black smoke. A bit of old lumber near the balcony carried the flames to the lower exterior wall, and soon the steps leading to the wooden balcony were cooking off.

None of it was catastrophic. Not yet.

But the danger was clear and obvious, and on a scale that left no doubt that a handheld fire extinguisher wasn't going to do the job.

Which was exactly what Slaton was after.

"Sir! Wake up!"

Li Qiang stirred from a fitful sleep. He saw Junfeng hovering over him, worry etched deep in a face that seemed to have no other expression. "What is it? What's wrong?"

"There is a fire! We must move to a different room!"

"Fire?" No sooner had the word left Li's lips than he smelled it. An acrid, chemical tang lacing the air. "Where?" he asked.

"We don't know. My men are investigating."

Junfeng pulled him to his feet, and began ushering him toward the staircase. He'd been sleeping in a corner of the basement. In a spill of light at the doorway, Li could see it now—smoke curling through the hallway.

"We should get in the cars and leave!" he said.

"No, that is the last thing we should do. It is possible someone is trying to flush us outside where you are vulnerable."

Li nodded, his mind still lagging reality.

"We will go to your bedroom. It's the farthest away from the smoke, and we can easily get to the front door if needed."

"Shouldn't we call the fire department?"

"I already have . . . they are on the way!"

Li was halfway up the staircase, Junfeng leading the way, when he suddenly stopped. "Wait!" He went back down, retrieved the shotgun, and hurried back to the steps.

Monkh was warming his dinner, half a cardboard carton of leftover takeout, when one of his alarms sounded. He quickly went to the laptop, scanned six divided images, and saw an alert on the top right. A flashing red border around the feed from camera three.

Monkh had pilfered the monitoring system from Chinese intelligence, one of a handful of going-away presents he'd honored himself with. The software was designed to watch for changes in video surveillance feeds. In theory, it was advertised as a backup for security monitoring, but as a practical matter it covered for snoozing guards at camera stations. The system had never found favor with the Ministry of State Security, but for Monkh it had proved a valuable tool—it allowed him, as a solo operator, to maintain continuous surveillance on targets.

Essentially a motion detector on steroids, the software could be configured to alert when certain conditions were recognized in a camera's field of view: the entrance of humans, animals, or vehicles would generate an alarm, as would the occurrence of muzzle flashes or plumes of smoke. At the moment, it was the last of these, surprisingly, that had generated the alert.

On the east side of the residence a great plume of smoke was rising from somewhere near the home's foundation. Monkh tried to recall what exactly had been in that area, but he drew a blank. It was a serious development, and one that might require action. His plan for eliminating Li was both simple and opportunistic. With the compound heavily guarded, he thought the most straightforward strike would be to hit Li as he departed. Not knowing exactly when that would be, and still ruminating over ideas for creating a need for his departure, Monkh had planted a network of cameras to monitor the house. On the first sign of activity suggesting that Li might depart, Monkh would hurry into position and make the kill.

It seemed highly likely that the scene he was looking at now would create that chance.

He immediately began gathering his gear, all of which was ready. He had already performed a dry run, and knew that he could reach his staging point on the road in fifteen minutes. The last thing he retrieved was a large canvas rucksack containing his weapon of choice. He shrugged it onto his back, and was about to head for the door when he hesitated. He turned back to the laptop.

The scene he was looking at seemed too good to be true. Almost the kind of event he might manufacture himself.

Wave after wave of black smoke pulsed in camera three. Monkh shifted to the other views—as a born-and-bred gamer, he was an expert at split-screen observation. His eye snagged on a flash of movement in camera five. Northeast corner, with a partial view of the road and driveway. A dark figure moved along the perimeter, masking expertly behind the foliage. The shadow got no closer to the house, but was arcing counterclockwise. A shark circling its prey.

Monkh watched intently, and suddenly he was struck by a sense of familiarity. The build, the movement. This was someone he knew.

His first impression was disbelief. Next came shock. But no, he was not mistaken.

Monkh felt like he was looking at a ghost—and maybe he was. He knew perfectly well he had shot this man. Watched him tumble into a rage of whitewater. Yet the body had never been found. And now here he was, days later, stalking the target he'd missed. Monkh respected that kind of tenacity. He had heard much about this legendary assassin. Most of it, of course, was second-and third-hand prattle, accounts of audacity and daring that were surely more fiction than fact.

He began to run a matrix, his usual pregame assessment of strengths and weaknesses. The man was experienced, having operated across the globe. How many targets he had taken out, Monkh had no idea.

He himself had sixty-one kills to his credit. Not the virtual kind he'd racked up for so long, but living targets of flesh and blood. It would be a good score in any game, but in real life it was intoxicating. His count had nearly gone to sixty-two, and might still get there, if only Elayne Cleveland would die. Monkh's proficiency was not sourced from his gaming background, at least not directly. He was simply a good assassin for the same reasons he was good with a joystick. His focus, his intensity, his rapid reactions. He had worked in Sri Lanka, Congo, Romania, and Singapore. Now the United States. Yet most of his kills had come in China, and he was intimately familiar with Hong Kong.

In the end, he decided his advantage over the CIA man would be the same as ever: he was younger and quicker, able to sight and shoot without match.

Then his calculations hit a hitch. Why was he even considering a comparison?

The assassin had come to eliminate Li, which left two possible outcomes. Either he would succeed, doing Monkh's job for him, or he would fail and be killed. He watched the man move smoothly toward the road, and soon camera one picked up an excellent view. As far as Monkh could tell, the assassin wasn't even armed. It made sense. *I gave him a rifle when he arrived, but he lost it on the hill. And to acquire a gun in Hong Kong these days is not so easy.*

Still, he marveled at the man's hubris. He was invading a fortress compound, brimming with armed guards, but carrying no weapon.

Monkh set his gear down by the door, pulled up a chair behind the laptop, and brought camera one to full screen. Like all successful operators, he was well-versed in the history of warfare, and the words of Napoleon came to mind.

Never interrupt your enemy when he's making a mistake.

He sat down and waited for the show to begin.

SIXTY-FOUR

"Where the hell is she?" Matt Gross shouted.

Eraclides was not accustomed to raised voices. Staid legal briefs, negotiations in conference rooms—that was more his style. The occasional pointed remark might be dropped, but it was an inherently civil business. Shouting matches in the Oval Office, in front of an acting president, had never been on his radar.

"I'm not sure where Anna has gone," he said. "She procured a jet through agency channels early yesterday, but I don't know where she went. Her pilots haven't been responding to the usual operational messages, although that's not unheard of. Owing to the nature of its mission, SAC/SOG air assets often operate off network."

"*'Off network'*? You make it sound like a damned mobile phone plan. We are trying to navigate the nation through a crisis, and the woman who got us in this bind has gone AWOL!"

"It wasn't her fault that—"

"Enough!" Quarrels commanded.

Silence took hold. Ten minutes earlier, every chair in the room had been taken in a full meeting of the national security council. When the meeting ended, Quarrels had ordered Gross and Eraclides to remain behind.

Quarrels asked, "Could it have to do with our disaster in Hong Kong?"

Eraclides tried to ignore the characterization. "I've seen nothing to suggest it, but that does seem to be the focal point lately. When Anna gets in touch, and I'm sure she will soon, I'll get some answers and let you know."

Gross said, "And when you're done getting answers, you can tell her she's fired! We can't have the damned head of clandestine operations going off on rogue missions."

Eraclides was about to raise his voice in response when he noticed the vice president nodding. If he'd learned one thing during his years as the agency's attorney general, it was that some battles were unwinnable.

Richard Cleveland entered his wife's room to find Dr. Singh leaving.

Singh shot him a peeved look. "This charade can't go on much longer," he said in a clipped tone. "If necessary, I will declare this patient to be not of sound mind and mandate better care despite her protests."

"I don't think that will be necessary, doctor. Give us one more day."

Singh fumed, but didn't argue further.

"How is she, by the way?"

The doctor sank a pen into his breast pocket. He'd forgotten to click it shut, and it left a blue streak just beneath his nicely scripted name.

"She's doing remarkably well, everything considered. But if we don't start certain therapies in the next twenty-four hours, I will not be held accountable for her progress going forward."

"Give me a minute with her. I'll see what I can do."

Singh disappeared through the door. The makeshift curtain was already shut.

Richard approached the bed and took his wife's hand. "Hey, Darlin'."

Elayne Cleveland opened one eye, checking that the coast was clear. When the other popped open, she looked more alert than Richard had seen her since the crash.

"Therapy my ass!" she said. "I'm feeling more myself every day."

"Evidently."

"Any news?"

"Actually, there is." He removed his phone from his pocket and handed it over.

Elayne took it with her good left hand. She noticed a call was active. "Who is it?" she asked.

"Miss Sorensen. She says she has some good news."

The president put the phone gently to her left ear, which was partially covered by a post-surgery bandage. "Anna?"

"Hi, boss." Sorensen's voice came with a time lag that sounded distant.

"Where are you?"

"I'm not exactly sure . . ."

Elayne Cleveland doubted that, suspecting Sorensen didn't want to give away her position on a line that could be compromised. It was probably the right answer. "All right then, tell me what you can . . ."

Twelve minutes after the emergency call was logged from the residence on Victoria Peak, two fire trucks arrived. It would have been sooner, but there was a delay getting through the gate at the bottom of the hill.

They parked on diagonals on the street in front of the house, one adjacent to each corner of the residence. With smoke pouring from the base of the home, crews bundled from the trucks and got to work. There were twelve firemen in all, dressed in full gear.

The fire chief took charge. He ordered two men to circle the house to seek out hot zones, wanting an idea of what they were facing. Another set of three he assigned to the house, tasked to ensure there was no one still inside. This team rushed to the front door, donning their oxygen masks to keep the thick smoke at bay. The rest of the men scurried around the trucks, unreeling hoses and turning on pumps. Two men dragged a supply hose down the street to find the nearest hydrant, which, according to their map, was seventy meters to the east.

Smoke was engulfing the rear of the house, and while there was no sign of open flames, the sound of wood crackling filled the night air. To any bystander it would have looked like controlled chaos. Truth be known, it looked that way to the chief himself. No matter what the level of training or experience, the first minutes on the scene of any raging fire was nothing short of bedlam.

Of the three men tasked to clear the house, two went inside to begin the search. The third remained stationed at the front door. By protocol, this man had very specific duties. He was to keep track of who went in and who came out. He would direct any civilians who emerged to a safe holding area, and also serve as a backup should anyone inside report problems over the communications network—each man inside carried a radio beneath the collar of his thermal jacket.

It all went as planned for sixty seconds. The man at the door heard chatter between the two inside, and then they reported that survivors would be coming out soon. On cue, three burly men appeared, all of them coughing and holding their shirt collars over their mouths. He instructed them to go to the street and gather behind the nearest engine. The men looked at one another questioningly, but then complied, disappearing in that direction.

Nothing happened for a time, and the door man contemplated inquiring as to the situation inside. This was, as he would recount ten hours later from a hospital bed, and with a very large lump on his skull, the last thing he remembered about his call-out that night to Victoria Peak.

SIXTY-FIVE

In a perfect world, the fireman who'd ended up isolated from the others would have been roughly Slaton's size. With any luck at all, he would have been a few sizes larger. Unfortunately, the man he'd overpowered turned out to be five inches shorter and built like a matchstick. His thermal suit fit Slaton like a rubber sweater. It was far too small, leaving his wrists and ankles exposed. The boots were four sizes too small, so he simply kept his trail shoes on. He doubted it would matter. Given the level of confusion, the smoke, and the rapidly changing conditions, it would take an astute observer to notice ill-fitting gear.

The good news was that the filtered mask and helmet were staying in place. They would provide camouflage as well as fresh air. The only drawback was that the faceplate limited his field of view in the periphery. Breathing compressed air through the mask would be vital in the coming minutes. Slaton didn't know how fast the fire would spread, or for that matter, whether the crews outside could contain it. Mossad, in its infinite and cynical wisdom, provided training to all its assassins in the fine art of arson. The first lesson, however, had been the most instructive: fire was inherently unpredictable.

He had attempted to create a governed inferno,

more smoke and disorder than flames and death. As Slaton went through to the main living area, he thought he might have overdone it. The smoke was so dense he could barely see the windows and balcony at the far side of the room. Swirling plumes of black vented from a partially open sliding glass door, some kind of Venturi effect taking hold.

He tuned it all out to focus on his mission.

Slaton had set the blaze on the lowest level of the house, maximizing the effect on the central basement by loosening an exposed ventilation duct. That, based on the floor plan he'd memorized, as well as tactical common sense, was probably where Li had holed up. When the fire began cooking, he figured Li would have two options: either move to a higher level, hoping the fire could be contained, or bolt out the front door to escape. Slaton had been watching the front door closely. So far, three men had emerged, and none were Li Qiang. Aside from Li, he estimated that between three and five men remained inside, along with the two firefighters he'd seen go in.

Slaton saw no one in the main room, but he did hear voices to his right. The main living area was sided by bedrooms, and the master suite was on the top floor, accessed by a lone staircase to his right. From a security standpoint, the top floor would be the most defensible. In terms of fire safety, the two main floor bedrooms allowed an easier escape. Slaton decided it came down to who was running the show: a suspicious security team, or a frightened Li Qiang.

Slaton moved toward the first bedroom on the main floor. He was halfway there when he saw commotion in the doorway. Three of Li's security men came out coughing. Two were carrying handguns, but not in a threatening way. They looked at Slaton and said something in Chinese. He shouted unintelligibly into his mask, enough to make a muffled noise. He then pointed to his mask, and waved frantically toward the barely visible front door.

Hired guns were a predictable lot, and these held to form. Faced with a choice between abandoning their protectee and burning alive, they bolted for the door and disappeared. Slaton hoped they didn't circle to the west side of the house, where he'd deposited one unconscious fireman near a tree—bound and gagged for good measure.

He could feel the heat through his thermal jacket, pulsing waves from the stairwell that led to the basement. He quickly cleared the two rooms on the main floor, but saw no one else. Then Slaton heard shouting from the top floor. He posted to the bottom of the rising stairwell and looked up. Through swirls of haze he saw a fireman at the top. He had dropped his mask and was talking on a radio.

And that, Slaton realized, was a problem.

Monkh sat transfixed behind his laptop.

He'd watched in fascination as Corsair had disabled a fireman and donned his protective gear. He next dragged the unconscious man out of sight, around the far wall. Why he simply hadn't killed the man, Monkh had no idea. Perhaps he had done so after getting him out of sight. Was Corsair that ruthless? Or was he curbed, as were so many Western operators, by boundaries of law and honor?

With no camera coverage inside the house, Monkh was blind to what was happening. He watched more of Li's guards emerge from the front door and run away. Then nothing happened for a time. Flames were advancing on the east side of the house, licking up the siding and consuming the balcony. The fire crews were losing the battle, backing away rather than advancing, and for some reason they seemed to be running low on water—one of his cameras showed a crew up the street still hunting for a fire hydrant.

The situation was becoming critical, forcing Monkh to a decision. His surveillance network was not accessible on his phone—a mistake on his part. If he left the safe house he would have no eyes on the target area. Yet if he stayed where he was, given the fast-moving situation on the hill, Li might rush to escape and his chance would be gone.

One finger tapped on the laptop's case. He was agonizingly close to tying up the last loose end. If Li disappeared now, it could take weeks, even months to track him down.

Monkh snapped the computer shut, retrieved his bag, and headed for the door.

SIXTY-SIX

Slaton was certain that Li was upstairs. Unfortunately, with the disaster he'd created growing out of control, time wasn't on his side. He saw only one option—he was going to have to go up and get him. Before he entered the fray, however, Slaton wanted to control what he could.

He reached into the biggest pocket on his thermal coat and removed a radio—no doubt, the same model every man was carrying. The transceiver was already turned on, the volume set to midrange. He heard a constant back-and-forth on the comm net, much of it coming from the chief, he guessed.

Slaton studied the compact handset. Other than a side-mounted press-to-talk button, he saw only two controls. Both were labeled with Chinese characters, but it wasn't hard to deduce their purpose. One was an on-off switch, the other a thumbwheel to control the volume. Most importantly, he saw no knob for changing frequencies. This was different from many tactical radios, but it made sense in the situation— multiple channels weren't necessary for fighting fires since jamming wasn't an issue.

He looked down at the left sleeve of his jacket. For reasons he didn't completely understand, a thick strip of red tape encircled the upper arm above the elbow.

It was probably an identifier, a way to signify a particular firefighter's job or duty when masks prevented facial recognition.

His plan evolved, and Slaton looked around for one more component. On a nearby bookcase shelf he saw, of all things, a box of ammunition, the cardboard flap open on one end. From a purely tactical point of view, it reminded him that the guards were armed and ready. Conversely, leaving boxes of ammo lying around implied complacency. Until twenty minutes ago, they had felt safe in this place.

Slaton ungloved one hand, opened the box, and found it half-full of 9mm hollow points. He extracted a round, set it on the shelf, and then unwrapped the red tape from his arm. He held the bullet over the radio's press-to-talk switch, pushed it down, and wrapped the tape tightly to keep it in place.

The speaker went to static, with intermittent clicks and garbled words as others tried to talk over the continuous transmission. Slaton turned up the volume on the speaker, and instantaneously feedback made it all worse. It was a classic "hot mic" and would render the channel useless. Communications jamming in its simplest form.

He set the radio on the shelf and again peered up the stairwell. The fireman who'd been there was no longer in sight, but Slaton heard shouting in Chinese. He'd seen most of Li's men leave the house, and he figured two remained upstairs. Plus or minus. Along with the two firemen and Li himself. All in one very small space.

Slaton mentally reviewed the diagram he'd seen of the upper floor: master bedroom, connecting bathroom, two closets. He prepared himself for what was going to be a frenetic scene: two men in thermal yellow suits, a minimum of two edgy guards, and the last remaining member of The Trident. All in one smoke-filled room.

He took a deep breath of compressed air and rushed up the staircase.

Outside, the fire chief was furious. The blaze was getting out of hand, and now somebody was running around with a hot mic, ruining their voice network. Right before the comms had gone down, the two men in the house had reported that three individuals on the top floor were refusing to leave. The chief tried to order the man he'd posted at the door to go up as a reinforcement, but he hadn't answered the call.

Just when he thought things couldn't get worse, the two men who'd gone down the street returned on a dead run.

"Sir," one said, "the hydrant isn't where the map shows it to be."

The chief looked at the reservoir gauge on the command truck. It was nearly empty. The second truck had to be in roughly the same shape. If they didn't get a supply line soon, they were going to lose the house. He was faced with a terrible choice. He could send these two inside as reinforcements to get everyone off the fourth floor, but that meant abandoning the search for a hydrant. Do that, and they would definitely lose the structure. He decided that the worsening conditions, if nothing else, would convince the civilians to evacuate.

The chief pointed up the road in the opposite direction. "The map must be wrong! Go look that way!" The two men hustled away.

The chief moved to get a better look at the back

of the home. The flames were working higher and a window had been breached. He looked at the front door, but saw no sign of anyone emerging.

Why would anyone stay inside a burning building? he wondered.

As it turned out, the chief would never get an answer to that question. Nor would he get one for a second question that arose hours later, in the aftermath of the blaze, when the mystery of the unlocatable water supply was resolved.

Why would anyone would hide a fire hydrant beneath a fake plastic boulder?

Sorensen was completely alone. Which was exactly how she wanted it.

She was sitting quietly in a small room, deep in a fortified bunker in a country that was rife with them. As deputy director of the CIA, she was accustomed to exchanging favors with peers in foreign countries. Right now she was running up a tab that, if it ever got repaid, would likely not be on her watch. Whether her efforts succeeded or not, the risks she was incurring would surely end her career at the agency.

Leery of any connection to headquarters, she was using assets that were entirely local. A computer station had been provided, as well as two reconnaissance feeds—one was a stealthy drone, the other a commercial satellite stream.

She stared intently at the monitor before her. A split-screen image of Li Qiang's residence stared back. Her theory had been purely speculative. If she were honest, something closer to hope. Yet what Sorensen had seen in the last twenty minutes validated her hunch. Li's house was going up in flames, and there was activity all around. First responders, mostly, and a handful of people evacuating the residence.

But is it what I think it is? she wondered.

If she was right, now was the time to act. And if she wasn't?

Sorensen smiled humorlessly. *Now's the time to act.*

She picked up the internal phone and called her counterpart in the local intelligence agency, a man who, thankfully, owed her a good number of favors. "I'm going to need one more thing," she said when he answered. "And it's a very big ask . . ."

SIXTY-SEVEN

When he reached the top of the stairwell, the first thing Slaton saw was a gun. This was good for two reasons. First was that he needed to acquire a weapon. Second was that it wasn't pointed at him.

He held three steps short of the top, scouting the upper floor. The staircase was misted in smoke, and he doubted anyone without eye protection would be able to see him. The direness of the situation was accelerating—the shouting on the top floor had turned to coughing. Very soon, Li and his guards were going to make a bad choice. They were going to decide that the fire was the greatest threat they faced.

The guard with the gun was standing near a window along the front wall. His weapon was at his side, and his opposing forearm was raised over his face, the sleeve of his jacket covering his mouth in a feeble attempt to filter the smoke. Slaton edged one step higher. His right hip remained sore, and while he tried to tune out the pain, it was a reminder that he was still not a hundred percent.

He peered around the top of the stairwell and saw the rest of the crowd: two firemen, another guard, and Li himself. The second guard was standing next to Li. His jacket was open in front and Slaton saw a

372 | WARD LARSEN

holstered weapon on his abdomen, configured for a right-hand draw. Li was gesturing wildly at the man and had a death grip on the back of an upholstered chair. He obviously didn't want to leave. The guard was pulling him by the elbow and saying something in Chinese. Something along the lines of, *Let's get the hell out of here!*

Slaton was weighing which guard to engage when he saw something that changed the equation entirely. Leaning against a wall nearby was a semiautomatic shotgun. Slaton recognized it as a Benelli M4. The weapon had a magazine tube in place, and was presumably loaded. The safety near the trigger was set for a right-hand grip.

Instinct took over.

Slaton rushed into the open, a working fireman cresting a flight of stairs. Both guards glanced at him, but seeing only one more first responder, neither reacted. One of the firemen began shouting through his mask and gesturing at Slaton. The other fiddled with his useless radio. Slaton barked through his mask to confuse things further, unintelligible words in no particular language.

He was five steps away from Li.

Three from the nearest guard.

Two from the Benelli.

Planning his next three moves, Slaton lunged for the shotgun. He gripped it with both hands, flicked off the safety, and whipped the barrel toward the guard with a weapon in his hand. The guard made Slaton's next decision for him—he began to raise his gun. Slaton fired.

The gun bucked. The close-quarters shot hit the man squarely in the chest and he flew back into the window.

Glass shattered and he fell through, dropping fifteen feet to the ground outside.

Slaton absorbed the recoil and kept the Benelli moving, settling the barrel on the second guard. He reached for his weapon, again forcing Slaton's hand. But he was also very close to Li. Slaton shifted to the guard's left side and fired again. The off-center hit was devastating enough. The guard spun to the floor, his weapon flying out of his hand.

Slaton settled the barrel on Li, then paused to assess the situation. Li stood frozen. His eyes looked watery and he was coughing, yet he was immobilized by fear. The firemen's expressions were hidden behind their glass faceplates, yet their body language suggested that they too were stunned. Neither made any attempt to fight or flee.

Cradling the gun steadily with one arm, Slaton raised his free hand. Then he lowered it, palm down, twice—the international calming gesture. The crackling of the fire was getting louder, and the broken window had created a chimney effect, a torrent of dense smoke flooding up the stairwell.

Slaton had to work fast.

Neither of the guards appeared to be alive, and both had dropped their handguns. Slaton picked up the nearest, a Sig Sauer, and pocketed it. The other was a Beretta, and he ejected the magazine and the round in the chamber, and threw the weapon out the window. He quickly gauged the room and began making decisions.

With the shotgun crooked under his arm, he shuffled sideways to a closed door. He opened it and saw a mostly empty walk-in closet. He backed away and used the Benelli's hot barrel to direct the two firemen inside. One complied instantly, but other began protesting in muffled Chinese. Slaton raised the shotgun to his shoulder menacingly, bridging any language barrier, and the second man relented.

Once both firemen were inside, Slaton pointed with his free hand to what one of them was carrying on his equipment belt—a fireman's hand axe. With one eye on Li, Slaton closed the closet door. Along the wall next to the door was a sturdy dresser. Slaton pushed it in front of the door using his good hip.

His most immediate problems were solved. Li's security team was neutralized, and the firemen were out of the picture. The dresser blocking the closet door was heavy, but the two of them could easily push their way out. Or hack their way through with the axe. At that point, they would either risk running down the stairs, or more likely go to the window and shout for a ladder. If that failed, the jump wouldn't kill them. All of that would take a few minutes.

Which was all Slaton needed.

Li had dropped to his knees. He was coughing uncontrollably, overcome by the smoke. At that moment, even the simplest of questions would be outside his mental blast radius. Slaton knew the next step had to be executed with care. He took the Benelli in both hands, flicked the safety on, and reversed his grip. He took careful aim and brought the matte-black stock down on the base of Li Qiang's skull.

SIXTY-EIGHT

The fire chief was relieved to see one of his men finally emerge from the front door. He couldn't tell who it was because the man had somehow lost the strip of tape around his upper arm. Feng, he guessed, or possibly Kwan. Whoever it was, he had an unconscious victim over his shoulders in a fireman's carry.

The chief shouted to get the man's attention, but he didn't seem to hear. He ran behind one of the trucks, still hauling the survivor, and disappeared.

The chief was on the verge of incandescence. They had lost control of the fire, and he still had two men inside the house, not to mention an unknown number of civilians. Desperate to get a grasp on the situation inside, he tossed his useless radio into the wet dirt and set out to get a look for himself. He hadn't gone two steps when he heard shouting from above. The chief looked up and saw his missing men at the upper window on the west side of the house.

Their masks were off, despite the billowing smoke, and they were shouting for a ladder.

From a distance the scene was nothing short of chaos. Monkh saw two fire trucks in front of the house, and the blaze had advanced rapidly in the ten minutes since he'd left the flat. Flames were scalding the back roofline and currents of smoke pumped into an obsidian sky. Curiously, the only firefighters he could see were manning a hose that was nearly useless—it looked like they were working a garden hose. He wondered if that was Corsair's doing. But only for a moment.

Of course it was him.

He caught a glimpse of motion near one of the fire trucks. A fireman in full gear was carrying a survivor away from the house, the limp body draped over his shoulders. There was an optic buried in the canvas bag Monkh was carrying, but he had no time to retrieve it before the fireman disappeared behind the truck. Again, he reprimanded himself for not having mobile access to his camera feeds.

Had the survivor been Li Qiang? Monkh hadn't gotten a good look, but it was quite possible. If so, what did it mean? Was Corsair still in the building, overcome by the fire he'd set? No, he was better than that.

What was happening then?

Monkh had to get closer. He shouldered the big ruck and pushed eastward through the dense foliage. He was fifty meters from the house when the front façade came into view. There, on the right side, he saw an even more curious sight. Two firemen were climbing down a ladder from an upper-level window.

He didn't know what to make of it. His own plan for eliminating Li was completely sidelined. The primary weapon he'd brought, hidden in the ruck, was ready to go. Yet as powerful as that was, it didn't suit the situation. Li might now end up in an ambulance or a fire truck, not the soft sedan Monkh had been counting on.

When the two firemen reached the bottom of the ladder, they launched into a heated conversation with what looked like a supervisor. There was a lot of gesturing and handplay. Then the supervisor pointed behind the nearest truck, to the point where the fireman carrying the survivor had disappeared.

Disappeared.

And with that, the switch flicked in Monkh's head. Now he understood.

The trace of a smile creased his lips. He had just seen Corsair in action. Then the smile ghosted away. But why had he hauled Li clear? Why not just kill him and be done with it, and then escape in the heat of the moment? The answer came swiftly.

Because he hadn't come to kill him.

The implication of that—why Corsair had *rescued* Li—was as clear as it was sobering. It meant that Monkh, along with his employer, might be facing a new peril—the threat of exposure.

A pang of discomfort wormed into his gut, a sensation Monkh had never felt before.

Fear? Not exactly.

Closer to resentment. At every turn, Corsair seemed to be one step ahead.

How much more had he gotten wrong about the man? Had Corsair intentionally missed his second shot that night? Preserving the life of the one man who knew enough to ruin everything?

It made perfect sense. Yet it also implied a measure of control, a self-assuredness, that few men possessed.

Now Corsair had invaded Li's compound, defeated a large security detail, and hauled him away under everyone's nose. The last remaining member of The Trident was in the hands of the enemy.

Then Monkh had a new revelation. Having worked out what was about to happen, he realized *where* it would take place.

He set out quickly through the pitch-dark forest.

SIXTY-NINE

Li moaned weakly, which was a good sign. At least, from Slaton's point of view.

Head blows were a delicately nuanced art. Hit a guy too hard, and you got a brain bleed and death. Don't hit him hard enough, and you'd just piss him off. Slaton had metered his blow with the Benelli just about right. He'd stunned Li, but he had never lost consciousness.

After hauling Li from the inferno that had been his house, Slaton needed a safe space for an interrogation that hopefully wouldn't take long. Ten minutes, he guessed, twenty at the outside. If he didn't have what he needed by then, he wasn't going to get it. Thankfully, the house under construction, where he'd set up six nights ago, was still available. And it wasn't too far to carry a dazed hundred-and-eighty-pound man.

Best of all, at this time of night it was bound to be empty.

Slaton found a battery-operated work light as he entered the place, and after turning it on he hung it from an exposed nail. He deposited his detainee in what would become the main living area of the residence. High above was the partially finished roof; the skeletal trusses he'd seen days ago were now half-covered with plywood, and the remainder was open to a starlit night sky. Below, mirroring Li's residence, was a lower level basement accessed by a roughed-in stairway.

All around were piles of lumber, drywall, and boxes of screws. A thick sheet of glass, destined for a large window, stood vertically on a rack near one wall. Food wrappers and empty drink bottles accumulated in the corners. A half dozen power tools had been left behind haphazardly by yesterday's crew—implying they were owned by the construction company and not the workers themselves—and extension cords ran riot across the floor. Li was presently propped against a mortar mixer in a sitting position, his shoulders covered with crumbs of dried stucco. His eyes were open but not entirely focused.

Slaton would remedy that soon.

He worked quickly against a running clock that he himself had started. Three hundred and six meters away was a house burning to the ground. In and around it were two dead bodyguards, and two witnesses who'd seen the victims killed with a shotgun by an assassin in fireman's gear. And of course, one fireman, minus his protective clothing, was probably also back in the mix.

Tick tock.

Slaton began with the five-gallon bucket next to the mixer. It was half full of murky water, no doubt intended for thinning mortar during the mixing process. He held the bucket over Li, tipped it slowly, and three gallons of cold, thin mud splattered onto his head.

Li's arms and legs spasmed, and his eyes saucered open. He sputtered and coughed, his overwhelmed lungs now violated by liquid after so much smoke. Slaton bent onto one knee, putting their faces level. Li stared at him with the eyes of a man who was alone and afraid. The eyes of a man who understood the depth of his disadvantage.

Slaton knew that Li spoke English—it had been in his file—but he didn't know his level of proficiency. He would keep things simple.

"Do you know who I am?"

The round face calmed a bit, rational words setting the world just a little straighter. Li studied Slaton for a moment as he contemplated an answer. "I think so."

"Good. Do you know why I'm here?"

Li's dark eyes assessed the room, wondering where "here" was. And probably searching for an escape in a place that held none. "You have come to kill me," he said.

"Originally, yes—four nights ago. But at the last moment, I changed my mind. I had you lined up in my sight, finger on the trigger, when it occurred to me that you might have some very valuable information. So I let you live. Consider that my gift. And I gave you another today, when I pulled you out of a burning house."

Li looked at him disbelievingly.

"Yes, I know what you're thinking—that I'm the one who put you in these difficult situations. But that's not entirely true." Slaton gestured to the half-finished house around them. "The truth is, you put yourself here, Qiang. You and whoever is controlling The Trident. And that's what I want to talk about. Who gives The Trident its orders?"

Slaton let that sit for a few beats, watching Li digest the question. He would be weighing a great many things. He would wonder whether answering, or not answering, affected his chances of survival. He would wonder if a deal could be made.

Slaton himself wasn't sure. He had been sent to Hong Kong to kill Li, but the very source of that order was now in question. Had it come from a traitor? The same person, possibly, who had sent Thomas after him?

Li said, "If I tell you what I know, you will kill me anyway."

"Probably. But if you don't tell me, I'll definitely kill you. And it won't be quick."

Slaton reached into his pocket and Li tensed. It wasn't an unwarranted reaction. There had been no way to keep the Benelli when he hauled Li out of his burning house, yet the Sig was in his pocket. That wasn't what he was reaching for. Slaton had searched Li carefully after arriving and, as expected, found no weapons. He had, however, discovered two items in his hip pocket that were disturbingly familiar.

Slaton pulled out a high-end phone and a battery, displaying one in each hand.

Li's reaction was slight. But it was there.

"I was wondering about this phone," Slaton said. "It looks a lot like one I was issued when I came here. The fact that you've removed the battery seems suspicious to me." Slaton pried the back cover from the handset and seated the battery in place.

"What are you doing?" Li asked.

Slaton turned the phone on, and after it spun to life, he rotated the screen and put it close to Li's face. The phone unlocked.

Slaton tapped up the contact information. There was only one number in the entire registry. It didn't look familiar. Slaton smiled, put the phone to speaker, and tapped down.

Somewhere, a phone began ringing.

SEVENTY

The call went unanswered. Slaton wasn't surprised. Whoever owned the receiving handset was aware of Li's execution order. They probably also knew it hadn't been carried out. A call from this phone would incite panic. Which, from Slaton's point of view, was sufficient reason to try. He was mildly disappointed there had been no voice mail prompt. If the call itself wasn't enough of a shock, a message from the ghost of an assassin would have been the devil's playground.

Satisfying as all that was, it got Slaton no closer to the answer he needed. Who was the traitor responsible for killing so many American servicemen? Who had tried to kill the president? Who had tried to kill him?

The countdown in his head was nearing zero.

It was time to incentivize Li.

He pocketed the phone, bent down, and gripped Li by the collar. Slaton hauled him to a standing position, marched him a few steps sideways, and slammed him into the roughed-in banister. Behind the raw wood rail was an unfinished staircase leading to the floor below.

"Do not move," Slaton said.

He turned toward the mortar mixer. It was a commercial-grade item, a big red bucket cradled on a frame the size of a barbecue grill. Beneath the mixing

bucket was a small engine that powered the contrap-
tion.

Having seen its potential, Slaton had already made
a quick operational check while Li was still groggy. It
worked like a champ. He pulled the starter cord and
the engine fired to life. Li, who as instructed hadn't
moved, stared wide-eyed. Inside the bucket were
mixing paddles that resembled curved lawn mower
blades, a mechanical helix designed to blend water
and aggregate. Slaton pulled a lever and the blades began their scything rotation.

Slaton retrieved Li and dragged him nearer the
mixer. As a method of harm, the machine was crude
and marginally lethal. As a method of terror it was
brilliantly effective.

Li tried to backpedal.

Slaton pushed him closer.

Slaton was still feeling the effects of his injuries, and
he tried to divert stress to the points where he was stron-
gest. Li fought weakly at first, but then Slaton locked
out one of his arms and pushed it toward the spiraling
blades. Li descended into full-on panic. He flailed and
began screaming. "No, please! I will tell you!"

Slaton froze things there, Li's hand inches from the
mixer blades. Then Li made a decision that surprised
Slaton. He tried to fight.

Li struck Slaton with his free elbow. What would
normally have been an ineffectual blow hit him
squarely on the healing wound on his abdomen. The
pain rocked Slaton, but he never lost his grip on Li's
arm. The shift in balance sent them reeling together,
neither in control of the momentum. Unbalanced, Li
pitched forward and his hand sank into the mixer. The
pitch of the little engine slowed as the blades came in
contact with flesh and bone.

Li screamed, and Slaton twisted to pull him free. Both men tumbled to the floor.

Slaton was instantly back on his feet, set in a solid stance. Li lay whimpering, clutching his hand, which was bloody but intact. His face had collapsed in defeat, and Slaton stared at him for a long moment. If Li could have given up his employer, he would have done so before engaging in a hopeless fight.

The bleak truth crystallized: he truly didn't know who was controlling the Trident.

It made sense in a way. Li would have suspicions, certainly. Yet the traitor in Washington would be diligent in concealing his identity. Now, looking at a traumatized man on the floor, Slaton saw only one more dead end.

Slaton stood a bit straighter, and was wondering what else Li might know when a distant flash in the periphery caught his eye.

The next moments came at the speed of war.

Slaton was overcome by instinct. He had seen such flashes many times, and even before he could turn his head and focus, he was moving—the reaction of a survivor who had spent countless years in countless hotspots.

He never actually saw the rocket hurtling toward the house. He was too busy diving toward the stairwell.

The explosion rocked the night. The fire chief had heard many blasts before, usually gas tanks or chemical reservoirs lighting off. This one, however, sounded different. Even more curiously, it wasn't sourced from the house that was torching in front of him.

He looked up the road, and saw a few tendrils of

flame dancing in a distant structure. It all seemed to die down quickly, which was just as well. He had no water supply, one of his men was injured, and reinforcements were slow in arriving. The last thing he needed was another fire to deal with.

In the scant light reflecting from the city, the chief noted wisps of smoke fading into the night. Whatever it was, it would simply have to wait.

Slaton's call to the White House went unanswered, but not unnoticed.

The owner of the receiving phone had just left a high-level meeting in which, despite his pressing, there had been frustratingly little news on the situation in Hong Kong. After making sure he was alone, he sequestered himself in private hallway and checked the phone. When he saw the missed call, it mystified him for a moment. He had been expecting a call, but from Monkh. Why would Li, after all that had happened, try to reach him?

Then he began to worry—because the only answers were damning.

He quickly powered the phone down.

The dead handset seemed inordinately heavy. He briefly wondered how he could best dispose of it, only to realize what a handicap that would create. It was his only link to Monkh. His only link to what was happening in Hong Kong. He pocketed the phone.

He *would* get rid of it soon.

But not until he'd confirmed that the job was done.

Slaton's ears were ringing from the blast. He struggled to a sitting position on the bottom stair and did a quick self-assessment. No new pains, no obvious bloodstains, no jagged slashes in his yellow jacket and pants. He stood tentatively. Everything seemed functional, outside the tympanic orchestra in his ears.

The incoming round, a rocket-propelled grenade, he guessed, had impacted directly on the floor above—roughly where he'd been standing seconds earlier. Slaton had fallen halfway down the plywood stairs, tumbling out of control, when the projectile struck. He'd been protected by the wood stairs and wallboard. Looking upward, he saw the wall on the higher floor shredded with shrapnel perforations. For all the destruction, the mixer was still churning away obediently. He regarded the basement around him. The walls here were concrete block, giving solid protection. In one corner a small generator sat silently, and from it a heavy extension cord threaded up the stairwell.

He considered who would be outside using heavy weapons. Only one name came to mind. *Thomas.* Slaton cautiously climbed back to the main floor, wary that a follow-on shot might be imminent. The damage came into view gradually, and it was significant, but not extreme. The room was only partially enclosed, and the lack of walls had helped disperse energy, mitigating the usual overpressure. The round had impacted the far wall, a smoking black hole centered in a sheet of plywood. He saw shrapnel damage all around.

He crested the stairs and finally saw Li. He was right where Slaton had left him, motionless in a fast-spreading pool of blood. Keeping low, Slaton crawled across the floor, which gave concealment from the point outside where he'd seen the RPG launch. Reaching Li's side, he checked for a pulse. There was none.

The right side of his face and neck were peppered with shrapnel, and a gaping wound on his chest was surely fatal.

Slaton kept moving.

If Thomas was outside, he would likely come to verify his kills. Slaton crawled low and fast toward a gap in the back northern wall. He looked out and tried to pinpoint the distant spot where he'd seen the flash. At first, he saw nothing, only the edge of the treeline—very near the point where he himself had paused to wait and watch on his first night here. Then movement caught his shooter's eye, a momentary flash in the light of a rising moon. After that, nothing.

Slaton weighed his options. Thomas was still over a hundred meters away, but he would come to the house. He knew because that's what he would have done. Slaton had a Sig with one full magazine. His adversary was packing an RPG and god-only-knew what else. Thomas would be cautious, but he couldn't wait long. The explosion would attract attention, and first responders were near.

Tick tock. The very same clock he had been facing.

Slaton was faced with a choice. He could easily run. He could head for the street and disappear over the far side of Victoria Peak. But that wasn't going to happen. This man had tried to kill him twice and failed. Almost surely, he would try again.

That made him a threat to Slaton's family.

Which was all the reason he needed.

SEVENTY-ONE

There was a time for speed and a time for caution. Monkh was feeling the latter as he approached the house under construction.

He knew time was limited—the collection of strobing lights in front of Li's house was growing fast, and the first police cars had joined the fray. His immediate problem was fifty meters of open ground between the treeline and the house under construction. Monkh was sure he'd seen Corsair and Li in his optic right before launching the RPG, and the round had struck his aim point perfectly. Until he confirmed the kills, however, restraint was warranted.

As he neared the house, he was struck by unexpected sounds. He heard at least two small gas engines churning away inside. He guessed that at least one was a generator—there had been a light illuminated on the main floor, which conveniently backlit his targets.

He covered the final twenty meters quickly, and put a shoulder to the foundation wall. His Glock was ready in his dominant right hand. He worked his way to the shell of a doorway and peered inside. The generator was there, humming along, and a thick extension cord ran above. The second engine, whatever it was, seemed to be located on the second floor. Monkh saw one problem. The only apparent way to access the upper floor was by a lone unfinished staircase. He thought that too predictable, on the off chance that one of the men had survived. In an abundance of caution, he searched for another way up.

Monkh spotted it immediately.

He darted to a network of scaffolding and began to climb.

Twenty seconds later he was on the balcony of the main floor. He took in every angle, the poised Glock sweeping in unison with his eyes. The balcony was clear, and he hurried to an empty window frame and got his first look inside. He saw the second source of noise, a barrel mixer of some kind chattering away. On the floor next to it was a body. He breathed a small sigh of relief—it was the one he had hoped to see, dressed in a fireman's coat, pants, and breathing apparatus. *Corsair.* He had fallen forward, and what Monkh could see of his face was a mess. The cheek and jawline were ruined by shrapnel, and a shattered faceplate covered the rest.

He saw no sign, however, of Li Qiang.

Monkh moved inside, wary, the Glock steady in front of him. He noted two partial walls on the far side of the room, a half dozen piles of wood and debris. He saw the top of the stairwell that he'd noted from below. There was no shortage of concealment. If Li had somehow survived, he would most likely have run—he wasn't a tactically oriented individual. Then again, God had a soft spot for amateurs.

It took two minutes to clear the entire floor. He then ensured that Li was not in the basement below. Monkh ended up next to the body, his irritation rising. If Li had indeed escaped, then his mission was incomplete. He would have to spend weeks tracking him down.

As he stood contemplatively, weighing where Li might have gone, something new and uncomfortable lodged in his head. An inconsistency.

No, an improbability.

Corsair had been killed, yet Li survived?

Monkh looked down, and immediately bile began to rise in his throat. The limp body puddled on the floor seemed changed. The yellow coat and pants fit differently. When he had seen Corsair earlier . . .

He bent down and turned the body over. Monkh pried away the shattered face plate and saw the other side of the face, the undamaged side. His heart seemed to seize.

A shot of adrenaline spiked, and before he could even look up the entire house came alive. Noise and motion seemed to come from every quadrant. Left and right, above and below. He threw himself to one side and rolled, ending up on his back. Directly overhead he registered movement on the plywood ceiling. Without even focusing, he brought the red dot to bear and fired four shots vertically. Four holes perforated the ceiling, bracketing the target perfectly. One of them, surely, would have taken out anyone on the roof above.

Then more motion to his right, something clattering near a floorboard. He shifted aim and fired twice, then made a lightning shift to a third target, more rounds striking what turned out to be a falling piece of lumber.

He altered his aim repeatedly, engaging one threat after another.

Then, all at once, Monkh stopped.

His weapon was still, the red glow of his sight

hovering over a vibrating reciprocating saw across the room.

He pushed all the distractions away, the noise and the movement. Very slowly Monkh looked up, and in the dim spray of the work light he saw what appeared to be the blade of a circular saw extending from a cut in the ceiling. He checked his second target, saw a heavy electric drill, now stilled by a slightly off-center hole. The generator and mixer churned away. The noise was deafening, disconcerting, robbing him of the sense of sound. He stood and spun two slow circles, the Glock poised, clearing the entire sphere around him for the true threat. He ended up facing the balcony.

"Don't move," said a voice from behind.

A voice Monkh knew.

He fell completely still.

SEVENTY-TWO

Slaton held the Sig casually by his side. Not that Monkh, whose back was to him fifteen paces away, could see it.

Slaton used his free hand to tap the kill switch on the mixer. Its engine sputtered to silence. Then he slid a foot sideways and disconnected the main extension cord to the power tools, only two of which were still running by their jury-rigged switches. The only sound at that point was muted, the generator on the lower level.

His target stood statue-like, the Glock still in his hand.

"I could ask you to drop the gun," Slaton said. "But I don't think you would. I can see the slide isn't locked back. Given that it's a Glock 19, with what appears to be a standard magazine, I'm pretty sure you're down to one round."

"Two," said the man Slaton knew as Thomas.

"Really? Maybe my count got off. But you should be very sure about that before you do something rash. One might not be enough. Hollow-points are good, but unless you manage a head shot, and a good one at that, I'll probably still be functional. Of course, that assumes you can turn and shoot faster than I can pull a trigger. And I've got a full magazine."

"You will be dead after the first."

"Doubtful. You already missed me once, down at the spillway. No, you will definitely need more than one shot."

He could see Monkh trembling with rage.

"Who are you working for?" Slaton asked.

Monkh didn't reply.

"Yeah . . . that's what I figured. I'm guessing you don't even know."

Monkh had never felt such fury. But then, he had also never found himself at such a disadvantage. He knew his only chance was to fight. Yet Corsair knew it as well. He tried to concentrate, channel his anger into the most perfect move he'd ever made. Turn, sight, and shoot in a flash. Two rounds. He was *sure* he had two left.

He whipped to the right, his quickness blurring, and instantly sighted on the assassin's silhouette. Monkh got off two shots and the slide on his Glock locked back. He knew both were on target. Strangely, Corsair didn't return fire. Nor did he fall. He just . . . stood there.

Only then did Monkh realize why.

"Not bad," Corsair said.

On the inch-thick sheet of glass in front of him, two coin-sized impressions, three inches apart, were fixed directly in front of his face.

"And you were right," he added. "You did have two rounds left. Too bad you didn't save one." Corsair stepped out from behind the glass.

Monkh's hand flew into his pocket. The touch of the polymer heel of his spare magazine was his last sensation on earth as two bullets pierced his forehead.

The entry wounds were less than an inch apart.

SEVENTY-THREE

Slaton stood still next to the massive window.

He knew a great deal about glass—that, too, was a sniper thing. The thick sheet next to him, standing on an iron glazier's rack, was one of the best bullet-proof varieties manufactured in the world. A Level 3 product, its polycarbonate plastic layers could absorb enough energy to stop at least three rounds from a .44 Magnum. Whoever was building this house had issues, some acute combination of money, enemies, and paranoia.

Slaton lowered the Sig. His only regret was that he hadn't gotten more information. The two men on the floor, he suspected, were both employed by the traitor in Washington, albeit for very different purposes. Now both were dead ends.

A glint of light swept across the back balcony rail—not an RPG launch this time, but a threat all the same. A car was approaching on the road, its side-mounted spotlight sweeping the trees. The police were finally getting in the game. He went to Thomas and performed a quick search of his pockets. He found nothing of use, no phone or identity documents. Hardly a surprise.

Slaton rushed down the stairs, and turned toward the rear-facing door. His best egress option was again the forest, the familiar creek leading to the drainage network where he'd nearly drowned.

He cleared the door and was breaking into a run when a shadowed figure appeared on his right. Slaton slid into a low crouch and sighted the Sig on the amorphous shape.

"*No, no . . . wait!*" A female voice. Very familiar.

Slaton let the barrel drop. "Anna? What the hell are you doing—"

"I'll explain later. We need to get out of here!"

"Agreed."

"This way," she said, beckoning him toward the up-hill portion of the road.

"No, that only leads to the top of the peak. It's a dead end."

She came closer, her face catching a spray of light. "Trust me on this."

He tipped his head to one side.

"Okay," she said, "maybe I should phrase that differently . . ."

Slaton gave her a half smile. "It's been a long week, Anna. But in case you forgot, I entrusted my family to you."

Sorensen explained her plan.

He looked up toward the top of the peak. "Seriously?"

"How do you think I got here?"

"Okay."

A minor explosion rumbled in the distance, and together they looked at Li's residence. The fire was raging, painting the night sky in slashes of orange.

"Probably the propane tank on the barbecue grill going off," he speculated.

"Probably." She looked up at the half-finished house. "I'm not exactly sure what you've been up to, but is there anything you need to do before we leave?"

Slaton looked toward Li's house. It was surrounded by first responders, including multiple police cars. The firemen, he guessed, were probably still looking for a fire hydrant. Tomorrow morning the police would comb through wreckage and process the bodies of two men killed by a shotgun-wielding madman. Invariably they would come to this house. They'd smell the tang of explosives, and confirm the explosion of an RPG. And of course, they would discover two more bodies.

He weighed Sorensen's question. Then he thought about Mali, Chinda, and Aranya. They would have to wait just a bit longer. "No," he said with certainty. "I think my work here is done."

Sorensen was a practiced distance runner. Even without his injuries, Slaton would have had a hard time keeping up. After the beating he'd taken in recent days, he was sucking wind by the time they reached the top of the peak fifteen minutes later.

"I thought you were in shape," she said, the barest sheen of sweat on her face.

Slaton bent down, his hands on his knees. He ignored the taunt, and asked, "Where is this ride?"

The road ended near the fenced-in tower array. The farm of tall aerials loomed over them with symbolic menace. Sorensen led the way to a siding where a plot of level ground was hidden behind outcroppings of vegetation. In the center of the small clear area was an aircraft. At least, Slaton thought it was an aircraft.

There were two concentric rotors on top, and the entire machine was no bigger than a standard sedan.

The skin was dark with a strangely mottled paint scheme. Sleek and angular, it reminded Slaton of one of Davy's Star Wars Lego kits.

"What the hell is that?" he asked.

"The official designation is VX-26."

Slaton noted that the fin flash was not U.S., but Taiwanese Air Force. "It's not one of ours?"

"It's not anyone's yet. It's experimental, a joint project between our two air forces. SAC/SOG also has some skin in the funding game. That's how I knew about it."

"So this is how you got here from Taiwan?"

"Yep."

"And how did you get that far?" he asked warily.

"I took an agency jet. But don't worry—other than the two pilots, nobody knows I'm even in this hemisphere. And the pilots have strict instructions to keep their mouths shut. When I arrived in Taiwan, I reached out to my counterpart in their intelligence agency, the National Security Bureau. They've been very accommodating. The VX-26 is a technology demonstrator—it was designed to test a new concept."

"The concept of life after death?"

She frowned. "Covert insertion in high-threat theaters of operation. It's small, has decent speed and range, and is more or less stealthy."

"More or less?"

"Yeah, I know. It's not as sleek as some stealth birds. But I'm told it has very effective coatings that minimize radar return. It got me here from Taiwan, and as far as I can tell there were no alarms raised. It's a pretty good hike to get back, almost two hours, but once we're airborne we'll be in international airspace in less than twenty minutes."

Slaton edged closer and looked at the front of the

aircraft. "I don't see where the pilot sits." He spun a slow three-sixty. "Come to think of it, I don't see a pilot."

"Well . . . that's part of the experiment. It flies autonomously."

"You mean it's a drone?"

"Basically, yeah. That way it can deliver supplies into really hot zones." A siren wailed briefly somewhere down the road. Sorensen scurried to the side of the aircraft. "Look, I can give you the full briefing later. We need to get out of here."

She opened a small access panel on the side of the aircraft, pressed a button, and a door that looked like the tailgate on an SUV hinged open vertically. There was a red light inside, and by its eerie glow Slaton saw a rectangular compartment the size of a dining room table, roughly four feet high.

Sorensen climbed in.

Seeing no seats, Slaton said, "What kind of load is this thing rated for?"

"I'm not sure how many pounds, but the contract specs called for four men in full combat rig."

He looked doubtful. "Are you sure this is a rescue mission?"

She stared at him pointedly as he limped toward the door. "Are you sure you're my best operator?"

Slaton actually smiled. "Yeah, well . . . I guess we're both screwed."

He clambered into the tiny helo. It was tight with just the two of them and no gear. The floor was bare metal, and overhead he saw hydraulic lines and the bottom of a turbine engine.

"It's very loud," she warned, handing across a pair of earmuffs.

Slaton clamped them on as Sorensen referenced on

the only instrument in sight—a touchscreen panel. She typed in a command, and within seconds the machine came to life. Mechanical noises dominated, clicking and whirring. When the loading door closed, Slaton realized there were no windows. In the glow of the red light it felt like a double-wide coffin.

With a clunk, the engine starter engaged and the turbine began spooling up. Thirty seconds later, the engine paused at idle, then accelerated. He felt the rotors engage, and soon the vibration level rose. He could feel the takeoff, a gentle rise, and then the deck seemed to pitch forward.

Even with the earmuffs, the noise was deafening.

Sorensen stopped her interactions with the touchscreen. "It's out of my hands now!" she shouted.

Slaton thought of a few clever replies, but the noise precluded them, so he simply nodded. There were a lot of things he and Sorensen needed to talk about. A lot of intel to share. None of that was going to happen until they reached Taiwan.

He saw Sorensen point to the watch on her wrist, then hold up one finger, then four, followed by a fist. Then she made a motion with her hands, one flat, the other zooming in for a landing.

They would be on the ground in an hour and forty minutes. That is, assuming the experiment they were riding in didn't crash, or that they weren't shot down by a Chinese interceptor or a surface-to-air missile.

Slaton gave her the middle finger back.

He could hear Sorensen's laughter over the roar of the engine.

SEVENTY-FOUR

Hours later, as embers were cooling amid the remains of Li Qiang's house, and as Hong Kong homicide investigators were getting their first look at the second of two murder scenes, a mid-afternoon meeting got under way at the White House.

The meeting had been called by Charles Eraclides, who'd promised to keep the vice president and his chief of staff apprised of any developments in Hong Kong. And there had been substantial developments.

"This is Li Qiang's house," Eraclides said, sliding an overhead photo onto the Resolute desk. "Or what's left of it."

Quarrels and Gross leaned in and saw the outline of a fire-ravaged structure.

"When did this happen?" Gross asked.

"Roughly six hours ago."

"Was Li inside?" Quarrels asked.

"No," Eraclides responded. He slid his finger to a different point on the same photo. "His body was found here, in a house under construction nearby. Coincidentally . . . or not . . . it's the very place where Slaton set up last week on his mission targeting Li and Zhao."

Quarrels and Gross exchanged a look.

"Are you certain it was Li?" Gross asked.

Another photo went onto the desk, this one far more graphic. It was a close-up of Li Qiang in death, one side of his face ravaged. "We're not exactly sure what happened to him," Eraclides explained, "but the photo has been matched for a positive ID. The picture came in less than an hour ago. It's part of an evidentiary file the Hong Kong police are building in the course of a quadruple murder investigation—NSA wormed their way into their database to acquire it."

"*Four* murders?" Quarrels inquired.

"Two in each of the residences. I'll spare you photos of the remains of two of the victims, one of which was burned beyond recognition in the fire. The salient point is that both died from shotgun wounds. Based on interviews, it appears they were members of Li's security detail. The last body, which ended up next to Li Qiang at the neighboring construction site, hasn't been identified." The CIA director slid the final photo across the desk.

"He looks Asian," Quarrels ventured.

"Possibly."

Gross pointed to two circular wounds in the victim's forehead. "Are those—"

"Yes, bullet holes. He was executed."

There was silence for a moment, no doubt induced by the gruesome images.

Gross said, "Well, this is good news. The last member of The Trident is dead."

"Yes," Eraclides allowed. "But this fourth man concerns me. I don't see where he fits in. And I also don't understand who wreaked all this havoc, and why."

The CIA director looked inquisitively at the vice

president, then his chief of staff. Neither appeared inclined to voice an opinion on the matter.

The company Gulfstream cut cleanly through smooth air as it climbed out over the western Pacific. Slaton and Sorensen had the big cabin to themselves, and the only sound was a steady hum from the engines. It was a far cry from the cramped and thunderous VX-26, but in Slaton's view the experimental drone was a resounding success. It had delivered them unscathed to Pingtung Air Base in southern Taiwan. They'd been met there by Sorensen's counterpart in the NSB, and she gave the aircraft a glowing recommendation before cutting free to continue her "highest-priority mission." Within an hour of landing, they were on the Gulfstream and taxiing for takeoff.

Slaton was genuinely impressed with Sorensen. Not only for her acumen and logistical wizardry, but by the fact that she'd put her life on the line to bail him out of a bind. He told her as much once they were airborne.

Sorensen set a pot of coffee brewing in the aircraft's galley. The G650, extended range version, was one of the longest-range business jets in the world. Even so, the flight to Andrews would stretch it to the very limit. With a decent tailwind and a light load—two passengers, and one small bag for Sorensen—they would reach Washington in fifteen hours.

After making sure the pilots were sufficiently caffeinated, Sorensen brought two cups to the mid-cabin club chairs.

"Thanks," Slaton said, taking one.

"No problem."

She went back up front, and moments later returned with two white cardboard boxes. She set one in front of him on the small table. "I asked the pilots to arrange for food, but all they could come up with was box lunches."

"Military bases aren't known for their fine cuisine." He opened his box and saw raw fish wrapped in clear plastic, a square of dried noodles, an apple, and a cookie. He took out the apple and cookie and pushed the box away.

"It's time for a little information-sharing," she said.

"Right. But before we get into that, I have a request."

"A request?"

"Actually . . . demand might be a better word."

She looked at him skeptically.

Slaton told her about his interactions with Mali, Chinda, and Aranya, and explained the promise he'd made.

Her expression softened. "I was afraid you were going to ask for a raise."

Slaton smiled.

"I think we can probably get them out."

"It needs to be in the next few days." He explained their predicament.

"I'll put someone on it as soon as we land."

"Thanks."

"So," she began, "Li is dead?"

"He is. Along with the NOC you brought in to help me."

Her eyes narrowed. "Dare I ask what happened to him?"

"I'll spare you the details. Suffice to say, the mission to take out Yao went perfectly. On the second op, though, the guy set me up. He hired some mercs to go after me, and when that didn't work out, he took matters into his own hands and shot me himself. Thankfully, he wasn't the marksman he dreamed he was."

Sorensen closed her eyes as she recalled what she'd been told. "The NOC reported that you'd been killed. He said he'd seen it with his own eyes."

"Oh, he saw it—right over the notch on the end of his barrel. And he almost succeeded."

"We lost contact with him after that." She paused, then added, "I'm so sorry, David. The whole thing was rushed . . . it was a fail from the start, and I take full responsibility."

His eyes drifted to the window. "It worked out in the end."

"Any idea who he was?"

"I can tell you he was trained. But he wasn't former military."

"How do you know that?"

"The way he moved, his mindset—no doubt he was an operator. But if he was a military product, he would have had a better gig line."

"A better what?"

"Gig line. He was wearing a chauffeur's uniform, but the button line on his shirt, the flap on his pants zipper, and his belt buckle were all out of alignment. Nobody who's ever been through basic training in the military does that—it's ingrained for life. Tactically, though, he was solid. I'm guessing he was recruited by a big intelligence agency, probably either China or Russia."

She shook her head. "That doesn't make sense—it puts us back to The Trident being state-sponsored."

"Not if he went private at some point."

"A freelancer?"

"That'd be my bet."

She leaned back in her chair. "Okay, clearly we've got a lot to cover. How about you go first."

Slaton did, covering the entire sequence of the last week. Sorensen did the same in return, including the revelation that Elayne Cleveland was secretly on the road to recovery. They eventually meshed the two accounts, challenged them from every conceivable angle. Two pots of coffee later, somewhere north of the Mariana Islands, they had a shared mental model of what had taken place. Unfortunately, it put them no closer to answering the thousand-dollar question. Who was the traitor in Washington?

"I'm glad Elayne pulled through," he said.

"Me too. As far as figuring out who our traitor is, I do have one ace in the hole. Vince Seward at Homeland Security. He's the one person I confided in. He understands what's at stake, and he's been researching the calls to the White House I told you about."

"Has he found anything?"

"Last I talked to him, no. But that was two days ago. I've been off-grid ever since."

"Can you reach him now?"

"I can. But if I use the comm suite up front, we'll be advertising where we are. A lot of people will know we're on the way home."

"That's only half true," Slaton said. "They'll know *you're* on the way home. As we speak, my star is about to be engraved on the Memorial Wall."

She thought about that for a time, then nodded.

Sorensen went up front, disappearing into the cockpit for nearly twenty minutes. Slaton looked through the oval window as the new day woke, a red dawn breaking ahead. He wondered if they would fly over Canada to reach Washington. He hoped so. He wanted to see the mountains and the forest. Wanted to think about the two-and-a-half people hidden deep within it.

Sorensen returned and took a seat, a freighted expression on her face.

"Seward figured out where the calls went," Slaton surmised.

She nodded.

"So who's our traitor?"

Sorensen told him.

Neither spoke for a long time, until Slaton said, "That's going to be complicated."

"It was always going to be."

He looked at his watch. "Well . . . we've got twelve hours to come up with a plan."

SEVENTY-FIVE

Matt Gross lived in a brick rowhouse on the edge of West End, although "lived" was an aspirational term. He hadn't been there in nearly five days, having spent his nights lodging in guest quarters at the White House. These were heady weeks, a historic transition of power taking place, and he was determined to be involved every step of the way. In truth, it did little to alter his life. Gross was a bachelor with no roommates and no pets, and had conveniently broken up with his girlfriend last month.

There would be time for all of that someday. Today, however, was about making history.

He checked his mailbox, found it full of junk, and mumbled a perfunctory hello to a passing neighbor, an octogenarian spinster heading out with her Jack Russell for a walk. The dog yapped at Gross. The woman ignored him.

Gross had lived in the rowhouse for nearly a year, yet he'd never had much interaction with his neighbors, most of whom were either old or Democrats. More often than not, both. He doubted any of them knew who he was or what he did for a living. To be the vice president's chief of staff was, on most days, the equivalent of being invisible. That, however, was about to change.

He keyed back the deadbolt, entered his apartment, and disabled the alarm system. Gross hung his jacket on a hook near the door and flicked on the living room light.

Nothing happened.

He paused and looked at the switch in the dim light. The LED clock on the microwave shone bright, so the power wasn't out. He was reaching out to cycle the switch when a lamp clicked on behind him. The room filled with light.

Gross whirled around and saw a man in the big chair by the window. He was sitting casually, his hands on the arms of the thickly upholstered chair. Gross recognized him instantly—a face he had last seen on the tarmac at Joint Base Andrews.

His eyes flicked to the nearby kitchen drawer. "I have a gun," he said.

"No, you don't." Slaton reached down to his hip and retrieved Gross's Beretta. He set it next to the lamp on the chair-side table.

"What do you want?" Gross said, trying for an authoritative tone.

"Truth. Integrity. A lot of things you can't deliver."

"I don't know what you're talking about."

"The mission you sent me on is essentially complete. Now I'm here to give you one, so listen closely."

The instructions Slaton gave were detailed, even intricate, but nothing a vice president's chief of staff couldn't grasp. When he finished, the look on Gross's face was not incomprehension, but obstinance.

"Why would I do any of that?" he asked.

Standing slowly, Slaton moved a few steps closer. His gray eyes locked on Gross with a distant haze, and he said at a near whisper, "For one very good reason. Because I'm not the judge. I'm not the jury. I'm the other guy."

Slaton walked to the door and was gone.

SEVENTY-SIX

The following morning dawned slowly, a heavy overcast shrouding the entire D.C. metroplex.

"I don't remember this being on the schedule," Lincoln Quarrels said as he stood at the foot of the South Lawn.

"We added it a few days ago," said Matt Gross. "Elayne was booked to give the keynote speech to the U.N. General Assembly. It fell off the radar in all the recent commotion, but things are settling. It's time for you to take the mantle as head of state, and this is the perfect opportunity."

"New York City?" Quarrels scowled. "When will we get back?"

"You'll be back in time for dinner."

The sound of a helicopter began rising, and Quarrels spotted it swooping past the great dome of the Capitol Building. It was a VH-92 from Marine Helicopter Squadron One. "Are you sure this is safe?" he asked, visions of last week's disaster still in his mind.

"The Marines and the Secret Service have adopted entirely new security protocols for presidential air travel."

"So quickly?"

"There was no higher priority—they got it done.

The alternative would be a motorcade all the way to Andrews, which is probably riskier."

Quarrels had his doubts, but there was no chance to argue as the big chopper roared to a gentle landing on the South Lawn. The two men set out across the manicured grass. Quarrels's reservations dissipated as the scene played out. This would be his first flight on Marine One as acting president. And after that, Air Force One—a symbol of power like no other on earth—would whisk him to New York. It was a perk he had certainly earned.

Marine One lifted off and turned west. Through the tiny window, Quarrels saw no sign of other choppers or fighter cover overhead. Still, he never doubted measures had been taken. He soon fell distracted as Gross began going over the speech he would give at the U.N. The theme was dear to his heart—to build a coalition of law-abiding nations that would stamp out aggression. Russia wasn't specifically named, but the target on its authoritarian back couldn't be clearer.

Gross seemed unusually reserved as he went through the talking points. The flight took longer than Quarrels remembered—he'd accompanied Elayne Cleveland previously on flights to Andrews—and an odd sensation struck as the chopper touched down. He looked outside and saw not a concrete tarmac, but verdant green grass. Then Quarrels was struck by another peculiarity, this one even more disturbing. He realized there was no security on board Marine One. He didn't know the exact protocols, but there had always been Secret Service agents and at least one Marine escort. As far as he could tell, he and Gross were the only ones on board besides the pilots. And he couldn't even see them—the door to the cockpit was closed.

"What the hell is—"

Before he could finish the question, the side entry door opened abruptly. Without a word, Gross jumped to his feet and hurried outside. The instant he was gone, another man appeared. Quarrels had never met him . . . but he knew who he was looking at.

His thoughts spun furiously as he sensed events slipping out of his control. "*You . . .*" he managed.

"Yeah," Slaton said. "Me."

"They . . . they told me you were dead."

"Don't always believe your intel."

Quarrels's eyes darted to the closed cockpit door.

"Don't bother," Slaton said. "You're on your own."

"I am the acting president of the United States!"

Slaton checked his watched. "Actually, as of twenty minutes ago—no, you're not."

"What are you talking about?"

"Not for me to explain. You need to come with me."

Quarrels didn't budge.

"All right," Slaton said, with just the trace of a smile. "Have it your way . . ."

Quarrels found himself being hauled across the dew-covered grass with one arm wrenched behind his back—more painfully than was necessary. In front of them was a large colonial house perched on the top of a minor hill. The acres around them were forest and rolling hills. The driveway disappeared into a distant swale, and there wasn't another residence in sight. Quarrels didn't see a single Secret Service agent. Matt Gross had disappeared.

"Where are we?" he demanded.

Slaton didn't reply.

"You can't do this!"

They reached a broad set of stairs leading to the front door, and Quarrels did his best to keep up. "You've got this all wrong!" he shouted.

The front door wasn't locked, and Slaton barged straight through using Quarrels's head to push the door open. He marched the vice president to the middle of a large atrium, then yanked him to a stop. The house was old and elegant, although with little furniture and no personal effects of any kind—it was simply the shell of a stately old mansion. Slaton pointed to a double door on one side, then gave Quarrels a shove.

The vice president stumbled but caught himself. He shrugged his rumpled jacket back in place, then gave Slaton a defiant look. He walked cautiously to the door, turned the handle, and went inside. After two steps Quarrels froze, stricken by the sight before him. Five people stood staring at him. On one side, Anna Sorensen and Charles Eraclides. On the other, Ed Markowitz and Richard Cleveland. Yet the most unnerving sight of all was in the middle: Elayne Cleveland seated in a wheelchair.

All five stared at him accusingly, leaving no need for words.

Quarrels started to shake his head, the beginnings of a denial rising. Then the momentum faded. It was, he realized, too late for that. The faces he was looking at were not inquisitive. There would be no accusations or questions. The time for that had passed. Quarrels felt suddenly older, more fragile. His posture sagged.

Elayne said, "The Cabinet convened early today for an emergency meeting. The members were surprised, as I'm sure you are, that my recovery has taken such a positive turn. I explained to everyone in attendance that, while I still have a long recovery ahead, I feel sufficiently capable of resuming my constitutional duties. Your absence at that meeting was noted, and it was explained that you yourself had suddenly been taken ill, and that doctors were evaluating your condition. The two events together, my recovery and your sudden affliction, created an imperative situation. The vote was unanimous to re-instate me as president, and all constitutional requirements have since been met."

She paused there, as if possibly expecting a protest. Quarrels gave none.

The president continued, "Had the Cabinet shown any reluctance to put me back in power, I was fully prepared to convey proof of the treasons you have committed against this country. I think the idea of having a murderer in the Oval Office would easily have swayed them. Thankfully, none of that was necessary."

Quarrels could take no more. "*Treason? Me?* I have risked everything to stand up to our greatest enemy! I have—"

"No!" shouted Elayne Cleveland. She produced a cane and pushed herself to her feet. Her stance was wobbly, yet her tone took on a forcefulness that hadn't been heard in weeks. "You have sacrificed men and women of our armed services, of our intelligence services, and tried to assassinate the commander in chief. You'll try to say you've done all this to pursue some quixotic hatred of one country, but I think we all know the true reason. You coveted the power of the nation's highest office."

Quarrels's eyes darted between the others. He saw no trace of support.

"The question," the president went on, "is what should we do with you?"

"Elayne, I—"

She held up her hand, and the look that descended on her face was one of agony. "I have made some difficult decisions in my time in office." She looked at Quarrels squarely, dispassionately. "But this one . . . this one was easy."

The president sat back in her wheelchair. Markowitz went behind it and began pushing her toward a door at the side of the room. The rest followed, leaving Quarrels alone. Almost. He turned to see Slaton behind him. Everything made sense. The lack of Secret Service, the remote location.

"So that's it," he said to the assassin. "I suppose they'll say I had a heart attack or something?"

"Or something."

"I'm curious . . . will it weigh on your conscience to kill a defenseless old man?"

"In your case, it wouldn't. But I don't get the honors."

Quarrels looked at him quizzically. Then he heard heavy footsteps, and a figure reappeared at the side door. It was Richard Cleveland, a six-shooter in his hand. Quarrels took on a panicked look.

Slaton pulled back into the atrium, closing the big double doors behind him. He was outside, well down the driveway and picking up speed, when the distant shot sounded.

SEVENTY-SEVEN

Two hours later, a limo was nearing Dulles Airport. Slaton and Sorensen were in back, an agency driver in front. The privacy screen was raised.

Sorensen ended a string of phone calls that had been going on for twenty minutes.

"I ordered the original security team back to your house," she said. "It might take a day or two to get everything squared away."

"Thanks."

"There was also a message from Jammer. They're on their way back, just stopped for fuel. He says they'll arrive at the ranch not long after you do."

"Great. I owe him big time."

"I think he enjoyed the company. It sounds like he's really taken with Davy."

"My son has that effect on people." He looked at her pointedly. "Jammer would make a great dad."

Sorensen acquired a pained look.

"Did I say something wrong?"

She shook her head—not for a negative reply, but more to clear her head of something. "They've decided to wait a few days before announcing Quarrels's cerebral hemorrhage."

"Is that what they're going to call it? I think waiting

makes sense. Don't want too many shocks to the Constitution all at once."

A long pause, before Sorensen said casually, "Elayne wants to make me her vice president."

His expression went through a hard double-clutch. "*What?* Are you serious?"

Sorensen frowned. "You don't have to sound *that* surprised."

"No, I mean it's an honor to be asked, and you'd be terrific. I just never saw it coming."

"Trust me—neither did I."

"You were talking about leaving the CIA a few days ago." He tried to catch her gaze, but it was locked on the window. "Are you going to do it?"

She heaved out a sigh. "I don't know. The thought of politics scares the crap out of me. All the back-slapping and fundraising and media garbage."

"Buuut . . ."

"But it would be a chance to make a difference. The kind of chance few people ever get."

"What does Jammer think about it?"

"I haven't told him yet."

Slaton laughed. "You need to sell tickets to that event."

She ignored the comment. "If I did decide to do it, it would leave the SAC/SOG position open. Eraclides asked me for recommendations."

"Head of SAC/SOG? Who the hell would want—" He cut the thought short. Something in her tone. "Oh, no. No, no, no. Not a chance."

"You understand special ops better than anyone I know, David."

"I want to be kicked out of special ops more than anyone you know, and with a do-not-resuscitate order."

"Don't you see? That's what this would be. Get out of the field, run the show."

"Me, sit behind a desk? I don't have a security clearance. I'm not even a U.S. citizen!"

"That can be remedied."

He shook his head. "You've seriously been thinking about this."

The limo pulled to a stop at the departures curb.

"Just give it some thought, David. That's all I ask."

"No, never. Not in a million years!" He got out, and before closing the door, said, "What's Jammer's favorite whiskey?"

"Coors Light."

Slaton grinned. "Great! I'll give him your regards." He closed the door. As he began walking away, the back window spun down. His first instinct was to ignore it. Instead, he turned back, leaned in, and with a raised index finger, said, *"Never!"*

SEVENTY-EIGHT

Slaton stood by the dormant ATV, hoping Christine still had the key. The sun was getting low, its light shimmering on the lake. The mountain air at dusk was cool and dry. It had taken him over an hour to hike here from the house, but he'd been in contact with Christine and she said they expected to arrive before sunset. The blue phone was now compromised, but the immediate threat had passed. He'd already bought her a new burner. Just in case.

He heard the plane before he saw it, and soon it was swooping low over the lake. It touched town softly, and minutes later was nosing onto a small sand bank at the shoreline.

Slaton was there to meet it, and Davy was the first one out. He jumped out on the pontoon, leapt onto the sandbank and flew into his father's arms. Slaton could have held him forever, but Davy wasn't so inclined. He pushed back and began regaling him with stories of their adventures. Slaton listened raptly, thinking them far preferable to his own.

Christine was next. She came to him more slowly, perhaps a bit wearily, and they simply held each other in silence for a time. Davy, wanting no part of the yucky parent stuff, was soon throwing rocks into the lake.

Last came Jammer. Slaton shook his hand, and said, "Big time, brother."

"We had fun! Nothing you wouldn't have done for me."

"Can you stay with us tonight?"

"Don't see why not. I can leave the Beaver here, no problem. Just need to secure a few things for the night."

"Good. I've got spaghetti in the slow cooker and beer in the fridge."

"Sounds perfect." Jammer headed back to the airplane and recruited Davy for postflight duty.

Christine looked her husband up and down.

"No playing doctor," he said.

"I'm going to find out eventually."

He frowned. "A few stitches here and there. Might need a little PT on my right hip."

"Who did the stiches?"

"A half-dentist."

She gave him a suspect look, and was about to ask for amplification when Davy came to the rescue. "Jammer says we can take you for a spin over the lake! Will you come, Dad? I want to show you how I can fly!"

He glanced at Christine, then said, "How could I say no? Tell him I'll be right there."

His son ran off.

"Davy the Undefeated," Christine said, using their pet parental nickname.

"He looks happy."

"That's because he didn't know what was happening."

"You look happy."

"I am . . . now. I trust you put in for retirement before you left Washington?"

He knew she'd meant it as a joke, but his discomfort must have been apparent.

"What?" she asked.

"Oh, something Anna told me. Jammer's got a surprise coming."

"A good surprise?"

"I'm not sure." He looked at her awkwardly, and said "I'll tell you about it later."

"Okay. But before we go for our sunset cruise here, there's something I've been wanting to tell you."

"What's that?"

She pulled him closer and put his hand on her bumped belly. "The genetic test came back. It's a girl."

And just like that, all the burdens Slaton had been feeling were gone.

ACKNOWLEDGMENTS

Assassin's Mark is the tenth installment in my David Slaton series. I could never have imagined, so many years ago, that I would still be on this journey. Nor could I have foreseen all the help required to bring it to pass.

Thanks first and foremost to my family, ever-growing as it is. You have all been there for me from the start, and I know I can always count on you going forward.

Much appreciation to my friends in the thriller-writer community: Kyle Mills, Jeff Wilson, Brian Andrews, Jack Stewart, Simon Gervais, Mark Greaney, Tony Tata, Marc Cameron, and Don Bentley.

James Abt and his team of reviewers at Best Thriller Books (Best ThrillerBooks.com) have been essential in helping spread the word about my stories. So too, David Temple (*The Thriller Zone* podcast) and Mike and Chris (*No Limits: The Mitch Rapp Podcast*). Thanks as ever to Susan Gleason, my longtime agent.

The Tor Publishing Group brings all the moving parts together. Thanks to Linda Quinton, Robert Davis, Libby Collins, Angus Johnston, Andrew King, Sam Glatt, and Eileen Lawrence. Also, to the talented P.J. Ochlan, who brings the audiobooks alive.

And finally to my editor, Bob Gleason—you claim to have retired, but a handful of us know better.